TOUCH THE DARK

by Karen Chance

Can you ever really trust a vampire?

Cassandra Palmer can see the future and communicate with spirits—talents that make her attractive to the dead and the undead. The ghosts of the dead aren't usually dangerous; they just like to talk…a lot.

The undead are another matter.

Like any sensible girl, Cassie tries to avoid vampires. But when the bloodsucking mafioso she escaped three years ago finds Cassie again with vengeance on his mind, she's forced to turn to the vampire Senate for protection.

The undead senators won't help her for nothing, and Cassie finds herself working with one of their most powerful members, a dangerously seductive master vampire—and the price he demands may be more than Cassie is willing to pay….

0-451-46093-6

Available wherever books are sold or at
penguin.com

Roc Science Fiction & Fantasy

ROC BOOKS BY KAREN CHANCE

Touch the Dark

Claimed by Shadow

KAREN CHANCE

A ROC BOOK

ROC
Published by New American Library, a division of
Penguin Group (USA) Inc., 375 Hudson Street,
New York, New York 10014, USA
Penguin Group (Canada), 90 Eglinton Avenue East, Suite 700, Toronto,
Ontario M4P 2Y3, Canada (a division of Pearson Penguin Canada Inc.)
Penguin Books Ltd., 80 Strand, London WC2R 0RL, England
Penguin Ireland, 25 St. Stephen's Green, Dublin 2,
Ireland (a division of Penguin Books Ltd.)
Penguin Group (Australia), 250 Camberwell Road, Camberwell, Victoria 3124,
Australia (a division of Pearson Australia Group Pty. Ltd.)
Penguin Books India Pvt. Ltd., 11 Community Centre, Panchsheel Park,
New Delhi - 110 017, India
Penguin Group (NZ), 67 Apollo Drive, Mairangi Bay,
Auckland 1311, New Zealand (a division of Pearson New Zealand Ltd.)
Penguin Books (South Africa) (Pty.) Ltd., 24 Sturdee Avenue,
Rosebank, Johannesburg 2196, South Africa

Penguin Books Ltd., Registered Offices:
80 Strand, London WC2R 0RL, England

First published by Roc, an imprint of New American Library,
a division of Penguin Group (USA) Inc.

First Printing, April 2007
10   9   8   7   6   5   4   3   2

Copyright © Karen Chance, 2007
All rights reserved

ROC REGISTERED TRADEMARK—MARCA REGISTRADA

Printed in the United States of America

ACKNOWLEDGMENTS

Thanks are due to Marlin and Mary for literally providing shelter from the storm. Katrina was a nightmare, but you helped turn that year into something positive. And special thanks to Anne Sowards, my editor, who saw this book through its many versions with unending patience. You deserve collaborative status for all the great ideas, but since they won't put your name on the cover, I'll put it in here.

Chapter 1

Any day that starts off in a demon-filled bar in a casino designed to look like Hell isn't likely to turn out well. But all I thought at the time was that a brothel should be more fun—especially one for ladies only that was staffed by handsome incubi. But the demon lovers slumped miserably at their tables, holding their heads as if in pain, and completely ignoring their companions. Even Casanova, lounging across from me, looked unhappy. His pose was unconsciously seductive—a matter of habit, I guess—but his expression wasn't so nice.

"All right, Cassie!" he snapped, when one of his boys suddenly began weeping uncontrollably. "Tell me what you want, then get them the hell out of here! I have a business to run!"

He was referring to the three old women who were perched on stools at the bar. They were giving the satyr serving drinks a wilt in a place rarely seen at anything but full attention on one of his kind. That wasn't surprising: none of them looked under a hundred, and their most obvious attribute was matted, greasy locks—gray since birth—

that streamed in a web of tangles to the floor. I'd tried to wash Enyo's, whose name appropriately means "horror," last night, but the hotel's shampoo hadn't made much of an improvement. I'd given up after finding what looked like half a decayed rat in a snarl under her left ear.

The hair did have the benefit of distracting attention from their faces, though, so you didn't immediately notice that they had only one eye and one tooth among them. Enyo was currently trying to take back the eye from her sister Deino ("dread") because she wanted to check out the horrified-looking bartender. Meanwhile, Pemphredo ("alarm") was using the tooth to rip open a bag of peanuts. She finally gave up and stuffed the whole cellophane-wrapped package in her mouth, gumming it happily.

I had once assumed that the Graeae were merely myths thought up by bored (and fairly peculiar) Greeks a few thousand years before the invention of TV. But apparently not. I'd recently acquired—okay, stolen—a bunch of items from the Vampire Senate, the body that controls the actions of all North American vampires, and had been trying to figure out what they were. The first one I'd examined, a small iridescent sphere in a black wooden case, had started to glow as soon as I picked it up. A brief flash of light later and I had houseguests.

I couldn't figure out why the trio had been imprisoned, especially in so grand a place as the inner sanctum of a vampire stronghold. They were as annoying as hell but didn't seem particularly dangerous, other than to my room service bill. I'd brought the gals along because it was either that or leave them unsupervised in my hotel room. They had a lot of energy for old women, and I'd had a hell of a time keeping them amused so far.

I'd sat them in front of three nickel slots while I went on my errand, but of course they hadn't stayed there. Like three ancient toddlers, they had very short attention spans. They'd wandered into the bar shortly after I did, carrying a load of no-doubt ill-gotten souvenirs. Deino, clutching a little red devil plush under her arm, had dropped a snow globe off with me before heading for the bar. It contained a plastic image of the casino that, instead of being surrounded by fake snow, had tiny flames that danced about whenever you shook it. I thought it would be just my luck to get arrested for shoplifting something that tacky.

Despite the annoyance of babysitting the weird sisters, the expression on Casanova's face as he regarded them told me it might work to my advantage. I smiled and watched the flames of Hell consume the tiny casino again. "If you don't help me, I may just leave them here. They could use a makeover." I didn't bother to point out how bad that would be for business.

Casanova winced and tossed back the rest of his drink, giving me a glimpse of a strong, tanned throat under the loose collar of his dress shirt. Technically, of course, he wasn't the historical Casanova. Possession by an incubus demon tends to increase mortal life span, but not that much. The Italian cleric who was remembered for having unmatched success with the ladies died centuries ago, but the reason for his reputation lived on. And there was nothing to complain about in his newest incarnation. I had to regularly remind myself that I was here on business and he wasn't even trying.

"I don't care about your problems," he told me fiercely. "How much to take them away?"

"This isn't a money matter. You know what I want." I

tried to discreetly pull the tight satin shorts I was wearing into a more comfortable position, but I think he noticed. It's hard to look intimidating in a sequined devil costume complete with pointed tail. Sinful Scarlett did not go well with my strawberry blond curls and whitest of white girl's complexion. I looked like a kewpie doll trying to play tough guy—no wonder he wasn't impressed. But I'd had to think of some way to reach him without being recognized, and borrowing a costume from the employee locker room had seemed like a good idea at the time.

Casanova lit a tiny cigarette with a brushed gold lighter. "If you have a death wish, that is your affair, but I won't put my head in a noose by crossing Antonio. The man is psychotic about revenge. You should know."

Considering that Tony, a master vampire and my old guardian, was at the head of the list of people who wanted me in an urn on their mantel, I couldn't argue the point. But I had to find him, and the person I strongly suspected was with him, or the urn wouldn't be necessary. There wouldn't be anything left of me to require a funeral. And since Casanova had once been Tony's second in command, it was a good bet that he knew where the crafty old bastard was hiding.

"I think Myra's with him," I said shortly.

Casanova didn't ask for details. It wasn't exactly a secret that Myra was the most recent person to try and help me shuffle off the mortal coil. It hadn't been personal—more of a career move, you might say—until I'd put a couple of holes in her torso. It was safe to assume it was personal now.

"My sympathies," Casanova murmured. "But I am afraid that is all I can offer. You understand that my position is somewhat . . . tenuous."

That was one way of putting it. That Casanova had occupied such an important place in Tony's criminal organization was unusual, to say the least. Demons are normally considered unwanted competition by vampires, but incubi aren't exactly tops on the demonic power scale. In fact, most other demons view them as something of an embarrassment. Casanova was an unusual incubus, though.

He'd taken up residence in an attractive Spanish don centuries ago, thinking he was simply trading an aging host body for a newer version. He hadn't realized until the possession was in progress that he'd actually invaded a baby vampire, one too young to know how to evict him. Before the vamp figured it out, they'd reached an understanding. The centuries of practice Casanova had in seduction helped the vamp feed easily, and having a body that wouldn't age and die on him suited Casanova. So when Tony decided to organize the incubi of the States into a moneymaking deal for him, Casanova was the perfect choice to run it.

His Decadent Dreams spa is located in a monstrosity of a building adjacent to Tony's Vegas casino, Dante's. While vacationing husbands throw away the family fortune at the roulette wheel, their neglected wives take consolation in the extravagant spa treatments, among other things, on offer next door. Tony gets rich from the proceeds, the incubi get more lust to feed from than even they can use, and the ladies come out with a glow that lasts for days. It's actually one of Tony's less reprehensible businesses, except for being highly illegal—unlike some people seem to believe, prostitution is not okay with the Vegas PD. But then, vamps have never paid much attention to human law.

"What's the penalty for slaving these days?" I asked idly. "Bet it makes that noose look pretty good."

For the first time, Casanova lost his superior look. He dropped his cigarette, and hot ashes splattered his suit, leaving tiny burn marks on the silk before he could brush them away. "I never had anything to do with that!"

I wasn't surprised at his reaction. Tony had been breaking both human and vampire laws by engaging in the very profitable but extremely dangerous trade of selling magic users. The Silver Circle, the council of mages who act for the magical community the way the Senate does for vamps, are violently opposed to the idea, and their treaty with the vamps specifically outlaws it. Ignoring the treaty risked war, and the Senate would have staked Tony for that alone, if they didn't already have plenty of reasons to want him dead.

"You'll have a hard time convincing the Senate of that if your boss tries to pin the whole thing on you." Judging by his expression, Casanova felt that was a good possibility. He knew his employer as well as I did. "But if I find him first, Tony will be out of the picture and you'll be in the clear. It's to your advantage to help me." I expected that line to work—self-interest was usually the best way to get a vamp's cooperation—but Casanova recovered quickly.

He lit another cigarette with steady fingers. "Why are you so sure that I know where he is? He doesn't tell me everything. He has that Alphonse character to help him now."

Alphonse was Tony's current second in command and personal bodyguard. He was easily the ugliest vamp I've ever seen, and his personality was no more attractive than his face. But I much preferred him to his boss. Alphonse didn't actually like me, but I doubted he'd hunt me down if Tony wasn't around to give the order.

"Tony had to leave somebody in charge when he disappeared. I'm betting it was you, and that you know where he is."

He regarded me through a haze of smoke for a long minute. "I'm in temporary control," he finally admitted, "but only of Vegas. You want to contact Philly."

I shook my head emphatically. That was what I definitely didn't want. There were too many people in Philadelphia, Tony's main base of operations, who remembered me less than fondly. Way less. "Uh-huh. They might give me something, all right, but it wouldn't be information."

Casanova's lips twitched, and the amusement in those whiskey-colored eyes was even more attractive than his usual smoldering seduction. I swallowed and pretended indifference, which won me an actual grin. But no information.

"You know as well as I do that the family does not take disloyalty well," he murmured. "That is especially true from a demon/vampire hybrid that most regard as a freak. And the fact that I have recently taken over temporary control on this coast hasn't won me any more admirers. There are many waiting for me to put a foot wrong, and betraying the boss would definitely qualify."

I hadn't been prepared for candor, and it threw me. I stared at him as a surge of fear fluttered through my stomach and up to my throat. I tamped it down; I couldn't afford to show uncertainty now. If I didn't find some way to get Casanova to open up, pretty soon Myra would be doing the same to me—with a knife.

I leaned across the table and played my best card. "I understand all about the family's idea of revenge. But think about it. "If Tony gets staked by me or the Senate, you'll be in a perfect position to grab some property. Wouldn't you like to own this place yourself?"

Casanova ran a hand through his shoulder-length chestnut hair, which fell in perfect waves without any obvious artifice. He was dressed in a raw silk suit in a rich brown that almost matched his eyes. I wasn't an expert on men's clothes, but his saffron-colored tie looked expensive, as did his gold watch and matching cufflinks. Casanova had caviar tastes, and I doubted Tony overpaid him—generosity wasn't one of his character traits.

He looked around longingly. "What I wouldn't give to re-decorate," he said. "Do you have any idea how difficult it is, getting patrons past the ambiance?" I could see his point. The gloomy opium-den interior and dragon's-head bar, complete with an occasional wisp of steam emanating from its carved nostrils, didn't exactly scream romance. "My boys have to work twice as hard as they should. I engineered a water leak last month to give me an excuse to gut the lobby, but there's so much left to do, and don't even get me started on the entrance! It scares off half the would-be customers before they make it in the door."

"So, help me out here."

He shook his head regretfully, expelling a thin stream of smoke with his sigh. "Not possible, *chica.* If Tony found out, he'd ruin me. I'd have to find a new body after he staked this one, and I've become somewhat attached to it."

It figured Casanova didn't want to risk it. Hanging out on the sidelines, waiting to see who won, was the practical move—and practicality is pretty much the defining vamp characteristic. Unfortunately, that option wasn't open to me.

A legacy from an eccentric seer had recently left me Pythia, the title for the world's chief clairvoyant. Agnes' gift came with a whopping amount of power that everyone wanted to either monopolize or eradicate, but I was stuck with it for the moment since she'd thoughtlessly died before I could figure out how to give it back. I hoped to pass it on to someone else, assuming I lived so long, but in the meantime, Tony wanted to kill me, the Senate wanted to make me their stooge and, oh, yeah, I'd also managed to piss off the mages. What can I say? I'm an overachiever.

"Tony isn't going to win against the six senates," I said flatly. "They have reciprocal agreements—if one is hunting him, they all are. Sooner or later, they'll catch up with him and he'll start blaming everyone else for what happened. They'll stake him anyway, but ten to one he'll incriminate you and a lot of others before then. Help me out and maybe I can get to him before they do."

Casanova studied me while he stubbed out his cigarette in a black lacquered ashtray. Dark eyes swept over my outfit, and a faint smile came to his lips. "Rumor has it that you're Pythia now," he finally said, stroking the back of one long-fingered hand lightly over mine. "Can't you use your power to deal with this? It would be worth a lot to me." My skin felt warmer than usual where he touched me, a feeling that spread outward along my arm. His voice dropped an octave, going husky. "I could be a very good friend, Cassandra."

He raised my hand, turning it over to run a finger lightly down the middle of the palm. I was about to make a sarcastic comment about my so-called power when he bent his head. His lips brushed along the line he'd drawn, silken soft yet feeling like they left a brand, and I forgot what I'd been about to say. He looked up at me through dark lashes, and it was like staring into the face of a stranger, one with a darkly beautiful visage and a hypnotic gaze. I remembered the old saying that the only difference between Don Juan and Casanova, the world's two greatest lovers, was that when Don Juan ended relationships, the women hated him, and when Casanova left, they still adored him. I was beginning to understand why.

I snatched my hand back before I was tempted to use it to drag him over the table. "Cut it out!"

He blinked in surprise and reached for me again. This time, the warm feeling was stronger when we touched, sending a frisson of heat dancing across my skin. I had a sudden image of sultry Spanish nights, the scent of jasmine, and warm, golden skin sliding against mine. I closed my eyes, swallowing hard, trying to reject the sensations, but that only seemed to help them become more real. Someone pushed me back against a thick feather mattress, practically burying me in its plump folds, and I could actually feel the soft weave of the sheets under my hands. A fall of silken hair spilled all around me and strong hands skimmed down my sides, a teasing touch that barely registered but flooded my veins with heat.

Then, with no warning, the sensation changed, going from seductive warmth to scorching heat. For a moment, I thought Casanova's touch would actually burn me, but he released my hand before it edged over into real pain. I opened my eyes to find us still sitting in the bar; the only signs that anything had happened were my flushed face and pounding pulse.

Casanova sighed and sat back in his seat. "Whoever did the *geis* knew what he was doing," he told me, signaling for a refill. "Out of curiosity, who was it? I would have said there were none I couldn't break."

"I have no idea what you're talking about." I rubbed my hand where it felt like he'd left an imprint of his fingers behind, and glared at him. I didn't appreciate the attempted distraction—I was not his afternoon snack—nor whatever had ended it so painfully.

"The *geis*. I didn't know anyone had a prior claim or I wouldn't—"

"What's a gesh?" He spelled it for me, which didn't help. A waiter brought us both new drinks and I gulped some of mine, my mood blackening by the second.

"Don't play games, Cassie; you know what I am. Did you think I wouldn't see it?" he asked impatiently; then something in my expression made his eyes widen. "You really don't know, do you?"

I stared at him resentfully. More complications; just what I needed right now. "Either make some sense or—"

"Someone, a powerful magic user or a master vampire, has put a claim on you," he said patiently, then corrected himself. "No, not a claim. More like an immense KEEP OFF sign a mile high."

I sat there, feeling a new wave of heat creep up my neck. I remembered a cultured, amused voice telling me that I belonged to him, always had and always would. I was going to kill him.

"What does that mean, exactly?"

"A *geis* is a magical bond, usually involving a taboo or prohibition over personal behavior." He saw my confusion. "Do you remember the story of Melusine?"

A childhood memory surfaced, but it was vague. "A fairy tale; French, I think. She was some half fairy who turned into a dragon, right?"

Casanova sighed, shaking his head at my ignorance. "Melusine was a beautiful woman six days of the week, but was cursed to appear as a half serpent on the seventh. She married Raymond of Lusignan after he agreed to a *geis* prohibiting him from ever seeing her on Saturday, even though she refused to say why. They had many happy years together until one of his cousins convinced Raymond that Saturday was the day she spent with her lover, and he spied on her to find out the truth. That broke the *geis*, causing Melusine to become a dragon permanently and losing Raymond the love of his life."

"You're telling me that story was real?"

"I have no idea. The point is, that's how a *geis* operates." His hand hovered over mine, but he didn't attempt to touch me again. "This one is the strongest I've ever felt, and it's been in place for some time now. It has a good grip."

"Define 'some time.'"

"Years," he said, concentrating. "At least a decade, maybe more. And a decade isn't a simple matter of ten years. For purposes of the spell, it's measured as a percentage of your life span. You're what, early twenties?"

"I'll be twenty-four tomorrow."

He shrugged. "Well, there you have it. For roughly half your life, someone has owned you."

A new rush of blood flooded my face. I remembered a cultured, amused voice telling me that I belonged to him, always had and always would. I was going to kill him. "No one owns me," I said shortly, but Casanova didn't look impressed. "What does this *geis* do, other than to warn people off?"

I soon wished I hadn't asked. "The *dúthracht geis* is a strong magical connection—one of the strongest. During the Middle Ages, paranoid mages with nonmagical wives employed it as a variation on a chastity belt. I've also heard of it being used in arranged marriages, to smooth out initial awkwardness."

He concentrated for a moment before continuing. "As far as I can determine, it allows whoever put it in place to know your emotions—your true ones, not whatever you're trying to project—so you can't lie to him. It also gives him a rough idea of where you are at any given time. He may not know your exact location, but he'll certainly be able to narrow it down to a city, and possibly further."

I remembered the arrogant jerk who I strongly suspected was behind this telling me that he had been able to find me once because he'd had help from the Senate's intelligence network. Maybe he had, but it seemed there had been more to it. I wondered how many other times he'd told me only part of the truth.

"And, last but not least, it heightens the attraction between you, with each meeting becoming more intense. Eventually, you won't want to run."

I felt myself go cold. "Then nothing I feel is real." I couldn't believe he'd stooped that low. He knew damned well how I felt about having my thoughts or feelings altered.

The jerk in question was Mircea, a five-hundred-year-old vampire whose biggest claim to fame was being Dracula's older brother. He'd also been my first crush. I hadn't cared about his family name, or that he was a first-level master and a Senate member. I'd been far more interested in the way his rich brown eyes crinkled at the corners when he laughed, in the mahogany hair that spilled over his broad shoulders and in that wickedly perfect mouth, still the most sensual I've ever seen. Among his other titles, Mircea was also the vamp Tony called Master. It was something that should have made me question the sincerity in that handsome face a lot sooner.

"The *dúthracht* doesn't create emotions," Casanova corrected me. "It isn't a love spell. It can only enhance what is already there. Which is why it's odd that anyone would have used it on you at what, age eleven, twelve?"

I nodded numbly, but the truth was that I didn't find it odd at all. My mother had been heir to the Pythia's throne before she eloped with my father. The fact that she'd been disinherited meant nothing as far as my chances for succeeding were concerned, however, because it isn't the old Pythia who chooses the new one. The final selection is made by the power of the office itself. In all but a handful of instances over thousands of years, it has selected the designated heir, the one groomed as a successor by the old Pythia. But Mircea had gambled that I would be one of the exceptions and had spared no effort to ensure that I'd still be eligible when the moment arrived.

For reasons I didn't fully understand, the heir has to remain chaste until the changeover ritual begins, and Mircea hadn't wanted to risk a teenage infatuation removing me from contention. So he'd marked me as off-limits by putting a claim on me himself. Bastard.

"You said it boosts emotion," I said, thinking about the first time I encountered Mircea as an adult. "Are you only talking about mine?" Mircea hadn't appeared exactly uninterested when I saw him last, but it was difficult to be certain. Most vamps are excellent liars, but he is the undisputed, number one champ, possibly because it's his job. He's the Senate's chief diplomat, the guy sent into tricky situations to get whatever they want through persuasion, seduction or deceit. He's very good at what he does.

"No, it's a two-way street, one of the spell's big drawbacks in most people's opinion." Casanova leaned forward, apparently enjoying lecturing me. "Think of it as an amplifier on a stereo: every meeting edges it up a notch. You have to give it something to start with, but once it's up and running, you're on the path to obsession with each other whether either of you likes it or not."

I turned away so he wouldn't see my expression, and tried to ignore the hard knot in my chest and the tight ache in my throat. I didn't know why I felt so betrayed. It wasn't as if I had ever completely trusted Mircea. I knew that no master vampire, especially a Senate member, fell into the category of nice guy. He couldn't have achieved his current position by being anything less than ruthless. But I would have given odds that he wouldn't do something like this. Tony, yes; that I could see, but I'd foolishly believed that his boss was different. Stupid. Who did I think had trained him?

I looked back to find Casanova carefully expressionless. "You're saying this is dangerous."

"All magic is dangerous, *chica*," he told me gently, "under the right circumstances."

"Don't hedge!" I didn't need my feelings spared, I needed answers. Something that would help me figure a way out of this.

"I'm not hedging," he insisted. A woman let out a high-pitched scream and his eyes shifted to a spot behind me. "Damn!"

I looked over my shoulder to see that my three roommates had decided to take up darts, despite the fact that the bar was not actually equipped with a board. While I'd been distracted, Deino had positioned herself at one end of the bar and Pemphredo at the other, while Enyo stood in front blowing toothpicks at the hapless bartender. Before we could make a move, Enyo blew another mouthful of tiny projectiles, leaving the poor satyr looking like a very unhappy pincushion. The woman screamed again as a forest of little red dots sprouted on his chest, and Casanova gestured for her companion to take her away. He went to rescue his employee and I followed to rescue him. The girls sometimes listen to me—when they feel like it—although I get the impression that I'm considered a spoilsport.

Casanova sent the trembling bartender on a much-deserved break, while I placated the girls by fishing some cards out of my purse. It's a standard tarot deck I received for a birthday present years ago that is charmed to act as a sort of metaphysical mood ring. It doesn't do specifics, but its forecasts of the overall climate surrounding a situation tend to be eerily accurate. I was not happy to see the card that poked up from the deck as soon as I touched it.

Despite the common misconception, the Lovers rarely has anything to do with finding a soul mate or even having a good time. The Two of Cups normally indicates that romance is on the way, but the Lovers is more complex. It points to a looming choice, one that will involve temptation and pain. And, like the depiction of the card in my deck—Adam and Eve being thrown out of Eden—the final decision will have huge consequences for everything that follows. Needless to say, it has never been one of my favorites.

While I confiscated the remaining toothpicks and gave the girls their new toy, Casanova arranged for another bartender. Finally, we rendezvoused back at our table. "It all depends on your point of view," he said, picking up the conversation as if nothing had happened. I suppose he'd dealt with worse over the centuries than a few bored grandmas. "Of itself, the *geis* is harmless. But then, so was Melusine's—as long as it wasn't broken. Your version merely causes devotion to one person. If nothing interferes with that relationship, both of you live happily ever after."

The fact that I might not want to live, happily or otherwise, in a magically induced state of mind was obviously not important. "What if something does interfere?"

Casanova looked faintly uncomfortable. "Love is a many splendored thing, as I have cause to know. But it has its ugly side, too. If anyone or anything is perceived as posing a threat to the bond, it acts to remove that threat." He saw my impatience and elaborated. "Say a person, nonmagical obviously, was to take an interest in you. A norm would be unable to sense the *geis*, so the warning would go unheeded."

"What would happen?"

"It would depend. If the bond was new and the two of you had not spent much time together—if the amplitude, in other words, was set on low—maybe nothing. But the higher the volume, the more the interference would be resented. Eventually, one or both of you would move to eliminate the threat."

"Eliminate? You mean, as in kill?" My jaw dropped. Mircea must have been out of his mind.

"It probably wouldn't come to that," Casanova assured me, and I felt my stomach unclench slightly. "Most suitors would exit quickly enough when you started screaming abuse, or your lover began threatening them."

Great, I thought as my stomach went back to its former knotted state. I could go cuckoo's nest at any moment, thanks to Mircea's idea of insurance. "But what if the originator of the *geis* wanted someone to seduce me?"

It wasn't an idle question. Mircea had sent a vampire named Tomas to befriend me when the Pythia's health began to fail. Lady Phemonoe, the Pythia better known to me as Agnes, had realized she was dying and had begun the rites that would free the power to go to a successor. And that had started a whole new ball game. Agnes could initiate the ancient ritual, but only I could complete it—by losing the virginity Mircea had guarded so carefully. He had designated Tomas to take care of that little item for him to avoid getting caught in his own trap. Mircea had been born before the notion of a woman choosing her sexual partners was fashionable, and Tomas was the servant of another master vampire and expected to follow orders. So, of course, neither of us had been consulted about any of this.

Tomas was one of those rare vamps able to mimic the human condition so perfectly that we lived as roommates for six months without me guessing what he was. We became close, although not as close as Mircea would have liked. I was reluctant to involve anyone in my crazy life and thought I was protecting Tomas by keeping him at a distance. But all it had done was force Mircea himself to have to stand in for the ritual.

As it turned out, we had been interrupted before the main event, something I'd been grateful for once my head cleared a little. Completing the ritual meant that I would be stuck as Pythia for life—a no-doubt extremely abbreviated period of time considering how much of a target that made me. Not that my life expectancy at the moment seemed all that great, either.

"The originator of the *geis* can lift it for a particular person," Casanova confirmed. "I've heard of instances when the spell was used on heiresses by their guardians, to ensure that they remained chaste until appropriate suitors were selected. The devotion aspect of the spell was supposed to guarantee that they would happily accept whomever was chosen."

I didn't like Casanova's expression. "What happened?"

He fumbled getting another cigarette out of a slim gold

case. Considering how graceful his movements usually were, I had a feeling I wasn't going to like the answer. "The *geis* fell out of favor because it tends to backfire," he explained, lighting up. "Sometimes it worked, but there were cases when girls committed suicide rather than marry someone other than their guardians."

At my appalled expression, he hurried to explain. "It is a very difficult spell to cast properly, Cassie. Devotion can mean so many things. The *geis* is designed to ensure loyalty, but how many human emotions do you know that have only one facet? Loyalty easily transmutes to admiration—for why, do you think, would I be loyal to someone who is not, in some way, admirable? Admiration becomes attraction, attraction into love and love usually leads to the desire to possess that which is loved. You follow?"

"Yes." Apparently, my body was a few steps ahead of my brain, because my arms had broken out in goose flesh.

"Possessiveness commonly develops an aspect of exclusivity—this person should belong to me and no other, we were meant to be together, that sort of thing." He waved a hand, causing his cigarette smoke to weave drunkenly on its way towards the ceiling. I felt kind of like that, too. My brain was stumbling about, trying to make sense of this mess, and my emotions were all over the place.

"That leads to covetousness," Casanova was saying, "which can convert to despair or hatred if thwarted. Even when cast properly, the spell often causes problems, with how many and what kind depending on the personalities of those bonded. And because it's so complex, it can easily be screwed up. Most mages won't even attempt it anymore. Your admirer is either a powerful magic worker or he knows someone who is."

"He can afford the best," I said absently. It must have seemed the perfect solution: leave me with Tony, one of his supposedly loyal servants, and put me under the *geis* so I would remain untouched until he saw whether the power was going to come to me. It was a great plan, if my feelings were discounted. And, of course, they had been. Master vampires tend to treat their servants like pieces on a chessboard, moving them about with no concern over little things like what the piece itself might want.

"It can't be Antonio," Casanova mused, regarding me speculatively. "You were at his court for years before you ran away. The spell would never have allowed you to leave him, nor would you have wanted to try."

I winced. Even the thought of being infatuated with Tony was enough to make me slightly sick. "Can it be removed?"

"By the person who originated it, certainly."

"No, without him."

Casanova shook his head. "I couldn't do it, and I'm very good, *chica*." He gave me an arch look. "Of course, if I knew more about who we're discussing, it might help. Perhaps one of my contacts . . ."

I didn't want to tell him. Tony was his immediate boss, but Mircea was Tony's master. He therefore had a claim to anything Tony had and to anyone who owed him loyalty. There was normally a certain amount of maneuvering that had to be done before a senior master could simply take one of his underling's possessions, at least if that subordinate had reached third-level master status, as Tony had. But since Tony was now in open defiance of both Mircea and the Senate, everything he owned had reverted to his master's control. Which was a roundabout way of saying that Mircea was Casanova's master. The incubus was unlikely to defy him, but he obviously wasn't going to give me any help without more information.

I sighed. I didn't like being backed into a corner, but who else was I going to ask? "Mircea," I said, after checking to make sure we weren't being overheard.

Casanova looked blank for a moment, then jumped up as if someone had given him a hotfoot. "You might have mentioned that earlier, Cassie!" he hissed in an alarmed whisper. "Getting this body skinned alive is *not* on my daily agenda!"

"Sit down," I told him in irritation. "Tell me how I get rid of this thing."

"You don't. Take some advice, *chica*," he said seriously. "Go home to the nice master vampire, beg forgiveness for causing him any inconvenience and do whatever he tells you. You do not want this one angry with you."

"I've seen Mircea pissed off," I said. That was true, although so far it had never been at me. I nudged Casanova's chair with my foot. "Sit down. People are starting to stare."

"Yes, they are," Casanova agreed, "which is why I'm going straight to my office, picking up the phone and giving the big boss a call. If you don't want him to find you, I suggest you use the time between now and then to run like hell. Not that it will do you any good."

"You're afraid of him!"

"Let me think," he said sarcastically. "Yes! As you should be."

I stared up at him in confusion. The vamp I knew wasn't someone to be trifled with, but I'd never seen him do anything that would explain why an ancient demon would be shaking in his designer shoes. "We're talking about Mircea, right?"

Casanova glanced around, then slid into the seat next to

me, looking almost comically grave. "Listen to me, little girl, and pay attention, because I am never saying this again. Mircea is the greatest manipulator I've ever known. There's a reason he's the Senate's chief negotiator—he always gets what he wants. My advice: make it easy on him, and perhaps he'll go easy on you."

I grabbed his tie to keep him from running for the phone and jerked his face close to mine. I'm not normally the violent type—I saw too much of it growing up to want any part of it—but at the moment I was too mad to care. "You've had your speech, now listen to mine. I know all about manipulation. I haven't lived a day when someone wasn't pulling my strings. Even this whole Pythia gig wasn't my idea. But you know what? It does change things, doesn't it? Mircea doesn't own me, no matter what he thinks. No one does. And anyone who tries to jerk me around from now on is going to find that I make a very bad enemy. Do you get it?"

Casanova pantomimed choking and I released him. He fell back in his chair, looking more amused than frightened. "If you're so powerful, why do you need my help?" he asked archly. "Why not remove the *geis* yourself, and rain down your wrath on Antonio while you're at it?"

"It doesn't work quite like that," I said dryly. "And what is so damn funny?"

The grin that Casanova had been attempting, unsuccessfully, to restrain broke over his face. "Inside joke," he chortled. "You'd have to be an incubus to understand."

"Give me the condensed version."

He looked coy. The expression should have appeared odd on his strong-featured face, but he pulled it off. "Anticipation, you might say. Like looking forward to the next heavyweight championship match. In this corner," he said, his voice taking on the cadence of a veteran ringside announcer, "we have Lord Mircea, never defeated in five hundred years of political and social maneuvering. And in this corner, his opponent, the deceptively sweet-looking Cassandra, newly elevated to the Pythia's throne." He grinned even wider. "You have to understand, Cassie. For an incubus, it doesn't get much better than this. If I wasn't so protective of this body, I'd be wrangling for a ringside seat."

"You're babbling," I said in disgust. "Tell me something I can use!"

"Why don't you tell *me* something for a change?" he countered. "What, precisely, do you think you're going to do if you find Tony? He's been around for a long time. He isn't going to be easy to kill. Why not relax and let Mircea handle him? He'll find him sooner or later and then you and I are both—"

"Mircea can't deal with Myra!" I couldn't believe Casanova still didn't get it. "He might be able to protect me in the here and now, but it isn't the present that worries me." Myra had been Agnes' heir until she fell in with some very bad company and was disinherited. But her fall hadn't taken away her abilities, meaning that she could slip into the past and attack me long before I even knew who she was. She could even kill one of my parents, insuring I was never born. And Mircea couldn't do a damn thing about it.

"But if Antonio is protecting her, how do you expect—"

"I have a few surprises for Tony. What I need from you—"

"Is likely to cost me greatly. You cannot believe—" He broke off at my expression. "What is it?" I jumped to my feet, wobbling a little in the heels, and stared over his head at the sight barreling in the bar's entrance.

My least favorite war mage was heading across the lobby

at a dead run. His short blond hair looked like it had been hacked at by a machete, and his icy green eyes were angry. Not that that was unusual: I'd never seen him smile, and normally considered it a good day if he wasn't trying to kill me. Considering that he was wearing his usual knee-length leather coat, the one that bulged with concealed weapons, it didn't look like today would be one of those.

Chapter 2

"Is that who I think it is?" Casanova gave a panicked glance at the mage, whose coat had blown open to reveal enough firepower to take out a platoon. Even vamps are cautious around war mages—wizards and witches who have been trained in human and magical combat techniques by the Circle. They have the *Shoot first, ask questions if you feel like it later* mentality that human law enforcement left behind with the Wild West. Of course, police officers don't have to face the kind of surprises the mages frequently get.

I'd already seen as much of this particular mage as I wanted, and apparently Casanova felt the same. Without waiting for me to answer, he let go of dignity and dove under the table. I was wondering whether it was worth the effort to try to run, when Enyo hopped down from her bar stool and jogged over. She gestured at the mage and raised bushy eyebrows that in her case protected only empty folds of skin. I'm not sure how I knew what she was thinking, because she didn't say a word, but the point came across. I shook my head emphatically. I wasn't actually sure what he was, but "friend" didn't sound right.

Enyo whirled to face the mage, who was only a couple of tables away. He stopped dead in his tracks and a second later I realized why. The three sisters weren't pretty by anyone's standards, but they looked harmless enough. Enyo's squashed face—containing so many folds that the absence of eyes wasn't all that noticeable—toothless mouth and straggling hair normally made her resemble a particularly homely bag lady. But she didn't look that way now.

My mythological knowledge is not great, composed mainly of bits and pieces left over from long-ago lessons with Eugenie, my old governess. This was one of those times I wished I'd paid more attention. Where a diminutive old lady had been, a towering Amazon stood, clad only in matted ankle-length hair and a lot of blood. Enyo's transformation was so quick that I hadn't seen it take place, but Pritkin's face, which had shut down to the pale, closed look he gets when truly terrified, told me there was more to her story than I recalled. I decided I didn't want to know.

I have never claimed to be a hero. Besides, Casanova had started to crawl away, using the tables as cover, and I still didn't know where Tony was. I dropped to the floor and followed on his heels. The next second, it sounded like all hell had broken loose behind us, but I wasn't crazy enough to look around. I've had lots of practice running away, and I've learned that it's best to keep your mind on the goal.

Half of a black lacquered chair flew over my head, but I just ducked lower and crawled faster. Casanova appeared to be heading for a blank stretch of wall, but I knew better. This was one of Tony's places, and he never built anything that didn't have at least a dozen emergency exits. I was pretty sure that somewhere up ahead was a door hidden by a glamour, so when the top half of Casanova's body disappeared into the red Chinese wallpaper, I wasn't surprised. I grabbed a handful of his suit coat, scrunched up my eyes and followed. I opened them again to find that we were in a utilitarian corridor with industrial fluorescent lighting.

Casanova tried to pull away, but I held on for dear life. It wasn't easy since the impromptu escape had left me with a serious wedgie and he was stronger than I was. But he was my best link to Tony and I wasn't about to lose him. "Oh, all right!" he said, dragging me to my feet. "This way!"

We raced to a door that led to a much more luxurious corridor carpeted in thick scarlet plush. The gold brocade wallpaper boasted a line of salacious prints and reeked of musky perfume. I gasped, but Casanova was too busy punching the elevator call button a dozen times to notice. It finally came just as I was about to give up on the idea of breathing altogether, and we jumped on board. Casanova hit the button for the fifth floor and I managed to choke out a protest. "Shouldn't we be heading down, to the parking level? If we stay in the building, he'll find us."

He shot me a look. "Do you really think he came alone?" I shrugged. I'd never seen Pritkin work with other mages, so it seemed possible. He did enough mayhem all on his own. "He almost certainly has backup," Casanova informed me, running shaking hands down his slightly rumpled suit. "Let the internal defenses deal with them."

The elevator let out into a spacious office that looked a lot like a boudoir. There were mirrors and fat chaises everywhere, and a bar almost as big as the one downstairs lined one wall. A good-looking secretary, who was probably going to be recruited by the incubi if he hadn't been already, tried to offer us refreshments, but Casanova waved him off. We barreled through a set of doors to a plush inner office.

Casanova ignored the huge four-poster bed sitting incongruously in the corner and the two scantily clad women reclin-
ing on it. He stepped through a multicolored modernist
painting that covered most of one wall and I followed, ignoring the scowls the girls sent my way. On the other side was
a narrow room that was bare except for a table, a chair and
a large mirror hanging on the wall. He waved a hand over
the mirror's surface and it shimmered like a mirage in the
desert. I figured out that this was his way of checking on his
employees.

I'd seen similar devices before. Tony had never been able
to use security cameras, since anything run on electricity
doesn't do well around powerful wards and his Philadelphia
stronghold had bristled with them. I'd had to learn about his
surveillance equipment in order to elude it when up to things
I preferred him not to know about, like stealing his personal
files and setting him up with the Feds. Not that that had
worked out too well, but at least I hadn't been caught during
the preparations. I'd discovered that any reflective surface
could be spelled to act as a monitor linked to other shiny ex-
teriors within a certain radius. Considering the number of
mirrors and all the polished marble around the place,
Casanova could probably check on anything within the spa.

He muttered a word, and an image of the bar appeared. I
wondered about the distortion until I realized that he was
using the large Chinese gong behind the bar as his spy hole.
It was convex, so the image was, too, along with being tinted
faintly bronze. I saw the backs of three people whom I identified as war mages by the amount of hardware they were
wearing. I didn't see Pritkin and was slightly worried that
Enyo had eaten him.

She certainly looked capable of it. The vague old woman

had been replaced by a blood-covered savage whose head brushed the edge of the fringed lanterns that swung from the central chandelier. Her hair was still gray, but the body had gotten a definite upgrade and she now had a full compliment of teeth and eyes. The former were longer and sharper than a vamp's and the latter were yellow and slitted like a cat's. She looked pissed off, maybe because she was encased in a magical web, courtesy of the mages. She slashed at it with four-inch-long talons and it ripped like paper, but before she could move, the slender cords reknitted themselves, holding her fast.

It looked to me like a standoff, and I wondered why her sisters, who were still lounging at the bar, didn't intervene. I'd barely had the thought before Pemphredo glanced up at the gong. Since it was her turn with the eye, she was able to wink at me before cutting loose.

I remembered that, when I'd looked up some information on the sisters after they dropped in, Pemphredo had been called "the master of alarming surprises." I hadn't been sure what that meant, but since the three had been given the task of protecting the Gorgons, I assumed they each had some kind of warlike talent. Considering what had happened to Medusa, though, it didn't seem like they'd been too effective.

As if she'd heard me, Pemphredo suddenly turned her gaze on the nearest mage, a delicate Asian woman, who didn't even have time to scream before the heavy lacquered chandelier came crashing down on her head. Pieces of splintered wood went flying everywhere, and the woman disappeared under a pile of red silk lanterns. It seemed the gals had been practicing.

The mage managed to crawl out from under the fixture a

few seconds later, looking battered and bloody, but still breathing. She was in no condition to rejoin the fight, though, and her companions were having trouble holding Enyo on their own. She was tearing through the net almost faster than they could reform it, and it was starting to look like a question of who would tire first. I couldn't tell whether she was getting weary, but even with their backs to me, the mages looked strained, with their raised arms visibly shaking.

"We have a problem," Casanova said.

"Duh." I watched as Pemphredo glanced at one of the other mages, who promptly shot himself in the foot. Deino was sipping beer and trying to flirt with the new bartender, who had crouched behind the bar with his arms over his head. Casanova was probably going to get requests for combat pay after today. I decided that I could live without learning what her special talent was.

"No. I mean we *really* have a problem." I glanced up at Casanova's tone to see a pissed-off mage standing in the doorway, a sawed-off shotgun leveled on us.

I sighed. "Hello, Pritkin."

"Call off your harpies or this will be a very short conversation."

I sighed again. Pritkin has that effect on me. "They aren't harpies. They're the Graeae, ancient Greek demigoddesses. Or something."

Pritkin sneered. It was what he did best, other than for killing things. "Trust you to side with the monsters. Call them off." An edge of anger threaded through his words, threatening to grow into something more substantial soon.

"I can't." It was the truth, but I wasn't surprised that he didn't believe me. I couldn't recall Pritkin ever believing anything I said; it kind of made me wonder why he bothered talking to me at all. Of course, conversation probably wasn't foremost on his list. It'd be somewhere after dragging me back to the Silver Circle, throwing me in a really deep dungeon and losing the key.

I discovered that a sawed-off, double-barreled shotgun sounds very loud when cocked in a small room.

"Do as he says, Cassie," Casanova chimed in. "I like this body as it is. If it acquires a large hole, I will be very annoyed."

"Yeah, and that's really what's worrying us." The comment came from the ghost who had just drifted through the wall. Casanova swatted in his direction as you might a pesky fly, but missed him. "I thought incubi were supposed to be charming," Billy said, wafting out of the way.

Casanova couldn't see Billy, but his demon senses could obviously hear him. His handsome forehead acquired an annoyed wrinkle, but he didn't deign to respond. I was glad about that, since it meant that Pritkin couldn't be sure that Billy was there.

Billy Joe is what remains of an Irish-American gambler with a love for loose women, dirty limericks and cheating at cards. Because of that last item, he cashed in his chips for the final time at the ripe old age of twenty-nine. A couple of cowboys hadn't liked his faint Irish accent, his ruffled shirt or the fact that the saloon girls were paying him a lot of attention. But the real kicker had come when he won too many hands at cards and they caught him with an ace up his sleeve. Billy was soon thereafter introduced to the inside of a croaker sack, which in turn made the acquaintance of the bottom of the Mississippi.

That should have ended a colorful, if abbreviated, life.

But a few weeks earlier Billy had won a variety of favors off a visiting countess—at least he claimed she'd had a title— one of which was an ugly ruby necklace that doubled as a talisman. It soaked up magical energy from the natural world and transmitted it to its owner, or in this case, to its owner's ghost. Billy's spirit had come to reside in the necklace, which gathered dust in an antique shop until I happened along looking for a present for my notoriously picky governess. I've been able to see ghosts all my life, but even I was surprised by my gift with purchase.

We'd soon discovered that not only was I the first person in years who could see him, I was also the only one of the necklace's owners who could donate energy in excess of the subsistence it provided. With regular donations from me, Billy was able to become much more active. In exchange, I got his help with my various problems. At least in theory.

He caught my look and shrugged. "This place has too many entrances. I couldn't watch them all." He glanced behind the mage. "He's got his helper with him."

He was looking at what appeared to be a man-sized clay statue. I had mistaken it for one the first time I'd seen it, but it was actually a golem. Rabbis versed in kabbalah magic were supposed to have invented them, but these days they were popular among the war mages as assistants—maybe because it's hard to hurt something with no internal organs.

I reviewed possible strategies, but none of my usual defenses seemed like a good idea. The lopsided pentagram tattooed on my back is actually a ward that can stop most magical attacks. It was crafted by the Silver Circle itself and I had seen it do some fairly amazing things, but I didn't know if it would stop a nonmagical assault of that caliber. This didn't seem like the best time to test it.

I also had a bracelet made of little interlocking daggers that seemed to dislike Pritkin even more than I did. It had once belonged to a dark mage who had used it mostly to destroy things. He'd been evil, and I suspected his jewelry was, too, but I couldn't seem to get rid of it. I'd tried burying it, flushing it down a toilet and feeding it to a garbage disposal, but no go. No matter what I did, the next time I looked it was on my wrist again, whole and shiny and new, glinting at me impudently. Sometimes it came in handy, and mostly it obeyed my commands, but it never passed up a chance to relive old times. All on its own it had sent two ghostly knives to stab Pritkin the last time we met. The hand with the bracelet was firmly in my pocket at the moment; no need to escalate this further. Fortunately, I had another option.

"Hey, Billy. Think you can possess a golem?" Pritkin's eyes didn't waver, but his shoulders twitched slightly.

"Never tried." Billy floated over and eyed the golem without enthusiasm. He doesn't like possessions. They sap his energy level and often don't work anyway. Instead, his favorite trick is to drift through someone, picking up any stray thoughts and leaving a hint or two of his own behind. But that wouldn't help us now. "Guess there's only one way to find out," he muttered.

As soon as Billy stepped into the thing, I found out why experiments are done under controlled conditions. The golem began careening about the outer office, knocking over tubs of plants and sending the girls screaming into the next room. Then it altered course and crashed into Pritkin, sending him sprawling.

I couldn't tell whether that had been deliberate, but I sort of doubted it when the creature started ricocheting around our tiny cubicle like a pinball on speed. It knocked me a glancing blow on its way to destroy the table and sent me stumbling into the mage. I started to yell at Billy to get out of the thing, but my breath was knocked out by Pritkin's knee, which came into contact with my stomach when I fell on him. To be fair, my high heel might have gotten him in a sensitive spot, but it had been an accident. I didn't think his knee was.

As I was struggling to get enough breath back to tell him off, a very familiar and extremely unwelcome feeling came over me. Time shifting is supposed to be under the Pythia's control, not vice versa, but someone needed to tell my power that. I had only enough time to think, *Oh no, not now*, before I was flailing about in that cold, gray area between time.

After my short free fall, the ground rushed up and hit me in the face. When my vision cleared, I identified the surface as carpet with a red and black oriental pattern thinly stretched over very hard wood. For a stunned minute I thought I'd ended up back in the bar, but then I noticed the two sets of feet in front of me. They didn't look like they belonged to tourists.

The woman was wearing tiny black silk heels with a scattering of jet beads on the toe. They matched the beadwork on her elaborate black evening gown, the hem of which was about a foot in front of my face. The beading ran up the front of the dress to an impossibly small waist, then disappeared, I assume so it wouldn't detract from the fortune in diamonds she wore draped around her slim throat and clipped into her golden curls. I glanced at her lovely blue eyes, narrowed in distaste as she regarded me, and quickly looked away. It isn't a good idea to stare a vampire in the eyes for long, and that is unquestionably what she was.

I scrambled to my feet and got another shock. I almost

fell again—only Tony would be sadistic enough to make waitresses wear three-inch heels—and a hand reached out to steady me. A very familiar hand.

Like the woman, her escort was obviously dressed for evening, in a black swallowtail coat over a low-cut vest, white shirt and white bowtie. His highly polished shoes shone more than his understated jewelry—plain gold cufflinks that matched the clip holding his hair in a ponytail at the nape of his neck. The discreet accessories didn't surprise me—Mircea has never liked showy clothes. What threw me was the abrupt, overwhelming sense of joy that spread over me as soon as our eyes met.

I was suddenly struck by the sheer masculine beauty of him. He was so gracefully made that I caught my breath, all long limbs and elegant lines, like a dancer or a long-distance runner—or what he was, the product of noble blood going back for generations. Only one feature didn't fit that picture: his mouth was not the thin-lipped aristocratic version, but had the full, beautifully sculpted lips of a sensualist.

Maybe there had been more peasant stock in the gene pool than the family would admit, people who might not have had the airs and graces of their lords, but who knew how to laugh and dance and drink with a passion the aristocrats had forgotten. Dracula was supposed to have been the one born of a fiery gypsy girl, but I'd sometimes wondered whether the old rumors had gotten things mixed up, and instead it was Mircea who had Romany blood. If so, it suited him.

His hand was under my elbow in a light, impersonal touch, but for some reason it made my whole arm tingle. I tried to sense the *geis* Casanova had talked about, but nothing registered. If I hadn't known better, I would have sworn there was no spell to find.

I realized vaguely that my hands had begun smoothing the thick silk of Mircea's waistcoat. It was crimson with red dragons embroidered on it and seemed a little flashy for him, although the tone on tone made the designs almost invisible unless the light hit them just right. The embroidery was smooth against my fingertips, a beautiful, intricate design. I could even see the tiny scales on the dragons. Then my wandering hands discovered something more interesting, the faint prick of nipples, barely discernable under several layers of fabric.

My fingertips traced them delicately, my whole body vibrating with pleasure from that small sensation. Being near Mircea caused none of the mind-numbing effects of Casanova's attempt at seduction. I could have pulled away; I just couldn't think of anything I wanted less.

Mircea also wasn't going anywhere. He just stood there, looking bemused, but the hand on my arm began pulling me gently towards him.

I went willingly, lost in admiration for the way the gas light gleamed in his hair, and a thrumming energy suddenly ran up my arm. It hit my shoulder, then dove back down to jump from my fingertips like electricity. Mircea jerked slightly as the sensation hit him, but he did not let go. The feeling echoed back and forth, holding the two of us in a loop of sensation that made the hairs on my arm stand up and my body tighten.

The dark eyes examined me as slowly and thoroughly as I had inspected him. The sensation of that gaze made me shiver, and Mircea's eyebrow climbed a fraction at my reaction. His hand moved to the small of my back but encountered only the tough frame of the corset. His touch slid down to the curve of my hip, his fingers splaying over the thin satin of my shorts as he pressed us close.

I took a deep breath and tried to cope with the waves of emotion that were rolling over me, but it did no good. Mircea didn't help by reaching up to delicately brush my cheek with the backs of his fingers. A spark of gold leapt in his pupils, a color that I knew from experience indicated heightened emotion. When he was truly angry or aroused, cinnamon amber light spiraled up to fill his eyes, giving them an otherworldly glow that others found frightening but I had always thought beautiful.

Someone cleared his throat in a harsh bark. Pritkin's voice sounded over my shoulder. "My deepest apologies, sir, madam. I am afraid one of our actresses is not well. I trust she has given no offense?"

"Not at all." Mircea sounded distracted, and he made no move to release me.

"I will take her backstage, where she can rest." Pritkin put a hand on my arm, to haul me away, but Mircea's hand tightened on my hip. His eyes had begun to glow, the green and light brown flecks no longer visible against the rising tide of reddish gold.

"The child does not look well, Count Basarab," the female vamp said, taking his free arm, mirroring Pritkin's stance with me. "Let us not detain her."

Mircea ignored her. "Who are you?" he asked. His accent was thicker than I had ever heard it, and his tone was filled with the same wonder I felt.

I swallowed and shook my head. There was no safe reply. I didn't know where or even when I was, but since the female vamp had a slight bustle on her gown, I didn't think it was anywhere I'd find familiar. There was a good chance I wasn't even born yet. "Nobody," I whispered.

Mircea's companion gave what in a less elegant person would have been a snort. "We will miss the opening," she said, tugging on his sleeve.

After a noticeable pause Mircea released me, the invisible energy stretching between us like strings of taffy as his hand slid away. He allowed his companion to lead him down the corridor, but he looked back at me in puzzlement several times. The energy arced between us but didn't break, as if there was an invisible cord spanning the distance, tying us together. Then they disappeared into a small curtained archway to what I vaguely recognized as a theatre box.

As soon as the red velvet curtains swooshed shut behind them, cutting off my view, the connection between us snapped. I was immediately hit with a longing so intense it was actually painful. It clenched my stomach like someone had sucker punched me, and started a headache pounding behind my eyes. I barely noticed Pritkin dragging me to the end of the corridor, where a set of stairs climbed towards, presumably, another set of boxes. An orchestra started to tune up somewhere nearby, which explained why there were no more people in sight. The entertainment was about to begin.

The stairs were lit by a series of small lanterns along the wall, with deep areas of shadow in between. As a hiding spot it wasn't great, but I was too preoccupied to care. My hands were shaking and sweat had popped out on my face. I felt like a junkie who has been shown the needle but denied her fix. It was horrible.

"What did you do?" Pritkin glared at me, his short blond hair standing up in tufts as if it was angry, too. It was a pretty fierce expression, but I'd seen it before. And compared with what had just happened, it was almost trivial.

"I was about to ask you the same question," I replied, massaging my neck to try to clear my head. My other arm was clenched across my stomach, where it felt like a hole had been ripped into me by Mircea's absence. This could *not* be happening—I wouldn't let it. I would not spend the rest of my life salivating over him like some teenager with a rock star. I was not a groupie, damn it!

Pritkin gave me a little shake and I eyed him without favor. On the only other occasions when I had been dragged back in time, the trip had been triggered by proximity to a person whose past was being threatened. "I have to tell you," I said frankly, "if someone is trying to mess with your conception or something, I'm not feeling a pressing need to intervene."

His face, normally ruddy anyway, flushed a deeper shade of red. "Get us back where we belong before we change anything!" he spat.

I didn't like being given orders, but he had a point. And the fact that I had a strong urge to run down the hallway and throw myself into Mircea's arms was another good reason for getting out of there. I closed my eyes and concentrated on Casanova's office at Dante's, but although I could see it clearly, there was no rush of power sweeping me towards it. I tried again, but I guess my batteries needed a recharge because nothing happened.

"There might be a slight delay on this flight," I said, feeling queasy. All sorts of fears began crowding my brain. What if there was a time limit on the ritual that the former Pythia had forgotten to mention? What if I couldn't shift again, period, because the power had gotten tired of waiting for me to seal the deal and had passed to someone else? We could be stuck whenever this was permanently.

"What the bloody hell are you talking about?" Pritkin demanded. "Take us back immediately!"

"I can't."

"What do you mean, you can't? Every moment we spend here is a danger!"

Pritkin was shaking me again and I think he was getting worried, because his voice had roughened. I had no sympathy—whatever he was feeling was nothing compared to my mood. Wasn't my life messed up enough without having to handle the Pythia's responsibilities, too? Couldn't whoever was running this show let me deal with a few of the items on my personal problem list before dragging me off to sort out other people's? It wasn't fair and I'd about had enough. If I was supposed to do something, fine. Bring it on.

"Let me spell it out for you," I told Pritkin, shrugging out of his grasp. "I didn't bring us here. I don't even know where here is. All I know is that I can't shift us out, either because the power has decided it doesn't like me anymore, or because it wants me to do something before I leave." I was betting on the latter, since I didn't think landing at Mircea's feet had been an accident.

Pritkin didn't look like he believed me, but I didn't care. I turned away from him, intending to find out whether Mircea had any bright ideas, but Pritkin's hand clasped around my wrist in a viselike grip. "You aren't going anywhere," he said grimly.

"I have to find out what the problem is and deal with it, or neither of us will be going anywhere," I snapped. "So, unless you can tell me where we are and why we're here, I don't see much choice but to go exploring, do you?"

"We're in London, in late 1888 or early 1889."

I raised an eyebrow. I hadn't seen any clues to help narrow things down, other than the woman's clothes—Mircea's were standard formal wear that could have come from any period in a wide span of time. It was a little disconcerting to learn that Pritkin was a connoisseur of women's fashion. I said as much and he actually growled at me before thrusting a piece of paper into my hands.

"Here! Someone dropped this." I looked away from his perpetual glower to peruse the yellow and black flyer he'd given me. It showed a man staring up a hill at three old crones. They sort of reminded me of the Graeae, only they had better hair. It informed me that it was a souvenir of the Lyceum Theatre's performance of *Macbeth*, beginning December 29, 1888.

"Okay, great. We know the date. It's a start, but I don't see it getting us too far." I tried to pull away again, but he stopped me, this time with words.

"The more you feed the *geis*, the stronger it will become. Not to mention that prostitutes in this era wear more clothes than you currently have on. You can't go anywhere without causing a riot."

"How did you know?" It was disconcerting to find out that I'd been wearing the equivalent of a sign on my back for years. Could everybody see it but me?

Pritkin gave a one-shouldered shrug. "I knew the first time I saw you together."

I considered the situation and figured it was worth a shot. "I don't suppose you could do something about it? We are in this together, after all, and I could probably think more clearly if—"

"Only Mircea can remove it," Pritkin said, dashing what

little hope I'd had. "Even the mage who cast it for him couldn't do it without his assent. The best you can do at present is to stay away from him."

I frowned. It was pretty much the same thing Casanova had said, but I wasn't buying it. "I don't know much about magic, but even I know there's no such thing as a spell that can't be broken. There has to be a way!" Pritkin's expression didn't change, but a momentary flash in his eyes told me I was right. "You know something," I said accusingly.

He looked evasive but finally answered. I suppose he decided it would be faster to humor me. "All *geasa* are different, but most have one thing in common. Each has built into it a . . . a safety net, if you like. Mircea would not want to be hoisted by his own petard, so he would have designed the *geis* with a way out of the spell, should something go wrong."

"And that would be?"

"Only Mircea and the mage who cast it know that."

I stared at him, trying to figure out whether he was lying. His words rang true, so why did I get the feeling he wasn't telling me everything? Maybe because no one ever did. "If this is 1888, Mircea hasn't done anything yet. There is no *geis*. Or there shouldn't be," I added, since obviously something was happening.

"You have a habit of getting into unprecedented situations," Pritkin said with a scowl. "I've never heard of this particular scenario. I don't know what will occur if the two of you spend time together in this era, but I doubt you would like the consequences." He adjusted his long coat to minimize the ominous bulges underneath. "Stay here. I will look about and see if anything strikes me as unusual. I lived through this period and am more likely to notice anything out of place than you. I'll return shortly and we will discuss our options."

He left before I could react, leaving me staring witlessly after him. Magic users live longer than norms, true, but not enough to look about thirty-five at a century more than that. I'd known since soon after meeting him that there was more to Pritkin than met the eye, but this was getting really weird.

I sat down on one of the steps and hugged my knees, staring at a patch of threadbare carpet. The minimal outfit was cold and the horns were adding to my headache. I took them off and stared at them instead. The gold glitter was starting to flake off in pieces, showing the hard white foam beneath. I felt a little bad about that. Assuming we ever got back to our time, the girl whose locker I'd burgled was going to have to pay for a new one. Of course, if I didn't get back at all, she'd need a whole new outfit.

I noticed that the stairway was getting colder but didn't worry about it until a woman suddenly appeared in front of me. She was dressed in a long blue gown and seemed as solid as any regular person, but I immediately knew she was a ghost. That was due less to my keen sense of the paranormal than to the fact that she had a severed head tucked under her arm. The head, which had a Vandyke beard that matched its dark brown hair, focused pale blue eyes on me.

"A dashed improvement over Faust!" it said, rolling its eyes up to its bearer.

The woman stared at me with no expression, but when she spoke her voice did not sound pleased. "Why do you disturb us?"

I sighed as deeply as I could manage with the damn corset cutting me in two. Exactly what I needed, a ticked-off ghost. I was just thankful I hadn't shifted as a spirit myself, or I'd have a lot more reason to be worried. I have time traveled before without my body, appearing in another era as a spirit or in possession of someone. But both states create bigger problems than putting up with an uncomfortable costume for a while.

Leaving my body behind means risking death unless I find another spirit to babysit it while I'm gone. Since the only one usually available is Billy Joe, this is something I try to avoid. Especially in Vegas, where all his favorite vices are so near at hand. The other downside is that traveling in spirit form saps my energy too quickly to allow me to do much unless I possess someone and draw energy from him or her. But I don't even like drinking from the same cup as someone else, much less using their body.

After becoming the Pythia's heir, I acquired the ability to take my own form along for the ride, although that has a downside, too. One possession resulted in an injury to the woman I was inhabiting—in the form of an almost-severed toe—but I'd been able to leave the wound behind when I shifted back to my own body. But if anything happened to me now, I was stuck with it. The upside of my current condition was that ghosts don't have a lot of power over the living. They can cannibalize other spirits under certain conditions, but attacking a living body usually drains them of more power than they gain. Still, there was no reason to provoke her.

"I'll be leaving soon," I said, hoping it was true. "I have an errand to run and then I'm out of here."

"You aren't in the show, then?" the head asked, looking disappointed.

"Only visiting," I said quickly, since the woman's eyes had started to glow. That's not a good sign in a ghost—it means they're calling up their power, normally just prior to letting you have it. "Really, I *want* to leave, but I can't yet. Hopefully, this won't take long."

"The other said the same," she intoned, her dark hair starting to blow gently about her face as her power rose. "But after poisoning the wine, she did not go. Now you are here. This must stop."

"She?" I didn't like the sound of that. "The only person I brought with me is male. Maybe you've seen him? About five eight, blond, dressed like the Terminator? Sorry," I said, as her forehead wrinkled slightly. "I mean, he's wearing a long topcoat over a bunch of weapons. He'll be back soon and we'll get this sorted out."

"It is not the mage that concerns us," the ghost said sternly. "You and the other woman are the threat. You must leave."

"She is somewhat territorial, I fear," the head said, looking sympathetic. "We've been here such a long time, y'see. This land belonged to my family long before they built a theatre on it, and it sustains us." He gave me a cheerful leer. "'Tis more fun these days. The demmed Roundheads closed all the theatres, as well as the pubs, the whorehouses, and all besides that wasn't a church. They even prohibited sports on Sunday! They were kind enough to behead me before I had to live through that. But we triumphed in the end, didn't we?"

"Uh-huh." I was barely listening. Every ghost I've ever met wants to tell me the story of his life, and if I hadn't learned how to nod and smile while thinking of other things, I'd have been driven crazy a long time ago. And I had a lot to mull over.

From the little I had managed to discover about my

position, mostly from rumors Billy Joe overheard, the setup worked like this: if someone from my own era was messing with the timeline, the ball was in my court. It was my problem, and I'd have to fix it. But if someone from another time was trying to interfere, that was the province of the Pythia from that person's time. If that was true, the interference that had brought me here should have come from my lifetime. But the only person I knew who could skip around between centuries was in no position to do so. Billy had checked with some of his ghostly contacts and assured me that the wounds I put in Myra's spirit form would have manifested as physical injuries as soon as she returned to her body. And there was no way she'd have healed damage like that in a week.

But if the woman the ghosts had mentioned wasn't Myra, she could only be another Pythia. Maybe my power had gotten confused, or I'd been called in as help on a difficult problem. Since I didn't know how this gig worked, anything was possible. If I could find her, I could plead for a little professional courtesy and get her to send Pritkin and me back where we belonged.

"Can you show me this other woman? Maybe I can convince her to leave and to send me home, too."

The woman looked unsure, but the head seemed happy to help. "Of course we can! She's not far," it babbled cheerfully. "She was in one of the boxes earlier."

The man's enthusiasm seemed to help the woman decide, and she nodded brusquely. "Quickly, then."

The ghosts followed me down the stairs, politely not passing through me, then led the way to the box beside Mircea's. I parted the curtains and peered inside, but it was empty. Onstage a woman in a green medieval gown with huge, red-lined sleeves was gesturing dramatically. I barely noticed her. My eyes fixed on Mircea, who was staring at the elaborate gilt frame of the stage instead of the actress, with the fixed gaze of someone who isn't really seeing it. I felt the same. One look at him and everything else suddenly seemed irrelevant. I had been bespelled before, but it had never felt like this. Then I'd known it was fake; I just hadn't cared. But even knowing this was due to a *geis*, it still felt unbelievably real. I could hate that he'd done this to me, but I couldn't hate him. The very thought was absurd.

"There." The ghost pointed a finger in front of my face. "The wine has already been delivered."

She indicated a tray with a bottle and several glasses that sat on a small table behind the seats occupied by Mircea and the blonde. "What are you talking about?" I forced my eyes to look at the ghost instead of Mircea, and something like rational thought returned. "Are you telling me that bottle is poisoned?"

"She said she would stay until it was consumed, but perhaps her power was insufficient." The ghost looked pleased for the first time. I could almost hear her thinking, *One down, one to go.*

I ignored her, my panic at the thought of anything happening to Mircea so overwhelming that I could hardly bear it. I ran out of the box and collided with Pritkin, who had been standing there looking annoyed. He steadied us both or we would have ended up on the floor. "Let go!" I batted at his hands, which were gripping my upper arms painfully. "I have to get in there!"

"I told you to stay away from him. Do you want to become completely besotted?"

"Then you do it," I said, deciding he might be right. I wanted to go in that box way too much for it to be a good idea. "There's a bottle of wine in there, and it may be poisoned. You have to get it!" I didn't know whether poison would kill a vamp, but I didn't intend to find out.

He tried out his usual glare for a second, then his face changed and I knew I was in trouble. "If I do this, do you swear to speak with me for as long as I wish without shifting times, attempting to kill me or placing any spells, curses or other impediments in my way?"

I blinked at him. "You want to *talk*?" We never talked. Stabbed, shot at and tried to blow each other up, sure, but never talked. "About what?" I asked nervously, but Pritkin only gave me an evil smile. He had me over a barrel and he knew it. "Fine. Whatever. We'll talk as long as *you* agree not to try to kill me, imprison me or drag me off to the Circle— or anybody else. And you don't get an indefinite time, either. One hour, take it or leave it."

"Agreed." To give him credit, he didn't waste time once the bargain was struck, but immediately let me go and slipped past the curtain. For several minutes I waited anxiously, but nothing happened. Finally, I couldn't stand it anymore and went back to the empty box so I could at least see what was going on. It wasn't good.

Onstage, a skinny Macbeth with a drooping moustache was starting the dagger-of-the-mind soliloquy, while in the box, Pritkin had a real dagger at his throat, courtesy of the blonde. She was being shielded from the audience by Mircea, who stood behind her, but my box was closer to the stage and I could see them clearly.

Before I could think how to help Pritkin, things got worse when Mircea started to open the bottle. His eyes were on the mage and there was a slight smile on his lips. I didn't like that look. Mircea has always been a strong believer in letting the punishment fit the crime. If he'd decided that Pritkin was trying to poison them, he was fully capable of forcing the entire contents of the bottle down the mage's throat and waiting to see what happened.

Normally, Pritkin might have been able to get out of this kind of thing on his own, but he was trying not to call attention to what was happening. I sympathized with his dedication to the whole integrity-of-the-timeline thing, but getting killed over it seemed a little fanatical. I was Pythia, at least temporarily, and I wasn't willing to go that far. Normally I wouldn't lose much sleep over Pritkin's death, but he had gone into that box because I asked him. If he died, it would be partially my fault.

I sighed and raised my wrist. A dimly glowing dagger practically jumped out of my bracelet to hover beside my arm. It was fairly buzzing with excitement over the prospect of a fight, but I wasn't sure this was a great plan. Among other things, I had a feeling that it might decide to stab Pritkin instead of shattering the bottle. They had a history and, as far as I knew, had yet to fight on the same side.

"Take out the bottle *only*," I told it sternly. "Don't attack the mage—you know how he gets. I mean it."

I got a faint bob of what I hoped was agreement before it was off. It flew over the balcony, straight for the bottle, which Mircea had just raised to Pritkin's lips. It shattered the thick glass easily, causing dark red wine to cascade over the mage's coat and splash Mircea's formerly pristine white shirt. Mircea whirled around, the bottle's neck still in hand, and saw me. He opened his mouth as if to say something, then stopped and just stood there, looking dazed.

Unfortunately my knife didn't follow his example but decided to ham it up. Onstage, Macbeth was asking if this was a dagger he saw before him. My flashing, luminescent knife dipped and swooped over the startled crowd, causing gasps and even a few screams, before coming to a halt in front of the actor's stunned face. It bobbed up and down for a minute, as if taking a bow, then flew back to me. Thunderous applause broke out all over the theatre, drowning out the rest of the actor's lines.

As soon as the attention hog melted back into my bracelet, I felt the disorientation spread over me that indicated that a time shift was coming. "Grab my hand, quick!" I yelled at Pritkin. "Takeoff is any second."

He had used the moment of distraction to jerk away from the blonde. She was between him and the way out, but he got around that problem by vaulting onto an unused seat and launching himself across the divide between the boxes. He almost slipped on the edge, but I caught his hand. The next minute, we were once more spinning through time.

Chapter 3

We landed in a heap on a white tile floor, and something fell with a *splut* right in front of my nose. My eyes crossed trying to identify the pale pink item. As soon as I did, I shrieked and scrambled back, knocking Pritkin off balance in the process. A crooked hand with skin the color and texture of old stone grabbed the offending item and returned it to a silver tray. "No guests allowed," I was informed in a gravelly baritone.

I didn't reply, being too busy staring at the platter of severed fingers that the owner of the voice was clutching between long, curved claws. I should have been more concerned by the greenish gray face, like mildewed rock, that was peering at me over the tray. It had a deep scar running from temple to neck and its only remaining eye, a narrowed yellow orb, was fighting for forehead space with two black, curled horns—not something you see every day. But I couldn't seem to tear my attention away from the severed digits.

There had to be twenty or more, all index fingers as far as I could tell, that had been shoved between pieces of

bread. The crusts had been trimmed away and a piece of ruffled romaine lettuce carefully wrapped around each one.
Finger sandwiches, some part of my brain observed. I
choked, caught between a retch and a hysterical giggle.

My gaze moved around what I now identified as a busy
kitchen. Another of the stone-colored things—this one with
glowing green eyes and bat wings—stood on a stool at a
nearby island, pressing something into small, finger-shaped
molds. My frozen brain finally thawed enough to recognize
the smell. "Oh, thank God." I sagged against Pritkin in relief. "It's pâté!"

"Where are we?" he demanded, dragging me to my feet.
I had trouble standing, both because I'd somehow lost a shoe
and because a larger gray thing barreled past, knocking me
back with a flailing tail. It was wearing a starched white
linen chef's outfit, complete with little red scarf and tall hat.
The breast of the tunic had a very familiar crest emblazoned
on it in bright red, yellow and black—Tony's colors.

"Dante's." When Pritkin had fallen on me at the theatre,
my concentration must have wobbled. We'd ended up a little off course.

"You're sure this is the casino?" The mage was eyeing a
nearby platter, which contained radishes that had been partly
skinned to resemble human eyeballs. They had olives for
pupils, and it almost looked like the pimentos were glowering at us. I took a closer look at the shield, a copy of which
adorned every uniform in sight and appeared over a set of
swinging doors across the room. It looked very familiar.

Antonio Gallina had been born into a family of chicken
farmers outside Florence about the time Michelangelo was
carving his fawn for old man Medici. But, some two hundred years later, when the impoverished English king

Charles I started selling noble titles to fund his art obsession, the illegitimate farmer's son turned master vamp had had more than enough stashed away to buy himself a baronetcy. I personally thought that the heralds, the men who had designed Tony's coat of arms, had spent a little too long at the pub the night before. I guess it could have been worse—like the poor French apothecary who was granted arms showing three silver chamber pots—but the comical yellow hen in the middle of Tony's shield was bad enough. It was supposedly a play on his last name, which means chicken in Italian, but the fat bird bore an uncanny resemblance to its owner.

"Pretty sure," I said. I would have elaborated, but one of the creatures doing the cooking, a diminutive specimen with a hairnet confining its long, floppy donkey ears, scurried by. It ran over my bare foot with clawed toenails, causing me to wince and press farther back. That resulted in Pritkin getting smashed into a slotted cart filled with trays of tiny black caldrons.

"What *are* those things?" I demanded. I kicked off my remaining shoe to keep from breaking my neck in case we had to run for it. I kept a wary eye on the creature in front of us, but he didn't seem overtly hostile, despite his looks. The only thing he was doing to back up his request was to point forcefully at the swinging doors with a spoon.

"Rum torte," a tiny chef croaked in passing. He was wearing only the top half of the usual tunic-and-trousers set, which in his case brushed the floor. A long, lizardlike tail protruded from beneath it.

He resembled most of the other creatures in the room, the majority of which had bat wings, clawed hands and long tails, but there the similarity ended. Their heads were everything from avian to reptilian, with a few furred ones here and there. Some had horns and others droopy ears, and their height ranged from maybe two feet to tall enough to stare me in the chest. Their eyes varied in color and size, but all of them seemed to glow, as if lit from inside by a high-powered bulb. It was unnerving, especially since they reminded me of something, and I couldn't quite figure out what.

"Gargoyles," Pritkin said as we stumbled through the swinging doors into a short hallway. At the end, a door that looked like old, carved wood but was too light to be real let out into a much longer and wider corridor. It was lined with medieval weaponry and cobweb-covered suits of armor, and dimly lit by flickering torches—fake, of course. Dante's wards were minimal on the upper floors, so electricity worked okay except for the occasional splutter. And real torches would have been hard to get past the fire codes.

I stopped and glared at the mage, who was looking around like he expected something to jump him at any moment. It would really be nice if the universe could stop throwing creatures out of fables, myths and nightmares at me. "There's no such thing as gargoyles!" I said just as two of the little monsters pulled a cart out of the door and began tugging it down the hallway. The floor, painted to look like weathered stone, was carpeted with a narrow strip of old maroon plush barely two feet wide that ran down the middle. It didn't do much decorwise, and it threatened to tip the cart over whenever one of the wheels encountered it. "It's just a name for fancy rainspouts," I insisted, even as my eyes told me otherwise. "Everyone knows that."

"How can you have lived so long in our world and know so little?" Pritkin demanded. "You must have seen stranger things. You grew up at a vampire's court!"

By this time, the servers had navigated the corridor and paused in front of an elevator. One of them pressed the call button with the tip of a pointed tail. He had the face of a dog and a bat's body, while his companion was covered in grayish scales and was drooling around a two-foot-long tongue.

"The strangest thing about our cook in Philly," I told Pritkin dazedly, "was that he was almost deaf from years of blasting heavy metal. But he was human. Well," I amended after a moment, "until that time Tony promised an important visitor fettuccine Alfredo, only the cook somehow heard bacon, lettuce and tomato. . . . Anyway, shouldn't they be off decorating a cathedral somewhere?"

"The creatures on medieval cathedrals aren't gargoyles; they're grotesques," he replied pedantically, while we moved in the direction of the cart.

"Stop it! You know what I mean! Why are they here?"

"Illegal aliens," he said shortly. "Cheap labor."

I stared at him suspiciously, but if the mage had a sense of humor, I'd yet to see any sign of it. "Aliens? From where?"

"From Faerie," he replied in the clipped tones he uses when annoyed. That seems to be most of the time, at least around me. "They have been coming into our world for centuries. But the numbers have greatly increased recently because the Light Fey have been making things difficult for the Dark—among whom the creatures we call gargoyles are numbered. The mages who handle Fey affairs have been complaining about the number of unauthorized arrivals we've been getting as a result."

"So they come here and do room service?"

The elevator came and the gargoyles tugged their laden cart onto it, ignoring the loitering humans. "They were traditionally employed as guardians for temples in the ancient world and for magical edifices in later centuries. But advances in warding have lessened the call for that kind of thing. Unlike the Light Fey, they can't pass for human, so their entrance is restricted." He scowled. "Their legal entrance," he amended.

"I guess around here, they just kind of blend in with the ambiance," I said, but Pritkin wasn't listening. He had crouched and was looking around a corner as warily as if he expected to find an army on the other side.

"Stay here," he ordered. "I'm going to check out the area. When I return, we will have that talk you promised, or the next time we meet won't be so pleasant."

"Pleasant? What weird definition of that word are you—" I stopped because he'd left, melting around the corner and into the shadows like a character in a video game. The guy was obviously cracked, but I had promised to hear him out. And if there was any chance of cutting a deal to get him and his Circle off my back, I wanted it.

I didn't think that going back to the kitchen was a good idea, so I hung out in the hallway. The suits of armor were interspersed with ugly tapestries, with the closest showing a Cyclops eating his way through a human army, a soldier in each hand and an arm dangling out of his bloody mouth. I decided to concentrate on the armor.

That turned out to be more fun than I'd expected. The suits stood on individual wood platforms bearing brass plaques, each of which had a Latin inscription. I'd had to learn Latin growing up, thanks to my governess's idea of what constituted a proper education, but the only time I'd used it outside the schoolroom was when Laura, a ghost friend, and I had amused ourselves thinking up mottos for

Tony. Her favorite had been *Nunquam reliquiae redire: carpe omniem impremis* (Never go back for seconds: take it all the first time). I'd preferred *Mundus vult decipi* (There's a sucker born every minute), but we settled on *Revelare pecunia!* (Show me the money!) because it fit better on the shield. I was rusty, but it didn't take long to figure out that, like our efforts, the inscriptions at Dante's weren't as serious as they looked.

Prehende uxorem meam, sis! (Take my wife, please!), begged the placard on the nearest knight. I grinned and moved down the hall, translating as I went. Some of the most amusing were *Certe, toto, sentio nos in kansate non iam adesse* (You know, Toto, I have a feeling we're not in Kansas anymore), *Elvem vivere* (Elvis lives), and *Estne volumen in amiculum, an solum tibi libet me videre?* (Is that a scroll under your cloak, or are you just happy to see me?).

I was crouched in front of a knight about halfway down the hall, trying to figure out the joke, when Pritkin came running full tilt back around the corner. I knew there was a problem before he opened his mouth—the fact that he was trailed by a line of hovering weapons sort of gave it away. "Get up!" he yelled as one of the floating arsenal—a knife long enough to be considered a short sword—took a swipe at him. If he hadn't dodged at the last second, it would have taken off his head. As it was, an arc of bright red blood went flying from his half-severed ear.

I admit that I just stood there for a moment. In my defense, the last time I'd seen Pritkin surrounded by levitating weapons, they had been his own. Before I could figure out why his knife was attacking him, two other figures rounded the corner. I recognized them as the mages who had been facing Enyo in Casanova's earlier. "They aren't with you?" I asked stupidly.

He didn't bother to reply. "Shift us out of here!" he yelled, throwing out an arm like someone doing a bad disco move. The other mages came to an abrupt halt. I didn't know why until I reached out and a tangible wall of energy met my outstretched hand. Pritkin's shields glimmered around us, faintly blue and wavelike in the flickering light from a nearby torch. "Do it!"

"Give us the rogue, Pritkin," one of the mages demanded. He was tall, with a prominent Adam's apple, pallid skin and a booming voice that didn't match his skinny frame. "She isn't worth this."

"She'll get a fair hearing," the bulkier, African American mage at his side added, although the look he sent me wasn't friendly. "Come peacefully while you can."

"What's going on?" I asked. The only answer I got was something large whizzing past my face, all of a millimeter from my nose. I jumped back with a shout, just as a heavy mace collided with a nearby suit of armor. That was a lucky break, since the heap of old metal had been about to bring a sword down on my head. The mace caught the thing in the chest, leaving a big dent and sending it staggering back into a tapestry.

I looked around wildly, not understanding what was happening. The mace had sliced through Pritkin's shields as if they weren't there. Even more worrying was the fact that the mages hadn't thrown the thing—it had come from somewhere behind us—but there was nobody back there. One of the knights was missing its weapon, but there was no one around to have thrown it.

A clanging sound caused me to whip my head back

around and, for a second, I thought the mages were attacking. But although they were looking even more grim, I was no longer the focus of their interest. Their eyes and weapons were leveled on the damaged suit of armor. Instead of simply falling over, it appeared to be fighting its way out of the tapestry. Once it threw off the heavy material, it started feeling around for its sword, which the impact of the mace had knocked away. But Pritkin grabbed the weapon first and, despite it being almost as tall as he was, leveled it menacingly on the creature.

The knight appeared unfazed. It righted itself, then wrenched a shield off the wall and sent it sailing at us like a hundred-pound Frisbee. Pritkin threw himself at me, smashing us into the wall just as the heavy iron sphere sliced through the air where we'd been standing. It crashed into a stained glass window at the end of the hall, causing a cloud of multicolored shards to rain down around the back staircase.

I didn't even have time to catch my breath before Pritkin hit the floor and jerked me down beside him, pushing my head so low that my nose found out by experience just how hard fake stone can be. I didn't complain, though, because the next instant my hair was ruffled as another shield blew through the air right above us. It took a bite out of the wall across the hall, embedding itself halfway into the plaster and sheet rock.

The two war mages must have done something that drew the armor's attention, because the old relic suddenly started moving towards them, flakes of rust drifting to the ground behind it. I clutched Pritkin's arm, stunned and disbelieving. "How did that thing get past my ward?" The first shield had come within about a foot of us, and the second had missed me by maybe half an inch. How close did a threat have to get before my star decided to pay attention?

Pritkin ignored me. He jumped to his feet, grabbing the sword he'd dropped when we had to get up close and personal with the wall. It turned out to be a bad move. The knight's visor-covered face immediately swiveled back in our direction. I guess it didn't like anyone else touching its weapon. It couldn't fight all three mages at the same time, but somehow that didn't make me feel better.

That was especially true a second later when the corridor echoed with the sound of a couple dozen metal figures simultaneously stepping off their plinths. It seemed that the internal defenses Casanova had talked about had decided to up the ante. The approaching metal army looked like the medieval version of a chorus line, all moving in perfect synchronization, but instead of doing high kicks they were shouldering weapons.

"The Circle found a way to block your ward—it won't work," Pritkin said shortly as I scrambled to my feet, ignoring the pain from my bruised nose and scraped knees. He was scanning the approaching line for some sign of weakness. I really hoped he saw one, because the closest knights had started to whirl heavy maces around their heads almost too fast to see, and the ones right behind them had unsheathed very sharp-looking swords. Then what he'd said hit me. I reached over my shoulder to grab the top of my lopsided star. It was still there, but its slight ridges lay quiescent under my fingertips.

"The Circle can't remove it unless they have you in their power," he added. "But it won't flare. Don't depend on it."

"And you were planning on telling me this when?!"

Pritkin didn't answer, being busy pulling an old-fashioned

.45 from his belt and pumping rounds into the nearest knights. The bullets all connected, leaving sizable holes, but there was no spray of blood or mangled bodily tissue. The torchlight glimmering through the punctures in the nearest armored head showed why—all I could see was the empty interior of the helmet and part of a tapestry on the far wall. There was no one in there to hurt.

Pritkin must have figured this out, because he shoved the gun back into its holster and sent a bright orange fireball at the line instead. It was powerful enough to catch one of the banners hanging down from the ceiling alight, quickly reducing it to a few burning shreds of material. But when the flames cleared, I saw that it had had less of an effect on the knights. The closest two emerged looking like contestants in a three-legged race, lurching along with their bodies melted together from the hips down. But they were still coming, and the others had only been scorched and knocked off their feet.

"Their weapons are enchanted," Pritkin said grimly. "And I've been using my shields almost nonstop all day. They won't last, and few spells will work within the casino's wards. Shift us out of here!"

I'd have liked nothing better, but there was a slight problem. I might be in possession of a whopping amount of power, at least temporarily, but I really didn't want to use it. Power wasn't free, especially in such large amounts. I'd been around magic users enough to know that if you borrow power, eventually you get a bill. I didn't like not knowing what that bill might be, or who might be sending it.

"Why are the knights attacking us?" I asked, hoping for another solution—any other. "We haven't done anything!" Maybe I was misreading the situation, and the casino's defenses were actually trying to take out the mages for us. In that case, all we needed to do was get out of the way.

Pritkin quickly destroyed that hope. "Andrew and Stephan triggered the automatic defenses by drawing arms inside the casino. I didn't respond, so we should have been safe, but they came too close. The defenses have confused us with the aggressors, and now we're all targets. Shift us now!"

I didn't have time to explain my views on my new power, because I had to dodge a spear thrown by a knight down the corridor. I jumped aside just before it slammed into the floor where I'd been standing, sending bits of painted concrete flying up at me. I felt liquid slide down my left cheek and raised a shaking hand to it. My fingertips came back painted red, but my ward never so much as twinged. I stared incredulously at my blood-smeared hand. So much for supernatural protection.

"Do it!" Pritkin yelled.

"I can't!" I would break my resolution, but only if I was sure that the only alternative was death. If anyone sent me a bill for London, I could reasonably argue that I had been getting myself out of the mess I'd been dragged into against my will. I'd have no such excuse for calling the power now, and I didn't intend to end up owing somebody my life if I could avoid it. That sort of debt in magical terms can be a very bad thing.

Pritkin might have argued, but the charred knights were quickly regaining their feet. He sent his animated arsenal into the crowd, the wildly weaving knives giving the knights some new targets. I added my daggers to the mix, just in time to take out a mace spinning straight at Pritkin's skull. He hadn't noticed it because he was using the sword to block a pike that had been about to run him through from the other direction. The last opportunity I'd had to see Pritkin fight, he'd looked like he was enjoying himself. His face showed no such emotion this time. Of course, the dangling ear might have had something to do with that.

I looked around for a way out, but there didn't appear to be any. The back stairs were surrounded by a minefield of broken glass, not that it was a huge obstacle. My bare feet wouldn't have enjoyed it, but if Pritkin could lift that huge sword, he could probably haul me across. But I doubted he could manage that while also fighting off the line of knights between us and that part of the hall. The same was true for the door to the kitchen. It was blocked by a fallen suit of armor, which was being dismembered by one of my gaseous knives, and the thing's three companions, which were still on their feet.

"Are there hidden stairs?" Pritkin asked in a calm voice that sounded really out of place at the moment. "They should have difficulty navigating them."

"How should I know?" I looked around frantically, but my attention was monopolized by a knight brandishing a wicked-looking two-headed axe. Alphonse, who collected weapons of all kinds, had an identical item on his safe-room wall. It had looked menacing enough just hanging there; it was a lot worse now that it was almost close enough to take off Pritkin's head—or mine.

"Check the tapestries!" Pritkin ordered, darting forward to take a swing at the armor's knees. "There might be a hidden door!" His blade took off one of our attacker's legs, causing it to topple over. But it kept coming, dragging itself forward by its arms and using the remaining leg to push. Even more disconcerting, its severed limb wiggled along the ground behind it, trying to catch up to the main event. To stop one of these things, we'd have to completely dismember it, and there were too many of them and too few of us for that to be practical. We'd be in pieces long before they would.

I yanked the nearest curtain aside, but nothing except more faux stone met my eyes. I felt around, hoping to encounter a hidden door, but no such luck. I glanced at the elevator, but the indicator light showed it to be five floors away. Not to mention that the two mages were having a hell of a battle right in front of it.

While I snatched aside the other tapestries in our dwindling safe zone, looking for nonexistent exits, the armor's detached leg reunited with its body. The metal at the top of its thigh grew liquid, like quicksilver, and the two parts merged seamlessly. A second later, you couldn't tell there had ever been a wound. I finally accepted that we were in an impossible situation. Even dismemberment was no more than a brief inconvenience for these things. Tony was a cheap bastard, but not when it came to security. Damn it.

"No stairs!" I yelled.

Pritkin whirled around, sweeping another knight's feet out from under it, and clipped me with his elbow. I fell in front of an empty plinth, my ears ringing. My brain automatically translated the phrase in front of my eyes: *Medio tutissimus ibis* (You will be safest in the middle). It was a quote from Ovid advising moderation, and seemed really strange at Dante's, home of the extreme.

While I struggled to sit up, the six knights from the far end of the corridor, which had been making their cumbersome way towards us, got within striking distance. That gave us the choice of being skewered by them or being dismembered by their buddies on our other side, since it was obvious that we weren't going to hold them all off for long. I was about to damn the consequences and shift us away when I noticed something interesting.

One of Pritkin's larger knives was slicing busily away at a nearby knight. The armor had lost its weapon, which was clenched in the fist that had just been severed at the wrist. But it was making no effort to retrieve it, despite the fact that it lay on the carpeted strip only a few feet away. The mailed hand was also motionless, not trying to rejoin its body as the other knight's leg had done. I suddenly realized that I had a clear view of it because not a single knight was anywhere near the center of the hall.

They were grouped on either side of the narrow strip of carpet, which they were going out of their way to avoid touching. I glanced back at the fight behind us and it was the same story. The knights on one side had gone after the mages, those on the other had come after us, but neither group came in contact with the ratty-looking piece in the center. For a brief moment, I almost felt like giving a cheer for paranoid Tony, who always designed a way out of every trap, even his own.

Pritkin had been driven to his knees blocking another pike attack, while a second and third knight converged on his position with raised swords. I didn't wait to see whether he would be fast enough to deal with the predicament, but launched myself at him, hitting him with a thud that rolled both of us onto the carpet strip. We landed catty cornered, with Pritkin's left leg and my whole right side dangling off the edge. Before I could do anything about that, a knight brought a sword down, spearing Pritkin's calf where it stuck out from between my legs.

"Don't move!" I yelled as the mage pushed me aside and plunged his sword into the knight's belly. The blow forced the heavy thing backwards, but it also ripped the sword brutally out of Pritkin's leg. He gasped but started after the knight as if there weren't almost a dozen others within striking distance, converging on us from both sides. I climbed up his body and sat on him, grabbing a handful of hair to swing his face around. "Safe!" I screamed to be heard over the clanging sounds of battle. "We're safe in the middle!"

I tugged his bleeding leg onto the maroon plush and put all my weight on the undamaged parts of his body. Even though he was injured, I couldn't have held him for long, but as soon as we were no longer touching the floor, it was as if the knights simply didn't see us anymore. They began lumbering down the hall toward where the mages had retreated around the corner. Pritkin looked stunned but followed my pointing finger to the inscription on the plinth and comprehension dawned.

"We need to get back to the kitchen," he said, getting to his knees. He was careful not to touch anything except carpet, but he swayed slightly, scaring me. I looked down and understood the problem. His trouser leg was drenched with red, making it a match for the jacket below his injured ear. There was so much blood that I suspected a major artery had been hit. He leaned on me heavily as we made our way along the narrow safe way, reinforcing the impression.

Sounds of a furious battle came from around the corner, no doubt from the mages, but we ignored it. Personally, I was rooting for the casino. I knew how to deal with it now, but the mages didn't have a time-out zone.

We burst back into the kitchen. "We need an ambulance!" I yelled, squinting around. It was hard to see, since the room seemed blindingly well lit after the hall, but I got a vague impression of a bunch of squat shapes pausing to stare at us out of huge, glowing eyes.

"No. I can deal with this." Pritkin collapsed just inside the door. He pulled off his boot and gouts of purplish red blood flooded the previously pristine kitchen floor. His face lost what little color it had.

I grabbed up a nearby dish towel and held it to the wound. Resolution or no resolution, I wasn't going to watch him bleed to death. "I'm going to shift us to a hospital," I said, but he drew back from my touch.

"No! I can heal this." He muttered something under his breath and the blood flow did decrease, but I didn't like the shallow, panting breaths he was taking or the clammy pallor of his face. It also seriously creeped me out to see his hanging ear slowly climb back up the side of his face and reattach itself.

"Why don't you want a hospital?" I demanded, trying to ignore the ear, which gave a final twitch to align itself with the slant of the other one. Suddenly, some pieces of the puzzle fell into place. "Wait a minute. Those mages weren't just after me, were they? The Circle's chasing you, too!"

Pritkin didn't reply, being too busy chanting something inaudible. I felt a presence looming over us and looked up to see a gargoyle with red eyes and, incongruously, dainty ruby earrings in its pointed, catlike ears. It pushed me aside gently but firmly.

I stood there awkwardly, unsure whether to protest or not. I didn't say anything, mainly because I didn't get a feeling of evil from the thing. That might have had something to do with the jewelry, or the fact that it had chocolate icing on its fuzzy chin. It seemed to have been the right decision. A hand that looked more like a paw hovered over Pritkin's leg for a moment, then slowly, the jagged wound began to close.

The process appeared to be helping him heal, but judging by the way his eyes were bulging, it wasn't pleasant. He looked like he wanted to say something, so I leaned in a little, staying out of reach of his balled fists. "*Me oportet propter praeceptum te nocere* (I'm going to have to hurt you on principle)," he gasped.

"Very funny."

"You could have shifted us out of there all the time!"

"Not without a price."

Pritkin's glare almost set a new record. "What price? You could have been killed! So could I!"

"*Stercus accidit* (Shit happens)." While he was deciphering my bastardized Latin, I went in search of another way out. I did not intend to set foot in that corridor again, nor was I planning to shift after going to such lengths to avoid it.

What I found was very satisfactory. If I hadn't been so weirded out by the gargoyles, I might have thought to take a look around earlier and saved us that whole scene in the hall. After passing a couple of huge, built-in freezers, a cool room and a storeroom for nonperishable stuff, I found a loading dock that let out onto the back of the casino.

I looked over the sunlit parking lot and was seriously tempted to take off while the mage was healing. I so didn't have time for this, whatever this was. I had to persuade Casanova to tell me where his boss was hiding. Not that I was 100 percent certain that Myra was with him, but it was a good guess. They both worked for the same guy, the leader of the Russian vampire mafia, known as Rasputin in the history books. What the books don't say is that he found other uses for his formidable persuasive abilities once a Russian prince "killed" him. After lying low for a while, he brought much of the drug running, counterfeiting and illegal magical weapon–selling rackets in Eastern Europe under his control. He'd recently decided to add the North American vamps to his growing business empire by taking over the Senate, and he'd succeeded in killing off four Senate members. But that got him nowhere unless he took out their leader, and the Consul had proven tougher than he'd expected. The whole thing was very Cold War–ish and didn't interest me much, except for the fact that I had accidentally blundered into the middle of it.

After the failed coup, Rasputin had simply disappeared. Thousands of vamps and mages were searching for him, but had so far come up with zilch. Since there aren't many good hiding places, and since Tony and Myra had vanished at the same time, I was betting they were all together. But wherever she was, I had to find her before she recovered from our last meeting, or she would certainly find me. And I doubted I'd enjoy the experience. Or survive it.

But I had promised, and it was intriguing to think that Pritkin and I might be on the same side for a change. The enemy of my enemy might not, in this case, be precisely my friend, but I'd take anything short of outright hostility. I could use all the help I could get, and Casanova had looked very nervous when Pritkin showed up. That might be useful. I dodged a couple of gargoyles wrestling a crate of cabbages up the ramp and started to go back inside. That was when the fun really began.

Chapter 4

"Cassie!" Casanova flew up the loading ramp, trying to minimize his time in the sun. A moment later, my three delinquents came into view, following leisurely in his wake. Great. I'd actually managed to forget about them for a while.

The gargoyles took one look at the trio and began a high-pitched keening that made me want to cover my ears. "Did you see what your stupid enchantments did?" I asked Casanova furiously as he skidded to a stop in front of me. "I could have been killed!"

"We have worse problems."

I jerked Enyo away from the smallest gargoyle, which she'd been poking at with a stick. The cowering, birdlike creature and his companion went running inside, squawking loudly. "And where were you?" I demanded, too angry to care that annoying an ancient goddess wasn't smart. "You three are always spoiling for a fight, but the first time I need help, you're off getting a manicure!"

It was true—Deino was sporting a new set of bright red nails—but less than fair, considering that they'd helped out

in the bar. But I was in no mood to care. The Circle blocking my ward had me seriously rattled, now that I had time to
think about it. It was the only defensive weapon I had, and
being without it made me feel extremely vulnerable.

Enyo looked offended but let me keep the stick. Pemphredo and Deino crowded around while I resumed my rant
at Casanova. "Now Pritkin's half dead," I informed him,
"and the mages are sure to be—"

He gripped my arm so tightly that I yelped. "Where is
he?" He began fumbling in his coat frantically. "Why can I
never find my damn cell phone when I need it? We have to
get him medical help, quickly!" For a minute I thought he
was being sarcastic, but one look at his face told me otherwise. The guy looked absolutely terrified.

"What is wrong with you? Since when do you care if—"

Casanova left me standing there talking to myself, while
he ran indoors. I followed, the Graeae trailing after me.
Enyo picked up a broom on the way in and formed it into a
weapon by snapping off the head to leave a jagged point. I
didn't try to wrestle her for it. She was back to old-lady
mode, but she'd probably win anyway.

I reentered the kitchen to find a livid Pritkin being pawed
at by a frantic Casanova. The mage knocked the vampire
aside hard enough to send him sprawling and glared at the
gargoyle who'd helped him. Since he was back on his feet, I
had to assume that her remedy, whatever it was, had worked.

"Take it off me," he barked. "Now!"

Casanova picked himself up off the floor. Not only did he
not respond in kind, he actually seemed to cower slightly. "I
can have a healer here in five minutes!"

I stared at the vamp as if he'd lost his mind, which maybe
he had. Vamps and mages have an adversarial relationship,

born out of the fact that they both claim to be the leading force in the supernatural world. The sight of a vamp as old as Casanova fawning over the war mage who'd just belted him was surreal.

"I don't need a healer. I need the damn *geis* removed," Pritkin said furiously.

That got my attention. "She can remove it?" I ran forward, hardly daring to believe it could be that simple, and the Graeae moved with me. I didn't get an answer because the gargoyles suddenly started to shriek like Armageddon had arrived, their combined voices loud enough to shatter several nearby glasses.

I covered my ears and dropped to my knees in shock, only to have Deino fall on top of me. I'm not sure whether she tripped, or whether she was trying to shield me from the hail of food—rolls, pastries and assorted molded-pâté body parts—being thrown at us from all sides. Either way, the landing jarred the eye loose from her face and sent it skittering across the floor. She screeched and scrambled after it, knocking gargoyles out of the way left and right. Her sisters waded into the fray as backup and I took refuge under the main prep table, where I found Casanova and Pritkin.

"You could get hurt! I can't allow you to go out there!" Casanova was practically screaming in order to be heard, and he had a two-handed grip on Pritkin's right arm. "The gargoyles view the kitchens as a sacred trust, as they once did the temples that fed them. They see the Graeae as a threat, but I'll explain—"

"I don't give a damn about your personnel problems," Pritkin snarled, grabbing the vamp by the front of his designer shirt. "Get her to remove my *geis*, or you will have more trouble than you've ever dreamed."

"Hey, I'm the one with the *geis* here," I interrupted. "Remember? If anyone is getting anything removed, it's me."

"This isn't about you!" Pritkin said as something heavy hit the tabletop and rolled off onto the floor. It was the little gargoyle with the hairnet and the donkey ears, and he wasn't moving.

I dragged him under the table with us but wasn't sure how to check for a pulse, or even if he was supposed to have one. What I was sure about was that the greenish colored blood he was leaking onto the tile wasn't good. "Okay, that's it."

I crawled out from under the table and stood up. The noise level was unbelievable and, in the few seconds I'd been preoccupied, the kitchen had been completely trashed. Deino had retrieved the eye but was staggering about on the far side of the room, four gargoyles hanging off each arm while another perched on her back, hitting her over the head repeatedly with a rolling pin. Enyo, in all her blood-soaked glory, had the gargoyle with the earrings raised over her head and was about to throw her across the room. The throw alone might kill her, but if not, landing on the knives a grinning Pemphredo was holding out certainly would.

I took a deep breath and screamed, louder than I'd believed possible. The gargoyles ignored me, but the three Graeae stopped and looked at me inquiringly. None of them appeared overly upset. The only expression anyone wore was a lopsided grin on Pemphredo's face. "Stop it," I told them in a slightly more normal tone. "When I said I needed you to fight, I didn't mean them."

Pemphredo cackled and pumped her fist in the air. Enyo looked at me sourly but sat the gargoyle down anyway, who hissed at her and staggered off, looking dizzy. Deino managed to lurch over to Enyo to hand her the eye, but her sister waved her off less than graciously. Pemphredo came skipping over and plucked it out of Deino's hands, looking triumphant. I suddenly got it. "You were betting on me?"

Enyo slumped onto the prep table, knocking some radish eyeballs out of the way and looking dejected. I wasn't sure why—obviously she could see without the eye, or come to some approximation of it—but she seemed very depressed about missing her turn.

The gargoyles had stopped the attack once their leader was safe, but were eyeing the Graeae with understandable concern. Several of those nearby were starting to check on their fallen comrades, with one pulling Donkey Ears away. His hairnet had come loose, but at least he was starting to come around. I hoped he'd recover, but the only thing I could do for him was to be sure we didn't cause any more harm. I reached under the table and pulled Casanova out by his fancy tie. "Explain to them that we'll be leaving now."

"We bloody well won't!" Pritkin crawled out, looking like a madman with his bloodstained clothes and matted hair. He scowled about until he located the female gargoyle Enyo had released. "We aren't going anywhere until she removes the *geis*!"

"Miranda!" Casanova called in a strangled voice, and I realized I might be holding the tie a bit too tight.

The gargoyle came over, but although it was hard to read her fur-covered face, her body language didn't look cooperative. If someone can walk sullenly, she managed it. She poked Pritkin in the stomach, maybe because she couldn't reach his chest. "You well. We sssafe. Good trade." He tried to grab her but she dodged his hands with a fluid movement that seemed impossible unless she'd dislocated something.

Maybe she had, because her ears went back and she hissed at him, showing off a very nonfeline forked tongue. She crossed her arms and took a wide-legged stance behind Casanova, her long tail whipping about behind her.

"I do not deal with Fey affairs," Pritkin said haughtily, as if such a thing was beneath him. "It is of no concern to me whether you are here legally or not. You have nothing to fear. Now, take it off!"

"What's going on?" I asked Casanova, who was straightening his tie. He gave me a less-than-friendly look, which I guess was fair under the circumstances.

"In exchange for healing him, Miranda put a *geis* on him not to reveal their existence to anyone. If the Circle finds out they're here, they'll be deported."

"Is that all?" I turned narrowed eyes on Pritkin, who didn't notice because all his attention was on Miranda. Considering the whopping *geis* I was carrying, I didn't have a lot of sympathy for his tiny one. "If you're not planning to tell on them anyway, what difference does it make? Let's go. Those mages could be back any minute."

"I'm not going anywhere until she removes it," he repeated stubbornly. The tone made me want to kick him. Instead, I prodded Casanova, who rolled his eyes.

"Miranda—" he began in a long-suffering voice, but she set her jaw. She didn't say anything, but she didn't have to.

"Damn it, Pritkin!" I said angrily. "I'm not standing here until the Circle sends someone else after us. You want to talk, fine. Let's go talk. Otherwise, I'm out of here."

"There's an idea," Casanova said brightly. "I'll call you a car."

Billy Joe came streaming through the door and got swatted at by half a dozen gargoyles on his way over. Normally,

I'd have been surprised that they could see him, but after the day I'd had I didn't even blink. "He's with me," I told Miranda, who nonetheless began hissing at Casanova in the strange language the gargoyles used. She had obviously had enough unwanted visitors for one day.

"Ixnay on the car," Billy said, looking worried. "Is there an exit that bypasses the front, back and side doors? 'Cause they're all being watched."

"By who?" Now what was wrong?

"Oh, I don't know," Billy replied sarcastically. "Whose mages did you just beat the crap out of? The Circle knows you're here, and they're out there in force. There's gotta be two, three dozen—I stopped counting. The trio we met in the bar was their advance crew, their way of asking you to come along nicely. But considering the way you returned 'em, I don't think they're interested in negotiating anymore."

"They attacked first," I said defensively, then paused to wonder whether that was strictly true. I hadn't seen what happened in the bar between the time I left and when Casanova and I tuned in to find Enyo throwing down with the mages. If Pritkin hadn't been with them, then they'd walked into a mess not of their own making. No wonder they hadn't been in a good mood when they met us again.

"It doesn't matter," Pritkin said, almost like he'd been reading my mind. "They want you dead. Making it easy for them won't change that."

I swallowed. I'd suspected that the Circle wouldn't cry much if I had an accident, but hearing it stated so baldly was hard. You'd think I'd be used to people trying to kill me by now, but for some reason it doesn't seem to get any easier. "You sound certain."

"I am. That's part of what we need to talk about." He looked at Casanova, who sighed.

"There are several emergency exits, but none are good options." He flapped a hand at me. "Can't you do whatever you did earlier, and shift away? With the internal defenses targeting you as well as them, I can claim you came here to bully me for information about Antonio and then left after trashing the place." He glanced around. "Oh, wait, that would even be true."

"Speaking of which, you were going to tell me where Tony is."

"No, as I recall, I was doing quite a good job of *not* telling you." He tried to hand me a handkerchief, I guess to wipe off the cupcake that had gotten smeared in my hair at some point, but I ignored it. "I'll help you get out of here, *chica*, and I will gladly tell lies to the Circle to throw them off the trail, but as for Antonio—"

"That vampire." Miranda spat on the ground. "He in Faerie. He bring usss here, then betray. We work like ssslavcsss."

Casanova looked sick. I smiled at the gargoyle, who was actually rather attractive if you concentrated on her slanted red eyes. "Thank you, Miranda! Tell me more."

She gave a feline sort of shrug. "Not much to tell. He in Faerie." She looked at Casanova. "This sssircle, they come here?"

He ran a hand through his slightly tousled hair. Somehow, he had managed to avoid all the flying food. The only visible damage was a few wrinkles I'd put in his tie. "Possibly. It seems to be our day for unwanted guests."

"No!" she told him, poking his leg with extended claws. "We have work! No more messss!"

I noticed that a couple of valiant little gargoyles were trying to get a laden cart, which had somehow avoided the carnage, through the disorder to the door, and that another was grunting into a phone and scribbling an order on a pad. I was about to agree with Miranda that we needed to get out of their hair—or horns or whatever—when yet another visitor arrived. Pritkin's golem came through the doors and the keening noise started up again from every side.

I groaned and stuck my fingers in my abused ears. Pritkin stared intently at the golem for a minute, as if some sort of nonverbal communication was going on, then glanced at me. He made a gesture, and blissful silence descended. I knew it had to be some kind of spell, because the pandemonium didn't diminish, but the cacophony quieted to a faint background noise. "They're coming. We have to go."

I nodded. "Fine. Then get lover boy there to tell us where Tony's portal into Faerie is. And don't lie," I told Casanova. "I know he has one."

"Yes, he does, but I don't know where it is," Casanova said distractedly. "Miranda! Can you calm your people down, please? It isn't going to destroy anything!" He looked at Pritkin. "Is it?"

"It will if you don't tell us the truth," I said grimly.

He looked askance at the golem, which looked back as far as the vague indentations it called eyes would allow. It had no fangs, horns or other oddities. It was just a badly made statue, like something a potter had started and then forgotten. But I didn't like it any better than Casanova did when it turned those empty eyes on me.

"I don't know where the damn portal is!" Casanova insisted. "Tony was selling witches to the Fey, but he had a special group who dealt with that side of the business and I wasn't one of them. He took most of them with him when he disappeared, and the rest left with the last shipment a week ago. They aren't here."

I glanced at Miranda. "You must have come through the portal. You have to know where to find it!"

She shook her head. "On other ssside, we sssee. But here, no." She draped a dishcloth over the head of a nearby gargoyle. "Like ssso." The blind gargoyle ran into Pritkin, or more accurately into his legs, which was as far as the tiny thing could reach. The mage removed the towel and sent him back to Miranda with a little push.

"They must have been blindfolded before they were sent through," Casanova translated. "I suppose Tony didn't want them to know how the setup worked, in case the mages got hold of them."

"What about you?" I asked Pritkin. "The Circle must have access to a portal."

"We use the one at MAGIC."

I sighed. Of course. It made sense that MAGIC—short for the Metaphysical Alliance for Greater Interspecies Cooperation—would have one. It's a sort of supernatural United Nations with representatives from the mages, vamps, weres and Fey, and the delegates from Faerie had to get there somehow. On the plus side, it was nearby, in the desert outside Vegas. On the negative, MAGIC was crawling with the very people who were looking for me, and not to wish me a happy birthday. It remained to be seen whether I'd live long enough to celebrate my twenty-fourth, but sticking my neck in the noose didn't seem like the best way to ensure that. Unfortunately, portals into Faerie aren't exactly thick on the ground, and any others would doubtless be guarded, too. On the theory that it's better to go with the devil you know, I decided to opt for MAGIC. At least I'd been there before and knew a little about its layout.

"Do you know exactly where it is?" I asked. MAGIC had a big compound; it would be nice if he could narrow things down.

Pritkin looked at me incredulously, but whatever he might have said was drowned out by the sound of sirens going off. They were just a faint, tinny klaxon through the silence bubble, but Casanova swore loudly. "The mages have entered in force—that's a general alarm."

"Get the humans out," Pritkin ordered.

Casanova nodded, not protesting the grip the mage had on his arm. "It's already being done—standard protocol is to claim a gas leak whenever there's an emergency and to evacuate everyone. And the mages are supposed to avoid hocus pocus in front of norms, aren't they?"

"Normally, yes. But they want her badly." Pritkin jerked his head at me.

Casanova shrugged. "Any fireworks will be thought to be part of the show, as long as no norms are injured. This place was designed to look this way for a reason—we've had slipups before." From Pritkin's scowl, I was guessing they had gone unreported. "Let's get all of you safely away from here, then I can concentrate on damage control."

"Where's the nearest emergency exit?" I asked.

"Thanks to you, most of them are overrun. Your best bet is the one leading to the basement of a liquor store on Spring Mountain, just off the Strip." Casanova moved towards the room service phone and plucked it out of the claws of the gargoyle taking orders. He glanced over his shoulder. "I'll have a car waiting out back of the store for you, but that's as much as I can do."

"Wait a minute. You have a house safe, right?"

"Why?" Pritkin asked suspiciously.

"Oh, crap," Billy said.

"You want to risk taking them into Faerie with us?" I demanded.

Billy groaned and looked at the Graeae, who were chowing down on finger sandwiches. "Considering what popped out last time? Hell no."

I looked at Casanova, who was in the middle of a phone conversation. "They're bypassing the security system almost like it isn't there," he informed us, relaying a report. "A group of mages have been stalled in Headliners, but there are two other teams and—*mierda*! They shot Elvis. Tell me it doesn't show," he demanded of someone on the other end of the line.

"They shot an impersonator?" I was surprised, if not precisely shocked. The mages were supposed to protect humans, not use them as target practice, although they seemed to forget that where I was concerned.

Casanova shook his head. "No, the real thing." He turned his attention back to the phone. "No, no! Let the necromancers worry about the patch-up job; what do we pay them for? And have them raise Hendrix again, we're going to need a sub."

I lost track of the conversation because the swinging kitchen doors came flying off their hinges, straight at me. Pemphredo, whom I hadn't even seen move, caught them and sent them spinning back across the room at the group of war mages who were pouring through the entrance. Enyo tried to stuff me under the table, but I caught her wrist. "How would you like to have some fun?"

She gave me a withering look. Obviously, she felt that

our ideas of fun differed. "I'm serious." I nodded at the mages, who were being attacked by a wave of hissing gargoyles that had apparently not appreciated the destruction of the doors. The mages were practically buried under a sea of thrashing wings and slashing claws, but I knew it wouldn't last. "Enjoy yourself. Just don't kill anybody."

A big smile broke over Enyo's face, making her look like a kid on Christmas morning, and the next thing I knew she'd picked up the massive prep table and thrown it into the breach left by the missing doors. She and her sisters ran across the room and hopped over it, cackling like the fiends they were as they took the offensive to the second wave of mages trying to get in.

"Bought us some time," I told Pritkin, who was looking conflicted. He might be having problems with the Circle, but he obviously didn't like the idea of them being play toys for the Graeae. Since the mages' idea of justice was to drag me off to a kangaroo court and a quick death, I had no such problem. "Come on!"

Pritkin ignored me and pulled a mage out from under three gargoyles, who'd been introducing the man's face to a cheese grater. Apparently, shields didn't work so well against the Fey—judging by his agonized expression, it was a lesson the guy would probably remember.

Pritkin knocked him unconscious, then grabbed Miranda. She tried to bite him, but he had her around the throat and held her back from his face. That didn't help the rest of him from getting badly clawed, but he grimly hung on. His concentration must have wobbled, however, because the silence bubble suddenly collapsed. He said something, but I couldn't hear it over the klaxons, which drowned out even the gargoyles.

I couldn't believe Pritkin was still fixated on that stupid *geis*. It seemed harmless to me, especially now that the Circle was finding out about the gargoyles all on their own. But I knew him well enough not to bother arguing.

"Miranda!" I screamed, literally at the top of my lungs. "Remove the *geis*! Casanova will hide you from the mages!" That got her attention, and she turned those slanted cat eyes on me. She didn't take her claws out of Pritkin, but I didn't really care.

"You promissse? We not go back?" she asked, her voice somehow cutting through the din.

"I promise," I yelled, nudging Casanova, who had waded through the battle to us. He looked alarmed, but I didn't give him a chance to protest. "You know you can do it. Tony has all kinds of bolt holes around here."

He rolled his eyes. "¡*Claro que sí*! Just go!"

Miranda smiled, a really odd expression on her furry face, since it flashed a lot of fang. "I remember thisss," she told me, and suddenly Pritkin was holding a spitting, hissing and squirming ball of fur. A set of four deep scratch marks appeared on his face, and I punched him in the shoulder. "Let her go and she'll help!"

Pritkin finally dropped her, and Miranda stood, smoothing her fur and preening for a moment. Then she waved a paw at him in a curiously graceful gesture. I didn't notice any change, but I guess he must have because he grabbed my hand and yanked me after Casanova, looking as irritated as if I'd been the one holding things up.

"I'll show you the tunnel, but we have to hurry. I can't be seen with you," the vamp was saying. I looked around for Billy Joe, but he'd disappeared. I hoped he was on my errand and not off somewhere interfering with a game of craps. He could move small things if he really concentrated, and thought it was funny as hell to rig the casino games.

The golem appeared in front of us, a meat cleaver sticking out of its clay chest, but it didn't seem to notice. We ran for the cool room and Casanova moved a large plastic bin of lettuce. He pointed at what looked like a solid concrete block wall. "Through there. The car is already in place and the driver's going to wait to hand off the keys. Give me whatever you want put in the safe and go!"

"I'll give it to the driver. Look, I really appreciate—"

Casanova cut me off with a gesture. "Just make sure I don't end up putting this place back together for that *bidonista*," he said grimly.

"You have a deal," I told him. I just hoped I could keep up my end of the bargain.

The man waiting for us at the end of the long, stifling tunnel was leaning casually against a luxurious new BMW, arms crossed, obviously bored. I gaped, my mind immediately flooded with images of hot nights, rumpled sheets and excellent sex. It wasn't just the rich black curls, as shiny as the car behind him, which begged any female under eighty to run her hands through them. It wasn't just the lean, muscled body, dressed in skintight jeans and T-shirt, and tanned that beautiful burnished color only olive skin gets. There was an instant attraction, a pull from those liquid dark eyes, that I knew couldn't be real. I might admire a guy's looks, but I don't get that interested until I've known him a little longer than ten seconds.

Incubus, I thought, my mouth going dry. And judging by the level of interest my body was taking, a powerful one. I swallowed and summoned up a smile.

He immediately smiled back, taking in my abbreviated

uniform with an appreciative eye. "Have you heard about our employee discount, *querida*? Twenty percent off all services."

"Casanova sent us," I clarified.

"Ah, of course. I am Chavez. It means Dream Maker—"

I cut him off before he could offer to make all my dreams come true. "We, uh, really need to go."

I noticed that he'd brought along a friend, I guess to drive him back after he turned over the keys. The handsome blond was wearing a Dante's baseball cap and a mesh tank top that gave tantalizing glimpses of a muscular upper body. He sent me a cheerful, beach boy smile from the driver's seat of a flashy convertible. The expression managed to call up sandy blankets, salt-laced wind and sultry, passion-filled nights.

"I'm Randolph," he said in a broad midwestern accent, gripping my hand firmly in his big, suntanned one. "But you can call me Randy. Everyone does."

"I bet."

In the end, I had to take Chavez's card, three brochures and a flyer advertising an upcoming two-for-one night before they would listen to me. I persuaded Randy to take Pritkin to a tattoo parlor where he said a friend would patch him up. I found that story fairly fishy, since most of his wounds had already closed, but maybe his friend would have a change of clothes or a shower. All that blood made him more than a little conspicuous, and we desperately needed to blend in.

"And where are you going?" Pritkin demanded, looking suspicious.

"I said we'd talk and we will," I assured him, sliding into the BMW next to Chavez. "I'll meet you later. But I can't run around dressed like this."

Billy had shown up while we were talking and started to flow in through the rear window, but I stopped him with a look. I didn't trust the mage. It sounded like Pritkin and the Circle were on the outs, but it could be a trap. I needed a pair of eyes on him while I was busy elsewhere, and ghostly eyes would do. Billy grimaced but floated back to Pritkin after dropping something small and metal in my hand.

"You can't go back to your hotel," Pritkin said. His tone made it a command rather than a recommendation.

"You think?" I pushed him back so I could close the door. "Chavez can run me by the mall. I need something to wear—even in Vegas, this outfit sticks out." Not to mention being really uncomfortable. "I'll even pick up lunch if you ask nicely." Pritkin frowned, but there was no way he could force me to go with him, as he seemed to realize. After a momentary pause, he moved back so Chavez didn't run over his toes. I decided that for him that counted as civil, so I'd grab some food after my errand.

"I need to go ice skating," I told Chavez as we blasted out of the lot behind the liquor store, salsa music blaring from the car's excellent sound system. He shot me an inquiring glance but didn't press. I guess working for Casanova, you learned to take things in stride.

Vegas has a good bus system, but there are no public lockers at the downtown station so I'd had to get creative for a place to stash certain items. Leaving them at the hotel hadn't sounded like a good idea, considering that the mages and vamps could locate my room any minute. We'd been switching hotels every day and I was using a fake name, but with MAGIC's resources, that didn't mean much. I'd been jumping at every sound and looking over my shoulder all week, although part of that had been caused by guilt over my newfound profession as a casino cheat.

Billy had been helping me pick up living-expense money by making sure dice and roulette balls fell where I wanted. I didn't feel good about it, but I hadn't dared to access my checking account or credit cards for fear that someone would trace me. I could stop by an ATM now that everyone and their brother knew I was in Vegas, but I'd lied about needing to shop. I'd stuffed a change of clothes in a duffle along with my purse and the loot from the Senate before heading off to Dante's. The bag had gone into a locker at the ice rink, and the key had been stowed in a dark corner of Dante's lobby. The fact that Billy hadn't bitched about having to retrieve it showed that he shared my enthusiasm for getting certain items off our hands.

The ice rink is a popular spot on hot desert days, and the free-skate period had just started when we arrived. A crowd of tourists looking for a family-friendly activity and a smattering of locals streamed in the doors along with us, letting out a collective sigh of relief at the climate change. The rink had a sub shop, so Chavez offered to load up on fast food while I retrieved my bag. I offered to pay for the food, but he laughed and declined. "Although I will be happy to quote you a price for other things, *querida*."

I ran off before I was tempted to take him up on the offer. I ducked into a ladies' room and changed into sneakers, a wadded-up pair of khaki shorts and a bright red tank top. It wasn't the picture of elegance, but it beat my barefoot-and-sequins look. Even in Vegas that had garnered a few glances, despite Pritkin's blood being almost invisible on the crimson satin.

When I returned, Chavez was flirting with a dazed

checkout girl, who had apparently forgotten that she was supposed to receive more than a smile in return for the two big bags she passed over. I was willing to bet that his living expenses were pretty low. "Do I look okay?" I asked, wondering whether I'd gotten most of the evidence of the food fight off.

"Of course not." He gave me a slow smile as his eyes took in my new ensemble. "¡*Estás bonita*! You will always stand out."

Since my hair was sticky with cupcake residue and my clothes were wrinkled enough that a homeless person wouldn't have had them, I took that comment for what it was—a knee-jerk reaction. Chavez was probably literally incapable of insulting a woman, no matter how she looked. It would be bad for business.

"Thanks, can we—" I stopped, my heart in my throat, and stared across the rink at a man who had just skated onto the ice. For a split second I thought it was Tomas. He had the same slender, athletic build, the same waist-length black hair and the same honey-over-cream skin. It wasn't until a little girl stumbled onto the ice after him and he turned to catch her in his arms that I saw his face. Of course, it wasn't him. The last time I'd seen the real thing, he'd been trying to hold his head up on a broken neck.

"What is it, *querida*? You look like you've seen a ghost."

I could have told him that seeing Tomas would be a lot more traumatic for me than seeing any ghost, but I didn't. My old roommate wasn't my favorite topic of conversation. He'd given Rasputin the keys to the wards protecting MAGIC in return for two things: help killing his master and control over me. The two went together, since his reason for wanting to get rid of his current master was so he'd be free to take out his old one. Considering that the vamp in question, Alejandro, was head of the Latin American Senate, Tomas had decided he'd need help. Maybe one day I'll meet a guy who doesn't think of me primarily as a weapon. Or, knowing my luck, maybe not.

Things hadn't gone quite the way Tomas had planned. I assumed he'd survived the battle, since a first-level master isn't easy to kill, but whether he'd eluded MAGIC's wrath I didn't know. But if he'd fought his way free, he was running for his life, not skating an afternoon away in full public view. "It's nothing," I said.

Chavez leaned on the railing beside me. "A handsome man. *Muy predido*, a turn-on, as you Americans say."

I shot him a glance. His expression was appreciative, even slightly predatory, as it followed the skating figure. "Aren't you an incubus?" I'd been under the impression that they preferred female partners. I certainly hadn't seen any male patrons hanging about Casanova's.

Chavez gave a Latin shrug. "Incubus, succubus, it's all the same."

I blinked. "Come again?"

"Our kind has no innate sex, *querida*. At the moment, I inhabit a male body, but I have possessed women at times. It is much the same to me." His eyes gleamed as he leaned closer, trailing a warm finger down my cheek. It was a light touch, but it caused me to shiver. "Pleasure is pleasure, after all."

With his words came a swift tug of pure lust. It wasn't as overwhelming as Casanova's touch, nor did it get the attention of the *geis* as his briefly had. It was a simple invitation, no more, no less—the knowledge that any advance I chose to make would be received with delight and would end in pleasure. It made me furious, but not with him. It drove home the point that, as things stood, I had less control over my love life than a nun. Even if I lost my head and decided to exchange a lifetime of slavery as Pythia for a brief fling, I couldn't. Literally couldn't, unless I wanted to risk going crazy. Mircea had seen to that.

"Did I shock you?" He looked more amused than contrite. I could have told him that, after growing up at Tony's, not much shocked me anymore, but I settled for a shrug. "It wouldn't be the first time," he assured me. "My lover is both male and a vampire, so I have developed . . . what is the term? A thick skin?"

"I didn't think vamps and incubi had much to do with each other."

"We don't. I am considered quite perverse," he said cheerfully.

I smiled in spite of myself. "Can we go?"

Chavez tried to take the duffle, but I held on to it with the excuse that he was carrying the bags of food. If this offended his macho sensibilities, he didn't let it show. Once we were safely back in the car, I removed the stolen costume from the duffle after wrapping it around the remaining black boxes. I left the Graeae's empty one in place. I had plans for it.

"Casanova said he'd stick these in the house safe for me, and not charge the girl who, uh, loaned me the clothes." I passed the bundle to Chavez as he turned over the engine.

"I'll see to it, although he may be busy for some time." He slid a flirtatious glance my way. "You left quite an impression, *querida*. I think Dante's will never be the same." He casually tossed the bundle in the back seat, and I suppressed a wince as it bounced on the padded leather. I wondered, not for the first time, whether I shouldn't put the boxes back in the locker and call MAGIC with their location. But with the Senate facing war, I didn't trust them not to decide that they needed some extra help and turn whatever was inside them loose. Casanova wouldn't want any more guests like the Graeae running around, so the boxes were probably safe with him. At least until I could figure out what to do with them.

Chavez pulled up to a seedy tattoo parlor where, presumably, Pritkin was getting cleaned up. He took my hand when I started to get out of the car. "I do not know what you are planning, *querida*, but be careful. Mages, they are never to be fully trusted, you understand? And this one especially. When dealing with him, remember: 'Look like the innocent flower, but be the serpent under it.' " I stared in surprise at the quote, and he laughed. "What did you think, that I was merely good looks?"

I stammered out a negative, although he'd gotten it right and we both knew it. "You have my card, yes? Call if you need assistance." He grinned, teeth startlingly white against his smooth olive skin. "Or anything else. For you, Cassie, my rates are negotiable."

I laughed, and he drove off, burning rubber. It only occurred to me after he'd gone to wonder how he'd known my name. I'd never actually gotten around to introducing myself. I shrugged it off; Casanova must have told him.

Chapter 5

I went inside the store lugging my duffle and the bags of food. It was almost as hot as outside, with a rattling window air conditioner threatening to give its last wheeze at any moment. The desperate sound matched the rest of the decor, which consisted of stained ceiling tiles, dung brown carpet and a battered laminate counter. Only the hundreds of brightly colored tattoo designs adhered to almost every surface gave it life.

The counter separated the front from the back of the shop, which I couldn't see because a brown curtain cut off my view. There was no attendant in sight, so I rang the bell, frowning at an issue of *Crystal Gazing* that was in full view on the counter. The self-proclaimed guardian of free speech in the supernatural community had its usual screaming headline: DRACULA SIGHTED IN VEGAS—THE SCOURGE OF EUROPE ALIVE! Yeah, he was probably sitting by the pool at Caesar's, eating Moon Pies with Elvis. I tucked it out of sight under the counter, thankful that no one had yet dug up my name. I had enough problems—I didn't need the paparazzi, too.

A few seconds later a skinny bald man with a long gray mustache appeared from behind the curtain. Except for the parts hidden by a pair of cutoff jeans, he was covered in tattoos from his scrawny neck to the tops of his flip-flop-clad feet. Even stranger, the inked images moved. The cobra coiled around his neck paused to flicker a tongue in my direction, while a painted lizard crept across his forehead before catching sight of me and scuttling away behind his left ear. The eagle on his chest flapped its outstretched wings lazily, eyeing me out of a single dark eye.

It looked like I'd found the right place.

The painted man took one look at my fascinated expression and laughed. "The shops that do butterflies and flowers are across town, love." Despite looking like a retired Hells Angel, he had a faint accent. I thought it might be Australian. "And I've canceled all my appointments today—rush job came up."

"I'm not here for a tattoo," I told him, trying not to watch the athame inked onto his stomach, which every few seconds dripped a spot of red from its tip that ran down his skin into the frayed top of the cut offs. "Pritkin said to meet him here. I brought lunch." I held up the bags and the man's expression brightened.

"You'll be Cassandra Palmer, then," he said, looking surprised. I nodded, wondering what he'd expected. I decided not to ask how Pritkin had described me. "Well, why didn't you say so? I'm Archie McAdam, but my friends call me Mac."

"Cassie," I said, taking the proffered hand. All around his larger tattoos was a forest of painted leaves and vines that rustled slightly, as if in a slight wind. From the dark areas under the foliage, a pair of narrowed orange eyes watched me malevolently.

Mac held back the curtain and I squeezed around the counter to duck inside. The first thing I saw in the back was Pritkin, lying facedown on a padded bench, his shirt off and his head turned away. Given how much trouble he regularly got in, I'd have expected his back to be a welter of old and new scars, but it wasn't. Only a fine tracery of whitened ridges marred one shoulder blade, looking almost like claw marks. Otherwise, flawless skin covered better muscles than I'd expected, unblemished except for the pale purple outline of a tattoo that had been stenciled onto his left side. The outline was about half inked in, although no color had been added yet. It was a stylized sword, very finely drawn, almost delicate. I thought that now was an odd time for body art, but it was his hour. He could spend it as he liked.

Mac held up a mirror to show his customer the design, and Pritkin scowled. "I still say it's too elaborate. A plain sword is all I need."

"What are you on about?" Mac asked incredulously. "Look at the lines, the artistry. I've outdone myself!"

Pritkin snorted, and I somewhat sympathized. It looked like he was in for a long day. The sword's blade trailed along the whole length of his side, ending on top of his hip. His jeans had been pushed down enough to bare the top of one buttock to the stencil. Most of his back was, like his arms and face, a light gold color, as if he spent a lot of time in the sun but didn't tan easily. But his lower back and hips shaded into peach and then to cream, although there was no obvious tan line. I found myself wondering whether there was a difference in texture between the areas, and how they would feel under my fingertips, before I abruptly snapped out of it.

I looked away, horrified that I'd been checking out *Pritkin* of all people. Obviously, proximity to incubi has some weird side effects.

"Take a break, John," Mac said heartily. "This pretty young thing brought lunch!"

Pritkin sat up, scowling, and kept his back to us while he zipped up his jeans. He'd either bought new ones or borrowed some of Mac's, because these were blood free. I grinned at him to cover the awkwardness. "John?"

"It's a good, honest English name," he snapped, angry for no reason I could see.

"Sorry," I held out the bag of food placatingly. "It just doesn't sound like you."

"Which part?" Billy Joe asked. He floated over from the back of the room, near where the golem stood propped against the wall, as silent as the statue it wasn't. "The good, the honest or the English?"

I ignored him and grabbed half a meatball sub before handing the rest of the food to Mac. The smell in the car had reminded me that the only nutrition I'd had all day was a handful of peanuts at Casanova's. The sandwich did a lot to improve my mood, and after a few bites, I was even able to muster another smile for Pritkin, who was tugging on a green T-shirt. "You forgot I was dropping in?"

"I wasn't sure you would be," he said curtly.

I decided I could either waste time getting into an argument over the value of my word or I could eat the rest of my sub. I chose the latter. A glance around showed that the back room was no more interesting than the front, and wasn't going to provide much in the way of entertainment. Its bare brick walls contained a metal thing that looked sort of like a washing machine but probably wasn't, a mini fridge, a cot piled high with old books, an overflowing wastebasket and the tattoo table and equipment.

I swallowed the last bite and wiped tomato sauce off my chin. "Tick tock. You have fifty minutes left. If you want to spend them eating or getting tattooed, go right ahead. But when your time is up, I'm outta here."

"To go where?" Pritkin demanded, peering at his sandwich as if he thought I might have slipped something nasty inside. "If you have the ridiculous notion of surviving a trip into Faerie on your own, allow me to point out one small fact. Your power won't work there, or will be very unpredictable if it does. For that reason, Pythias have made it a habit to leave the Fey strictly alone. You can go against tradition, but with your power unreliable and your ward blocked, you won't last a day."

He sat on the cot and began dissecting his sandwich while I mulled things over. Mac was perched on a stool by the table, munching his way through the other half of my sub and staying quiet. Billy floated over and tipped his hat back with a hazy-looking finger. "He's got a point," he commented.

"Gee, thanks so much."

Billy hoisted his insubstantial backside up onto the edge of the table and looked at me seriously. That was an expression he used so rarely that it got my attention. "I don't like the guy any more than you do, Cass, but if you're determined to do this thing, a war mage could be a real asset. Think about it. We got to get into Faerie, which ain't exactly easy anytime and will be 'specially hard with all the security from the war. Then we got to avoid the Fey, who don't like trespassers, while we look for the fat man and that seer chick. And, assuming we manage all that, we have to deal with them at the end of it. And if the Fey are hiding 'em, that ain't gonna be fun. We could use some help."

"We haven't had an offer yet," I reminded him. Mac seemed surprised by my apparently random comments, but Pritkin ignored them. I suppose he'd learned that, wherever I was, Billy wasn't far behind.

"If he didn't intend to help, he could have stepped aside and let the mages have you back at the casino."

"I could have managed on my own," I said shortly. Even to my ears it sounded sulky, but that didn't mean it wasn't true. I didn't need Pritkin, or anybody else, to come riding to the rescue.

"Yeah, but I thought you were trying to avoid using the power."

This conversation was starting to irritate me. "Are you just going to sit there and eat, or what?" I asked Pritkin crossly.

He glanced up, a look of distaste on his features. I wasn't sure whether it was for me or the sandwich, so I let it pass. "We worked together before when we had a common cause. We have one again. I am proposing that we join forces long enough to deal with our mutual dilemma."

"You have a grudge against Tony? Since when?" That was awfully convenient.

"The Circle has issued a warrant for him, but that isn't my interest."

I crumpled up my sandwich paper and tossed it at the trash. I missed. "Then what is?"

Pritkin took a drink from one of the Cokes Mac had passed around, and grimaced. "I want you to help me recover the sybil called Myra," he informed me.

"What?" I stared at him. It was disconcerting and more

than a little suspicious that the first name on my list also topped Pritkin's.

"None of our locating charms have turned up anything. Therefore it is a fair guess that she is hiding in Faerie, where our magic doesn't work. In return for your help, I promise not to take you before the Circle, and to assist you in dealing with your former master."

I narrowed my eyes at him. "I don't even know where to start. First, you aren't taking me anywhere, and second, why should I help you bring back my rival? So your Circle can kill me and reinstate her? For some reason, that doesn't appeal."

"The Circle has no plans to put her in your place," he said grimly. "As for the other, do not overestimate your abilities, or underestimate mine. If I wanted to capture you, I would. Even if I refrain, eventually someone else will. The Circle will never stop chasing you, and they have to get lucky only once. You, on the other hand, have to elude all of their traps, with little knowledge of the magical world to aid you. Only with my help can you hope to avoid the fate the Circle has planned for you—and for her."

"Oh, right. They're going to kill the only fully trained initiate they have. Why do I doubt that?" The Circle might want me dead, but they had every reason to keep Myra alive and well. There was a war on, and they badly needed the help a malleable Pythia could provide.

He glanced at Mac, who was looking dour. "Some of us have noticed a disturbing tendency in the Circle's leadership lately. They seem to care less for our traditional mission and more for power every year. The Silver have always been separate from the Black, not only in how we obtain power, but in what we do with it. I fear the Council has forgotten that."

Mac nodded. "And now they have a new candidate for Pythia, one of the more docile initiates. If both you and Myra die, they believe she'll inherit." He shook his head wearily, causing a dragonfly on his right shoulder to flutter glittering green wings. "I knew we had some rot at the core, but this is worse than any of us guessed. The power chooses the Pythia. That has been a maxim for thousands of years, because to have the wrong person in that office is to invite disaster. Dark mages are always trying to find ways to slip through time, to remake the world the way they want, and every once in a while one succeeds. Without a proper Pythia on the throne, our entire existence is in danger! The council must be stopped!"

"Uh-huh." I looked into Mac's homely, earnest face and tried to give him the benefit of the doubt. But it was difficult. The world I'd grown up in was run on the carrot-and-stick principle: everything was done to gain reward or to avoid punishment. And the more risky the job, the higher the rewards or the greater the punishment had to be. Considering the risk level Mac was talking about, the payoff had to be out of this world.

Pritkin had stayed quiet throughout his buddy's rousing speech, contenting himself with glowering into the distance. I snapped my fingers in front of his face. "So, what's your story? Are you also in this out of the goodness of your heart?"

His perpetual scowl deepened. "I am in it, as you say, because I resent being made into a murderer. I was given the assignment of locating Myra for trial, even though the verdict in her case is a foregone conclusion. Others are searching for you, and I have no doubt that their instructions were the same as mine. If I did not think she could be taken alive, I was free to use extreme measures to ensure that she did not continue to threaten the Circle's interests."

One word in all that had caught my attention. "Trial?" It was hard to believe that anyone would prosecute Myra for attempting to kill me. It seemed more likely that the Circle would give her a medal. "What did she do?"

"She has been implicated in the death of the Pythia."

For a minute, I thought he was talking about me, after all. Then it clicked. "You mean Agnes."

"Show some respect!" Pritkin said heatedly. "Use her proper title."

"She's dead," I pointed out. "I doubt she minds."

"But Myra couldn't have done it!" Mac broke in. "The Council's argument doesn't make sense. What would she gain by it?"

I thought that was kind of obvious. "She probably thought she'd be Pythia, if Agnes died before she could pass the power over to me."

"But that's just it, Cassie," Mac insisted. "As John pointed out to the Council, the power won't go to an assassin of another Pythia or heir designate. It's an old rule, to keep the initiates from slaughtering each other for the position."

My mind screeched to a halt. "Run that by me again?"

"The power has never yet gone to the killer of a Pythia or her heir," Mac repeated slowly.

"You didn't know that?" Pritkin demanded.

"No." And I wasn't sure I believed it. I really wanted to, because it meant that offing me might not be on Myra's agenda after all. But I was having a hard time with the idea that she intended to let bygones be bygones. It didn't seem like her style, especially not with two knife wounds from my weapon in her torso. Not to mention that, even if she did decide to take the high road, I couldn't see Rasputin letting her concede defeat. He needed her to be Pythia if he had any chance of winning, or even surviving, the war. Something was wrong here.

"Didn't Agnes die of old age?" I asked Mac, since he seemed the more forthcoming of the two.

"That's what we believed, at first. But strange sores were noticed on the body when it was being readied for burial. A doctor was called in to look at them, and became suspicious, so an autopsy was ordered. She didn't die because of her age, Cassie. She was poisoned. And considering the amount of precautions taken to safeguard the Pythia, it couldn't have been easy."

"They used arsenic, rather than a potion or curse that would have been detected by the wards," Pritkin added, apparently appalled that Agnes had been killed by something so mundane. "Here. What do you sense from this?"

I backed away fast, even before I got a good look at what he was holding out.

"I promised to talk, nothing else," I reminded him.

"With no witnesses, this is our best chance to find the killer!"

I stared at the small amulet in his hand. It looked pretty innocent, just a round silver disk with a worn figure embossed on it, swinging from a tarnished chain. I wasn't getting any warning signals from it the way I did from objects likely to trigger a vision, but I didn't intend to take chances.

"Well?" Pritkin thrust it at me, but I backed away rapidly.

"Your chance," I corrected, making sure the little bauble didn't brush against me. "This isn't my problem."

"Don't be too sure of that," he said cryptically.

I dodged behind Mac for cover and refused to take the bait. I glanced at my nonexistent watch. "Oops, look at the time. Guess I have to be going now. Let's not do this again sometime, okay?"

Before I could move, Pritkin was there, jamming the medallion into the skin of my upper arm. "Ow!" He looked at me expectantly. I glared at him. "That hurt!"

"What do you see?"

"A big red mark," I said irritably, rubbing at what would probably be a bruise. "And stop poking me with that thing!"

"If you are lying to me—"

"If I had a vision, you'd know it!" I told him furiously. "I don't just see the bad stuff anymore—I get a front-row seat. And lately, I take whoever's closest along for the ride! Or have you forgotten already?"

Pritkin didn't answer; he just continued to hold out the amulet, although he was no longer attempting to brand me with it. I sighed and took the damn thing. "How does it work, exactly?"

"That's just it," Mac said, sounding as if he was enjoying the mental puzzle. "We don't know. It contained arsenic— we opened it last night. But it was enclosed by the metal, with no way to touch the skin."

"The answer has to be there!" Pritkin insisted. "She was holding it when she died, and it contained the same poison that killed her. And where else could the poison have come from? No one would have been able to get to her to administer it, especially not repeatedly!"

I gingerly examined the tiny thing. It had been cut open

along the side, like a locket. Whatever it might once have contained, it was empty now. Which probably explained why I was getting nothing from it. The tampering had ruined its physical integrity, and in the process had ruptured any psychic skin that might have imprinted itself. But with Pritkin already looking as if his blood pressure was going through the roof, I decided not to mention that. "Repeatedly?"

"No one was suspicious, because the poison wasn't administered all at one time," Mac explained. "It was spread out over six months or more, administered in small doses that built up in her system until it finally overwhelmed her. Her worsening condition was put down to her age and to the strain of losing the heir."

"Six months?" The same time the Senate sent Tomas to babysit me. I didn't like the coincidence, but didn't say anything. Unfortunately, either my face gave me away or Pritkin had already made the leap himself.

"Myra couldn't have administered the poison," he said flatly. "She went missing months ago, long before Agnes took ill, and she has no motive. The Council wants her out of the way, so they are using the story of her involvement for their own purposes. Others had far better cause, but the Council can't afford to challenge them."

No, I didn't suppose so. The Circle was allied with the Senate in the war; they couldn't risk accusing their buddies of murder. I didn't like to think about it, but it really wouldn't surprise me if the Senate was guilty as hell. It fit the usual vampire modus operandi to remove obstacles in the most final manner possible. And it would have been worth it even if they'd only thought there was a chance that the power would come to me. They'd believed I was going to be their tame Pythia, the first in centuries under their control rather than the Circle's. For that kind of power, they'd have done far worse than kill one old woman. Of course, there was another strong contender.

"What about the Circle?"

Pritkin's eyes narrowed. "What about it?"

I shrugged. "You've implied that the Senate is guilty, but they're not the ones hunting down the only two candidates who stand in the way of the Circle's chosen heir."

Mac looked sick, but Pritkin brushed it aside. "The Circle had no reason to want a change in leadership. Lady Phemonoe was an excellent Pythia."

"Well, yeah, that's the point. Agnes being good at her job might have been the problem, if the Council really is going bad. Maybe she opposed them one too many times, and someone decided that a younger, more easygoing Pythia would be—"

Pritkin cut me off with a savage gesture. "You don't know what you're talking about! The Council would never stoop so low!"

I stared at him, amazed that he'd already forgotten our morning in hell. His precious Circle didn't seem to have a problem with taking me out, or with sending him after Myra. But I guess we didn't count. "Okay, so why are you after her? Because you think she knows something?"

"I declined to kill her untried," Pritkin said, "but by now the Circle has doubtless assigned another operative. If he finds her first, she will have no chance to tell her side of things."

"You must have turned them down pretty forcefully. Because they don't seem too fond of you."

"I found out that an informant had placed you at Dante's

this morning. I had to battle the Circle's team to reach you first, and one of them recognized me."

And, of course, they'd seen him in the hallway with me, too. That probably hadn't done his reputation any good. "Say you find her. What then?"

"Charges have been made that she needs to answer," he said shortly. "Her fate will depend on her responses."

I looked down so he wouldn't see the disbelief in my eyes. "Sounds like you have a plan. Now that you know where Myra is, why do you need me? As you pointed out, I won't be much use in Faerie, assuming we can get there."

"Because there is a chance that she can time-shift away from me without someone to hold her in place," Pritkin told me reluctantly. "Part of your power allows you to restrict a sybil's abilities. It is usually used for training purposes, to permit a Pythia to retrieve a sybil from the timeline if she falls into difficulties. You should be able to exercise the same control to ensure that Myra cannot elude me."

I sipped soda to hide my expression, and Billy merged with me so we could talk privately. "Either these two are the dumbest conspirators I ever met," he said in disgust, "or they don't think too highly of you."

"Both," I thought at him. *"Can you drift through either one, maybe find out what they're really up to?"*

"Nope. They're both warded all to hell and back. But we don't need that to know they're lying. If your power won't work in Faerie—"

"—then I couldn't hold Myra for them, even if I knew how. Yeah, I got that much. So what do they want me for?"

"That's kind of obvious, too, isn't it?"

"You think?"

Billy laughed, and it echoed inside my skull. "I'm gonna

go check up on Dante's, see what kind of hell the Circle is raising, if you think you can handle these two geniuses without me?"

I thought something rude and got another peal of laughter before he was suddenly gone. I stared at Pritkin and he looked back, completely expressionless. He did a good poker face, but it didn't matter. I didn't buy his flimsy story for a minute.

Pritkin knew full well that Myra had tried to kill me. He was probably betting that sooner or later she'd show up again for another go. Basically, I was bait. As for why he and Mac wanted to find her, that was also obvious. Locating her would give them a powerful tool to use in a coup against the Circle's leadership. Maybe they saw themselves as revolutionaries, remaking a corrupt system, or maybe they were just opportunists who figured she was their ticket to power. It didn't matter to me either way, but I did care about the fact that she would never help them for anything less than the full title. The only question was whether Pritkin would kill me himself once I'd served my purpose, or if he'd let Myra do it for him.

Of course, I knew they were kidding themselves if they thought she would just fall in line with their scheme. As Agnes had put it when she reluctantly handed power to me, her heir had joined Rasputin because she was evil or because she was weak, and either way she'd make a lousy Pythia. The fact that Myra had shortly afterwards attacked me had me leaning towards evil. I might not want the job, but that psycho wasn't getting it, either.

I thought it over. Billy was right—we needed more help than he could provide, and a couple of war mages were perfect. Pritkin wanted to use and then double-cross me?

Okay, but two could play that game. I'd let him help me through the obstacles ahead, and as soon as we found Myra, I'd dump him and use the trap that had housed the Graeae on her.

I smiled at the mage. "Sounds interesting. Maybe we can work out a deal, after all."

That afternoon was quite an education. Even though I'd been brought up at a vampire's court, my knowledge of magic wasn't great. Clairvoyants are viewed as the dregs of the magical world, people with little real talent who make a living telling norms what they want to hear. You know the type: "Your soul mate's name begins with *M*"— or *S* or *R* or any of the more common letters of the alphabet— but the clairvoyant needs subsequent sessions to figure out exactly who it is. Expensive sessions. I'd never done that, even when money had been more than tight. I might cheat casinos out of desperation, but I never mocked my gift. Most of the mages at Tony's, however, had put down any of my Seeings that came true to coincidence, and wanted little to do with me.

Vamps, of course, have an innate magic of their own, and I don't mean just the power that animates them. Most gain useful abilities if they survive long enough, and some of those can be pretty spectacular. I'd seen vamps levitate themselves and others, strip the skin off a body from across a room, and rip a beating heart out of a chest with little more than a thought. But the kind of magic the mages do is beyond them, and magic workers lose their ability if turned, so there are no vamp mages.

I think I learned more that afternoon about magic than ten years at Tony's had taught me. It started when Pritkin stripped back down to let Mac finish the tattoo, and I asked why he was bothering with that now. I was mainly asking to focus my attention on something other than his body, which was suddenly a lot more attractive than it should have been. I really hoped the side effects from encountering incubi were going to wear off soon.

"Like yours, my magic will not be reliable in Faerie," Pritkin said. He sounded like he'd rather tell me to go to hell, but since we'd just agreed to be allies, he had to play nice. I decided to press the advantage while it lasted, which I suspected wouldn't be long.

"What, you're going to flash your manly tattoo at the Fey?"

Mac laughed, but even though Pritkin's head was turned away from me, I could tell he was scowling. His shoulders tensed, and that tightened things further down in an interesting way. I got up to get another Coke.

"It's a special tattoo," Mac told me cheerfully, picking up something that looked like an electric toothbrush without the bristles. "If I do this right, it should imprint his aura—his magical skin—as well as the physical. When he throws his shields up, it'll manifest as a real weapon. And, as we learned the technique from the Fey, it should work in Faerie even better than here." He put the head of the toothbrush thing to the top of the sword and started to ink it in. Pritkin didn't flinch, but the muscles in his arms stood out a bit more. I sipped Coke and gave up trying not to watch him.

"I'm not getting it," I said after a minute. "You have weapons"—a serious understatement—"why not rely on them?"

Mac answered, although his attention remained on his victim's back, where he paused to wipe away some blood.

"Regular weapons won't do much against the Fey. You need magical stuff to hold up against the sort of thing they can dish out, but like John said, our magic doesn't work in Faerie." He went back to inking, and this time Pritkin did flinch slightly. "At least, most of it won't, and the sort of stuff that will, we don't have access to."

"What sort of stuff?"

"Oh, different things," Mac said, his little tool humming as it tore through Pritkin's skin. He paused to consult the large grimoire he'd propped on the stool next to him, then muttered something over the partly finished tattoo. The image gleamed for a moment, then died back down. Mac grunted and went back to work. "What would really help would be some null bombs. Only they're hard to come by, and it's a death sentence to use them without authorization. And even were we willing to risk it, for some reason the Black Market doesn't trust us—too many years putting them out of business, I guess."

"What are null bombs?"

"Wicked things, but good to have anywhere there's magic you don't know how to counter. No one knows who invented them, but they've been around for centuries. Dark mages take a null—a mage born with the ability to disrupt magic—and drain his life force into the sphere. It kills the mage but traps his lifetime's ability in one extremely potent package. If it's exploded, including in Faerie, all magic ceases or goes haywire for a while. How long depends on the strength of the null, and how many years of life he had left when he was drained."

"Interesting." I felt vaguely sick. "What do they look like?" I carefully did not glance at my duffle, which was sitting innocently on the floor near the fridge.

I thought I'd kept my voice casual, but Pritkin must have heard something in my tone, because his head whipped around to face me. "Why?" His eyes were narrowed, whether in pain or suspicion, to the point that only a thin green line showed through his pale lashes.

I shrugged. "I was just wondering. Tony used to have weapons lying around all the time. Maybe I've seen one."

Mac shook his head, his face intent on Pritkin's back. "Not likely, love. They cost a fortune, because nulls strong enough to make one are rare and well protected. Most of the ones floating about these days are left over from past centuries. The vamps used to hunt nulls before the truce, which is why there's hardly any left now. Most were wiped out, whole family lines destroyed to build up the vamp arsenals."

"You've never seen one of the bombs, then?"

"Oh, I've encountered a few through the years. The Circle buys any they come across, to keep them out of the vamps' hands. Donovan's auction house acquired one in London, back in sixty-three. The Circle wasn't happy when they refused our initial offer and put it up for public bidding, but old man Donovan told them it was perfectly legal. The thing was old—I examined it and it had to date from at least the twelfth century—and of course there were no laws against making them back then." He paused to wipe down the tattoo again and grimaced at the amount of blood on his rag. "You want to take a break?" he asked Pritkin.

"No. Finish it." Pritkin's jaw was clenched, but his eyes were on me. I didn't like the suspicion in them.

"What happened at the auction?" I asked, hoping Mac would get around to giving me a description sooner or later.

"Oh, we bought it," he said, going back to work. "No choice, really. Cost a fortune, though, I can tell you. I kept calling in for authorization to go higher until the council told me to quit bothering them and just get the damn thing, no matter the cost. I don't think they planned on spending a quarter million on a little silver ball, though, considering the complaints I heard when I got back. But there was nothing they could do to me—I was following orders."

The phrase "little silver ball" rattled around in my head while I tried to keep my expression vague. I must not have done too well. "You've seen one," Pritkin accused.

I wanted to say, "Yeah, there's two in that duffle over there," but I didn't know how much I could trust my new "allies." Pritkin needed my help, so I doubted he'd grab the bag and run, but what about Mac? A quarter million pounds in the 1960s would be worth what today? I didn't know, but the answer might be enough to make good old Mac's loyalty waver. His business didn't exactly look prosperous, and even mages could be tempted by an early retirement.

"Maybe. It's been a while."

I glanced at Mac, and Pritkin looked disgusted. "He is risking his life in this endeavor. You can trust him as you do me," he said impatiently.

I raised an eyebrow, and Pritkin exploded. His face had been reddening as the tattoo was inked in, inch by agonizing inch, and I think he wanted someone to yell at. "If you do not trust me, this will never work! There are going to be times, very soon, when our lives will depend on whether we can work together! If you cannot put faith in me, say so now. I would rather do this alone than get killed because you assume I am false!"

I drank Coke and remained calm. "If I didn't think I could trust you, to a point, I'd have left by now. Your hour was up a few minutes ago." I looked between him and Mac.

"Hypothetically, say I know where some weapons might be found. I'll describe them, and you tell me what they do. If we decide they could be useful, maybe I'll tell you where to locate them."

Pritkin looked outraged, but Mac shrugged. "Sounds fair." He paused to change ink colors, having finished all the gold areas on the sword. "Have at it."

"Okay." I didn't have to think about it, since the only thing I'd taken from the Senate besides the traps and the null bombs was a small velvet bag. Inside were a handful of yellowed bone disks imprinted with crude runes. They had holes carved in the top and leather thongs threaded through them like they were usually worn rather than cast. I described them to Mac, who stopped working to stare at me, openmouthed.

"That's impossible," he said. Pritkin didn't say anything, but it felt like his eyes might bore a hole through me at any minute. "I'm not calling you a liar, Cassie, but if a two-bit gangster like that Antonio has the Runes of Langgarn, I'll—"

"He doesn't." Pritkin cut him off. "Where did you see them?"

"This is hypothetical."

"Miss Palmer!"

"You can call me Cassie." Considering that he was probably planning to kill me eventually, formality seemed a little odd.

"Answer the question," Pritkin forced out through clenched teeth. Since Mac hadn't resumed digging in his back, I supposed I was the cause.

"I'll tell you what I know," Mac put in, "but it isn't much. Legend has it that they were enchanted by Egil Skallagrimsson in the late tenth century." At my blank look, he elaborated. "He was a Viking poet and general hell-raiser—took his first life at age six when he killed another boy over the outcome of a ball game—but he was one of the best rune-masters to ever live. Of course, some stories say that he stole the runes from Gunnhild, the witch queen of Erik Bloodaxe, king of Norway and northern England. And since Gunnhild was said to have Fey blood, it's possible the runes were enchanted long before in Faerie by someone else entirely—"

"Mac," Pritkin broke in when it sounded like his friend was about to go off on a tangent.

"Oh, right. Well, there are a lot of stories about Egil, most of which were recorded in his own poetry. He depicted himself as a larger-than-life figure who did impossible things—took on huge numbers of opponents and slew them single-handedly, set barns ablaze with a look, brought kings under his sway with only the power of his words and survived numerous attempts on his life. He made an enemy of Gunnhild, either by stealing her runes or by killing her son—stories differ—yet he lived to age eighty in a time when most men died in their forties. Interesting bloke, I always thought."

"So what do the runes do?" I tried not to sound impatient, but I needed useful facts, not a history lesson.

"It's rumored that there was a full set at one point, but it was broken up centuries ago. It doesn't matter, since they're used separately. Each has a different power associated with it, and their only limitation is that they have to recharge for a month after use. Those that remain are highly valued weapons. It's said that they can't be warded against and that even null bombs don't have much effect on them."

I shot Mac a skeptical look. I'd never heard of any magic that couldn't be countered. Casanova had tried to sell me that idea about my *geis*, but even Pritkin had admitted that there was almost certainly a way out of it. I just didn't know what it was yet.

Mac shook his head. "It sounds fantastic, doesn't it? But the Circle owns two of the set, and I was there twenty years ago when they used one to test a new ward they'd developed. This thing was a bear—nothing got through it, and I mean nothing. Twenty of our best mages hammered at it for the better part of a morning, hit it with everything they had, but it didn't so much as waver. Then old Marsden—he used to lead the council—brought out the runes. He decided to cast Thurisaz. I'll never forget that, not long as I live."

"What happened?" I prompted.

"If you didn't know Marsden, it may be hard for you to get a visual on this, but picture the oldest, scrawniest, least threatening man you've ever seen. His magic was still strong at that point—he didn't step down until a few years ago—but he was *old*. His hands shook and he almost always had food spilled down the front of him because he couldn't see worth a damn. He kept running into things but he wouldn't wear his glasses or use charms to enhance his vision. He kept saying he didn't need them; then he'd try to shake hands with coat racks. He looked like he ought to be in a retirement home, unless you crossed him. Then you found out why he led the council for seven decades."

"Mac!"

"Right, right. Well, Marsden cast Thurisaz on himself, and the next thing any of us knew, he was gone and there was this huge—and I mean *huge*—ogre standing in his place. It was so tall it had to hunch over to fit in the room, and the council chamber has ceilings almost twenty feet tall! It snatched up the council table, which was made of old oak and weighed God knows what, and hurled it the length of the chamber. When it bounced off the ward without doing any damage, the thing let out a bellow that deafened me for a good ten minutes, then charged. The ward had been set up to protect a small vase, and so far, not so much as a petal of any of the flowers had been disturbed. Less than a minute after Thurisaz was cast, the ward was down and the vase was dust."

"How . . . amazing." I had raided the Senate hoping for weapons; it looked like I'd finally lucked out and found some. Knowing Tony's penchant for nasty surprises, I was going to need them.

"Yes, well, that part was all right, but then we had a rampaging ogre on our hands, didn't we? And we couldn't kill it without also killing the head of the council. Not that any of us was keen to take on that thing. We ran over each other getting out the door, then hied away like frightened rabbits. We reassembled outside and argued for almost an hour over what to do once it destroyed the wards guarding the chamber and got loose. Then old Marsden came wandering out and finally bothered to mention that the spell only lasts an hour."

"What do the other runes do?" I asked. "Is there a book or something?"

He glanced at Pritkin. "Would Nick have anything? I don't know the individual powers, just the basic legend."

Pritkin ignored him. "How many do you have?" he asked me. The question was quiet, but a pulse was throbbing at his temple.

I hesitated, but if I wanted to find out what these things did, I'd have to give up some information. "Three."

"Good God." Mac dropped his etching tool. A small

tornado carved on his right bicep started whirling even more enthusiastically.

"Describe them." Pritkin was looking pretty intense, but he wasn't gob smacked like his friend.

"I already did."

"The symbols!" he said impatiently. "Which runes are they?"

Mac broke in. "If you draw them I can—"

I cut him off with a frown. They might think I was a dumb blonde, but come on. I was a clairvoyant—did they really think I didn't know my runes? "Hagalaz, Jera and Dagaz."

"I'm on it." Mac jumped up and went into the next room and I heard him pick up the phone. It crossed my mind that he could be calling for backup, but I doubted it. They didn't know where the weapons were yet, and nobody would think that I'd drag stuff like that around in my bag. Come to think of it, I wasn't so thrilled with the idea now, either.

"Where did you get them?" Pritkin demanded.

I couldn't think of a reason not to tell him. "Same place I got the Graeae. The Senate."

"They didn't simply hand them over."

"Not exactly." I decided to change the subject. "Um, you wouldn't happen to know how I get the ladies back in their box, would you?" I had been wondering how to figure out the spell needed to trap Myra in their place. It would be very convenient if Pritkin would simply give it to me.

"Tell me about the runes." Damn, but he was single-minded.

"Tell me about the Graeae and I'll think about it."

"They are required to work for you for a year and a day

after their release, or until they have saved your life. Then they will be free to terrorize mankind again."

I glared at him. "That's not what I asked. And I didn't let them out on purpose, you know!"

"You shouldn't have been able to do it at all! That is a very complex spell. How did you learn it?"

I decided not to mention that all I'd done was pick up the orb. Pritkin thought me enough of a danger already; no need to add to the impression. And maybe it didn't mean anything. The box could have been defective—there was no telling how long they'd been in there. Of course, if it wasn't working right, I couldn't use it on Myra. I wondered whether there was a way to test it.

"Well?" He was obviously not the patient type.

"Do you know the spell to put them back or not?"

"Yes." That was it, that's all I got.

"So maybe we can work out a trade. You give it to me, and perhaps I'll tell you where the weapons are."

"You'll tell me anyway," he countered. "You won't get near your vampire without me, so you'll never get a chance to use them. And even my assistance may not be enough. We need every advantage."

Mac returned before I could think up a good comeback. "Nick is very curious why I want to know, but I think I put him off." He consulted a scribbled note in his hand. "He says that two were purchased at auction from Donovan's back in 1872. The Circle was outbid by an anonymous bidder who paid a king's ransom for them. No one's heard from them since." He looked at me. "I'd really like to know where you found them."

"She didn't find them; she stole them. From the Senate," Pritkin said.

Mac whistled. "I want to hear that story."

"Maybe later," I said, hoping he'd get on with it.

"All right, but I'm going to hold you to that." He consulted his notes again. "This is composed mainly of hearsay, but Nick knows his rune lore, so it's likely as good as we'll get. Hagalaz cast upright causes a massive hailstorm that attacks everything in the vicinity except the caster and whomever he chooses to protect—I assume that means whoever is within his shields, although Nick wasn't sure. Cast inverted, it calms even the fiercest of storms."

I brightened. That could prove useful. Mac read a few lines silently and cleared his throat. He glanced at me. "Er, Jera is . . . well, it's said to be, that is to say—"

"It's a fertility stone," I said, hoping to move him along. "Stands for a time of plenty and a good harvest."

"Yes, quite. It is believed to cause . . . er, to aid in, rather, some believe that—"

Pritkin snatched the paper from him and read over the paragraph that seemed to be giving Mac so much trouble. "It was advertised as an aid to virility, something like a magical version of Viagra," he summarized, shooting Mac a withering glance. "Is that it? No other properties?"

Mac looked sheepish. "Nick didn't know. All he had to go on was the auctioneer's description, and those are known for being phrased to elicit the best possible bids. It may have other properties, but if so they weren't listed. But it was enchanted at a time when thrones ran through family lines. Ensuring the succession would have been seen as equally, if not more, important than any weapon. And having the power to take fertility away from your opponents would be a great asset, throwing their lands into turmoil and civil war at the death of each king, and giving you a chance to invade in the chaos."

Pritkin frowned. "Perhaps, but it is of little use to us. And the last? Dagaz?"

"A breakthrough," I murmured. "A new beginning." I could really use one of those.

Mac nodded. "Traditionally, yes, that's the meaning. But how it is interpreted in the case of battle runes . . ." He shrugged. "Nick doesn't know."

"Then what is his best guess?" Pritkin asked it before I could.

"He doesn't have one." Mac threw up his hands at our expressions. "Don't shoot the messenger! It wasn't purchased with the others—in fact, no one has heard of it ever being up for sale. So there's not a lot to go on."

I felt frustrated. One rune that was no use to me was bad enough, I didn't need two. "What about other sources?"

Mac shook his head. "Nick said he would double-check, but the man has a mind like a computer, love. I doubt he missed anything, not about his favorite hobby. The rune is mentioned in several old sources, but they're mute about what it does."

"There is one way to find out," Pritkin said. I raised an eyebrow. "Cast it."

"Did you sleep through the story about the rampaging ogre, or what?"

"I will cast it if you are afraid," Pritkin said, assuming a sneer. "Where is it?"

I sighed and thought it over. I really needed to know what the thing did, and if Pritkin wanted to risk his neck to find out, who was I to stop him? Besides, he had a point: without his help, I might never get to Tony in the first place, and even if I did, what if the rune was another like Jera? I needed to know before I used it on the fat man and just ended up making him horny. I shuddered at the mental picture and Mac shot me a questioning look. "You said the runes have to recharge after every use," I reminded him. "If we cast it, we won't be able to use it again for a month."

Pritkin answered before his friend could. "Perhaps. However, if it hasn't been used in centuries, it may have a cumulative charge built up that could last through many castings."

"I don't know whether it's been used lately or not."

"Or the cumulative effect may simply make the casting an especially strong one," Mac pointed out.

Pritkin looked annoyed with his friend, but I thought the guy had a point. "One thing is certain," Pritkin said testily. "We cannot plan how to use it if we do not know what it does. As it stands, it is useless to us. Casting it would not make it more so." I wanted to debate him but couldn't. "Where is it?" he demanded.

I sighed. "Promise you'll teach me the spell to trap the Graeae, and I'll tell you."

He didn't even pause. "Done."

I shrugged. "In that duffle over there."

Chapter 6

I thought the two mages were going to rupture something trying to get to the bag. Mac beat his buddy, but only because he was closer and Pritkin's unzipped pants tried to fall down on the way. I watched him zip up with some disappointment, then gave myself a mental slap. At the rate things were going, I was going to need therapy.

Mac started setting items on the top of the fridge, one by one. His actions were reverent, like someone handling nitroglycerine. The two null bombs gleamed softly silver under the overhead lights. Behind them was the insignificant-looking box that had housed the Graeae for who knew how many centuries. Finally, Mac fished out the velvet pouch and carefully, one at a time, set the rune stones in front of the rest of the items.

It took him several tries to find his voice. "Quite a collection," he said, breathlessly. The wolf totem tattooed on his back stopped in midhowl and peeked over his shoulder to see what all the fuss was about.

"Was this everything?" Pritkin asked. "Did you take all the Senate had?"

"Of course not! I know there's a war on—I was there when it started, remember?"

"What else do they have?" Pritkin inquired, while Mac stood and drooled at the items on his fridge.

"None of your business." I decided to let him think I'd been daring enough to carry out a highly dangerous raid on the Senate—it sounded better than the truth. In fact, I'd returned from a trip to the past with Mircea only to find the Consul waiting for us. She'd reached for me, I had instinctively jerked back and, thanks to my unpredictable new power, ended up three days in the past. I had shifted in time, but not in space, so I was still in the inner sanctum of the vamp portion of MAGIC. Since their cache of magical goodies was literally right in front of my face, I'd decided to help myself to a few items before making my getaway.

I'd been in a hurry because their wards had almost certainly informed them I was there. I paused only long enough to grab the stuff from one shelf and barely even noticed the rest. But since the unit housing the vamp's treasure trove was taller than me, there was a good bet I hadn't left them defenseless.

"We will need help in Faerie," Pritkin pointed out, making an obvious attempt to hold on to his temper. "If you stole these things, you could get others."

"I'm not going to take the rest of their weapons! They're at war!" I might be pissed at Mircea, but leaving him at the mercy of Rasputin and his allies wasn't in my plans. Not to mention that my old friend Rafe was with him. There were plenty of nasty vamps out there, but they weren't all tarred with the same brush, no matter what Pritkin liked to think. "Anyway, I couldn't get back in there without using my power, and I'm trying to avoid that."

"Why?" He looked genuinely puzzled. "It is the best weapon you have."

"It's also the scariest. As you pointed out, I don't know what I'm doing. And if I mess up, it could get a lot of people killed."

"Is that why you wouldn't shift us out of Dante's?" he demanded. When I nodded, an expression crossed his face that managed to be both puzzled and angry at the same time. "That makes no sense. You took us to the nineteenth century earlier, trying to get away from me!"

"I did not!"

"I was there, if you recall," he retorted angrily. "Your lover almost killed me."

Unless you counted one out-of-body experience, Mircea and I weren't lovers. And thanks to the *geis*, I couldn't risk us ever being so. However, I didn't intend to explain that to Pritkin. It wasn't his business, and I was sick of feeling like I was constantly on trial with him as judge, jury and, possibly, executioner.

"I don't care whether you believe this or not," I said, as calmly as I could manage. "But I didn't have anything to do with us ending up at that play. The power just flared—I don't know why. The only thing I did was to get us out of there as quickly as possible."

"The Pythia controls the power, not the reverse," Pritkin said, calling me a liar.

"Believe what you want," I said, suddenly weary. Fighting with him got old fast because it never seemed to solve anything. "If what you said earlier about us needing every advantage is true, I have a job for Mac."

Mac glanced up, still looking dazed. "What?"

"My ward," I said, tugging down the back of my tank to

show him the top of the pentagram. "Pritkin said the Circle deactivated it. Can you fix it?"

"I did not say 'deactivate.' That would be impossible," Pritkin corrected as Mac moved to take a look. "From a distance, the Circle can only block it, which they almost certainly did for fear that you would use it against them. They would not have closed the connection otherwise—whenever it flared, it gave them an approximation of your location and they want to find you badly." Pritkin suddenly moved forward until he invaded my personal space. "Your explanation of the power's actions makes no sense," he said, his voice harsh. "Not if you truly are Pythia."

I suppose he was trying to be intimidating, but it didn't work out quite that way. He had stopped about an inch from me with his bare chest right in my line of vision. It was lightly furred over muscles that were hard and sleekly defined, and the inadequate air-conditioning had caused rivulets of sweat to run in fascinating ways through all that hair. The only men I'd ever touched had been smooth, or almost so, and I had the insane desire to run my hands through those damp blond curls to see what patterns I could make with my fingers.

I didn't know why the mage, whom I didn't like in the least, was affecting me like this, but I felt like someone who's been on a starvation diet for weeks and just caught sight of an ice cream sundae. My hands were sweaty and my breath was coming faster, to the point that I'd be panting in a minute. I tore my eyes away from his torso before I lost control, but that didn't help since they only drifted lower, to what was concealed by that infuriating expanse of tight denim. I swallowed and struggled to get a grip before I gave in to the burning desire to rip the jeans off him.

I had almost succeeded in talking myself into stepping

back, even if it meant letting him think he'd intimidated me. That would, after all, be better than the truth. But then I made the mistake of looking him in the eyes. I finally figured out why he had always appeared a little odd: his sandy lashes and eyebrows were so close to his skin tone that, from a distance, he didn't appear to have any. This close, I could see that his lashes were actually long and thick, and that they framed clear green eyes—the rare kind with no hint of any other color.

Despite strict orders to the contrary, my hands were on him, tracing the muscles in his chest. His pupils expanded to the point that his eyes turned almost black and a shocked look crossed his face, probably more so than would have been true if I'd slapped him. But he didn't pull away. There was an odd tingle in my hands where they pressed against his pecs, and his skin felt warmer than it should have even with the shop's lousy air-conditioning. Or maybe that was me. I didn't care: very little thought was happening in my mind, except how to get that damned zipper down.

Before I could act on that plan, Pritkin grabbed my wrists. I'm not sure whether he meant to push me away or to pull me closer, and judging by the look on his face, I don't think he did, either. But neither of us had the chance to find out.

It suddenly felt like someone had doused me in gasoline and thrown on a match. It wasn't pain that flared through me; it was agony, and it seemed to spear every cell in my body simultaneously. I screamed and jumped back, hitting Mac and taking us both to the floor. Pritkin followed us down because he still had hold of my wrists, and I vaguely heard Mac yelling something at him, but I couldn't concentrate enough to understand. I arched my back and began convulsing like a fish out of water, only what I wanted wasn't air but relief from the excruciating pain.

I gained a real understanding of what it must feel like to burn alive, fire ripping its way up my spine, every nerve ending exploding with white-hot agony. I forgot where I was, forgot my problems, which suddenly appeared trivial to the point of absurdity next to the torture I was undergoing. I think I would have forgotten my name in another few seconds, but then, as abruptly as it had come, the pain was gone.

I found myself on the linoleum floor of Mac's workroom, trying to relearn how to breathe. I looked up to see him holding Pritkin's wrists captive. He'd obviously pulled him off me, and for that I could have kissed him, if I hadn't been shaking too hard to even sit up. Once he'd solved the immediate problem, Mac dropped Pritkin's hands and turned to me.

"Are you all right? Cassie, can you hear me?" I nodded, unable to do more at the moment. "Right." He looked freaked out, his usually laid-back, *G'day, mate*, attitude entirely gone. "Stay where you are and I'll be right back. Whatever you do, no touching!"

Mac disappeared through a door that led off from his workroom, and I heard water running. The pain had receded, but the memory of it was burned into my body the way an afterimage of a blinding light damages a retina. My nerve endings pulsed with vivid recall and, although I was no longer convulsing, a light tremor seemed to have settled in for good. I was terrified to move, afraid that I might accidentally trigger it again.

I vaguely realized that the gasping breaths I was hearing weren't all mine, and shifted my eyes to the side without moving my head. I got a glimpse of Pritkin, lying on his back, staring at the ceiling with eyes that showed white all around. His face was flushed, his muscles corded, and his breathing was as shallow as mine. It occurred to me that maybe I hadn't been the only one affected.

Mac returned with a damp washcloth, which he put on my forehead. I was about to tell him that I needed a bit more than that, like a shot of codeine or a bottle of whiskey, but the small gesture did seem to help. I watched a moth circle the halogen light overhead and tried to regain motor control. The very idea of sitting up sounded insane, so while Mac tended to Pritkin, I lay there and thought. I had been having what qualified, even after some memorable experiences in the past, as a crazy day. So maybe it was understandable that it would take me this long to figure something out.

I'd been reacting strangely all day around men. Normally, I noticed attractive guys as much as the next woman, but I'd had years to learn how to admire in a detached sort of way and then move on. Living on the run meant that any guy I became involved with got the added bonus of a death threat. Not wanting to get anyone killed, I'd made sure to keep my distance, and practice, as they say, makes perfect.

I'd found it hard to concentrate around Casanova and Chavez, but come on. They were both drop-dead gorgeous, not to mention being possessed by incubi. I'd assumed I was having the reaction any heterosexual female could expect around them, and had just been grateful that I hadn't dragged one or both into the nearest closet. But Pritkin was another matter.

Not only did I find him completely insufferable, and had ever since we met, but I'd also never thought him particularly attractive before today. Okay, I was willing to admit that his body was pretty good and that his face wasn't that bad, when it wasn't wearing its usual sneer. His hair was unfortunate, looking like it had been styled with a Weed Eater, but nobody was perfect. But Pritkin definitely wasn't my type. I've never been attracted to blonds, especially homicidal ones who probably have my name on their target list. Yet all of a sudden I was seriously lusting after him.

I abruptly sat up, feeling sick, and barely managed to grab the damp cloth before it fell in my lap. What if Mircea was fiddling around with the *geis*, trying to force me to finish the ritual? I knew he could do it, since he'd modified it once before to accept Tomas in his place. Maybe he could alter it to accommodate even more partners—a lot more, if today was anything to go on. I covered my eyes with my palms, pain of a different kind lancing through me. The idea that Mircea might not care who completed the rite, just so long as I ended up Pythia for good, was like a cold fist to the chest.

After a few minutes, I hauled myself up from the floor, using the tattoo table for leverage. Surprisingly, my body didn't protest. "Could Mircea have altered the *geis*?" I asked. I was proud of the fact that I managed to keep my voice steady.

Pritkin had also regained his feet and as an added bonus had put his shirt back on. He glanced at me, then quickly looked away. "Unlikely."

"Would somebody please tell me what the hell just happened here?" Mac asked.

"Then why am I suddenly lusting after every guy I meet?"

Pritkin was staring intently at the wall behind the fridge, and after I found myself starting to focus on the front of his jeans, I decided to do the same. "The pain was the *geis* defending you against an unauthorized partner," he told me. "It would not draw you to one."

I felt a sudden surge of relief, strong enough to make me weak in the knees. I clutched the table with both hands and fought not to grin like an idiot. After a few seconds, I managed to tamp it down. Maybe Mircea hadn't set me up—this time—but I obviously still had a problem. "So what is going on?"

"I . . . am not sure." Pritkin took in a ragged breath and closed his eyes. After a moment the flush in his cheeks faded a little. "Did anything go wrong during the ritual?"

"What ritual?" Mac was trying to catch up but not doing real well. I'd felt the same way all day.

"The transfer ritual," I clarified, "the one required to become Pythia. I don't know what it's called. Agnes started it but she said that I had to, uh . . ." I trailed off in deference to Mac's old-fashioned sensibilities.

"But Mircea took care of that," Pritkin said.

"Not exactly." I could understand his confusion. Other than for the play interlude, the last time he'd seen Mircea and me together we'd been nude and sweaty. Well, technically I'd been wrapped in a blanket, but you get the idea. "We were interrupted. Rasputin attacked, remember?"

"Vividly." Pritkin wrinkled his brow as if trying to get his mind around a difficult concept. "You're saying that you are still a virgin?" he asked bluntly. His voice held the same level of incredulity anyone else would use if told that a spaceship had landed on the White House lawn. Like something barely possible but highly unlikely.

I stopped looking at the wall to glare at him. "Not that it's any of your business, but yes!"

He shook his head in disbelief. "I would never have considered that."

I was getting ready to become seriously annoyed when I found myself admiring the way the damp hair at the base of his neck curled up. Damn, damn, damn! "Do you have a theory or not?"

"The most likely explanation is that the Pythian Rites are trying to complete themselves."

I stared at him blankly for a moment. He didn't notice, being too busy counting bricks in the wall. "Let me get this straight," I finally said, sounding a little strangled despite my best efforts. "Since Mircea isn't here, the unfinished ritual is starting to draw me to other men to complete itself. But the *geis* doesn't like that, and it's making its feelings known by torturing me and anybody who gets near me. Is that right? And more importantly, is it going to keep happening?"

"What *geis*? You're under a *geis*?" Mac asked.

"Her vampire master put her under a *dúthracht*. It is conflicting with the Pythian Rites, which have yet to be completed," Pritkin said curtly.

"Oh, bloody hell." Mac sat down on his stool, looking shell-shocked.

"Answer me!" If I'd dared to touch Pritkin, I'd have shaken him within an inch of his life.

"I don't know enough about the rites to say for certain if there is a way out at this point," he said unhelpfully. "The ceremonies are held within the Pythia's court, and there are few records kept on anything connected to the office."

"What about witnesses?" I hoped I didn't sound as frantic as I felt. "The ritual was done for Agnes once, right?"

"That was more than eighty years ago. And even if any witnesses still live, they would be of little use. Most of the ritual is carried out privately. The only people who know the complete procedure are the Pythia and her designated heir."

"Myra." Great, I was back where I'd started. "What about the *geis* then?"

"You are already doing what you can by staying away

from Mircea. That will at least slow down the process. There is no other remedy, other than having it removed."

"Then how do I do that?"

"You don't."

"Don't give me that! There has to be a way."

"If there is, I don't know it," he told me, sounding tired. "If I did, I would tell you. Unless the ritual is completed, it will continue to draw you to men, but the *geis* will oppose any except Mircea. And it will likely grow worse over time. The *dúthracht* is spiteful when it's opposed."

"But . . . but what about Chavez?" I asked desperately. "He touched me and nothing happened. I didn't go writhing all over the ice rink!"

"You were at the ice rink? Why?" Pritkin was back to looking pissed. I couldn't have cared less.

"To get that." I gestured at the duffle. "I didn't want to take it into Dante's."

"So you left it unattended in a public arena, where anyone might pick it up?!"

"It was in a locker," I said sullenly. "And can we get back to the point? I felt something start to build when Casanova touched me. It was nothing like what just happened, but it felt—I don't know. Like it could get bad fast. Only he dropped my hand before it flared. But Chavez didn't affect me at all, and that was later. So if you're right and the reaction is strengthening, shouldn't it have been worse?"

Pritkin looked uncomfortable. "I don't know."

"The only reason I can think of," Mac mused, "is that the *geis* determines the amount of threat by reading the interest level of any prospective partners, and reacts accordingly. Casanova was likely somewhat attracted to you and this Chavez wasn't. Casanova was therefore identified by the *geis* as the wrong match and as a potential problem, and warned off. But Chavez, although also the wrong one to complete the bond, was not interested in you, and therefore was not perceived as a danger."

Mac looked pleased with himself, while Pritkin and I stared at each other in mounting panic. As if by mutual consent, neither of us made the obvious connection. I did *not* want to go there. Ever.

"Of course," Mac continued obliviously, "when there's a mutual attraction, the reaction is stronger because the warning is going both ways . . ." He trailed off awkwardly.

"Okay." I put a hand to my head, which had started throbbing in time with my pulse. At this rate, I was going to be the youngest person ever to die from a stress-induced stroke. "How do I deal with this thing?" I asked Mac, because Pritkin was busy trying not to look horrified.

Mac scratched his stubble-coated chin. "Usually, there's a way out built into these things, especially the *dúthracht*. It has a habit of causing chaos, and I can't imagine anyone putting it in place and not giving himself an escape route. But only two people are likely to know what the safety net is."

"Mircea and whoever cast the spell."

He nodded. "And the mage was doubtless someone disavowed who was under the vamp's protection. He isn't going to risk losing that to help you, even if we could figure out which of the hundreds of rogue mages—and that's just the ones in this country—Mircea used. Of course, there aren't a lot with that kind of skill, outside of the Black Circle. But that doesn't help greatly. Say we could narrow it down to a few dozen, we'd still have to find him or her, and if that was easy it would have been done long ago."

"Is there anything that can slow this thing down, make

the reaction less . . . extreme?" I asked Mac, but it was Pritkin who answered.

"Once we cross into Faerie, it may not be an issue. Like the rest of our magic, the *geis* should not work well there." He was still apparently admiring the blank wall. "I, er, think this would go more smoothly if you waited elsewhere. Mac can look at your ward when he finishes with me."

I didn't argue. I grabbed another Coke, scooped my weapons into the duffle and left, taking it with me. It was a measure of how shaken Pritkin was that he didn't object.

I sat on a rickety stool at the counter and thought things over. There was little I could do, except to avoid attractive men until I could get into Faerie. I hoped Pritkin was right and the effects would be less there, maybe enough to buy me time to find Myra. It wasn't a great plan, but it was the best I could do. I drank my soda and looked around for something, anything, to keep my mind off the image of a mostly naked Pritkin getting a sword carved into his taut gold skin.

I sat out front for more than an hour, leafing through a couple of huge black binders filled with tattoo designs. There was everything from voodoo veves to Indonesian tribal designs, but most were traditional magical symbols and Native American totems. I figured out pretty fast from the descriptions under the photos that all of Mac's designs came with some sort of supernatural benefit. I didn't see the sword he was doing for Pritkin among them, but maybe it was a special order.

The two volumes were divided into categories and levels. First, someone selected the main thing they wanted the tattoo to do. Some were for protection, with specialties for cuts and abrasions, blood loss, fire damage, head trauma, poison and frostbite, among others. The length of the list made me wonder why anyone wanted to be a war mage. It also made me curious why, before today, Pritkin hadn't had any tattoos. There were some that sped up healing, but although I'd seen him heal almost as fast as a vamp, he hadn't been wearing them. Unless they were somewhere I hadn't seen. I dragged my mind away from that image and quickly flipped over a few more pages.

There were also a lot of offensive spells, with a division between stuff like better vision and enhanced hearing and a whole list of nasty things to do to your enemies. I didn't linger over that section, not wanting to know what the Circle's war mages had in mind for me. I also found out that not everyone could get every tattoo. What kind and how many you could have depended on your level of magical ability. The images drew their power partly from the natural world, so they worked to a limited degree like talismans, but they also fed off a person's innate magic. It sounded sort of like a hybrid car that used electricity to extend the gas mileage. There was a long, complex chart in the back of the books for assigning yourself a range from which to choose. I didn't completely understand it because I'd never been tested for that sort of thing. Magical children are usually graded by ability early, so they can be shunted towards an appropriate apprenticeship, but of course, Tony had already known what he had planned for me.

I discovered that there were limits to what even a powerful mage could support. Someone with a snow leopard tattoo to aid her in moving silently and a spider for help in weaving illusions, for example, had to subtract a certain number of points from her powerbase for the energy those two enhancements used up. Unless she was very strong, she probably wouldn't be able to support another major improvement. It was all very complicated, even with the chart, and I finally lost interest. None of this helped me figure out how to get past whatever block the Circle had put on my ward.

Pritkin finally emerged, looking pale and a little ill, and I took his place in back. I didn't mind Mac checking on my problematic protection. He and Pritkin needed me alive until they reeled in Myra, so he had a vested interest in fixing it if he could. I was a little worried about the *geis* acting up, but apparently I wasn't Mac's type. I didn't get so much as a twinge from the hellish thing, even when I removed my tank top. I wasn't wearing a bra, but I held the shirt in front of me and Mac's hands were as impersonal as a doctor's.

"Can I ask you a question?" He was poking at my back with something that resembled an extremely fuzzy pipe cleaner. It didn't hurt, but it made my aura itch.

I repressed the urge to wiggle. "Sure."

"Why are you doing this? You seem . . . that is, you don't strike me as particularly vindictive."

I glanced at him over my shoulder. "What am I supposed to be vindictive about?"

He shrugged. "John said you plan to kill this vampire, Antonio. I'm assuming he deserves it, but . . ."

"I don't strike you as a homicidal nut?"

He laughed. "Something like that. If you don't mind my asking, what did he do to you?"

I thought about it while he changed instruments. The easy answer was "everything," but I didn't want to get into a long conversation on a topic that, even on a good day, managed to depress me. But avoiding it entirely might not be smart either. I didn't need Pritkin to get any hints that Myra interested me a lot more than Tony at the moment. I decided on a partial truth. It wasn't like I didn't have plenty of legitimate grievances against the fat man.

"Revenge isn't my main goal. I guess you could say that I want to retrieve some personal property." I jumped as a spark suddenly arced over my skin. Mac's new instrument made my aura crackle, like it was filled with static. I sat very still to avoid shocking myself again.

"He stole something from you?"

I repressed a sigh. Apparently, Mac wasn't going to be satisfied with the short version. "Twenty years ago, Tony decided he wanted a competent seer at his court, someone he could trust. But accurate seers are few and far between, and honest ones aren't likely to work for a member of the vampire mafia. He finally decided that what he needed was to find one he could bring up from childhood to be loyal. And, as luck would have it, one of his human employees had a young daughter who seemed perfect for the role. But even though my father had been on Tony's payroll for years, he ignored the order to bring me to court."

"Your father was a rogue?" Mac asked. He seemed surprised.

"I don't know what he was. I was told he could communicate with ghosts, so I guess he had some clairvoyant ability. Whether he was a mage or not—" I shrugged. One of these days, I hoped to ask him—about that and a lot of other things. "All I know is that he was one of Tony's favorite humans. Until he told him no, that is."

"Surely he must have known what the vampire's reaction was likely to be."

"I assume he planned to flee with my mother and me, since refusing Tony isn't considered healthy, but he never got the chance. And Tony felt that the betrayal, as he viewed it, deserved more than a mere assassination. So he paid a mage to construct a magical snare, which he used to trap my father's ghost after he rigged my parents' car to explode. He's been using it as a paperweight ever since."

Mac's hands had gone very still on my back. I glanced behind me to see him staring at me blankly. "You aren't serious . . . are you?"

I turned back around. "Yeah. From what I understand, it's only about the size of a golf ball, so it could be anywhere. Tony has three houses and more than a dozen businesses, and those are just the ones I know about. I don't feel like searching through them all so I thought I'd let him tell me where it is." I actually assumed he had it with him. It would be Tony's style to carry his trophies along even when fleeing for his life.

Mac was just standing there, his hands on my shoulders. He looked stunned for some reason. "Haven't you ever been tempted?" he finally asked.

"Tempted to do what?"

"You're Pythia. You could go back, change what happened." He moved so he could see my eyes. "You could save your family, Cassie."

I sighed. Sure I could. "You don't know Tony. Besides, I thought the idea was for me to help guard the timeline, not to interfere with it myself. I could end up changing something vital and possibly make things even worse." Make that *probably*, with my luck.

His gaze sharpened. "But, technically, you could do it."

"Yeah, I could keep my parents from getting in the car that Tony rigged to explode, but if I did, my life would have been completely different, along with who knows how many other people's. And, knowing Tony, he'd have managed to kill them some other way," I smiled grimly. "He's persistent like that."

Mac regarded me searchingly, to the point of making me uncomfortable. "Most people would view the power as a great opportunity to advance themselves," he finally said. "It could bring you, well, almost anything you wanted. Wealth, influence—"

I gave him exasperated eyes. "The only thing I want is a nice, uncomplicated life. With no one trying to kill me, manipulate me or betray me." And where, if I messed up on the job, I didn't get anyone killed. "Somehow, I don't think the Pythia gig is going to help me with that!" I was tired of the inquisition and I wanted to get dressed. "Are you done?"

"Oh, right," Mac replaced his instruments in a small case and looked politely away so I could get dressed. "Do you want the good news or the bad news first?"

"The good." Why not try something different for a change?

"I think I can fix it."

I blinked at him in surprise. I'd been expecting to hear that there was nothing he could do and that I'd have to go into Faerie with no protection. "Really? That's great!"

"Do you know anything about how your ward works?"

I shook my head. "Not a lot. My mother somehow transferred it to me, but I don't even remember it. I was only four when she died. For years, I thought it was a regular ward that Tony had put on me as an added safeguard."

Mac looked almost offended. "Regular ward! No, I guarantee you'll never see another of the like. It's hundreds of years old and priceless, one of the Circle's real treasures."

"It's a tattoo, Mac, not a work of art."

"In fact, it's both." He stretched out his right arm and pointed to a small brown and orange hawk near the bend in his elbow. "Watch." He muttered something, then took hold of the loose skin in the crease of his arm and pulled. A second later a small, metallic bird glimmered on his palm, its wings outstretched in flight like the one on his arm. It took me a moment to realize that it *was* the one on his arm, or rather, the one that had been there. Now there was only a bare, bird-shaped patch of skin. I picked up the small metal object. The feathers and detail were gone. It looked and felt like solid gold. For a moment I suspected sleight of hand or some trick, but after letting me examine it, he put it back in place and I watched it dissolve into his skin.

"What is that?"

"A red-tailed hawk. It increases the power of observation. Doesn't help the eyesight, but if you want to notice more about your surroundings and retain the knowledge, you can't do better."

Something was bothering me. "The books out front said that there's a limit to how many tattoos anyone can support, even the strongest mage, because each one takes some of your magic to maintain itself, and even more when it's used." I looked him over, almost dizzy with the number of squirming images all over his body. "How can you wear so many?"

He grinned. "I'm not a super-mage, Cassie, if that's what you're asking. There are two types of tattoos. The ones I etch directly into someone's aura feed partially off his magic, so of course there's a limit to how many anyone can support. But ones like my hawk or your pentagram draw their power from outside sources, so there is no limit to those. Except, of course, to your ability to afford them. The enchantment process for even a small one can take months—I shudder to think what went into your ward."

"So you're an advertisement for what's available?" Personally, I'd have made people flip through the books outside rather than turn myself into a walking billboard.

"In my case, it isn't a choice. To other people these are enhancements—to compensate for some part of their magic that isn't as strong as they'd like or to add power in an often-used area. But to me they're necessities, unless I want to retire from our world entirely." He saw my confusion and smiled slightly. "I had a run-in a few years back with a spell that ate through my shields and attacked my aura. The physical wounds I sustained in that fight healed, but the ones in my metaphysical skin were permanent. That's why I didn't realize you were under a *geis* until you told me. With my own aura so damaged, I have to concentrate to read other people's."

I stared at him, horrified at what he'd so casually revealed. It wasn't only what had happened to Mac that freaked me out, but the knowledge that there were spells that could actually do something like that. The more I learned about the mages, the scarier they got.

"But with the wards, you're okay, right?" I kept my attention on his face so I wouldn't focus on my own aura, to reassure myself it was intact and undamaged. Under the circumstances, it would have been tacky.

Mac seemed to understand where my thoughts were going anyway. He waved a hand in the air and my bright red and orange flames suddenly sparkled between us like a cheerful fire on a cold night. "My wards compensate to a degree, Cassie, but they'll never again be like this—a seamless, perfect blanket of protection. Most people couldn't get past my defenses, but war mages aren't most people. Sooner or later one of the dark ones would have found the chinks in my man-made armor, the places where the wards don't overlap perfectly. I was removed from active duty as soon as anyone realized what had happened, and told I couldn't take the field again." He saw my expression and grinned. "It's not all bad. I'm in much less danger these days!"

He sounded casual, but there was something in his eyes that told me he wasn't being completely truthful. I didn't know what usually happened to old war mages, but it was obvious that Mac, at least, wasn't content to just fade away. He craved the adrenaline rush of battle, maybe even the danger.

I decided on a change of subject. "So, my ward drew its power from the Circle, until they cut it off."

He nodded. "Right, which gave it its strength, but also created a conduit between you. I suspect that John is right and the council got worried that you'd figure some way of turning their own magic back on them, so they shut down the connection."

"Or they thought I'd be simpler to kill that way."

Mac looked uncomfortable. "Perhaps. But what it means is that there's nothing wrong with your ward, except that your mother didn't have experience in doing the transfer so it got a bit warped. I can fix that, but its looks aren't the problem. The reason it doesn't work is the same as if a watch stopped. It needs a new power source."

"What new source?" I was getting an idea about what the bad news was.

"The only one big enough to support something like this, other than the Circle itself." He smiled gently, as if he understood my dilemma. "The power of your office—the energy that makes you Pythia."

"No. No way." I gestured at the curtain. "Give me one from the books out front." There were some pretty scary ones listed; surely we could find something that would work.

But Mac was shaking his head. "I have no way of knowing how strong your innate magic is. Your aura is confused with the Pythia's energy, and I can't separate them. There's no way to know whether you could support one of the larger protection wards on your own. If not, any tat I gave you would draw power from the reserve you inherited as Pythia, the very thing you want to avoid."

"Then give me a smaller one, an easy one!"

Mac regarded me somberly. "You're going into Faerie, a place most mages won't venture on a bet. None of the smaller stuff would do you any good there. And none of the wards I have would protect you as well at that one. Craftsmanship like that is rare these days."

"Maybe I'm stronger than you think." I was a clairvoyant; surely I could manage to support one measly ward.

Mac only shrugged, causing his lizard tattoo to scuttle for cover again, this time under the snake's scales. The snake didn't like that and swatted at the smaller ward with the end of its tail. The lizard jumped out of the way, then ran across Mac's cheek to the top of his head. It stayed there, peering out from behind a bushy eyebrow, regarding the snake with unfriendly black eyes.

I dragged my attention back to what Mac was saying. "Magic is like a muscle, Cassie, a metaphysical one but a muscle nonetheless. The more you work with it and train it, the stronger it gets. Whatever magic you have is raw talent. And that alone won't get you very far."

"Tony wouldn't allow me to be trained."

"He did you more of a disservice than you know. A powerful, untrained magic user is a target, nothing more. Power can be siphoned away if you don't know how to protect yourself. The Dark Circle has no compunction whatever about stealing magic from anyone they can. At the moment, you fighting a dark mage would be like a baby trying to arm wrestle a bodybuilder, unless you use the power of your office. You need training, at least in defense," he said seriously, "and the sooner the better."

"Yeah, I'll add that to my list," I said bitterly. Everyone was always giving me new items for my agenda, when what I needed was help in clearing off some of the old ones. "Right now, I have a few other problems." I turned, feeling Pritkin standing in the doorway even before I saw him. "Like how we're going to get into Faerie."

"We'll get in," he said grimly, and I noticed that he'd strapped on his arsenal. He had the long leather coat that acted as a slight disguise draped over his arm. "The problem will be getting out."

"Are we going now?"

"No." I tried not to look relieved at his answer. "Tonight."

"Tonight?" I followed him into the outer room. "But the vamps will be up then." I didn't know that Mircea was in his safe room at the moment—first-level vamps aren't bound by the sun cycle and can be active at any time of day. But most still sleep in daylight, since the night is much kinder to their energy levels. If Mircea was awake, he was probably sluggish. But tonight he wouldn't be.

"We are not trying to penetrate the vampire area," Pritkin reminded me. "And the portal is guarded by mages."

"I don't see how that'll help," I protested, not liking the idea of walking into a bunch of war mages any more than dealing with the vamps. In fact, it was probably even less smart—at least the Senate didn't want me dead. Probably.

"Some friends of mine are on duty tonight," Mac explained. "I think I can get you past them."

"I have some supplies to arrange," Pritkin added, throwing on his coat. I didn't envy him that, considering that it had to be over ninety degrees outside, but I guess he didn't have much of a choice. The police would probably object to his walking around looking like an extra from *Platoon*, and going about unarmed right now would be even less healthy than heat stroke. "I suggest you stay here, out of sight," he said, avoiding my eyes. "Rest if you can. You may not get another chance for some time. And have Mac rework your ward," he added as he headed for the door. "You'll need it."

He hurried out the door like all the hounds of Hell were after him. Mac looked at me and shrugged. "It's your call, but I'd advise you to consider it, love. Faerie is a scary place, even when it isn't on the brink of war. Right now, I can't think of a soul who'd want to go near the place."

"I'll think about it," I promised. I might have questioned him more, but my attention was distracted by Billy floating through the wall. He was making faces at me, so I figured he had news. "I'm tired," I told Mac. It wasn't a lie—sharing a room with the Graeae isn't exactly restful—but I mainly wanted some privacy.

"Got a cot in back," Mac said. "I cleared my appointment list for today after John showed up, so I won't need to go back there. Get some sleep, Cassie."

He meant well, so I managed not to roll my eyes at him. Yeah, sure. There were only about a hundred reasons why I'd have trouble sleeping.

Billy followed me to the back and I flopped down on the cot after shifting aside notebooks full of sketches, stacks of grimoires and old potato chip bags. "What's up?"

Billy took off his almost transparent hat and fanned himself. "I need a draw," he said without preamble.

"Well, hello to you, too."

"Hey, I have had a day, okay?"

"And I haven't? What happened at Dante's? Is everything all right?"

"Sure, if by all right you mean that the Circle has closed the place while they search it for a certain rogue sybil and the illegal aliens who helped her elude them."

"They're searching? But that's vampire property!" The reason I'd sent Casanova the remaining contents of the duffle was the longstanding treaty between the mages and the vamps. It contained strict prohibitions against any of one group entering the property of another without permission. "Are they crazy?"

"Don't know. Some of them sure act like it. Anyway, Casanova was pitching a royal fit when I left, and he'd sent a couple of reps to MAGIC to complain. But these are weird times, Cass. Tony owns the place and he's a known ally of Rasputin, the guy the Circle and the Senate declared war on a week ago. I don't know what the rules are in wartime, and I don't think Casanova does, either. Right now, he's playin' it safe. To keep from looking like he helped you, he pretended that you appeared and started wrecking the place because you're pissed at Tony. The mages jumped on the excuse to say that they'd make sure you weren't still in the casino, and started searching."

"Great. So now I'm some kind of lunatic who goes around starting fights."

"No, now you're some lunatic who goes around killin' people."

"What?"

"Yep. A couple of mages came right out and called you a murderer. I didn't get details, but I'm guessing they were talking about the two mages who ended up dead."

I felt sick. "Tell me the Graeae didn't—"

"They didn't. They tore up the place, but it looks like the mages were killed by Miranda's group. Some of the more powerful gargoyles stayed behind to buy the others time to get away, and the mages started slaughterin' 'em. Then the rest went ballistic and voilà. Two dead mages."

"But the gargoyles were acting in self-defense!"

"They might get away with claimin' that, 'cept they ain't supposed to be here in the first place. Casanova got the rest of Miranda's people out and hid them somewhere, and now he's blamin' Tony for bringing in unlicensed workers behind his back. He's doing a pretty good job of covering his ass, but he's leaving yours hangin' in the wind."

I fell back on the cot, feeling numb. None of this was happening. It had to be some kind of nightmare I'd blundered into and would wake up from any minute now. "If the Circle knows the gargoyles killed their men, why are they blaming me?"

"I don't know." Billy looked puzzled. "I saw the bodies and they have claw and teeth marks all over 'em. I guess it gives the Circle an excuse to brand you a dangerous lunatic."

"Shit."

"Yeah, that about sums it up. So like I said, I'm whacked. I hate to be a pain—"

"Since when?"

"Very funny, Cass. I spend half the day gettin' top-quality info for you and—"

I was too tired to go through our usual routine. "Fine. You can have a draw, but then you go back to Dante's. I need you to give Casanova a message."

"He may not be able to hear me," Billy protested. "Some demons can't, at least not in a human body."

"Then you'll have to get creative." Given Casanova's re-action to Billy's presence earlier, I was betting he could hear him just fine. But even if not, I wasn't going to let Billy weasel out of this. Casanova had to get the traps I'd sent him somewhere secure. Otherwise, with mages crawling all over the place, they were sure to find them and I doubted he could lie his way out of that one. Even if he did, it would only be by blaming it on me, and thereby giving the Circle yet an-other nail to put in my coffin. Not to mention a hell of a weapon, depending on just what was inside those boxes. I sighed. It looked like I should have kept them after all.

Billy left after taking what I considered to be an inordinately large draw, and I settled in for a much-needed nap. What I got instead was the disorientation that precedes a time shift. I tried to call out, to warn Mac that I was about to take a trip, but darkness reached out and grabbed me.

Chapter 7

M y knees made the acquaintance of another hard floor, this one marble, and my head hit something with an audible crack. A green blur wavered in front of my face, and I slowly blinked it into focus. It turned out to be a porphyry vase taller than I was, complete with leering Gorgon-head handles. For a moment, I just sprawled beneath it, staring up at their ugly faces while my head and knees vied for the title of most abused anatomical region. But the marble was cold against my bare legs, and I didn't think lying around in the open was too smart. I pulled myself into a seated position using the vase's pedestal for leverage, and got my first clear look around.

I was in an alcove alongside a large, round room. The dark green marble floor was incised with gold lines that formed themselves into a starburst pattern directly under an immense chandelier. Three others just like it lit up a sweeping staircase, their crystals showering pinpricks of light onto the crowd below.

People passed me in a dappled river of candlelight, satin and flowing shadows. Men in swallowtail coats escorted ladies dripping with jewels. Subtle brocades vied for attention with flashy silks. Fans fluttered and hems danced in a kaleidoscope of color and movement that did nothing to help my throbbing head.

Most of the fashions looked like the ones I'd seen at the theatre, but there were a few more exotically dressed guests including an African chief wearing enough gold to buy a small country and a guy in a toga. It looked like a costume party, but I knew better. I pulled my legs up and wedged myself as far as possible into the dark alcove. It wasn't much of a hiding place, though, considering the nature of most of the room's occupants. For a moment, I just looked around in stunned awe. I'd never seen that many vampires in one place in my life.

Then I noticed an even stranger sight. A diaphanous form, transparent enough to be almost invisible, glided along one wall. It blended so well into the shadows cast by the chandelier's long tapers that for a moment I doubted my instincts. Then it passed in front of a painting so dark with age that the subject was unrecognizable, and I saw it more clearly—an amorphous column of pastel iridescence. At first I thought it was a ghost, but the only discernable features on the protrusion I assumed to be a head were two huge, silver eyes. Whatever this thing was, it had never been human.

I was so intrigued that, for an instant, I almost forgot my predicament. There was a huge amount about the Pythia gig I didn't understand, but I knew spirits. I'd met old ones who'd been around for centuries, new ones who, in a few cases, hadn't even known they were dead, friendly ones, scary ones, and some things that weren't ghosts at all. But this didn't fit into any of those categories. I realized with shock that I didn't know what it was.

It drifted along with the crowd in the direction of a ball-room directly across from the stairs. I couldn't see much of the interior, which was lit for vampire eyes rather than mine, and received only an impression of laughing, candlelight-gilded faces and rich fabrics. But the thick, cloying scent of mingled perfume and blood that spilled out of its doors convinced me that I didn't want to get any closer.

A young man, probably in his late teens, paused a few yards in front of me. He looked strangely out of place in the formally dressed crowd, wearing only a pair of plum-colored trousers in a silky fabric that hung low on his hips. His chest and feet were bare and his long hair was loose around his shoulders. It had a slight ripple to it as it cascaded down his back, like dark silk against his pale skin.

I really wanted to move, to get out of a place where my heartbeat had to be audible to the entire room, but he was in the way. And the last thing I needed was to answer questions about my right to be here when I didn't even know where here was. Then one of the guests approached, a vampire with pale blond hair wearing what looked like a military uniform—red with gold braid and highly polished black boots. He stopped directly in front of the young man, his eyes sweeping over him in obvious appreciation.

The boy shivered, back tensing, buttocks tightening. He ducked his head shyly, causing light and shadow to play across high cheekbones and a cleft chin. His face flushed with a healthy glow, making him resemble the cherubs who stared down from flaking murals overhead, all but their pink faces lost to the dark.

The vamp stripped off one of the white gloves that went

with his uniform. His hand stroked possessively down the boy's side, fingers playing along the ribs until they came to rest on the thin silk clinging to his hipbone. The young man's chest started rising and falling faster, but other than for louder breathing, he made no sound. My eyes focused on the boy's bare feet, which were directly in my line of vision as I tried to melt into the floor. They were startlingly white against the dark green, and looked strangely vulnerable next to the vamp's heavy footwear.

The young man stiffened as the blond head bent towards him, probably from the first glimpse of fangs, but a hand splayed possessively on his trembling back, holding him in place. He gave a small cry when his neck was pierced, and a visible shudder ran through him. But within seconds, he slid an arm around the vampire's neck and began making low sounds in his throat, openly, generously eager.

The vampire pulled back after a minute, his mouth stained as red as his uniform. The boy smiled at him and the vamp ruffled his hair affectionately. He threw his short cloak around the young man's shoulders and they walked together into the ballroom.

With a lurch in my stomach, I realized why I hadn't seen any waiters passing with trays of drinks, or heard the chime of glasses. When the heart stops, blood pressure in the body drops to zero, the veins collapse and the blood starts to co-agulate. Not only is it less palatable in that form, but it's also harder to extract. Even baby vamps learn quickly—only feed on the living. At this party, the refreshments walked around on their own. And in my brief shorts and tank top, I looked a lot more like part of the beverage parade than a guest.

Almost as if he heard my thought, a vamp suddenly

looked my way. He had a graying goatee that matched the silver brocade on his robes. They were lined with what looked like wolf fur, and he wore a large pelt draped around his shoulders. There was also something almost wolflike in the way he paused, one foot on the last stair, his nose tilted as if scenting prey. His flat black eyes came to rest on me, and a look of fierce interest crossed his previously unreadable face.

I scrambled to my feet and stumbled into the drifting crowd, panic lancing through me. The only doors were to the ballroom, and I dove for them as if my life depended on it, which it might. Somehow, I made it ahead of him, probably because he was too polite to elbow fellow guests out of the way. But a glance over my shoulder as I entered the dark, cavernous space showed that he wasn't far behind. Anticipation had lit those expressionless eyes and I felt my stomach plummet. Some vamps preferred their food frightened and struggling; just my luck I'd find one on the first try.

I took a quick look around the ballroom, but there were no obvious exits. Of course, the stairs should have warned me—we were probably underground. I tried to focus, but it was difficult with power crawling along my skin like a cloud of insects. None of it was directed at me specifically; it was just overflow from the beings jostling me on all sides. I realized with a jarring shock that I wasn't seeing merely a room full of vamps; it was a room crowded with master-level vampires—hundreds of them.

Convocation, I thought numbly—it simply had to be. Every Senate had a biannual meeting where master-level vamps met to discuss policy. I'd never been to one, but Tony had spent days preparing for them, changing his mind about clothes and escorts as often as a teenager going to a prom.

His entire entourage had been designed to impress, and with good reason. The weeklong gathering was the one time when he and other low-level masters could rub elbows with the glitterati—their own Senate members and visiting dignitaries from other senates around the world. Boots were licked, deals were made and alliances decided for the next two years.

Tony had always gone armed to the teeth and surrounded by bodyguards, since it wasn't unknown for the entertainment to get a little out of hand. I darted towards the orchestra on instinct—their golden instruments were the brightest things in the room—and hoped I wasn't about to be another Convocation casualty. Of course, it was a bad idea. There were no service doors, hallways or exits anywhere I could see, just a large alcove surrounded by burgundy drapes. I looked back to see my pursuer almost within arm's reach, and all the breath left my lungs.

What I'd taken to be a wolf pelt, I realized with horror, wasn't wolf at all. The paws draped over his chest were normal enough, if oversized. But the head that dangled halfway down his back was pink-skinned with a shock of light brown hair. I didn't get a good look at it, just flashes under his arm as he reached for me, but that was more than enough. My eyes told me what my mind didn't want to believe. He'd skinned a werewolf halfway through the transformation, so that the gray fur shaded into human skin around his shoulders.

I tried to shift but felt too light-headed to be able to concentrate. I bit the inside of my cheek hard, to keep from passing out, and tried to climb into the orchestra pit. I'd hoped to find a hidden exit, but a clarinet player shoved me back out, hard enough that I went sprawling. I slid into oiled black boots that shone in the low light. A hand grabbed my hair, using it as a handle to jerk me upright.

I stared into black eyes dancing with dark fire and forgot about the pain in my scalp. "You reek of magic," the vamp said, his voice thick with an accent I couldn't place. "I did not think the English brave enough to provide us with such a rare treat."

My eyes fell to the skull-less head bumping lightly against his side. It was now less than a foot away, and my throat closed in horror. I could see it perfectly—the sagging features, the dull hair, the empty eye sockets—and the limp, lifeless thing frightened me more than the vamp wearing it. If it brushed against me, there was a chance I'd See part of the creature's life—and knowing my gift, it would undoubtedly be the last part.

I moved away from it as much as I could, not wanting to know what it felt like to be skinned alive, and the vamp moved his grip from my hair to my elbow. His thumb caressed the skin at the bend of my arm, lightly, gently, but it felt like liquid metal poured from his hand into my veins. Pain was too mild a description for the shock that reverberated through me, bringing tears to my eyes and blinding me to everything outside my own body. He moved down to my wrist, a delicate stroke, but it spilled a line of blood along my arm as if his touch was a knife.

"They usually cringe at the idea of feeding from magic users, too afraid of retaliation from the mages," he said contemptuously. "I will have to remember to thank our host." Panic flooded my system with adrenaline, but there was nowhere to go. I pulled backwards, even knowing it was a wasted effort, and he smiled. "Now, let us see if you taste as good as you smell."

A warm hand descended on my shoulder, and his smile faded. "This one is taken, Dmitri."

I didn't need to turn around to know who had spoken. The rich tones were unmistakable, as was the pleasure that danced down my arm, slicing through the pain, reducing it to a low throb. A flash of anger passed over Dmitri's face. "Then you should have kept her with you, Basarab. You know the rules."

A claret-colored cloak fell around me, so deeply red that it was almost black. "Perhaps you did not hear me," Mircea said pleasantly. "So close to that appalling orchestra, it is not surprising."

"I don't smell her on you," Dmitri said with open suspicion.

"Our host asked to see me shortly after I arrived. I did not think he would appreciate my bringing an extra pair of ears." The joviality had fallen from Mircea's voice.

Dmitri didn't seem to hear the warning. His eyes had fixed on the rapid pulse in my neck and he sneered, showing elongated canines. "She will not live to speak of anything she overhears." His grip tightened, his fingers pressing into my flesh hard enough to bruise. The split in my arm widened, spilling a rush of blood over my skin.

"That is for me to decide." Mircea's voice was soft but deadly cold. His arm encircled my waist, drawing me back against his body. His other hand caught Dmitri's wrist. White-faced, the vamp swallowed, his hand spasming in Mircea's grip. Power sparked between them, washing the air around us in a burning mist that felt like it would eat into my skin if I stayed there long enough.

I stood in the curve of Mircea's arm, all my strength needed just to keep my knees from buckling. Mircea's power spiked, setting a warm rush of energy dancing along my body. But Dmitri didn't seem to find the sensation so pleasant. He flinched noticeably, but stubbornly hung on, his grip so tight that my hand went numb. The two vampires stared at each other for a long minute, then Dmitri abruptly stepped back, gripping his arm and panting, eyes murderous.

Mircea took hold of my wounded arm, pulling it straight, baring my blood-streaked skin. He dipped his head, his eyes fixed on the other vamp as his tongue flicked out, sliding along my arm in determined, challenging strokes. I watched him lick the blood from me in a daze, unable to look away from the sight of that proud head bowed over my wrist, mesmerized by the warm wetness of the tongue smoothing over me. Mircea raised his head after a moment and I stared at my arm in disbelief. Where there should have been wounds, there was only pale, unblemished skin.

Mircea's eyes never left Dmitri. "If you wish to contest this further, I am at your service."

Dmitri's mouth worked for a moment, but his eyes slid away. "I would not affront our host by violating his hospitality," he said stiffly. He stepped back, anger in every line of his body. "But your abuse of the rules will be remembered, Mircea!"

As soon as he stalked off, the red haze around us dissipated like fog in sunlight. The adrenaline that had kept me on my feet abruptly left, leaving me cold and shaking, and if it hadn't been for Mircea's arm, I'd have hit the floor again. Some nearby guests, who had been watching with obvious anticipation, turned away in disappointment.

Mircea slowly pulled me backwards, into the shadows lining the wall. Nearby, a couple of vamps, a statuesque brunette and a blond, were feeding on a young woman. The female vamp was seated in a chair along the wall, the girl's body draped across her lap as she drank from her jugular. The young woman's head had fallen back, loose tendrils of blond hair tumbling around her shoulders, contrasting with the deep rose of the brunette's gown. The male vamp knelt in front of them, his long, sapphire robe spilling around him like a waterfall. Predictably, he went for another target.

He pulled the plum-colored, silky tunic the girl wore loose from the jeweled clasps at her shoulders, letting it slide through his hands slowly. The shimmering folds skimmed down her body to puddle around her hips. She moaned softly, whether in distress or encouragement, I couldn't tell. He stroked her sides and stomach soothingly for a moment, then moved a fingertip to trace the plump blue veins on her breast. Her hand crept up until it lay on his shoulder, a timid gesture of embrace.

He cradled one pale globe tenderly, his thumb brushing across the nipple in a light caress. The girl trembled visibly at his touch, but she leaned into it as his head followed his hand. She jerked violently a moment later as sharp fangs bit deep into her white flesh.

The female vamp's mouth drew the girl backwards, arching her body in a perfect bow, then the male vamp pulled her back toward him with hands and lips and teeth. Each movement flowed smoothly into the next, building a hypnotic rhythm. Her young body was soon shuddering helplessly under the dual suction. Her breath came in short gasps as she was rocked between sensations until she was begging incoherently for more.

I swallowed. The European vamps obviously didn't follow the Senate's approved method of drawing blood molecules through the skin or air. Maybe it was the era, or maybe they just played by different rules. Tony's vamps had fed publicly enough times that I thought I'd grown blasé about it, but theirs had been a far more basic act, without the sensual overtones. Given the choice, I thought I preferred their crude brutality. I'd rather know death was coming, see it as the enemy it was, than welcome it like a lover.

The male vamp had slipped a hand under the spill of plum fabric, and within seconds the girl was crying out in pleasure. But he wasn't looking at her; his eyes were locked on the brunette's, their shared gaze hot enough to burn. Feeding was an intimate act for vampires, and they never shared a body lightly. The girl appeared oblivious, or maybe she was just past caring. Her hips thrust up, accompanied by a groan loud enough to win a few amused looks from bystanders.

Shocked slightly out of my daze, I looked away. I wondered whether the girl realized that she was merely a conduit for other people's passion. I wondered whether she'd go to her death smiling, or if draining the refreshments dry was considered bad taste. Most of all, I wondered whether that was how Mircea saw me. Just a conduit—in my case, to power.

Warm lips found my neck. "The only humans here tonight are entertainment and food," he murmured, a husky whisper in the dark. "Which are you?"

His breath feathering over my nape and shoulders was enough to speed my pulse, to make my body tighten. He breathed deeply of my scent and I trembled, caught between fear and desire. The *geis* didn't care that this wasn't the Mircea I knew, that this was a master vampire who had no reason to protect me. It didn't understand that he was interested only in satisfying his curiosity over what had occurred at the theatre. It didn't care that he might be hungry.

"I'm here to warn you. You're in danger." It sounded lame even to my ears, but there was so much I couldn't tell him that it was almost the only thing left.

"Yes, I know. Dmitri is watching. And he does not release prey easily. We will have to be convincing, will we not?"

I saw the flash of heat in his eyes a second before a hand slid behind my head and a hot mouth descended onto mine. I'd expected passion, but not the rush of overwhelming relief that filled me and spilled over into a strange and quiet joy. It felt like I'd been holding my breath for too long and was finally allowed to breathe. My hands curled reflexively where they lay against his chest, and for a long moment I was motionless, letting myself be kissed. Then my hand moved off his shoulder and down the side of his torso to the warm, sleek swell of Mircea's hip. It wasn't meant to be a caress, but somehow it turned into one. A broad palm circled my waist, a warm tongue slipped between my lips, and the *geis* really woke up.

It was the difference between a single match and a bonfire. I inhaled a sobbing gasp, and tugged him downward. Fire gathered in that kiss, collected between our bodies and spilled over our skin, sending a shower of sparks through me. It was better than I'd thought it could be: strong and hard and hot and fierce. My hands seemed to exist only to tangle in that rich, dark hair, my mouth only to taste that smooth tongue.

Powerful arms swept me up and he backed me into the wall; then we were devouring each other with shuddering, desperate hunger. His arm tightened around my waist, his legs shifted to make way for mine, drawing my thigh

between the warm, muscular columns of his. I ached to feel
him inside me, and like the girl, I suddenly didn't care about
the surroundings, or the desperate noises I was making. I
wanted him with an ache that threatened to devour me.

The kiss finally broke for lack of air on my part and I
pressed my cheek against Mircea's chest, gasping for breath.
The pine scent that always clung to him engulfed me—it
was almost as if I could see the forest, verdant and deep,
spread out under an evening sky. I inhaled against the warm
heat of his body, and felt weak. The only thing holding me
up was his strength, bracing me against the wall, pressing
skintight against me.

Mircea drew back after a moment, looking a little shaken
himself, and I somehow found my legs. "You seem to have
a number of talents, little witch."

Any answer I might have made caught in my throat when
I noticed what he was wearing. His clothes at the theatre had
seemed a bit off, but this was really over the top. My hands
sank into a claret-colored coat voluminous enough to act
like a cloak. It was made of rich, heavy wool with a silken
nap, edged by a thick band of gold embroidery. It fell a little past his knees, brushing the tops of dark brown boots.
The outer garment opened to reveal a thin, golden brown
inner robe, so soft that it had to be cashmere. It was loose
but light enough that it clung to his body, outlining the
sharply defined muscles of his chest, the long waist, the narrow hips, and the heavy weight of his sex.

I assumed it was traditional Romanian dress for a noble
and, oddly enough, it suited him. But I doubted he'd chosen
it for fashion's sake. Mircea preferred simple clothes that
stood out because of superb tailoring. Tonight he was making a statement, the outfit a far more potent reminder of his

lineage than the vest he'd worn to the theatre had been. The dragons on the waistcoat had been almost invisible—although I assumed vampiric sight would have picked them out easily enough—a subtle reference to his family symbol. Where it had whispered a reminder of his rank, his current outfit screamed it. I wondered who the message was for, and why he would need to make it badly enough to go around looking like a barbarian chief.

The impression was reinforced by the sword hanging from a jeweled belt at his waist. The gold and cabochon rubies glinted dimly in the thin light, heavy and obviously old, like something out of a crusader's treasure. As perhaps it was. I'd never seen Mircea carry a weapon before—when you're a master vampire, it's a little redundant—and it startled me. "You're armed."

"In this company, certainly." He moved behind me, baring my body to the room, and an arm slid around my waist, pulling me tight against him. As he kissed along my shoulder, silky hair, longer than my own, fell forward over my throat, but that wasn't his destination. He brought my arm up and around his neck in a backwards embrace, and the pinpricks of fangs dented my skin.

He was directly over the artery in my upper arm, but he wasn't feeding—I'd have felt the energy drain, even if he didn't pierce the skin. But it probably looked convincing. It also put him in perfect position to whisper in my ear, his voice low and dangerous. "What concerns me is that you, who claim to be merely human, are not. You are either very foolish or . . . more than you appear. What urgent business brings you here tonight?"

The *geis* was enjoying the silk of Mircea's breath against my cheek. It flooded my body with molten sweetness to the point that I could barely breathe, much less talk. And what would I have told him? There was a problem, otherwise I wouldn't be here, but I had no idea what it was. And in this company, it was beyond ludicrous to think that I could affect anything. I was seriously beginning to doubt that my power knew what it was doing.

"You ruined the play for me," Mircea whispered. "I could not stop thinking about you. All I could see was that lovely body spread out for me . . . in my box . . . in my carriage . . . in my bed."

He pulled me around to face him and his mouth covered mine again, sweeping us away. The kiss was rougher and sweeter at the same time, threatening to overwhelm me with the mindlessness of pleasure. I could have no more broken away than I could have fought the whole room and won.

Mircea finally pulled back, eyes gleaming, cheeks flushed. "Why do I want to touch you so badly?" The voice turned rough. "What have you done to me?"

I thought that should be my line. "I'm here to help," I told him shakily. "You're in danger."

His fingers stroked along the curve of my face, slowly, tenderly, as if he were touching something far more intimate. I licked my lips, and Mircea's eyes dropped to my mouth. "I can see that."

"Mircea! I'm serious!"

"So we are already on a first-name basis. Good; I despise formality." As he spoke, the *geis* tugged at me with a persistent, unfulfilled ache. I felt the power of his shoulders under my hands and masculine hardness against my hip. It took an incredible amount of control not to let my body arch against him, silently begging to be taken. "As you know mine, do you think I could have your name?"

I almost told him; that's how far gone I was. Some tiny sliver of reason spoke up at the last minute, shouting a warning, and I bit my tongue to cut off the words. The pain brought me back to sanity, to the strains of a waltz and the hum of conversation.

I looked around, but all I could see beyond the orchestra was a flickering darkness studded with candle flame. The high ceiling disappeared into shadow, the only bright spots a few glints where candlelight splashed over cracking gilt in faded murals. Nearby, the two vamps had finished their meal, and surprisingly the young woman was still alive. The male vamp was giving her something to drink out of a flask, and she accepted it without hesitation. At this point, she'd probably dive headfirst off the roof if he told her.

Somewhere in all this was the problem I'd been sent to fix, and I had to concentrate if I had any hope of finding it. "It could be the woman—the one who was with you at the theatre—who's the target," I told Mircea. "Is she here?" It would be better to have them together, although what I was supposed to do if another master attacked them I had no idea.

One of those dark eyebrows lifted in a very familiar gesture. "Why should I tell you? I know what you are. I try to be open-minded about these things, at least when the sorceress is young, pretty and thoughtfully wears so few clothes." He ran a single finger up my spine, dancing lightly along the vertebrae. "You have less on every time we meet—I applaud the trend." His words were light, but his eyes were intense on my face. "But however trying Augusta may be at times, her death would be more so."

"Then help me prevent it!"

"But are you here to prevent it? You rescued a man who slipped us poison—"

"Someone else slipped it to you! He was trying to take it away!"

"—and will not even give me your name. Yet you ask for my trust."

"If you think I'm an enemy, why rescue me? Why not let Dmitri do his worst?"

Mircea's mouth curled into a predatory smile. "A show of strength is often useful on these occasions, and I do not care for the man. Dmitri's tastes are well known, and I find them . . . displeasing. Depriving him of a prize was no hardship." His hand smoothed down the bow of my back, and my spine turned liquid. "Now, little witch, you are going to tell me what you are doing here, and explain some very curious events at the theatre two nights ago."

I stared at him, my mind blank. The truth was impossible if I had any hope of not messing up the timeline more than it already was, but he would smell a lie before I finished getting the words out. There was only one possibility that might work. "Take me to Augusta, and I'll think about it." When he hesitated, I forced a laugh. "The great Mircea, afraid of an unarmed girl!"

His lips quirked upward with slow mirth. After a moment, his expression slipped into a true grin, one that made him look years younger. He raised my hand and kissed the palm. "You are quite correct, of course. What is life without a taste of danger?" He tucked my arm into his. "Come, let us see what Augusta can make of you."

Despite the crowded ballroom, Augusta was not difficult to find. She and another female vamp, a petite brunette, had commandeered a spot on the other side of the room and cleared a space on the floor. A crowd had gathered around them, laughing and calling out encouragement, although I couldn't see the attraction. The two vampires appeared merely to be standing in the middle of the circle.

We stopped by the vamp in the toga. "Your Augusta is making herself very popular," he observed.

Mircea looked pained. "She is not my Augusta," he murmured, and the vamp laughed. He'd seemed plain before, with flyaway brown hair that looked like he went to Pritkin's barber and a wind-chapped complexion. But laughter changed the face entirely, adding animation to the whiskey-colored eyes and charm to the expression. When he laughed, he was handsome.

"That's not what she says."

"As you should know better than anyone, Consul, some women are prone to exaggeration . . . and fits of temper."

"The more passionate ones," he agreed. "Although they are frequently worth the trouble. Speaking of passionate shrews, how is your Consul?"

"She is well. I wondered that you did not ask before."

"Your news fair drove all else from my mind."

"Shall I tell her so?"

That produced another chuckle. "Only if you wish to incite a war, my friend." The vampire hadn't so much as glanced at me, which I'd assumed was due to my status as party snack. But his eyes suddenly slid in my direction. "And who is this? Are you beginning a collection of dainty blondes, Mircea?"

The Consul smiled at me, but it didn't reach his eyes. Mircea's grip tightened a fraction. "Are we not permitted to bring guests, Consul?"

"Guests, yes. As long as they are one of us, or human."

He tilted my chin up with a finger. Something shifted behind his eyes, a killer peeking out from behind the jovial mask. "Very pretty. And very powerful. You will answer for her actions, of course."

Mircea bowed slightly and the Consul left to work the room, chatting and talking, back to charming in a blink. I repressed a shiver. "They don't seem to like magic users here," I said weakly.

"They can complicate matters. Different precautions must be taken than are needed for our people."

"I'm surprised he let me stay, then."

"You caught him in a good mood. Augusta and I recently removed a problem for him."

"I'm not planning to cause any trouble," I assured him fervently. Mircea just looked at me, a wry quirk to his lips. "I'm not!"

"Why would I doubt you? Merely because the first time we met, I was almost poisoned, and the second, I came very close to a duel?" His smile broadened. "Fortunately, I don't mind trouble. If, as the Consul said, the reward is worth it."

I didn't know what to say to that so we watched the women for a while. I still couldn't tell what they were doing, possibly because they had their backs to us. The brunette was in pale blue, the icy color embellished with too much lace, but Augusta wore a gorgeous off-the-shoulder champagne satin gown with a gold and cream brocade train. I might not like her, but there was no question that she knew how to dress. The full skirts blocked my view for a moment; then something tore through the middle of them, coming straight at me.

"Oh, no! He's loose!" Augusta's voice rang out over the room, shaking with laughter. A wild-eyed, naked creature scrabbled on hands and knees for the edge of the circle, leaving a trail of droplets behind him. They were black and oily looking against the deep green. Right before he could reach me, something snapped his head back, throwing him twitching onto his side.

Augusta had a leash in her hand as she walked towards him, one end of which was looped around his neck. He lay on his back, quivering in terror, as she stood over him. "Up," she said impatiently, tugging on the leash.

It forced his chin up, and I got a glimpse of his face through a snarl of greasy black hair. His mouth worked with pain, then tightened into a rictus of rage, distorting his features beyond recognition. But I knew those beetle black eyes. I'd seen them in more than a few nightmares.

"Jack," I whispered, and he stared up at me blindly.

"What's wrong?" the brunette called. "I thought you liked to play with women!"

"I think he prefers the helpless kind," Augusta said, trailing her long fingernails down his chest, hard enough to leave red welts among the sparse hair. "So they call you the Ripper, do they?" she crooned. "By the time I'm done with you, you'll truly deserve the name."

The man curled into a ball in a vain attempt to protect himself from those daggerlike fingernails, and I gasped when I saw his back. It had been lacerated until the skin hung in strips, what little there was of it. Mircea noticed as well. "If you don't let him rest soon, Augusta, he'll die and spoil your fun," he observed mildly.

She laughed. "Oh, I don't think so," she said with a coy look.

Mircea frowned and knelt by the man's side. He looked

up after only a moment. "You've made that madman one of us?" he asked incredulously.

Augusta shrugged. "I'll dispose of him when I'm finished, or you may, if you like, for all the trouble he gave you. But you will have to wait." She casually stroked the side of Jack's face, an almost tender gesture, and he gave a desperate, broken cry. I realized with sickened disgust that she'd thrust one of those long fingernails through his right eyeball. "I like this one. He screams so nicely."

Mircea shook off Jack's hand, which had grasped his trouser cuff in a silent plea, and Augusta dragged her captive back to the center of the space. Better to show him off, I supposed. Mircea glanced at me as I struggled to show no emotion. "How did you know who he is? Augusta only unveiled him tonight."

"I heard a rumor," I managed, after swallowing hard. "How did you find him?"

"He found us. We were looking for someone else." Jack screamed as the brunette ground her heel into his groin, and I flinched before I could stop myself. "She'll grow tired of him quickly enough, once he breaks," Mircea said. I didn't comment. They would find out soon enough that it's hard to break an already fractured mind.

My attention was diverted from Jack by the sight of two ghostly figures. They had moved from among the assembled spectators into the circle itself, unseen by the crowd. One was the intriguing creature from earlier, still a featureless blob; the other was Myra.

I froze. On the edge of the circle stood the chief pain in my butt in all her spiritual glory. It was easy to recognize her since the only other time we'd met she'd also been in spirit form. I could hardly believe my eyes, especially since she looked healthier than before I'd stabbed her. Her fair hair, which had hung in lank, unwashed strings the only other time we'd met, was combed and shining. Her face was pale but she looked like she'd gained a few much-needed pounds. How the hell had she recovered so fast?

"What are you doing here?" I demanded.

Mircea thought I was talking to him. "You wished to see Augusta. There she is, safe and sound."

"To right a wrong, of course." Myra's voice was high and sweet, like a child's. It didn't go well with her expression. If looks could kill, I'd already be out of her way. "Isn't that what we were trained to do?" She was staying near the brunette, not coming any closer. I wasn't sure whether that was because Augusta was there, too, or because the brunette's body offered her a shield from my knives. I freed my hand from Mircea's cloak, just in case, but he caught my wrist.

"That is a pretty trinket you're wearing, but I would not advise sending anything deadly at Augusta. You can see what she does to those foolish enough to attack her."

I ignored him. "What wrong?"

"Oh, but I forgot," Myra added sweetly; "you weren't trained, were you? How dreadful."

That singsong voice was really starting to get on my nerves. "This isn't a game, Myra."

"No," she agreed. "It's a contest, for very high stakes. The highest, you might say."

"Meaning what?"

Mircea followed the line of my gaze but of course saw nothing. "To whom are you speaking?"

"Meaning you aren't fit to be Pythia." She regarded me out of eyes that were such a pale blue, they were almost white. I assumed they weren't that light when she was in her body, but at the moment it was creepy. "Agnes was old and dangerously unstable when she appointed you. If her decision had gone through the usual review process, she'd have been laughed out of the hall. But she skipped all that, didn't she? She went behind everyone's backs and fucked up a system that's been in place for thousands of years. I'm here to fix that."

"By killing me?"

"Nothing so crude. Let me give you a little lesson, your first and last, all in one," she said pleasantly. "Any being that travels in linear time is defined by its past. Take that past away, or change it, and you redefine that being." She smiled, but there was acid in it. "Or do away with it completely."

"I know that." What I didn't understand was why she was here, in this time. If Augusta had just turned Jack, then it looked like I was back in the 1880s. If Myra wanted to change my past, she was a little early. "Do you have a point?"

"What is happening?" Mircea demanded, looking back and forth between the vampires and me as if he realized he was missing something.

"Do I have a point?" Myra mimicked. "God, you're thick. I know first-year initiates who catch on faster!"

She glanced at Mircea, and I tensed. I really didn't like her expression. "If you want to kill me, why attack him?"

"You still don't get cause and effect, do you?" Her voice held genuine astonishment. "Let me spell it out for you. Mircea protected you most of your life. Why do you think Antonio never lost his temper and killed you? Why did he open his arms and welcome you back after you ran away? If

Mircea is removed, his protection is removed. And that means you die, long before you become a problem for me."

The ghostly creature behind Myra jerked slightly, as if it didn't like this information any better than I did. It moved those huge eyes back and forth between the two of us, its color shading from a silvery hue to dark purple. Odd flutterings starting around the edge of its diaphanous shape and, with no further warning, it changed. The pale, almost featureless face grew a mouthful of deadly-looking fangs, and the eyes flooded with dark red, like old blood. I stared at it in shock, but Myra didn't seem to notice. Or maybe she thought I was grimacing at her.

"And did Agnes become a problem for you?" I demanded. I was assuming that Myra had been the woman at the theatre who had poisoned Mircea's wine. How she'd recovered so fast I didn't know, but if she was here, then she could have been there. And it wasn't as if there were a lot of other contenders. I couldn't know whether the poison she'd used was the same kind that had killed Agnes, but the similarity in method was interesting. "Is that why you killed her?"

Myra laughed as if I'd said something genuinely funny. "That's against the rules, or didn't you know?" she asked. Then she stepped into the brunette's body and disappeared.

Mircea gripped my upper arms. "Are you mad?"

"The brunette," I gasped. I didn't say any more, because the vamp Myra had possessed suddenly hurtled herself at Mircea. He grabbed her around the throat before I had a chance to blink, holding her away from him. She twisted and fought, but her reach wasn't quite long enough. Not that it would have made any difference if it had been. Apparently, to Myra a vamp was a vamp. She didn't understand that the brunette was a child compared to Mircea, and that he could break her as easily. But she was a fast learner. In less than a minute, Myra flew out of the woman, disappearing into the crowd.

The brunette collapsed, sobbing, clutching Mircea's feet and begging for forgiveness almost incoherently. "She was possessed—she didn't know what she was doing," I told him.

He lifted the hysterical vamp to her feet and looked at me over her head, his face darkening with anger. "Vampires cannot be possessed!"

I thought of Casanova but decided not to debate the point. "Not by most things," I agreed, my eyes on the crowd, which had grown with the advent of violence.

I'd invaded a vamp before, a first-level master. The difference was that I'd done it by accident, not knowing about that facet of my power, and almost scared myself to death. It hadn't done him much good either. But Myra could obviously manage it at will, and there was a whole roomful of vampires for her to choose from.

"What is out there?" Mircea pushed the sobbing vamp towards Augusta—her master, I assumed—and started to examine the crowd himself, those quick dark eyes taking it in, no doubt memorizing the faces. Too bad that sort of thing wouldn't help.

I didn't have to answer, because a woman who might have walked straight out of Versailles, in cream-colored panniers and a two-foot-tall headdress, lurched out of the crowd. She didn't make a beeline for Mircea as I'd expected, but staggered drunkenly about the circle, careening into Jack, who was huddled off to the side, trying to disappear into the shadows. They went down in a tumbled mass, naked, dirty legs entwined with embroidered satin, until Augusta snatched up his leash and yanked him away.

The vamp didn't get up, but stayed in the middle of the floor, limbs thrashing, head rolling, eyes showing white. It looked like she was fighting the possession, trying to throw Myra out. If she succeeded, it would really help. My knives could rip through flesh as easily as spirit, but I couldn't risk attacking when Myra was clothed in someone else's body. Her puppets might not deserve an untimely death, not to mention what it would do to the timeline.

Several vamps started toward the woman, looking concerned, and I grabbed Mircea's arm. "Get them back! I can stop this if I get a clear shot."

"No! You are not killing the host merely—"

"I'm not going to touch the host," I said as the woman screamed and clawed the air. "Once the spirit realizes it can't control her, it will come out. As soon as it does—"

I stopped, but too late. Normally, Myra wouldn't have been able to hear a whispered comment from yards away, but in a vamp's body, she also had a vamp's hearing. The woman's head raised and she gave me a smile that was halfway between a grin and a grimace; then she collapsed. One of the women who had been trying to help her suddenly darted back into the crowd, no doubt with a passenger on board. Damn it!

I searched the crowd for the new host, but when I finally spied her, she'd fainted into the arms of a young vamp. Myra was playing hide-and-seek. "Watch the women," I told Mircea, hoping Myra would overhear. She'd been in only women so far, possibly because she didn't like invading a male's body any more than I did. And those closest to Mircea were all women. If Myra overheard me and switched to men, he'd at least get a split-second warning before he was attacked again.

I went back to scanning the crowd of vamps, who were muttering among themselves but showing no signs of dispersing. In fact, more were drifting over every minute from around the ballroom, as people realized where the entertainment was currently to be found. And the more who crowded in on us, the harder it was to predict where Myra would strike from next.

Fear crept up my spine. All I could see was that ring of faces, avidly waiting to see someone bleed, something die. A male vamp, wearing a vivid green burnoose, fell onto the floor. He was up in an instant, looking around with a snarl, his fangs very white against his dark skin. Then I saw movement toward the center of the circle and caught a look of hatred on Augusta's face, her blue eyes narrowed to icy chips. The young man had been a diversion.

I clutched Mircea's arm and pointed. "Not him! She's in Augusta!"

A murmur went through the crowd—everyone knew something was wrong, but no one was likely to interfere. This was Europe, and both Mircea and Augusta were members of the North American Senate. If they wanted to kill each other, that was their affair. No one would lift a finger to hinder or to help.

"You can't kill her," I told him in a rush. "Just . . . disable her, or something." Enough to force Myra to come out and face me. Augusta grabbed up a huge iron candleholder the size of a coat rack that had been lighting the area. She hefted it like it was made of paper, and I realized a flaw in my plan. If she was a Senate member, she had to be a first-level master.

Just like Mircea.

Augusta came at us, brandishing the flaming candlestick, and Mircea swung me out of the way. She barreled past us but turned in a flash and was back for more, slashing with the candleholder like it was an extra-long sword. Sparks flew everywhere and all hell broke loose in the crowd. Vampires are mortally afraid of fire, and the way she was slinging it around, it could hit anyone. There was a mad rush to the door.

Augusta took another swing, Mircea dodged and a dark figure broke away from the crowd, dashing at him with an outthrust hand. Mircea hadn't seen him, but he felt it when the stake slammed into his side. I screamed, and Dmitri looked up for an instant, smirking; then the expression froze on his face. I saw a blade coming out of his chest in the perfect position to have sliced through his heart, and the hilt was in Mircea's hand. Dmitri gave it a disbelieving look and collapsed, his body spasming violently.

Mircea dropped to one knee, a hand to his side, and I knew it was bad. Mircea's blade was metal—meaning that Dmitri might eventually heal. But the stake Mircea pulled out of his side was wood. When I saw it, my world went gray. I tried telling myself that even if it had hit his heart, that alone wouldn't kill a first-level master. But that wasn't much comfort with Augusta around to finish the job.

She had stopped her attack, surprise on her features when Mircea went down. But she recovered almost instantly, running forward to rip the bloody blade out of Dmitri's chest. She looked at me and laughed. "You aren't even going to make this a challenge, are you?"

She turned back to Mircea and I didn't even hesitate. Killing Augusta would dramatically alter time, but so would letting Mircea die. I'd never been as scared as I was watching the blood pour from Mircea's side and having no power to stop it. I would not watch his head taken, too.

My knives leapt out of the bracelet and flew at Augusta. With vampire agility, she was able to get the candlestick up in time to shield herself, but in the process she knocked a candle free. It landed on her shoulder before bouncing to the floor, and a spark caught on the bodice of her dress. It burst into a tiny flame, smaller than that of a match. A human would have snuffed it out between her fingers with no concern, but Augusta started screaming and thrashing around like a drowning victim going down for the last time.

Apparently, the terror of fire was enough to override Myra's control, because Augusta promptly forgot all about the attack. Mircea tried to get her to hold still so he could smother the flames with his handkerchief, but she wouldn't listen. She slipped on a patch of Jack's blood and ended up on her elegant backside, and I had to jump out of the way to keep from having her roll right into me.

"Augusta! Stay still!" Mircea bellowed, but Augusta wasn't listening. Instead of putting out the flame, all her rolling around had caused more oxygen to get to it, and a finger of fire leapt to one of the long curls that framed her face. Her screams became more like shrieks, and she whipped off the fashionable curls, sending them flying. That explained why her head hadn't gone up like a gasoline fire— half of the golden coiffure was fake and probably made of human hair.

Myra rose out of her, abandoning ship now that she could no longer control it. I waved my arms and screamed frantically at my knives, which had zeroed in on the terrified Augusta. "No—not her! Get Myra!" They either didn't hear me or were having too much fun to obey.

The spirit creature was more single-minded. It dove through Myra, as insubstantial as a breath of wind, but she staggered backwards, clawing at her chest and screaming. After a stunned second, I realized that she'd been given the spiritual equivalent of a mugging. The spirit emerged from her back, so flush with stolen power that it was blinding silver, looking at it like staring into a searchlight.

I blinked, and when I looked again, it had faded out. Myra dropped to her knees, almost transparent, the energy that should have allowed her to remain here for hours gone. She turned a furious blue glare on me. "Doesn't matter. You can't guard him all the time."

She shifted out just as Augusta scrambled to her feet and careened into Mircea, screaming and clawing like she blamed him for the danger. I tossed him the cloak, and he wrapped it around her to smother the flames, just as I felt the tug of my power.

"Tell me, little witch," he gasped, holding the struggling vampire with obvious difficulty. "What happens when you *are* trying to cause trouble?"

A wave of dizziness and nausea swept over me, and I felt myself falling. I crashed headfirst into Mac's cot, where Billy Joe had been playing a game of solitaire, scattering his cards everywhere. "I fold," I said weakly, and passed out.

Chapter 8

I hugged porcelain in the bathroom for the next half hour. Once the power receded, I was wiped out and had a headache so severe I was nauseous. With my usual luck, Mac decided to check on me right after I returned and found me green and shaking. He left to round up a snack, apparently on the assumption that my problem was low blood sugar. If only.

Billy moved over so I could stretch out on the cot without having to lie through part of his body. "Did you see Casanova?" I croaked. I had commandeered one of Mac's beers to help my dry throat, and almost succeeded in making myself sick again when the alcohol hit my stomach. I hastily put it down.

"Yeah, but Chavez is AWOL. Maybe he's lying low until the mages vacate Dante's, I don't know. But Casanova said he'd lock up the stuff whenever he gets there." I nodded. It was as good as I could have hoped for. If Chavez had been smart enough to dodge the invasion of his workplace, the items he was carrying should be safe.

"Are you gonna do it?" Billy asked, shuffling the deck of

cards. He never lifts things unless forced or showing off, but I was too sick to be impressed.

"Do what?" I lay back on the cot, trying to convince my stomach that there was nothing left to throw up. I couldn't figure out what was wrong with me. I'd shifted in time before and never felt like this when I returned.

"Fix the ward."

I blinked blearily at him. I'd almost forgotten about that. My pentagram would have come in really handy with Dmitri, and it had proved capable of traveling through time with me before. Unfortunately, I couldn't risk fixing it. "Yeah, and I'd owe the power a favor, too."

"Seems like it owes you a couple, if you ask me. You've been running its errands. It's not like you wanted to go anywhere."

"But I don't know if it looks at things like that."

Billy blew smoke from an insubstantial cigarette, making a ring that floated up almost to the ceiling before disappearing. I asked him once why he could smoke ghostly cigarettes but couldn't drink ghostly booze, which would save me some embarrassing incidents and a lot of his whining. He'd said that whatever was with you, as in touching your body or within a few feet of it, when you died could materialize with you. It was all part of your energy, of course—so Billy was essentially smoking himself—but it was apparently satisfying on some level. Too bad he hadn't had a whiskey flask tucked away when he took his burlap swimming lesson.

"Why are we talking about this power like it's a person?" he asked thoughtfully. "You sound like it has a tally sheet and is marking down every favor so it can demand that you pay up one of these days. What if that's not true? Maybe it's a force of nature, like gravity. Only instead of keeping everything glued down, it responds to problems with the timeline by sending a repair person to fix it."

I shook my head. His theory was surprisingly logical, but some part of me knew that whatever I was dealing with was conscious, not a mindless force. It knew I didn't like being on its repair crew. It just didn't care. "I don't think so."

"Okay, let me make sure I understand this." Billy dealt out a hand of cards consisting of two black aces, a pair of black eights and the king of spades. It's called the Dead Man's Hand in poker because, according to legend, that's what Wild Bill Hickok was holding when he was shot in the back. Hickok died in 1876, almost two decades after my dealer, but Billy knew his poker lore—and how to be obnoxious with it. "You're going to refuse to fix the ward even though you've got more people after you than I can count *and* you're going into Faerie, where trespassers are usually killed on sight? Just so you don't maybe owe a possibly nonsentient power a favor, which it might not even bother to collect?"

I was too tired to glare at him. "I don't know."

"Oh, well, I'm glad you've at least thought it out."

"Why are you nagging me about this?"

"Because, turtledove, in case you've forgotten, we made a deal. I've kept my end and I expect you to keep yours— which you can't do if you're dead. Okay, yeah, you don't like being bossed around. Who does? But, newsflash, being dead is a lot worse. Have Mac reattach the damn ward. If you don't need it, great, you don't owe anybody anything. But if you do, it'll be there, and when the smoke clears, so will you."

"Uh-huh," I said testily, giving up on the idea of getting any sleep with Billy around. "And what if it flares when it isn't a life-and-death situation? I don't have control over what the power perceives as a threat. If it's fueling the ward, it'll be in charge, and it's already tried to trick me . . ." I trailed off because Billy hadn't been there when I'd assaulted Pritkin, and I didn't want to be teased about it. Luckily, either he didn't notice or he let it go.

"Okay, you're taking a risk, wagering a few chips that this thing won't be able to trick you. But that's a lot better than gambling your life on not needing the ward and then finding out you were wrong. Take it from someone who knows, Cass—never bet when you can't afford to lose."

We were interrupted by Mac returning laden with the four fast-food groups—salt, grease, sugar and caffeine—in the form of fries, burgers and extra large, sweetened coffees. I forced myself to eat, as it was the fastest way to regain some energy, despite feeling queasy. Halfway through the meal I told Mac that I'd decided to have the ward reactivated. Billy gave me a thumbs-up and I grimaced at him. The only thing more annoying than Billy when he's wrong is Billy when he gets something right. I'd hear about this one for a long time.

When Pritkin returned, I'd just finished dressing after Mac's adjustment. The ward remained lopsided because fixing aesthetics could wait. Mac said he thought that the power transfer had gone well, but I was skeptical. I couldn't feel anything—not a single spark or twinge. Of course, I usually didn't unless there was a threat, but I would have liked some sign that it was back at work. It didn't look like I was going to get one, though. I guessed I'd have to wait until someone tried to kill me to find out whether Mac was as skilled as he claimed. The way my life was going lately, that shouldn't be long.

"We need to go," Pritkin said without preamble. He tossed something over my head and it caught on my ear. I pulled it off and saw that I was holding some kind of charm—actually several charms—on a sturdy red cord. The little cloth pouch contained either verbena or a really ripe gym sock—they smell about the same—but I wasn't sure about the significance of the others.

"Rowan wood cross," Billy identified, "set with amber and coral—all three said to ward off Fey attacks. The pentagram is probably iron," he added, squinting at it despite the fact that that couldn't possibly help his eyesight. "It looks like he's serious about this crazy expedition. I'm beginning to think he's as nuts as you are."

Pritkin had pulled another, matching necklace out of the bulging pack on his back. It would have made him look like Santa Claus, except that I doubt the jolly old elf ever looked that grim. He threw it to Mac and scowled. "The Circle's closing in."

"As expected," Mac said lightly. He stood and brushed off some crumbs. We'd been talking about wards before Pritkin showed up, mainly because Mac had wanted to distract me from focusing on what he was doing to my star. He grinned at me now and held out his right leg. "Here's one I didn't have time to tell you about," he said, pointing to a small, square patch of empty skin below his knee.

"I don't get it."

Mac just grinned bigger and took a folded piece of paper out of his pocket. He spread it out on the cot and I identified it as a map of Las Vegas and its surroundings. It was old and yellowed, except for patches of bright red inked onto different areas. It reminded me of a subway map, except that, of course, Vegas doesn't have one.

"There," Pritkin said, pointing out an area close to MAGIC's canyon.

Mac nodded. "No worries." He raised an eyebrow at me. "Ever see *The Wizard of Oz*?"

"Uh, yeah. Why?"

"You might want to hold on to something," was the only reply I got before what felt like a giant earthquake hit the shop. I clutched the cot, which was bolted down, while Pritkin looped a foot around the table and held on with both hands. Only Mac looked unperturbed, ignoring the spinning, tilting and bucking room to trace a finger along a line on the map from the city to the desert. A few seconds after he finished, the building gave a last thudding shudder and was still. A few pieces of paper wafted down from where they'd been tossed near the ceiling, but otherwise, it was like nothing had ever happened.

"What was that?!"

"See for yourself." Mac waved a hand at the front of the shop, and after regaining my rubbery legs, I walked into the front room. Instead of the asphalt street and busy hamburger restaurant that had constituted the view out of the front window, there was only a bare expanse of desert, without so much as a cactus to break up the monotony.

"I think she needs a backup," Mac was saying as he came through the curtain.

"She has those damn knives."

"They're unreliable—they came off a dark mage and their loyalty is in question. They serve her now because it suits their purpose, but later?" Mac shook his head. "I don't like it. Not to mention that we don't even know if they'll work there."

"You reactivated her ward; that should be sufficient,"

Pritkin replied, dragging his sack out of the back room and starting to unload it on the counter. "She is more than strong enough already."

Mac didn't say anything, but he quietly reached up to his left shoulder and grabbed something that had been concealed by the gently waving leaves. He put a finger to his lips and glanced at Pritkin, who was lining up a collection of weapons on the counter. If he thought we were going to carry all of those, I hoped he'd brought a cart.

Mac reached for my arm and I looked down to see a gleaming gold charm in the shape of a cat being held to my elbow. As soon as it touched bare skin, it morphed into a sleek black panther with narrowed orange eyes. I recognized them as the ones that had been peering at me malignantly earlier, and they didn't look much happier now. The kitty didn't seem pleased to have lost Mac's generous camouflage, and after a brief glance around, it ran up my arm and disappeared beneath my shirt.

I could feel it almost like it was a real cat, with warm fur and little claws that pricked my skin. It was weird and it tickled and I didn't like it one bit. "What the—"

"Come on, Cassie, you need to finish lunch," Mac said, pushing me ahead of him through the curtain.

"What the *hell* is going on?" I hissed once we were in the back. Mac shushed me and made a weird gesture in the air.

"Silence shield," he explained. "John has better hearing without enhancements than most do with them."

"Mac, if you don't explain what—"

"I just gave you that other ward you wanted. Sheba will take good care of you. Top of the line, she is."

Ms. Top of the Line was crawling around on my stomach,

occasionally stopping to lick me, and it was creeping me out. "Mac! Get this thing off me!"

He chuckled. "Can't. That kind can only be transferred once a day. Sorry."

He didn't look sorry, and I had no way of knowing whether he was telling the truth. I frankly doubted it. "Mac!"

"You may need her, Cassie," he said more soberly. "You let me reactivate your ward, but it's like John said: your power may not work in Faerie, and if it does it could be sporadic. If the energy isn't flowing to fuel it, your ward won't function. Sheba's going to tag along to make sure you have some protection even if your main ward fails—think of her as a slightly temperamental backup. There aren't many wards that'll work in Faerie, but that one will. I bought it off the Fey who enchanted it. And I wouldn't be much of a gentleman to let you go off defenseless, now, would I?"

"But I'm not going alone." Sheba had now climbed around to my back and was doing something with her claws that was less than pleasant. I reached around to get her to stop and got swatted at by a small paw for my trouble. Fortunately, the next minute she curled up in a warm ball at the base of my spine and went to sleep. If I concentrated, I could hear her purr contentedly.

"You're assuming we'll all get past the guards. But it won't be as simple as just walking in tonight."

"You said you know them."

"I do, but they know me, too. I used to be John's partner before I retired. He's a wanted man now, after that exhibition you two put on this morning, so my walking in there out of the blue and making small talk is going to look strange. The idea is that I create a diversion and you two run into the portal while the guards are busy with me. But there's no saying it'll work. Even if it does, you and John are going to be on your own after the guards apprehend me."

I squirmed uncomfortably, both because Sheba's lazily twitching tail was ticklish, and because of Mac's easy non-chalance about defying the Circle. "What'll happen when they catch you?"

He shrugged. "Likely nothing. It won't be a slap on the wrist and Bob's your uncle, I'm back on the streets. But I know a trick or two. With a little luck, I should be able to convince them that John put me under a compulsion spell and forced me to help."

"And if you're not lucky?"

Mac grinned and patted me on the shoulder. "That's why we're going tonight. My old mates may not be happy to see me, but neither is likely to kill me. I pulled their nuts out of the fire a time or two—they owe me."

"But the Circle—"

"You let me worry about them," he said as Pritkin stuck a suspicious face through the curtain.

"What's going on?" I saw him mouth before Mac dis-solved the shield around us with an unobtrusive flick of his wrist.

"Finishing clogging our arteries," Mac said cheerfully. "I'd ask you to join us, but I know you've stretched your rules once today." He winked at me. "Never let John be in charge of the food, Cassie. He'll poison you with wheatgrass and prune juice."

"It's better than the kind of thing you call food," Pritkin said, but he disappeared back out front as if satisfied.

I ate a little more of my burger, but the grease had started to congeal, and anyway, I'd lost my appetite. I was tired of other people getting hurt because of me, and falling into the

Circle's hands definitely came under that category. Maybe people did owe Mac a few favors, but would it be enough? What if they tortured him to find out what he knew about me? I wouldn't put it past them, old soldier or no. I felt sick again, a combination of the type of food I'd consumed, nerves and worry. Mac didn't seem to have that problem, and ultimately finished off my burger himself.

I wandered back out front to find that Pritkin was loaded for bear. The mass of weapons was gone, but he didn't appear any more weighed down than usual. I realized why when I saw him clipping some very unusual charms to a link bracelet. "Iron," he explained as he fastened it around his wrist. "It saps Fey energy, tears through their defenses like silver does to a were."

"I didn't peg you for the jewelry type," I said, although I'd pretty much figured out what he'd done. Not even a homicidal mage wears a charm bracelet with tiny machine guns, rifles and what looked suspiciously like a grenade launcher dangling from it. The latter was especially telling, since he'd pulled a life-size model out of his sack earlier.

"I shrank them," he said impatiently. "It's the only way to carry that much weight for any distance."

"I thought you said our stuff doesn't work there?"

"I said our magic may not work properly, if at all. This"—Pritkin tapped the Colt on his belt—"isn't magic. And it's loaded with iron bullets. Speaking of which, here." He gave me a long coat that almost matched his own. "Put that on."

I took it from his outstretched hand and almost collapsed to the floor. It felt like it was lead lined. After a minute, I realized that was pretty much the truth. The added weight came from boxes and boxes of bullets of every conceivable caliber that had been stuffed into the coat's many pockets.

"You have got to be kidding," I said, dropping the thing on the floor. It landed with an audible thud. "I won't be able to run in that! I doubt I could walk in it!"

"You won't be running." Pritkin picked it up and stuffed it back in my arms. "We would never outrun the Fey on their own turf, so we won't try. If we come across any and they're hostile—"

"And they will be," Mac put in, emerging from behind the curtain. He had a small backpack into which he put the contents of my duffle and, with a wink, a couple of beers.

"Then we stand our ground and fight," Pritkin finished. "Running is a waste of time and would play into their hands if it separated us. No matter how grim a battle seems, don't panic."

"Of course not. I'll stand my ground while they mow me down." I was struggling into the hot leather and feeling cranky.

Pritkin checked his shotgun and, for the first time since our incident, he met my eyes. "If you're with me, you won't die," he said. He sounded so certain that, for half a second, I believed him.

I swallowed and broke eye contact. "Why can't you shrink my stuff, too?"

"Because I am not entirely certain that the reverse spell will work in Faerie, so I am carrying both shrunken backup weapons and regular-sized primaries. Your ammunition is for the primaries."

I was busy trying to sort through my emotions, which ranged from pissed off to terrified, so it wasn't until we stepped outside that I remembered our wild ride. Freakish though it had been, it actually ranked pretty far down the list of weird things that had happened to me lately. "How did we get here?" I asked Mac.

"I took a short cut," he said, pulling a wide-brimmed hat over his bald head. He turned around and tapped the blank square that decorated his knee. I stared at the very odd sight of a tattoo parlor sitting all alone in the middle of the desert, just before I was treated to the even odder one of it folding in on itself and winking out of sight entirely. Mac grunted and examined his leg, where a miniature version of the front of the shop, complete with bright neon sign reading MAG INK, had appeared. It fit perfectly into the bare spot I'd seen earlier.

The little sign on the tattoo flashed on and off just like the real thing. After a second, I realized that it was the real thing. "We've spent the whole afternoon inside one of your wards?" I asked incredulously.

"Right in one," Mac said. "My shop goes wherever I do."

"What do you do? Pick out an empty lot and then, *bam*! New retail location?"

He grinned. "Something like that."

"What about zoning? What about pedestrians walking by and all of a sudden, there's a building? What about the cops?"

"What about them? Norms can't see it, Cassie, any more than they can one of the tattoos." He took my arm companionably. "You've got to realize that the so-called magic you've seen all your life is only the tip of the iceberg. Those sad bastards the vamps use for warding and such are the bottom of the barrel. If they had any real talent, whatever issues got them disavowed would have been overlooked or they'd have been chastised and put back to work. Or, if it was something truly heinous, they'd have run off and joined the Dark—only even they won't take screwups. The type that ends up working for vamps are those with only enough magic to qualify as menaces—to themselves and everyone else. They couldn't do a complex spell if their lives depended on it. You stick with us, and you'll see some real magic."

Pritkin stopped and took something out of his pocket. "Good idea," he commented, and a second before he did it, I knew what was going to happen. It wasn't a Seeing, just my kind of luck. The idiot was going to cast the mystery rune.

I hit the dirt and tried to drag Mac down with me, but my feet got tangled in the hem of the heavy coat and I had to let go of him to break my fall. I scraped my palms on rock-hard dirt, and the pain and subsequent struggle to free myself from the leather distracted me for a few seconds. There was a flash of light and a popping noise, like a very large champagne cork. When I looked up again, Pritkin and Mac were gone.

Although I could see a good distance in every direction, there wasn't so much as a shred of cloth or a footprint to show that they'd been there. I felt around with my senses, but there were no unusual vibrations. That was almost as strange as the disappearance—a major magical object had just been set off, yet there wasn't so much as a metaphysical ripple for miles. The only thing I could pick up was the slight buzz of MAGIC's wards off to the northwest.

I didn't understand it. If the rune had killed Pritkin and Mac—even if it had vaporized their bodies—I should be able to see their spirits. And, so far, I couldn't. After walking a large circle around where the mages had vanished and coming up with nothing, I turned my attention to my own position. It wasn't good.

I was miles from Vegas with no food, water or transportation. Worse, the only nearby source of those things was MAGIC, where half the people hunting me currently resided. Breaking in by myself would have been daunting, even if Billy had been there to help. But he, like the mages, was currently a no-show. That thought started me worrying that perhaps the rune could destroy ghosts, too, and that was why I couldn't see Pritkin or Mac's spirits. I shied away from that concept quickly when I began to shake. Billy was a royal pain, but he'd been with me through some pretty crazy times. It was hard to think about being truly alone, without a single person I could claim as an ally—not even a dead one.

The only good news was that I was wearing enough ammunition to wage a small war. Unfortunately, I'd have to drive off my enemies by throwing it at them, because I didn't have a gun. Pritkin hadn't offered to share, and my own Smith & Wesson was in my purse, which Mac had stuffed into the backpack—a backpack he had been holding.

I was watching a gorgeous desert sunset with rising panic when I noticed something small and dark in the sky. It was only a tiny spec highlighted by the rays of the setting sun, but it was getting bigger fast. I barely had time enough to think that Mac had been right, it did remind me of Oz, before the thing grew so huge that it blotted out what was left of the sun. I hit the ground, huddling inside the thick coat while my brain flashed on an image of me lying under Dorothy's farmhouse, with only my dead legs sticking out. Too bad I'd lost the shoes from Dante's; they'd have been perfect.

My inner monologue began to babble as something huge hit the ground nearby with a bone-shaking thud. A hail of rocks and dirt rained down on me, and my brain lost it. It was hysterically insisting that getting crushed to death wouldn't be fair—I was only a slightly bitchy clairvoyant, not a wicked witch—when the dirt storm finally passed.

I peered out from inside the coat, but there were no Munchkins or yellow brick roads in sight. Yet there was a house. It took my dust-filled eyes a few seconds to realize that the structure sitting so incongruously on the desert sand wasn't a rogue Kansas farmhouse but an urban tattoo parlor, with its neon sign flashing as cheerfully as Mac's grin.

I was lying in the dirt, shaking, when the door burst open and Pritkin and Mac ran out. They looked pretty forbidding, but then Mac caught sight of me, gave a whoop and sped over to pick me up and spin me around in a circle, lead-lined coat and all. "Cassie! Are you all right? You had us so—"

"Where the hell did you two *go*?" I was sobbing and half hysterical, so relieved that I felt weak and simultaneously as mad as hell. I hit him in the chest and, although I doubt it hurt much, his eagle screeched and pecked viciously at my hand. I shrieked and tore away, ending up back in the dirt. I had just been attacked by a painted bird that was not now and never had been real. Despite my afternoon crash course on advanced wards, it didn't seem possible, but it was hard to argue with evidence that hurt that much. Then Sheba woke up and things went from bad to worse.

I felt the unwelcome fur ball stretch along my lower back and, when Mac bent over to help me up, she flowed along my torso and down my arm. I looked in surprise at the line of bright red that suddenly appeared on his forearm. Despite the size of her paw, the gash it left behind was three inches long and deep enough to need stitches. Even worse, I had no idea how to call Sheba off.

Pritkin jerked me away from his friend and sent me staggering, releasing his hold quickly before Sheba could get her claws into him. His lips were thin with anger. "Stop it, both of you! Before you activate the wards for real and tear each other apart!"

I looked down at my hand, which now sported a painful two-inch gash, and gulped in enough air to say, "For real?" How much worse did they get? I don't know what else I might have said, but I glimpsed Billy over Pritkin's shoulder and temporarily forgot everything else. I pointed a trembling finger at him. "Where were you? It's almost dark and MAGIC is right over there!"

"Calm down, Cass—it's okay. Everything's fine, but you need to get a grip or your new pet is going to do some serious damage."

"My ward didn't flare." I stared at Mac, who was busy healing his wound. Lucky him—I'd wear mine for a while. Yet, although it was Mac who was bleeding, it was Pritkin who was glowering at me. That was so unfair it was breathtaking, considering that all of this was his damn fault.

"That doesn't necessarily mean anything," Mac said. "It's a bit more advanced than those. It's designed to sense intent, and I didn't mean you any harm." He had managed to stop the blood flow, but a raw red weal remained behind to mark his skin, leaving a gap in the leaves that they brushed against but couldn't cross. "I'm sorry, Cassie—I shouldn't have grabbed you. But when you disappeared we—well, we didn't know what had happened."

So they'd thought I was dead, too. Mac's confession that he, at least, had been worried helped me calm down—that and the fact that I wasn't about to face an ambush alone. "I've been right here," I told him shakily. "You two are the ones who disappeared. Where did you go?"

"You were aware that we were gone?" Pritkin asked with a frown. He glanced at Mac. "We were wrong, then."

"Not necessarily." Mac looked at me keenly. "Maybe time displacements don't affect her like the rest of us. That could be why she didn't come along for the ride even though she was as close to you as I was."

"You went somewhere in time?" What, could anybody do it anymore?

"We think that thing"—Mac gestured at the rune Pritkin still held in his fist—"is a do-over."

"A what?"

"It carries the caster back in time about twenty minutes. So if you get in a tight spot, you cast it and have a chance to redeem a mistake."

I sent Pritkin a less-than-friendly glance. "Something that might have been very useful where we're going."

"I'm sure it will be," he commented, tucking it out of sight inside his coat.

I would have reminded him that the rune was mine, except that he would almost certainly have replied that I'd just stolen it first. I glanced at Billy and nodded slightly toward the mage. He floated over while I started an argument to distract Pritkin. "Well, it's useless now, at least for a month."

"We could not risk employing it without first learning what it does," Pritkin insisted, his eyebrows drawing together in their usual expression. "If it has not been used in as long as we think, it should be possible to cast it again soon."

"But you don't know that," I pointed out angrily. "You

can leave rechargeable batteries plugged in as long as you want, but they only hold one charge. Maybe the rune works the same way."

"Permit me to think that I know a little more about magical artifacts than you," Pritkin replied with disdain as Billy slipped an insubstantial-looking hand into his pocket. A few seconds later, my rune floated out as if levitated. It made its way to me and I surreptitiously pocketed it. "I am reasonably certain it will work," the mage added. "Now, if you have finished having hysterics, we should be going."

I said nothing but retrieved the backpack from Mac and took out my gun. It was fully loaded, but I checked it anyway. Pritkin's lips thinned out even more as he watched; pretty soon he wasn't going to have any at all. He obviously didn't like the idea of my carrying a weapon—maybe he was afraid I'd shoot him in the back—but he refrained from comment.

He struck out across the desert and I followed. Mac and Billy Joe trailed after us as soon as the mage again absorbed his mobile business. Not a word was said for half an hour, until the dim outline of MAGIC spread below us.

The complex is designed to look like a working ranch, just in case any norms with a little talent wander by and manage to see through the perimeter wards. But it's centered in a canyon with high sides, far away from any tourist facilities, so that isn't likely. Not to mention that there are all kinds of metaphysical KEEP OFF signs everywhere, starting about a mile out, that make norms very uncomfortable.

The starlight had turned the landscape into something like the moon's surface—all mysterious dark craters and endless silver sand. MAGIC itself was dark and quiet, with all the external lights off and no movement among the buildings. It looked like whatever was happening tonight was taking place underground.

I collapsed onto a relatively rock-free piece of sand while Mac and Pritkin debated approaches. The hike had been a bitch. I'd stumbled through the growing darkness, stubbing my toe about every fourth step and falling on my face twice. The coat kept getting tangled around my legs and made me feel like I was carrying another person on my back. I'd been too busy lately for regular gym visits and it showed. Running for my life was obviously not giving me enough exercise.

"Is he in there?" Billy asked, hovering a few feet off the sand.

I hugged the coat around me, grateful for its thickness now that the desert had started to cool off. "I don't know."

"Want me to check it out?"

"No." If Mircea was there, I didn't want to know. With luck, we'd escape into Faerie before he figured out that I'd been crazy enough to drop by.

"Is your ghost here?" Pritkin interrupted to ask. He surprised me by being cautious for once—maybe the idea of breaking into MAGIC scared even him. He had Mac describe his guard friends to Billy, who agreed to go see whether anyone had changed the duty roster unexpectedly. He streamed off across the sand, quickly becoming invisible against the night. In the meantime, we waited.

Once upon a time, when I was a child reading fairy tales, I'd ached to have my own adventures. Not that I'd wanted to be some drippy heroine languishing in a tower, awaiting rescue. No, I'd wanted to be the knight, charging into battle against overwhelming odds, or the plucky country lass who gets taken on as the apprentice to a great wizard. As I got older, I'd found out the hard way that adventures are rarely anything like the books say. Half the time you're scared out of your mind, and the rest you're bored and your feet hurt. I was beginning to believe that maybe I wasn't the adventurous type.

Billy returned after half an hour with news. The guards fit the descriptions Mac had given him and, lucky for us, there was a major uproar in the vamp area. "It's like a circus, Cass—everybody's there. The rest of the place is practically deserted!"

"Well?" Pritkin was looking impatient. "What does he say?"

"It's okay—the right guys are on duty." Billy, I noticed, was looking way too pleased about something. Maybe it was just relief that our job might be easier than we'd thought, but I doubted it. I knew his expressions almost as well as I knew my own, and he was practically ecstatic. "Okay, out with it."

Billy grinned and twirled his hat around an index finger. For some reason the finger was less substantial at the moment than the hat, so it looked like his headgear was doing a giddy little jig all on its own. "It's too perfect," he crowed, his grin threatening to split his face. "Talk about a good omen!"

"What are you talking about?"

"Is something wrong?" Pritkin demanded. Billy and I both ignored him.

"I know your birthday doesn't start for a couple more hours, Cass, but you're getting your present early."

"Billy! Just tell me already."

He laughed delightedly, to the point that it barely missed being a cackle. "It's that bastard Tomas. He was captured early yesterday morning. I think they're trying to decide what would be the most painful way to execute him. That's why everyone's crowded into the vamp section—they want to see the show." Billy threw his hat up into the air jubilantly. "I wouldn't mind taking a peek myself, if we had time."

The only thing that saved me from falling was that I was already sitting down. Tomas was about to be executed and might already be under torture? I sat blinking at Billy as my brain tried to comprehend it, and whatever showed on my face he didn't like. His grin faded and he started shaking his head violently.

"No. No way are you doing this! He deserves this, Cass, you know he does. He betrayed you—hell, he almost got you killed! For once, fate is taking a problem off our hands gratis. Let's smile, say thank you and stay the hell out of it!"

My face felt numb. I wondered vaguely whether that was due to the night breeze or to horror. I was betting on horror. "I can't."

"Yes, you can." Billy flickered like a candle flame in his agitation. "It's easy. We walk into MAGIC's nice, quiet halls, make our way to the portal and pass through. That's it, that's all. No biggie."

"Yes biggie." I stood up, wobbling a little, and Pritkin caught my arm. As usual he wasn't gentle, but this time that was a plus. I barely kept my balance even with his iron grip. "Very much biggie."

"What are you talking about? What's going on?" Pritkin was talking, but I barely heard him. All I could hear was Tomas' voice raised in agony, all I could see was him tied down like an animal, waiting for Jack.

If I closed my eyes, I could see a different scene. It was Tomas in the kitchen of our Atlanta apartment, frowning in puzzlement at the stove. It hadn't cooked the brownies he'd intended as breakfast for me, possibly because he hadn't known to turn the thing on. He'd been wearing one of my aprons, the one that said DOES NOT COOK WELL WITH OTHERS, over the smiley face pajama bottoms I'd bought to keep him from sleeping in the altogether. We'd had separate bedrooms, but just the thought of Tomas down the hall wearing only his skin had been keeping me up nights. I'd explained how the range operated and we'd eaten the whole pan of brownies before I went off to work, resulting in a sugar buzz that lasted most of the day.

That was the first time I'd let myself begin to hope that he might become a permanent fixture in my life. He'd already been my best friend for six of the happiest months I'd ever known. Against all odds, I'd actually started to create a more or less normal existence. I'd liked my sunny apartment, my wonderfully predictable job at a travel agency and my gorgeous roommate. Tomas had been a dream come true—handsome, considerate, strong, yet vulnerable enough to make me want to take care of him.

I should have remembered the old phrase about something that looks too good to be true, but I'd been too busy enjoying the gift fate had dropped in my lap. What followed had proven that the gift had been more of a curse, and the normal life only a mirage. All those rosy dreams had come crashing down around my head, leaving scars that hadn't even scabbed over, much less healed. I realized with a jolt that the brownie incident had been only a few weeks ago. That seemed impossible; it had to have been at least a decade.

Pritkin was shaking me, but I barely noticed. I opened my eyes, but it was Jack's pale face and crazed expression I saw. The Consul's favorite torturer loved his work, and he was very, very good at it. He'd probably had plenty of firsthand instruction from Augusta. I'd seen him in action on one very memorable occasion, and no way could I leave Tomas in his hands. No matter what he'd done; no matter how furious I was with him. There was no freaking way.

It looked like I got to be the knight on the white horse after all. Only never in my wildest dreams had I planned on the odds being quite this bad. There was such a thing as a heroic challenge and then there was suicide, and I had no doubt into which category this fit. If Tomas' death was being made into a public show, most of MAGIC would be there: vamps, mages, weres, maybe even a few Fey. And somehow we not only had to get past them and snatch him from under the Consul's nose; we also had to battle our way to the portal afterward. It was worse than a nightmare. It was insane.

"We have a problem," I told Pritkin, choking back an absurd urge to giggle at the understatement.

His eyes narrowed to pale slits. "What problem?" Since he forced the words past clenched teeth, it looked like he'd already figured out that he was going to hate this. That was good; it saved time.

"Billy says the halls are almost empty because everyone's in the vampire area. They're executing someone tonight, and it's drawn quite a crowd."

"Executing who?" Pritkin's icy green eyes stared into mine and I smiled weakly, remembering the last time he and Tomas met. To say that they weren't pals was missing the mark a bit. People don't generally try to behead their friends.

"Um, well, actually . . ." I sighed. "It's Tomas."

I couldn't keep myself from wincing slightly, but Pritkin barely reacted, other than to look slightly relieved. "Good. Then this should be simpler than I'd anticipated." He noticed my expression and his frown returned. "Why does this constitute a problem?"

I swallowed. I'd have preferred a little more time to lead up to it, like a year or two, but I couldn't afford to stall. Every second that passed was dangerous for Tomas. Jack liked to play with his victims before finishing them off, and no one would be happy with a short show. But it had been dark for well over an hour. Jack could do a lot of damage in that time.

I looked at Pritkin and worked up a smile. It didn't seem to help, and I gave it up. "Because we, uh, sort of have to rescue him."

Chapter 9

Pritkin looked as if he was trying to determine whether I was genuinely crazy, or just temporarily insane. "Do you remember what that place contains?" he asked in a savage undertone, gesturing at the dark outline of MAGIC. "If we had every war mage in the corps, it wouldn't be enough!"

Billy was nodding violently behind Pritkin's head. "Listen to the mage, Cass. He's talking sense."

I didn't even try to persuade Billy to do something for Tomas. He'd never liked him, even before the betrayal, which because of our arrangement he viewed as an attack on himself as well as on me. I glanced at Mac but didn't see much in the way of encouragement. He seemed like a fairly sympathetic guy, but he was also Pritkin's friend, not to mention that there was no love lost between mages and vamps. They tolerated each other, but they didn't risk their necks for each other.

I sighed. "If none of you want to help, then wait here. I'll manage without you." Tomas was not dying tonight.

"He tried to kill you!" Pritkin had apparently decided to reason with me.

"Actually, he tried to kill you. He thought he was helping me; he's just not that bright sometimes."

Pritkin moved, but Mac was suddenly there, a hand on his friend's chest. "Throwing her over your shoulder isn't going to help, John," he said quietly. "I don't know what this vampire is to her, but if we let him die I think we can kiss the Pythia's help goodbye."

"She is not Pythia yet," Pritkin said, teeth clenched so tight that I don't know how he got the words out. "She's a foolish child who—"

I started down the incline, wondering if I really had gone mad, but within seconds a Pritkin-shaped bulk appeared in front of me, blocking my way. "Why are you doing this?" he demanded, looking genuinely confused. "Tell me you're not in love with him—that you're not about to risk our lives because of some vampire's seduction techniques!"

I paused. I wasn't sure what to call the stew of emotions Tomas inspired, but I didn't think it was love. "He was my friend," I said, trying to explain so Pritkin would understand— which was difficult since I wasn't sure I did. "He betrayed me, but in his own warped view of things he thought he was helping me. He endangered my life, but he also saved it. I guess we're sort of even."

"Then you don't owe him anything."

"This isn't about what I owe him." And it wasn't. I wanted to rescue Tomas, but, I realized with sudden clarity, I also wanted something else. "It's about making a statement. Someone who is known to be important to me is being publicly humiliated, tortured and killed. Yet no one— not the mages, not the Senate, not a single individual in the supernatural community—ever once thought to ask my permission!"

"Your permission?" Pritkin looked dumbfounded. "And precisely why would they need that?"

I looked at him and shook my head. Screw this. If I had to deal with all the downsides of the office, it was about time I had a few of the perks, too. "Because I'm Pythia," I said quietly, and shifted.

I had assumed the Senate would be using its own chamber for this, and I'd been right. The usual echoing vastness was empty no longer. The huge mahogany slab that served as the Senate table was still there, although it had a new purpose now. The chairs that normally lined one side had been moved, arranged in a semicircle in front of the table. Behind them were row upon row of benches, crowded with weres, mages and vamps. The only no-shows were the Fey, unless they looked so much like the mages that I couldn't tell them apart. After my experience at Dante's, I kind of doubted that.

I had landed right where I'd planned, directly beside Tomas. I wasn't interested in subtlety, although there would have been no way to manage it in any case; I had to touch him in order to shift us away. Jack had stepped back a few feet when I flashed in, and to my surprise he made no move to grab me.

My eyes automatically scanned the rows, looking for one face in particular. I found him easily, sitting at the end of the front row of seats in the position nearest me. Mircea's stylish black suit was perfect in cut and fit, and the pale gray banded-collar shirt he wore under it was silk. Platinum cufflinks that shimmered faintly in the lamplight constituted his only jewelry. He looked as elegant and in control as always, but his aura was fluctuating wildly. It spiked when he saw me, but he made no move forward.

Behind him, many of the spectators had overturned their chairs in haste to get to their feet. The Consul stood with one hand up, some sort of signal to hold them off, I guessed. Each group's area inside MAGIC was sacrosanct, the same way an embassy on foreign soil belongs to its host government. The weres and mages had to behave themselves on vamp territory or they violated the treaties that protected them and it was open season.

I felt Sheba wake up and start licking a paw on my left shoulder blade. She was ready to rumble—too bad there was only one of her and about a thousand of them.

"Cassandra, you have returned to us." As always, the Consul appeared perfectly serene. The only movement was her outfit, which consisted of bare skin covered by a lot of writhing snakes. It was little ones this time, none longer than a finger, who slipped over her like a shimmering second skin. "We have been concerned for you."

Something suddenly rippled across me, an odd, skin-prickling sensation. It didn't hurt, but I didn't know what it was, and under the circumstances that wasn't good. I decided not to hang around and find out.

"I bet. Wish I could stay and chat, but maybe next time." I gripped Tomas' shoulder tighter and tried to shift, but nothing happened. I didn't feel the slightest surge of my power, even though it had been bright and strong just moments before.

"You cannot shift, Cassandra," the Consul said in her habitual even tones. She had a good voice, well modulated and slightly husky. A guy would have probably found it sexy; I was having a very different reaction.

Tomas moved slightly and I looked down at him. "It's a trap," he croaked weakly. "They said you would come for me. I didn't believe it—there was no reason. Why did you come back?" The anguished cry seemed to sap his strength and he collapsed into unconsciousness. I stared at the Consul, who looked calmly back, no hint of apology visible on that beautiful face.

Tomas was alive, but his wounds were bad—very bad. He was laid out on the dark wood like some bizarre form of art—something Picasso might have painted if he was in the habit of putting his nightmares on canvas. This might have been a trap, but it was obvious that, if I hadn't shown up, the Senate would have let Jack kill him. They probably planned to do so anyway, now that he'd served his purpose.

I narrowed my eyes at the Consul, but she made no response. I'd seen her kill two ancient vampires with little more than a look, when they were farther from her than I currently was. But I felt no sting of desert sand against my face, no warning rush of power. It suddenly occurred to me that, in a room full of magical creatures, I felt no magic at all.

"You used a null bomb on me, didn't you?"

The Consul smiled. It wasn't a nice expression. "You overlooked a few."

Considering everything, I didn't feel much like apologizing for taking their stuff. "Well, damn. I'll try to be more thorough next time."

"We don't have time for verbal sparring," an old mage interrupted, glaring at me. "The effect won't last much longer, and you know we can't afford to explode another—"

One of the Senate members, a brunette in hoop skirts, picked him up by the throat, choking off his voice as she hoisted him into the air. She looked inquiringly at the Consul, but the Senate leader shook her head. The damage was done. All I needed was to stall long enough for the spell to break. Then my power could get Tomas and me out of this. Unfortunately, I had no idea how long that might take.

"Look, all I want is Tomas," I told her. "You were about to kill him, so I guess you won't miss him."

My attempt to start a dialogue fell flat. "I wish this were not necessary, Cassandra," the Consul said quietly. She glanced at the vampires around her, some of the most powerful on the planet. "Take her," she said simply.

I didn't try to run. There was no point. Under other circumstances, it would almost have been funny. What did she think I was going to do that would require half a dozen first-level masters to stop? Without my power and with my ward acting up, the youngest vamp in the place could make me into dinner with no problem at all.

Then I realized that I wasn't the one she was worried about.

"Remove it!" Mircea had stopped short of the table, and although his face was impassive, his fists were clenched at his sides. Not a good sign on someone who normally controlled himself so well. The other vamps seemed to agree. They weren't looking at me—every eye was riveted on him.

"Mircea." The Consul walked up behind him and placed a smooth bronze-skinned hand on his shoulder. It looked like it was meant as a calming gesture, but he shrugged it off. The circle of vamps drew in a collective breath, and the southern belle actually gasped. The Consul's hand quickly became an arm around his throat, but it was as if he didn't even notice. "I suggest you heed him," she told me. I noticed that, despite her grip, Mircea was making slow progress forward, if only by inches. "What do you hope to gain by allowing this to continue?"

"Allowing what to continue?" I looked from her to Mircea in mounting confusion, only to see his calm facade slip a little more. I didn't need her to tell me that something was wrong. His face was as white as bone, but his eyes burned like two candles.

"This has gone on long enough," the Consul agreed. "Release him, and we will discuss matters amicably. Otherwise . . ."

"Otherwise what?" I might not understand what was happening, but I knew a threat when I heard one.

"I will let go," she said quietly. "Then we will see if you can deal with the results of your revenge. We have been doing it long enough." The dark eyes flashed, and I suddenly understood how she'd dominated an empire when only a teenager. "I need him, Cassandra! We are at war. I cannot have him like this, not now."

"Cassie . . ." Mircea had somehow managed to lift his right arm, despite the fact that a Senate member almost as old as the Consul was hanging off it. Tendrils of sensation radiated outward from his hand like smoke from a fire. At first I thought he was just leaking power, but then one wisp brushed against me and I understood. It felt like one of my old visions, the kind in which I saw flashes of the future. They had been absent since my run-in with the Pythia, and I had wondered whether they were gone for good. I'd half hoped so. They had been a part of me for as long as I could remember, but they'd never shown me anything good. This was no exception.

A fragment of vision curled around my arm despite my best attempt to dodge it. It was so hot that I expected to see a welt rise on my skin. What I got instead was worse—a mosaic of images, each more cruel than the last: a blood-covered Mircea battling for his life in a swordfight almost too fast to see; a triumphant-looking Myra running from the shadows to throw something at him; an explosion that was more felt than heard, reverberating through the ground and tearing the air; and then, where two elegant fighters had been, a sodden mass of flesh and bone gleaming slick and red in low light, so mixed up that it was impossible to tell where one body began and the other ended.

I screamed and jerked away, causing the scene to shatter. I stumbled backward, too desperate to get away from the images to worry about dignity. I stared around frantically, but most of the vamps were still fixated on Mircea. A few spared me a puzzled glance, but none looked as if they had seen anything unusual, much less the gory death of one of their senior members. But there was no doubt in my mind what I'd witnessed. Somewhere, somewhen, Myra had succeeded.

It felt like someone had dumped a bucket of ice cubes into my stomach. My visions always came true—always. I'd tried to change the outcome of things before, especially when I was younger. I'd gone to Tony numerous times to report upcoming disasters, believing him when he swore he would do everything in his power to stop them. But, of course, the only thing he'd ever done was to figure out how to profit from them. And, in the end, everything had always happened exactly as I'd foreseen. The same held true for a vision I'd seen as an adult, when I tried to warn a friend of his impending assassination. I didn't know whether he'd received the message or not, but it hadn't mattered. He still died.

But all that was before I became Pythia, or, at least, her heir. I had changed things since then, hadn't I? And, if Myra had won, why was Mircea still here?

I finally focused on the Consul. I needed answers and Mircea was in no shape to give them to me. "What is going on? Is this a trick?" Even as I said it, I knew it wasn't. I'd had enough visions to know the real thing when I felt it.

The Consul's eyes narrowed to slits. "Do you play with me?" she demanded, so quietly that I hardly heard her.

I looked down at Tomas and drew in a sharp breath. I wasn't the one playing here. "I want Tomas," I said, more unsteadily than I liked. "You obviously want something, too. Tell me what it is and maybe we can make a trade."

"You don't know." I finally saw emotion cross that lovely face. It was surprise.

Tomas made a small sound and I lost it. "Just tell me!" The vision had shattered my nerves, and I didn't feel like chatting while Tomas slowly bled out.

The Consul took a breath, which she didn't need, and nodded. "Very well. Remove the *geis* you placed on Lord Mircea, and I will give you the traitor."

I goggled at her. "What?" Somewhere along the line, I'd missed something. "The only *geis* around here is the one he put on me! It's been causing me hell."

"Hell?" Mircea laughed abruptly, but it was mirthless. "What do you know of hell?" He tore free of his living restraints and dropped to the floor. Two vamps dove under the table after him, but I never saw how close they came. All I know is, it wasn't close enough. I was suddenly crushed against a hard chest. "Try mine," he whispered before catching my lips in a bruising kiss.

The punch of his emotions came clearly through the *geis*, hitting me like a kick to the stomach. The same energy that arced between us whenever we met thrummed through Mircea, only it had grown. This was no vague frisson of passion. The craving had lain smoldering, waiting for the proper fuel, and now it ignited into a roaring blaze. It was like drowning in a river of molten lava. I felt it in his veins for an instant, pleasure as sharp as pain, before it poured into mine in a scalding wash of desire. I felt myself flounder, falling into heat, falling away from thought to a place that was all-consuming sensation. Fire. Sweet fire.

The kiss was hard and brutal, as if he would eat me alive. There was nothing gentle about it, nothing romantic. And it was just what I wanted. My hands closed convulsively on his shoulders, my nails digging into his coat. His mouth was relentless on mine, fierce and insistent, and a hard hand slid behind my head to hold me in place. One of his fangs nicked me and I tasted my own blood. He made a strangled cry and pulled back, his eyes wild, his face beautifully feral.

His tongue darted out to taste my blood on his lips; then his eyes closed and he shuddered. I ripped open his collar and his head tilted, almost blindly, towards the ceiling, giving me better access. My hands tore at his shirt, popping buttons, while my tongue and lips slid down the cords of his neck. My palms traced the contours of his chest and trailed along his ribs, reveling in the fact that his breath quickened under my touch. I kissed a path across the taut skin and hard muscle to a nipple, and when I bit down, he let out what was almost a scream. I knew how he felt—the energy between us sang in time with the throbbing of my pulse and I felt like I could combust at any moment.

Mircea pushed me against the sandstone wall of the chamber, but I was held there more by the physical impact of those fire-lit eyes than by the body pressing against mine. I looped a leg around one of his and slid a hand to the nape of his neck, molding myself to him. His hands dropped below my waist and lifted, and I gasped as his arousal pressed full against me. He was large and hard and it felt wonderful, but I wanted more. It seemed that he did, too, because he gasped my name in between savage, hard kisses, ran a hand through my hair and over my face, cursed in Romanian and generally forgot about dignity. I wasn't doing any better myself, making inarticulate demands whenever I could catch a breath.

I found myself straddling one of his legs, my thigh tight against his groin. Even through our clothes, the sensation was unbelievable: a combination of raw pleasure and yearning hunger. But then he wrenched away, abruptly putting inches between us. His expression was desperate and he looked almost ill, as if racked by the same need that tormented me. Yet, when I reached for him, uncomprehending, he flinched away as if my touch was painful.

Immediately the *geis* showed both of us what pain really was, flaring into a white-hot heat. Pain beyond imagination slammed into me, ripping from my throat scream after scream that all but shredded my vocal cords. The blood burned under my skin until I thought I would die from unfulfilled need. Hot tears fell over my cheeks onto Mircea's hands as he gripped my face, trying to calm me. But nothing helped; the pain was literally unbearable. My knees gave out when the screams stopped spearing me upward, and Mircea caught me as I sagged against him.

"Mircea! Please . . ." I didn't know what I was asking for, only that he make it stop, make it better. I closed the small distance between us and kissed him desperately. I had a few seconds to delight in the familiar warmth of his mouth and the clean scent of his flesh before he jerked back.

"Cassie, no!" It sounded tight, like he was forcing the

word out. He put both hands on my upper arms, holding me away from him, but they trembled, and the strong column of his throat worked in a silent swallow. He was fighting the *geis*, I finally realized, but I couldn't help him. His hands moved up to cradle my head, smoothing my hair. The pain and pleasure together were devastating. My body was wracked by alternating surges of agony and ecstasy, and my pulse roared so loudly in my ears that I could hardly hear.

Just when I thought I would tip over the brink into insanity, the energy flared and reformed into something completely new—a sparkling brilliance, like water under a desert sun. It broke over us like a tidal wave, and the pain was simply gone. In its place was an overwhelming sense of relief, followed by a rush of pure joy. I saw the astonishment in Mircea's eyes as it broke over him, too.

I realized abruptly that more tears were streaming down my face. It wasn't from memory of the pain, but from how good, how safe I felt being near him. It was every dream I'd ever had rolled up into one—home, family, love, acceptance—and so exhilarating that it blinded me to everything else. For an instant, I forgot about Tomas and Myra, about Tony and my whole laundry list of problems. They didn't seem to matter anymore.

I shook in dawning comprehension. I wasn't simply attracted to Mircea. Attraction didn't feel like this, didn't destroy my ability to breathe, didn't make me ache, didn't make me feel hopeless and desperate at the thought of being apart from him. I clung to him, knowing there was no way he could possibly return my feelings unless a spell compelled him, and I didn't care. It didn't matter if he loved me back. I craved him like a drug, needed him to feel alive and whole. Much more of this and I would do anything, anything at all, never to be parted from him again.

I felt an answering emotion in the tightness of his grip and finally understood. It seemed that passion was only one of the tricks in the *geis'* repertoire, and not the most devastating. Not by half.

"When did you place the spell?" the Consul demanded.

I gazed at her blankly, having forgotten she was even there. My thoughts were thick and sluggish, the very air around me heavy, and I had to fight to understand the question. I considered my options and they were sobering. "I don't know" wasn't likely to go over well, but pointing out the obvious fact that the Consul was mistaken wasn't likely to do any better. I had no idea what answer might satisfy her, or how long I needed to stall. And Mircea jabbing something into my rib cage wasn't helping.

I looked down to see that the offending object was a pale pink high heel that he must have been concealing in an inner pocket of his coat. It was oddly fragile looking, with the delicate satin material starting to flake off in places and a few darker colored sequins hanging by threads. It looked like an antique, except for the design. I didn't think they made three-inch spiked heels in the good old days.

After a minute, my brain caught up. I'd hobbled around Dante's kitchen that morning because I'd lost a shoe. It had been bright red, not shell pink, and had looked brand new, but otherwise it was the twin of this one. Luckily, Mircea's body mostly blocked me from view, because I doubt I managed to keep my face under control. The theatre. I'd lost that shoe more than a hundred years ago in a London theatre.

"Cassandra?" The Consul did not sound pleased at the delay, which was ironic considering her habit of fading out at inopportune moments. I didn't answer, remembering the spark I thought I'd imagined in that other time. The Mircea of that era had not been under the *geis*, but I had. The spell must have recognized him as the needed element to complete itself, and made the connection on its own. The implication hit me like a sledgehammer. I'd inadvertently laid a spell on him that had had more than a century to grow.

"How long?" the Consul repeated in the voice of someone not accustomed to having to say anything twice.

"I'm not sure," I finally said. My voice was hoarse, but I couldn't seem to clear my throat. "Possibly . . ." I finally managed to swallow. "It may have been the 1880s."

Someone uttered a profanity, but I didn't see who. It was as much as I could do to keep even part of my concentration on the Consul. The heat of Mircea's body and the horror at what I'd done to him were causing chaos in my emotions. Passion and guilt struggled for dominance, but fear was making a strong showing, too. My stomach contracted viciously.

The Consul did not look pleased. "The *geis* went dormant after you left, unable to complete itself without you," she mused. "And when the two of you encountered each other again, you were only a child—too young for it to manifest. But when you met as adults, it activated and its power began to build."

I managed to nod. Mircea had been caressing my hand to keep contact between us, stroking the bones in my wrist and sliding down to massage my palm with his thumb. But now he'd graduated to running his hands up and down my arm, as if craving more contact. And everywhere he touched left what felt like liquid pleasure behind. It soaked into my skin, making me as giddy as if his touch was an intoxicant, and maybe it was. I didn't know how the spell worked, only that it was far too good at what it did.

All I wanted was to stay there forever, the *geis* flowing around us like a dazzling waterfall. I knew it wasn't real, that it was just a spell that had had far too long to take hold, but it was very hard to care. When in my life would I ever feel like this again? I'd had twenty-four years of reality and never even come close. Wasn't a lie this good worth something? My body's answer was a resounding yes. Only, some tiny voice whispered, that wasn't really the question, was it? Not was it worth something, but was it worth everything, because that was what the spell demanded.

And that it couldn't have.

"The person who initiates the spell controls it," the Consul was saying. "But you left it untended for more than a century."

"Not intentionally!"

She arched a perfect eyebrow and repeated the unofficial vampire code. "We are discussing outcome, not intent." Vamps are extremely practical about such things. The results of an action are always more important than whether or not harm was intended. And the result of my action was catastrophic.

"What about the original spell—the one Mircea put on me?" I asked desperately. "If he removes it, maybe the . . . the effects will lessen." And buy us time to find a mage who could lift the duplicate.

"That has already been tried, Cassandra," the Consul informed me patiently. "The spell is proving remarkably . . . resilient."

"It won't break?" I tried to wrap my mind around that, but Mircea was making deep thought impossible. I tried to step out of his embrace, just long enough to clear my head, but he gave an inarticulate sound of protest and pulled me closer.

"It will not," the Consul said mildly.

I gave her a look meant to scald, uncaring for the moment how stupid that was. If she wanted to help Mircea, she was doing a lousy job of it. According to Casanova, the spell would grow faster with Mircea and me in close proximity, and we couldn't get much closer than we currently were. Soon, neither of us would care about anything else. And that meant there would be no one to stop Myra. I was beginning to see how my vision could easily come true.

For a moment, I contemplated trying to explain the situation to the Consul, but I doubted she'd believe me. I had zero proof to offer, and vamps aren't exactly known for taking things on faith. I moved slightly so that I was momentarily hidden from her sharp gaze and met Mircea's eyes. He'd thought to bring the shoe, which meant that, at some point, he must have figured out what had happened. I just hoped he remained lucid enough to understand what I needed to tell him.

"Myra," I mouthed. The mages were out of earshot, and with no magic they couldn't use enhanced hearing. But the vamps would hear any conversation just fine.

Mircea gazed at me for a long moment, and I could almost see him putting the pieces together. How much he understood I didn't know, but he'd been with me when Myra and I first met. He knew she'd tried to kill me and that she'd gotten away. And he'd heard me call her by name in London, assuming he remembered so minor a detail after so long. I frankly doubted it. He would probably guess that she was up to the same tricks, but not that he was her new target. And I had no way to tell him.

Not that there was much he could do even if he did know. Mircea might be able to defend himself in the present if forewarned, but Myra could attack him in the past. The fact that he was still here was proof she hadn't yet succeeded, but if I didn't remain sane enough to stop her, that wouldn't be true for long. History would rewrite itself, without Mircea in it. And with Myra as Pythia.

After what felt like a year, Mircea gave a slight nod. "Two minutes," he said silently. I stared at him in confusion until I figured out what he meant. He was telling me when the null bomb would wear off.

He was going to let me go.

I gazed at him in disbelief. "What about you?" I mouthed. He shook his head. I didn't know whether that meant he couldn't tell me with such limited communication or whether he didn't want me to know. I realized I was gripping his arms hard enough to bruise, had he been human. But it was only when I let go that a spasm of pain crossed his face. I felt an echo of it myself, a physical ache from the lessened contact, and had to force myself not to reestablish it.

"You must go," he said silently.

I swallowed. The second *geis* was new to me, but it had had a century to take hold of Mircea. If I felt like this, and the spell had had only a day to get its claws into me, what was he experiencing? Even if the Consul was right, and it had toned down after I returned to my own time, it had still been there, slowly maturing over decades. And judging by his reaction, when it woke up, it had done so with a vengeance.

The thought of deliberately putting him back in that hell was excruciating, but what other choice was there? I had to deal with Myra or we were both dead, and I couldn't take him with me and risk continued exposure. I looked up at him, letting my remorse show on my face. "I know."

He closed his eyes and his arms clenched around me for a long moment. I pulled him to me, kissed him and immediately the pain receded. The *geis* was satisfied as long as we were in close contact, and I knew why. I could almost feel the bond between us strengthening, the energy humming happily everywhere we touched. It was contented now, but what would happen when I left? I'd felt the agony he was in when I arrived and doubted this brief meeting would relieve the craving for long. In fact, it might make it worse, like offering a starving man a single bite of bread.

Mircea slowly opened his arms and pulled back. I had been expecting it, but the pain still almost drove me to my knees. I somehow kept my feet, but only half stifled an agonized noise. Wild shudders of shock radiated from my center, shaking me violently, and my hands went ice-cold. I hunched my shoulders against the blaze of longing that shook me, and wrapped my arms around myself to keep them from dragging him against me.

Casanova had made it sound like the bond was a slow progression, growing in stages over a long period of time. But ours wasn't acting that way. Maybe because it wasn't exactly new, at least on one side, or maybe because it had accidentally been doubled. All I knew was, it was vicious.

Mircea was standing close enough to give the impression that he was still holding me. The pain had cleared my head like smelling salts, allowing me to understand why. Although he might be willing to release me, the Consul most certainly was not. I'd refused to become her puppet, had stolen valuable merchandise from her and had placed her chief negotiator under a dangerous spell. The fact that the latter, at least, had been inadvertent was irrelevant from her perspective. I wondered what she had planned for me if her mages couldn't break the spell. Based on Mircea's action, I could make a good guess. Few spells outlive the demise of the caster. And if I wasn't going to be her pet Pythia, she had no vested interest in keeping me alive.

I met Mircea's gaze. "I'll find a way to break this," I told him. I didn't bother to whisper this time. "I promise."

He smiled slightly, but his eyes were infinitely sad. "I am sorry, *dulceață.*"

The Consul said something, but I didn't hear her. One minute, the chamber was quiet enough to hear a pin drop; the next, a howling arctic wind had filled the room, whipping my hair in stinging strands against my face. It paused for an instant, gathering strength near the high ceiling of the chamber, before exploding into the worst ice storm I've ever seen.

The slashing, brutal winds ignored me and a small space around me, and for a minute I thought my ward had finally decided to wake up, but there was no flood of golden light, no distinctive pentagram shape. Something else was protecting me, and for the moment I didn't care what—just so long as it kept it up. Everywhere outside that small island of calm, chaos raged.

Mircea stepped away and I gasped in pain as the *geis* realized that something had gone wrong. I would have grabbed him again, despite the consequences, but I couldn't see him in the swirling white void. "Mircea!" I screamed, but my voice was lost in the deafening winds.

Not knowing what else to do, I leapt forward and threw myself over Tomas. Thankfully, the clear spot went with me. It didn't cover him entirely, and his wounds were too extreme for me to stretch out on top of him, but frostbite on his lower legs was the least of my worries.

I fumbled for his restraints, but I couldn't see them, couldn't see anything next to the violent, thrashing world of white. Then something bounced on the table right beside me and I understood what the odd, thumping noise raining down all around us was. The wind carried hailstones the size of bowling balls, and since they were trapped between the four walls of the Senate chamber, they had nowhere to spend their fury except to ricochet off every available surface. It was like being caught in Hell's pinball game. If I didn't get Tomas loose soon, they'd crush his feet, and no way could I drag him anywhere.

I had to get us out of there and I had to find Myra, although how I was supposed to deal with her in my current state I had no idea. All I wanted was to curl into a little ball and wait for Mircea to find me—and if I stayed, I knew he would. Whatever strength had allowed him to pull away, the *geis* was stronger. It wouldn't be long now.

Something hit Tomas' right leg, jarring his whole body. I stretched but couldn't reach far enough to shield his lower limbs without leaving his head unprotected, and I couldn't pull his legs up because they were strapped down. I tried to shift, but although I felt something this time, like a slight tug, I still couldn't go anywhere. *Hurry up*, I thought desperately.

I finally figured out the release on Tomas' hand restraints and had just clicked them open when the room suddenly became a lot more crowded. A tattoo parlor was sitting in the middle of it, so close to the main table that it was almost on top of us. Mac's face, half obscured by snow even though it was only a few yards away, appeared in the main window under the flashing MAG INK sign. A second later, an arm covered in wriggling designs reached out the front door and grabbed Tomas by the leg, clicking off the right ankle restraint with practiced ease.

As soon as Mac hauled Tomas in the door, I scrambled across the table after them. The shop had landed on the impressive row of steps leading up to the dais on which the table sat, and was therefore tilted towards me. If I made it another few feet, my momentum should do the rest.

I had just managed to clasp the hand Pritkin held out when someone grabbed my ankle. My ward—damn it—didn't flare, but Sheba suddenly got busy. She had ignored Mircea, either because of the null effect or because she didn't view him as a threat. But whoever had grabbed me was another matter. I felt her flow down my body, then there was the sound of a snarling great cat and a surprised yelp from a dignified Senate leader. Sheba launched herself off my foot, and a second later the Consul let go of my leg.

"Come on!" Pritkin gave a heave and I almost flew the rest of the way across the slick tabletop. We tumbled in the door of the shop and suddenly I could see again. Neither Mac nor Tomas was in the front, but I didn't have time to worry about it. At Pritkin's yell of "We're clear!" the whole building started to shake.

The next minute we were barreling through pure stone, on a crazy zigzag course into the middle of MAGIC's foundations. We were making pretty good time, it seemed to me, although I was so busy holding on to Pritkin, who had a death grip on the counter, that it was hard to tell. I did see a dark blur, however, coming down the newly carved tunnel, and the next minute Kit Marlowe tumbled into the wildly lurching room.

He looked grim and determined, and there was an air of

danger about him that I didn't remember from our brief childhood meeting. Of course, that night he'd been enjoying Tony's best hospitality, not bleeding from half a dozen wounds. "Oh, bugger it!" I heard Pritkin mutter. He pulled me off his back, pressed my hands around the edges of the desk and yelled, "Hold on," loudly enough to threaten to rupture my eardrum. Then he let go and went flying across the room at Marlowe.

They grappled, but without magic it was down to old-fashioned dirty fighting and pure muscle, and they seemed about evenly matched. Marlowe was yelling something at me, but I couldn't hear him over the racket our tunneling efforts were making. And I was too consumed by the waves of pain coursing through me from the *geis* to care.

The farther I got from Mircea, the worse they became, to the point that I was barely aware of what was happening. Tears blinded me, spasms clenched my stomach and it was becoming increasingly hard to breathe. I remembered Casanova saying that people under the *geis* had committed suicide rather than endure the pain of separation and I finally understood why.

Marlowe got Pritkin in a headlock and the two stumbled into the desk, almost causing me to lose my already tenuous grip. Then Pritkin stabbed a knife into the vamp's chest and they broke apart. But the mage, looking dazed from the loss of air, didn't follow up his advantage and for some reason neither did Marlowe. He was grimly pulling out the knife when, with no warning, the shop shuddered to a halt.

My knees knocked painfully against the side of the desk and I barely kept from sailing over it. But I couldn't have cared less. The *geis* was suddenly gone, cut off like a stereo when someone turns a switch. I gasped for air and found that

I could breathe deeply again. My head swam with the influx of oxygen and with relief. But almost immediately I noticed another sensation: hunger.

It was only in the magnitude of its absence that I could tell the true strength of the bond. I wanted to laugh and cry at the same time. Relief from the pain had also brought an end to the addictive, all-consuming pleasure. And the craving started immediately.

I staggered around the desk, feeling strangely hollow and empty inside. Then I looked out the front window and did a stunned double take. What I saw was enough to take my mind off even the *geis*. In front of us wasn't another sandstone corridor or even an empty stretch of desert. Instead, I saw a large meadow filled with long grasses that bent to the left in a gentle breeze. By the sun's height I guessed it was midday, although the diffused light made it hard to tell for sure. In the distance lay a ridge of sharp blue mountains capped with snow, but the breeze that swept in through the shop's front door was warm and smelled faintly of wildflowers. It was beautiful.

Mac stuck his head out from behind the curtain warily, then gave a whoop of pure joy. "All right! And they said it couldn't be done! Bloody hell!" I noticed that his wards had stopped moving, frozen in place like normal tattoos, and light dawned. Mac, that crazy son of a bitch, had driven the tattoo parlor straight through the portal and into Faerie itself.

Chapter 10

I left Mac and Pritkin to deal with Marlowe and ran into the back. Tomas was strapped down on the padded table Mac used for doing tattoos. He didn't look comfortable, but at least he hadn't been thrown around the room. I hadn't had a chance to do more than glance at his wounds before, but now I tightened my lips to avoid saying something extremely rude about Jack. Then I decided to hell with it and said it anyway.

Tomas groaned and tried to sit up, but the straps wouldn't let him. That was just as well, since something would have probably fallen out otherwise. Jack had split him open from nipples to navel, like an autopsy specimen or an animal he was about to gut. I stared at the wreck of what had once been a perfect body and grew cold. I really wished Augusta had finished him.

I swallowed and looked away, partly because I had to or risk being sick, and partly because I needed to locate something to use as a bandage. Vampires had amazing recuperative powers—horrific as his wounds were, Tomas could probably heal them in time. But it would help a lot if the edges of the wound were somehow held together, and for that I needed fabric—a lot of it. I started for the cot, which had a fitted sheet and blanket that might work, when I tripped over something. I landed on my knees next to a dark-haired man wearing a bright red shirt. I stared at him in surprise—how had we picked up another stowaway without my noticing? Then he turned his head and I realized that he'd been there all along, just not quite in this form.

"I gotta tell ya," Billy said, sitting up and grabbing his head with both hands, "I haven't felt this bad since I got into that drinking contest with those two Russian bastards." He groaned and lay back down.

I cautiously reached over and poked him with a finger. He was as solid as I was. I lifted his wrist and felt for a pulse. It beat strong and firm under my fingers. I dropped his hand and scrambled back a couple of feet, only to encounter another impossible thing. I felt something solid against my back and looked down to see an orange-brown hand lying on the floor. It was connected to a similarly colored arm, which led to the naked torso of what my brain finally identified as Pritkin's golem. Only, despite the color, he wasn't clay any longer.

I didn't need to check for a pulse—he was obviously breathing, his oddly colored but otherwise perfect chest rising and falling normally. Or what would have been normal for a human. Since he was supposed to be a big pile of clay animated by magic, it wasn't normal for him. A glance that I swear was involuntary informed me that he was also anatomically correct, which he certainly hadn't been before, and that whoever had handled the changeover had been generous. The next second his eyes—real ones this time—flew open to regard me with utter confusion. They were brown, I noticed irrelevantly, and he didn't have any eyebrows or eye-lashes. In fact, he didn't appear to have any hair at all.

I looked back at Billy. He was pale and needed the shave he'd been putting off for a century and a half, but otherwise seemed fine. He quite simply had his body back, which was ridiculous because it had gone for fish food ages ago.

"What the hell?" I felt the floor move and looked around wildly. I did not need another of Mac's crazy rides. Only we didn't, I realized after a minute, appear to be going any-where. The room was definitely shaking, though, and I spared a second to wonder whether Faerie had earthquakes when Billy sat up, wild-eyed and panic-stricken. He felt his chest, then let out a scream and began thumping himself in the head, stomach and legs, as if his body was some unfa-miliar and horrifying bug that had crawled onto him.

He jumped up and started dancing around the room, shedding clothes and screeching. His antics and the room's gyrations upset the golem, which had left behind confusion for fear. His eyes widened and his lips opened to emit a high-pitched squeal that was a lot harder on the ears than Billy's screams. I stumbled across the room, avoiding both of them, and grabbed the sheet. After tearing it into strips, I bound up Tomas' wounds as best I could while the golem and Billy ran around, bumping into things and each other, and managing only to work themselves up more.

I freed Tomas before one of them could careen into him and dragged him under the table. I crawled in after him and put my hands over my ears, which felt like they'd start to bleed any second. Let somebody else deal with the crisis for a change—I was through.

It became obvious that abdication wasn't an option when half the roof was abruptly ripped off. For a second, only a patch of blue sky and a couple of yellow butterflies showed through, giving the impression that the tiny insects were responsible for the damage. Then a head the size of a small car poked in. It was green and covered in shiny, iridescent scales, with a snout big enough to eat a person without needing a second bite. No smoke came out of its nostrils, but I didn't need that to know what it was. Its orange eyes had narrow red pupils that dilated on sight of me like a cat that had just encountered a new form of mouse.

It poured through the hole in the roof, its head suspended on an impossibly long neck and its huge jaws cracking to show off jagged, dark yellow teeth. I froze with its warm, acrid breath in my face, so close that it made my eyes start to water. Then the golem really lost it, running naked and screeching directly across the dragon's line of sight, causing the orange eyes to focus on him instead. He plunged through the curtain and the dragon followed, its neck flowing past me in a river of scales, its talons trying to rip a large enough hole in the roof for its huge body.

I scrambled out from under the table and tackled Billy Joe, who had torn his shirt off and was clawing at his bare chest, leaving red welts behind. "Billy!" I grabbed for his wrist, intending to drag him under the table with me, but he was too fast. He ran to the back of the room, to the small door beside the cot that I had never seen opened. I didn't see it now. I had the feeling that it was solely ornamental, but Billy didn't get that. He beat on it and tore at the doorknob, which he finally managed to rip completely off.

I stared at him in confusion. I'd never seen him like this and wasn't sure there was anything I could say that would calm him down. Then there was the fact that, in human form, Billy stood almost six feet tall. No way could I subdue him without a weapon, and the only ones I had—my gun and bracelet—would likely kill him in his new form.

There was a lot of keening, swearing and some explosions from the front of the shop, then there was a rushing wind and a sound like a hundred helicopters starting up. I looked up to see the dragon lift itself into the air on black leathery wings, screeching and clawing at its face. Half its snout was missing, lost in a smoking hole, and there were gashes in the great wings that beat the air with the force of a small hurricane. A second later the creature was gone, soaring high over peaceful green fields toward distant, tree-covered hills.

Billy slumped against the door, his hands on the scarred wood, his fingers a bloody mess. He was sobbing in great, wracking heaves, but at least he was no longer manic. I was about to try to talk some sense into him, when Pritkin ran through the curtain, followed by Mac and Marlowe. The vamp wasn't, I noticed with rising anger, under any kind of restraint. And the first thing he did was head for Tomas.

"Pritkin! Stop him!" I crossed the room at a run, while the mage merely stood there, looking in disbelief at Billy's solid form. I dove under the table from the far side and grabbed Marlowe's wrist before he could drag Tomas into the light. "Get away from him!"

He looked surprised, as well he might. Why any human would think she could stop a master vampire from doing anything he wanted by holding his hand was laughable. I threw myself backwards, raising my wrist with the bracelet on it and hoping it would be enough to do the trick. I never found out, since nothing happened. I shook my arm and glared at the inert silver. What was wrong with it now?

"Our magic won't work here," Marlowe told me gently.

"I'm not going to hurt Tomas, Cassie. Believe it or not, I want to help."

Sure, which was why he'd sat by and watched him be butchered. Marlowe had a reputation that had started in Elizabethan England, when he'd been one of the queen's spies, and it had increased in infamy ever since. If even a fraction of the stories whispered about him were true, I didn't want him anywhere near Tomas. "Get away," I repeated, wondering what I would do if he said no. But instead of arguing, he slid gracefully out from under the table. I checked on Tomas' wounds, but they didn't seem to be any worse. His eyes were open a fraction and he even managed to raise his head.

"I can't hear him," he said obscurely, an expression of pure bliss passing over his face. Then his eyes closed and his head fell back, connecting sharply with the tile floor.

My heart almost stopped and I frantically felt for a pulse, which of course I didn't find. The fact that I'd even tried said something about my mental state. It looked like he'd fainted or was in a trance, but I couldn't be sure. Tony had once been involved in a clandestine and highly illegal feud with another master. One of our vamps lost an arm and was halfway gutted in the miniwar. When he was brought back to us I'd assumed he was dead, but Eugenie said he was in a healing trance. He'd stayed unmoving and immobile for several weeks, until one night he suddenly sat up, asking whether we'd won. I hoped Tomas was only in a trance, but there was little I could do for him either way. Vamps healed themselves or they didn't—there weren't a lot of medical or magical remedies that worked on their systems. The problem was to keep him safe long enough for him to have a chance to recover.

I glanced at Pritkin. "Why isn't Marlowe tied up or something?"

"Because we may need him," was the grim reply.

"Do you know who he is?" I demanded.

"Better than you." He tore his eyes away from Billy, who was now rocking back and forth, staring sightlessly at the wall, and turned the full force of his stare on me. He wasn't angry—that, at least, I'd almost come to expect, and it wouldn't have worried me. But this was different. He was pared down somehow, his eyes so intense that they looked like two lasers. It was the face of a predator when its own life is threatened—deadly, serious and completely focused.

"Let me explain the situation," he said, and even his words were faster and more clipped than before, as if every second counted. "We have arrived in Faerie, but not in the unobtrusive way I had planned. Most of our magic will not work, and we have a finite amount of nonmagical weapons. One of our company is gravely ill and two others are mentally suspect. To make matters worse, that dragon was the guardian of the portal, and having failed to defeat us itself, it has gone after reinforcements. If the Fey do not already know we're here, they soon will. And we cannot go back though the portal for obvious reasons."

"Will the Senate come after us?" I asked, uncertain that I wanted an answer.

Pritkin gave a short bark of a laugh. It didn't sound amused. "Oh, no, at least not until they can appeal for passes. To cross into Faerie without them is to risk a death sentence. As we have done."

"He means that we're all in this together," Marlowe added. "I, too, am without a pass, and the Fey are famous for not listening to excuses. If I'm caught, I could be killed." He smiled at me. "So I won't be caught, and shall endeavor to see you are not, either."

Mac snorted. "The fact is, we're all safer together. Nobody would last a day in Faerie alone right now."

Marlowe shrugged. "That, too. And, as my first comradely gesture, may I suggest that we leave this area as soon as may be? We have very little time to lose."

Pritkin had pulled Billy up by the wrists and now he slapped him, hard. "He's right. If the Fey find us, they will either kill us on sight or ransom us back to the Circle or Senate." After the second slap, Billy tried to hit him back, but Pritkin blocked his arm, then twisted it cruelly behind his back before pushing him at me. "Gain control of your servant," he said briefly. "I will deal with mine. Then we move."

I spent the next few minutes getting my ward checked out by Mac while I tried to reassure a very freaked-out Billy Joe. "Why are you so upset?" I asked, when he had calmed down enough to listen. "You have a body," I pinched him lightly on the arm and he flinched, the big baby. "Isn't that what you always wanted?" He certainly seemed to have a good time whenever he was borrowing mine.

Billy still looked stunned, although some color had started to return to his cheeks. Without warning, he leaned over and kissed me hard on the lips. I jerked away and slapped him, and shock made it harder than I'd intended, but he just laughed. His hazel eyes were bright with unshed tears as he gingerly felt his stinging cheek, but his expression was euphoric. "It's true; it's really true," he said in awe; then his eyes grew wide and he abruptly started rooting through Mac's backpack. He came out with one of the beers, clutching it like he'd found a treasure made of pure gold. It was unopened, and he scrabbled at it, trying to get the bottle cap off with his bare hands.

"You don't get it, Cass," he said, his eyes almost feverish. "Sure, I babysit your body from time to time, but nothing's really real, you know? Like there's a film over everything, and I only ever touch that, taste that." He gave a yell of frustration and tried to smash the bottle on the table, but it was padded and the glass bounced off.

Obviously, he was not going to be coherent until he'd had a drink. "Give that to me," I said impatiently, and he handed it over, but his eyes never left the dark brown bottle. I opened it on the metal underside of the cot and he snatched it out of my hand, gulping half the contents at one time.

"Oh, my God," he said reverently, falling to his knees. "Oh Jaysus."

I was about to tell him to stop the melodrama when Mac interrupted with a report. "There's nothing wrong with your ward, so it must be the *geis*. They tend to complicate things, with the more powerful spells causing the most interference. And the *dúthracht* is about the strongest there is."

"But my ward worked before, and the spell was cast when I was eleven," I protested.

"That could have been why you got away with it, because you were too young for the *geis* to be active. This particular ward is designed to fit over your aura like a glove does a hand, but it needs a stable field to keep a proper grip. An active *geis* is interpreted as a serious threat, and your natural defenses go into constant turmoil, trying to reject the invader. But, by doing so, they make it impossible for your artificial protection to do its job."

Light dawned. "That's why Pritkin was freaking out at

Miranda. He knew if she didn't remove the *geis*, he couldn't get that tattoo."

I was immediately sorry I'd said anything, since Mac demanded the whole story and seemed to find the idea of a small, female gargoyle getting the best of Pritkin hysterically funny. I finally managed to get him back on track, but he didn't tell me anything I wanted to hear. "It's like trying to put a glove on a small, squirming child, Cassie—which is why kids usually get mittens. It's too damn much trouble to get them dressed otherwise." Mac sounded like he knew, and I briefly wondered whether he had a family. Possibly there were people who would mourn him if Pritkin got him killed.

"So you can't fix it?"

"I'm sorry, Cassie. Get rid of the *geis*, and I can have it running in no time. Otherwise—"

"I'm screwed."

"It looks that way."

As if in comment on the way my day was going, Billy took that moment to throw up beer all over the floor in front of my sneakers. I snatched my feet back just in time. "Billy! What is the matter with you?"

He groaned and sat up. "Stomach cramps," he gasped. I sighed and went to get him a glass of water.

"Sip it," I warned. "You have a brand-new stomach. Nobody gives babies beer, so I guess you don't get any, either." I took the bottle away, and he groaned louder.

"Have a heart, Cass!"

I held the bottle up and shook it, letting the amber liquid slosh against the sides. "Get off your backside and help me with Tomas and maybe I'll give it to you."

"There's a pub in the town where we're headed," Marlowe said mildly.

"How do you know where we're going?" I asked suspiciously.

"Because we aren't spoiled for choice." Billy was regarding the vamp as if he'd just announced that he'd won the lottery. "Beer, pretty girls—of a sort—and excellent music, as I recall."

Billy jumped up as if propelled out of a canon. "Where's that poor unfortunate, then? We should get the lad somewhere safe so he can rest and heal," he added piously.

"What town?" I asked Marlowe.

"The local village and castle are populated by Dark Fey, a few of whom have done favors for my spies in the past. That has primarily taken the form of intelligence gathering—they spy on the Light Fey and my contacts among the Light spy on them. But occasionally they have helped out agents in distress—for a fee, of course."

"You spy on the Fey?" I asked in surprise.

Marlowe smiled. "I spy on everyone. It's my job."

"Discuss this later," Pritkin said, poking his head in through the curtain. The golem stood next to him calmly enough, but it flinched when the curtain brushed against its arm. "If the Dark Fey find us before we come to an understanding—"

"Point taken," Marlowe murmured. Together, he and Billy got Tomas out from under the table and into a makeshift sling made out of the cot blanket. I didn't believe Marlowe when he swore the Fey sun didn't harm vampires, but Mac backed him up. Since Tomas didn't burst into flames when the beams leaking through the ruined roof fell on him, I had to assume they were right.

Billy took one end of the sling and Marlowe picked up the other. His cooperation made me apprehensive enough to walk alongside the bearers to ensure that he didn't harm Tomas when no one was looking. I'd have preferred another helper, but there weren't a lot of options. I doubted I could carry even half of Tomas' weight for any distance, especially not weighed down by fifty pounds of ammunition. Mac was bringing up the rear and his hands needed to be free for weapons. And Pritkin, at the head of our motley group, had his hands full keeping his servant from freaking out again.

The poor golem was shaking and looking about wild-eyed, jumping at every breath of wind, chirping bird or Billy singing "I'm a rover and seldom sober," until Pritkin threatened to make him a ghost again if he didn't stop. It was like the golem had never seen any of it before—which I guess he hadn't, at least not through human eyes—and wasn't sure what was benign and what was a threat. I don't know what they rely on for senses, but based on his scream when a cloud of airborne dandelions brushed against his bare chest, I don't think it's the same five we humans use.

We finally made it to the tree line, but even I could follow the path of trampled grass in our wake. Anyone with tracking experience wouldn't even break a sweat following us. I stared at the dark woods ahead and hoped someone had a plan.

The next hour was a nightmare, slogging through a forest that, while amazing, was also intensely creepy. For one thing, it made the centuries-old trees that had surrounded Tony's farmhouse look like saplings. We passed two giant oaks going in, each of which had a trunk large enough to have driven a car through had they been hollow. Of course, that would have required building a ramp first, because the trunks started well above my head, resting on a massive root system taller than most houses. They were positioned like sentries at a castle's gate, their mossy arms raised as if in salute—or warning.

The tangled tree roots all seemed to stop at the same point, forming a rough path towards who knew what. Something brushed my shoulder as we pushed our way into the sea of brambles and tangled underbrush. For an instant I thought I saw a gnarled hand with bulbous knuckles and unnaturally long fingers reaching for me. I jumped before realizing it was nothing more threatening than a low-hanging branch, the moss on it damp and clammy against my skin.

Even worse was the way the place smelled. The meadow had been warm and fresh and flowery, but there was no pleasant green scent here. The forest was dank and mildewed, but below that was something worse—sour and faintly rotten. I thought about it as we plodded along, and it finally hit me. It was like being in the presence of a terminally ill person. No matter how good the hygiene, there is always a faint odor clinging to them that doesn't smell like anything else. The forest reeked of death—not the quick, red-clawed end of a hunted animal, but the long, lingering sickness of someone death has stalked for a very long time. I vastly preferred the meadow.

I pressed closer to Tomas, who was thankfully still oblivious, and tried not to look as spooked as I felt. But there was something unnatural about these woods. It was in the murky light that made it instantly twilight, and in the age, which pressed down like gravity had somehow increased as soon as we left the field. I couldn't even begin to guess how old some of the trees were, but every time I thought they couldn't get any bigger, they managed. And my tired brain kept seeing faces in patterns in the bark—old, craggy ones with mushroom hair, lichen beards and shadowy eyes.

Marlowe tried several times to start a conversation, but I ignored him until he gave up. I had other things to think about, like how I was going to find Myra and what I was going to do with her when I did. Now that I was here, I understood why she'd chosen to hide in Faerie. It was an entirely new playing field, and one I knew nothing about. Getting close enough to spring the trap was going to be difficult if my power was unreliable, and I had no idea how many allies she had. After seeing what happened to Mac's wards, I wasn't as confident about the Senate's weapons as I had been. What if they didn't work in this crazy new world?

My mood wasn't improved by more mundane considerations, like how heavy the damned coat was getting, how much I could really use a bath, and how badly I wanted to see Mircea. The craving hadn't diminished, and although it was bearable, it wasn't fun. I felt like a three-pack-a-day smoker at the end of a twelve-hour flight. Only, for me, there was no relief in sight.

We finally stopped for a breather. Wind rustled the treetops, but down at ground level, there wasn't so much as a breath of air. Billy, who had been bitching about Tomas' weight the whole way, swore we'd been walking for a day, but it had probably been only an hour or so. I stripped off the lead-lined torture device Pritkin had stuck me with, and it helped a little, but no breeze hit my soaked clothes.

I was bent over, panting and exhausted, sweat running off my face to drip onto the leaf-strewn forest floor, when I saw it: my first proof that this really was an enchanted forest. A tree root, covered in bright red lichen like a scaly arm, reached up from the path to position itself on the ground under my nose. I shied back, giving a surprised yelp, then watched as it sucked dry every leaf that held any of my sweat.

"W-What is that?" I pulled back a leg as the root came closer, rummaging through the leaves like a pig after acorns. It couldn't see me, but it knew I was there.

"A spy." Marlowe's resigned tones came from above my head. "I knew we couldn't avoid them, but I was hoping for a bit longer than this."

"A spy for whom?"

"The Dark Fey," Pritkin answered, coming alongside. "This is their forest."

"Very likely," Marlowe concurred. "But I should reach our allies before—"

"You aren't going," Pritkin interrupted. "Give me a token and I'll do it."

"Go where?" I asked, but no one was listening.

"They don't know you," Marlowe protested. "Even with an introduction from me, you could be in danger."

Pritkin smiled sourly. "I'll take the risk."

Mac cleared his throat. "It might be best if I go," he offered. "You've got enough trouble keeping that one in line"—he nodded at the golem, who was running his hands over the trunk of a nearby tree, an expression of wonder on his features—"and it doesn't know me. If something sets it off again, I can't guarantee I can control it."

"It's coming with me."

"It won't be much good in a fight right now," Mac said doubtfully.

"It isn't going to be fighting." Pritkin glanced at me. "I suppose you want to stay here and tend him?" He didn't name Tomas, but we both knew whom he meant. I looked at Marlowe before replying. He was adjusting the bandages around his curls as if they pained him, and grinned when he caught my eye.

"The storm didn't do my head any good," he explained, wincing slightly as his hand brushed a tender spot. "First Rasputin cracks my skull, and now this. You would think someone could aim for another part of my anatomy just once, but oh, no."

I didn't smile back. Marlowe might really be in pain, or he might be trying to convince me how weak he was. If the latter, he was wasting his time. I'd seen enough injured vamps to know: if they were conscious and moving, they were deadly. There wasn't much I could do for Tomas, but at least I'd make sure Marlowe didn't cut off his head. I looked back at Pritkin and nodded.

"Then I'll need to borrow your servant."

Billy had collapsed into a sweaty heap as soon as we stopped and was now tugging on one of his black boots and swearing. I guess he had tender baby feet to go along with the new stomach. "You sure? He's not much of a fighter."

"He's only there in case something goes wrong. To run back and warn you."

"He should be able to handle that." I nudged Billy. "You're up." He bitched, of course, but eventually beer won out over blisters and he agreed to go.

Marlowe scribbled a brief note on a piece of paper that Mac had located among our supplies. It seemed somehow wrong to be using lined notebook paper and a ballpoint to write an introduction to the Fey, but no one else seemed to notice. "I'm not sure my contacts are still there," Marlowe said, handing over the finished note. "Time doesn't flow the same way here. My spies have sometimes entered months apart to find that they arrived on the same day, or on other occasions that decades had passed. We've never been able to determine a pattern."

"I'll manage," Pritkin said, rummaging through my discarded coat for ammunition. He fished out three large boxes. I didn't ask what he thought he'd need that many bullets for. I didn't want to know.

He had exchanged his leather trench for a dark cape with a hood from Mac's pack and, after a brief struggle, managed to get the golem to accept being put into his coat. It wasn't a great disguise, considering that the golem was still orange, bald, seven feet tall and barefoot, but it beat the alternative. "Shouldn't he stay here?" I asked doubtfully.

Pritkin didn't answer me, but Marlowe smiled slightly. "If the mage does not bring a gift, he will never gain an audience. Fey protocol."

"A gift?" It took a few seconds to sink in. "You mean—but that's slavery!"

"He isn't actually alive, Cassie," Mac protested.

I looked at the childlike being blinking slowly at Pritkin as he was buttoned into the long coat. He seemed to find the buttons fascinating, and kept poking at them with an orange, but otherwise very human-looking, finger. "He looks alive to me," I said.

"I'll retrieve him later—he's merely to get me in!" Pritkin said crossly. "Or would you prefer to offer *your* servant instead?"

Billy gave me a panicked look and I sighed. "Of course not."

"Then refrain from giving advice about matters you don't

understand," I was told curtly before the trio disappeared into the foliage.

Over the next few hours, a number of things conspired to rub my remaining nerves raw. One of the most annoying was the roving roots that followed me around like nearsighted puppies. I was bone weary but could I sit down for five minutes? Hell, no. I had to play keep-away with the local flora while being stared at by the fauna.

A short time after Pritkin left, it seemed like every bird in the forest—ospreys, eagles, owls and even a few vultures—had congregated in the trees around us, along with some small mammals. They made no noise except for a fluttering of wings as the early arrivals shuffled around to make room for newcomers. After a few minutes their collective weight began to bow some of the smaller limbs they were using as perches, but none collapsed. They looked eerily like spectators assembling for some type of entertainment. Since we weren't doing anything interesting, I assumed the show started later, a thought that didn't improve my mood.

Neither did the tension of being able to do nothing for Tomas, who lay unmoving on his blanket. Not only could I not help him heal—if, in fact, that's what he was doing—I couldn't get near him for fear of bringing my bark-covered fans along. They absorbed sweat—who knew what else they ate?

The most irritating factor of all, though, had to be Marlowe's suddenly renewed interest in conversation. He waited until Pritkin was out of hearing range, then turned to me smiling cheerfully. "Let's chat, Cassie. I am certain I can put your fears to rest."

I hopped over a root trying to curl around my ankle. "Why do I doubt that?"

"Because you've never had a chance to hear our side of things," he said, giving me a warm, understanding smile that immediately raised my hackles. "We would have had this conversation before, but when you came back from your mission with Mircea you failed to give us the opportunity."

"I tend not to open dialogues with people who threaten to kill me."

Marlowe looked surprised. "I can't imagine what you mean. I certainly don't want you dead, and neither does anyone else on the Senate. Quite the opposite, in fact."

"Did you tell Agnes the same thing?"

Marlowe's brows knitted together into a small frown. "I'm not certain I understand you."

I brought out the small charm Pritkin had given me. He'd never asked for it back, so I'd stuffed it into a pocket. Now I let it swing in front of Marlowe's eyes like a pendulum. "Recognize this?"

He took it and gave it a once-over. "Of course."

I stared at him. It wouldn't be a shock if Marlowe had been the one to mastermind the assassination—it fit his reputation—but I hadn't expected him to just admit it. Did he think I'd be pleased that he removed Agnes and cleared my way to succeed?

"It's a Saint Sebastian medallion." He took it from my limp fingers. Mac had closed in, but he wasn't saying anything. Maybe he also thought we were about to hear a confession. If so, he was disappointed. "I haven't seen one of these in years. Of course, there's been no need for them."

"What need?" Mac had a look on his face that reminded me of Pritkin at his most suspicious.

"The plague, mage," Marlowe said impatiently. "Sebastian was the saint believed to be able to ward off disease.

These were still popular on the Continent in my day, although most were made in the fourteenth century, during the Black Death."

I leaned in for a closer look. "So this is what, a good-luck charm?"

Marlowe smiled. "Something like that. People wanted to believe they were doing something to protect themselves and their families."

"Kind of ironic," I said. Mac nodded, but Marlowe looked confused. "This was used to kill someone recently," I explained.

Marlowe's brows rose. It was the first expression I'd seen him wear that didn't appear contrived. "The Pythia was murdered?"

Mac said one of Pritkin's bad words. "And how would you know that if you didn't do it?" he demanded heatedly.

Marlowe shrugged. "Who else were we talking about?" He turned the thing over in his hands, frowning. "Someone's cut it open."

"We did that," Mac said, snatching it out of his hands. "It had arsenic in it!" He said the latter as if he expected it to stagger the vamp, but Marlowe didn't appear fazed.

"Well, of course it did." At my expression, he explained. "Powdered toad, arsenic—a whole host of substances were often put inside these things before they were soldered together. They were thought to ward off sickness, and added to the medallion's value—and its price, of course."

"You mean there was *supposed* to be poison in there?" I looked at Mac. "You're sure she was murdered?"

"Cassie—" he said warningly. He obviously didn't want to discuss this in front of Marlowe, but I couldn't see the harm. If Marlowe had arranged the Pythia's death, he already knew about it; if not, maybe he could provide a few clues.

"A medallion like this was found next to her body," I told Marlowe. "Is there any way it could have been used to kill her?"

He looked thoughtful. "Anything that comes in contact with the skin can be a danger. Queen Elizabeth was almost assassinated by poison rubbed into the pommel of her saddle. And I once killed a Catholic by soaking his prayer beads in an arsenic solution," he added nonchalantly.

He was creeping me out, but at least it looked like I'd come to the right guy. "Would that sort of method take a long time to kill someone?"

"An hour or so."

"No, like six months."

Marlowe shook his head. "Even assuming someone soaked her necklace in a weak solution, and she was in the habit of fingering the medallion, it wouldn't have worked. Arsenic causes redness and swelling of the skin over time— she would have noticed. That's why gradual poisoning is usually done in food. It's tasteless and odorless, and in small doses, its symptoms are similar to food poisoning."

"Her food was specially prepared and carefully tested," Mac said. "And Lady Phemonoe was extremely . . . careful about poisons. You might almost say she was, well, not paranoid exactly, but—"

"That's not what I heard," Marlowe broke in cheerfully. He seemed to like talking shop. "They say she'd become extremely superstitious with age, and had been buying all sorts of questionable remedies. A knife believed to turn green when passed over unsafe food, an antique Venetian glass supposed to explode if filled with a poisoned liquid, a goblet with a bezoar set into the bottom—"

"Maybe she Saw something." Agnes had been a seer, too, a powerful one. I shivered. How horrible would it be to see your own death, yet be able to do nothing about it?

"Perhaps." Marlowe was smiling at me again, and I didn't like it. "But if so, it appears to have done her little good. Which rather proves the point I am trying to make. The mages cannot keep you safe any more than they did your predecessor. We will be much more efficient, I assure you."

Mac shot the vamp an unfriendly look. "Don't listen to him, Cassie. If you don't want to talk, don't. He can't force you with me here."

"I wouldn't be too sure of that, mage. I know your reputation, but much of your magic is useless at present, and my strength is unchanged. Not that I would dream of forcing Cassandra to do anything against her will. I merely think she ought to know who her newfound ally is and what he wants."

"You stay out of our business," Mac said, his tone ominous.

"Ah, but it isn't yours alone, is it?" Marlowe asked. "She has a right to know with whom she's become involved." He turned to me, looking innocent. "Or do you already know that Pritkin is the Circle's chief assassin?"

Chapter 11

Mac choked on the contents of the flask he'd been sipping from, and then all but confirmed it. "That's neither here nor there!" he gasped as soon as he got his breath back. Marlowe didn't even look at him; his eyes were fixed squarely on me.

"I take it this is news?" he asked.

"Tell me."

"Cassie, you can't believe anything one of them says. It's all rubbish—" Mac began, but I cut him off.

"I'm too tired to debate this, Mac," I said, and the weariness in my voice was genuine. All I wanted was to find a soft patch of moss, one that wasn't too damp and was free of moving tree parts, and sleep for about twelve hours. I was mentally and physically near exhaustion, and my emotional state wasn't all that great, either. But Marlowe was right—I needed to hear this. I could decide whether to believe it later.

Marlowe didn't need a second prompt. "We wondered why a demon hunter had been assigned as the Circle's liaison to us. There are plenty of vampire experts available and many of them are far more . . . diplomatic . . . than John

Pritkin. The timing was also suspicious, with the Circle removing their old liaison and substituting Pritkin only hours before you were brought in. It was as if they knew you were coming and wanted him to be there."

"They hoped he'd mistake me for a demon and kill me," I said. This was old news, something Mircea had figured out early on. It had almost worked. Pritkin didn't know much about vamps, but he was an expert on demons. And some of my powers, especially possession, had made him very suspicious.

"I heard that theory, but it seemed strange that the Circle would simply assume you would do something to alarm Pritkin enough for him to attack you. Had things gone the way we planned—had you not escaped and Tomas not betrayed us—it would have been a quiet evening." I fidgeted at this evaluation of my first meeting with the Senate, which had been anything but quiet from the start, but didn't interrupt. "I thought there might be more to the story," he continued, "and began a discreet inquiry."

"You don't know anything," Mac said vehemently.

Marlowe raised an eyebrow, the look on his face one a king might have bestowed on a peasant who tracked mud across his castle floor. "On the contrary, I know a good deal. For instance, I know Pritkin has at least a thousand kills to his credit, and probably more. I know that he's the man the Circle turns to when they want to make absolutely certain someone ends up dead. I know that he is famous for using unorthodox tactics to bring down his prey"—he gave me an arch look—"like having one mark help him to locate another—"

Mac uttered an explative. "Don't listen to him, Cassie." He paused to stomp on a root that had been trying to curl around my ankle. It slunk off into the forest, but I had no doubt it would be back. I felt a strong yearning for an axe. "You may not know us, but you do know vamps. They lie more than they breathe. John's a good man."

Marlowe let out a contemptuous laugh. "Tell his victims that!" He glanced at me, as if trying to gauge my reaction to his news, but I'd hit that washed-out sensation that comes from too much exertion in too little time. I couldn't manage to make myself care very much if Pritkin wanted me dead. It wasn't exactly a novel idea; I'd been operating on that assumption all along.

I started searching through Mac's backpack for some dry socks. I'd had a pair in my duffle, but Mac must not have bothered to pack them. It's a clue that you are hanging with the wrong crowd when you have beer, guns and about a ton of ammunition, but no clean clothes.

Marlowe looked slightly put out that his bombshell wasn't causing the uproar he'd expected, but he continued nonetheless. "You've entrusted yourself to Pritkin's care, but you know virtually nothing about him! The Circle has obviously sent him to kill you."

"This is a perfect example of what vamps do, Cassie!" Mac thundered. "They cobble together some half-truths that leave them looking lily-white and the rest of us covered in shite!"

"He needs your help to find the other rogue," Marlowe told me earnestly, ignoring Mac. "But as soon as he has her, you're dead. Unless you let us assist you. The Senate only wants—"

"—to control your every move!" Mac broke in. "Cassie, I swear to you, John was appalled when he found out what the Circle intends. They've gone power-mad! Even if they get their way and both you and Myra die, they can't be sure their chosen initiate will become Pythia. There are hundreds, possibly thousands, of unknown, untrained clairvoyants in the world. What if it went to one of them? And what if the Black Circle found her first?"

I smiled slightly. "Better the devil you know, huh?" Mac looked somewhat appalled at what he'd let slip, but it was exactly because he hadn't made a rousing speech in my favor that I tended to believe him.

I glanced at Marlowe. "Mac has a point. Pritkin was declared a rogue himself today for protecting me, and was almost killed in the bargain. Seems kind of extreme for someone who is only setting me up."

"He is known for such tactics," Marlowe said, waving it off. He gazed at me intently, his eyes practically radiating sincerity. "Cassie, we have no desire to manipulate you. Our aim is to offer you an alternative to domination by the mages. That has been the fate of Pythias for generations, but it doesn't have to be yours. We can—"

I held up a hand, both because I didn't want to hear it and to keep Mac, who had grown dangerously red in the face, from going ballistic. "Save it, Marlowe. I know the truth. And I don't intend to be dominated by anyone."

"You know what you've been told," he replied urgently. "And you will need allies, Cassie. No great leader has ever ruled entirely alone. Elizabeth has gone down in history as a magnificent queen, which she was, but one of her chief talents was choosing able people to advise her. She was great partly because those around her were great. You cannot remain isolated. You will not be able to work that way. In the long term—"

"I'm not real interested in the long term right now, Marlowe." I was just trying to live through the day.

"In time, you will come to understand that you need allies, and the Senate will be there. Unlike the mages, we want to work with you, not control your every decision."

"Uh-huh. Which is why Mircea put the *dúthracht* on me?" There were a lot of things I wasn't clear on, but that one was crystal. The *geis* wasn't used to advise; it was used to control. The look on Marlowe's face said he knew that.

"We will find a way to break it," he promised. "And in the meantime, the Senate offers you its protection." I rolled my eyes and Mac snorted.

"Yeah," he said contemptuously, "just substitute 'prison' for 'protection' and—"

"You might wish to consider," Marlowe said smoothly, "that despite Lord Mircea's lapse of judgment, the Senate has protected you in the past. Whereas the facts make only one conclusion possible: the mages want their candidate on the Pythia's throne and will stop at nothing to see her there—including your death."

"Another lie!" Mac surged to his feet.

He looked angry enough to go for Marlowe's throat, but he didn't get the chance. I heard a rustling sound and, quicker than I could blink, the roots that had been bugging me all day wrapped themselves securely around Mac. He tried to say something, but I couldn't make it out. Within seconds, only his outraged eyes showed over a coil of rope-like roots, some of them as big as my arm. Struggling seemed useless, although he appeared to be trying anyway.

Marlowe was in much the same predicament, but he sat quietly, making no attempt to resist. I noticed that, despite Marlowe being the stronger of the two, he was bound less tightly than Mac, with roots coming up only to his chest. Maybe the less you fought them, the less tightly they held you. I followed his example, hoping that they'd continue to ignore me. Then I realized they weren't the only problem.

"We are not spies," Marlowe said loudly, apparently to thin air.

"You are in our land without permission," came the answer; "therefore, you are whatever we say you are."

"Who are you?" an imperious voice demanded. A doll-like creature flew out from behind Marlowe to hover in front of my face. It was about two feet long, with a mass of fiery red hair and a huge span of bright green wings. It took me a moment to place it—her—as the pixie I'd seen a week before at Dante's. Then she'd only been about eight inches high, but it wasn't like I could be mistaken. She was the first member of the Fey I'd ever seen, and the image sort of sticks with you.

"Don't give her your name!" Marlowe said urgently. The pixie frowned at him and a large root with a knot on it shoved its way between his lips. It's a good thing vampires don't need to breathe, because more roots followed, twining around his face so thickly that only a shock of brown curls could be seen. He was gagged so effectively that it didn't look like I'd be getting any more help.

"I'm the Pythia," I said, deciding that a title might be better than my name. As far as I knew, it couldn't be used in enchantments. "We met before, at Dante's, if you—"

"I'll be rewarded highly for this," she said, ignoring my attempt to trade on our brief acquaintance. "Seize them." A large party of shaggy things burst out of the trees, clubs and hide-wrapped shields at the ready. I don't know why they bothered with weapons—the stench coming off them in waves was enough to incapacitate anybody.

A couple of very odd-looking things converged on me. It looked like two gruesome trees had uprooted themselves and decided to go for a walk. The closest had a more or less human form, if humans were commonly four feet tall and at least as wide. But his hair was the color of the lichen on the roots, a bright flaming red despite the dirt that caked it, and his eyes were the same dung yellow as his teeth. He had skin as gnarled and pitted as old bark, and its color exactly matched the loamy forest floor. He was wearing only a small loin covering of oak leaves, which was almost hidden by the folds of his enormous belly.

His partner had him by about a foot in height but wasn't nearly as wide. Filthy gray hair trailed down to his knees, with the look and consistency of Spanish moss. Stringy muscles stood out on impossibly long arms covered in greenish gray skin. His body resembled a cragged tree trunk more than a living being, with knobby extensions all over like stunted branches. Instead of clothing he had long strings of dirty gray moss and a few ferns that appeared to sprout directly from his flesh.

I clapped a hand over my nose and wished that I, too, didn't have to breathe. "What *are* they?"

"Dark Fey," Marlowe managed to say. "Giants and oak men." The roots had withdrawn as quickly as they had come, baring him to the shoulders. I realized why when a ten-foot giant strode forward and knocked him in the temple with a club the size of a small tree. Marlowe sighed. "It's always the head," he murmured, then his eyes rolled up and he collapsed.

I backed away, lifting my hands to show how harmless I

was. Unfortunately, it was the truth. The pack with my gun in it was too far away to reach and I had no other weapons. The shorter one laughed and said something in a guttural language I couldn't understand. Judging by his expression, that was probably just as well. I backed away as they stalked forward, trying to keep an eye on them and also on the root-strewn trail. It didn't work, and I ended up sprawled in the scattered leaves. As soon as I was down, roots wrapped around my wrists, trapping me. The next moment, the taller thing was on me, his breath like a ripe compost heap in my face.

"Cassie!" I heard Mac's voice and looked up in time to see him slide through the weakened hold of the roots and sprint for me. Everything seemed to slow down, the way it does when you see what's about to happen but can't stop it. The roots dove for him, and before I could draw breath enough to scream, one had pierced him like a living spear. All I could do was lie there and watch as he twisted in pain, a wooden limb as sharp as a knife erupting from the flesh of his upper thigh. He wavered and went down hard, dropping to his knees as I finally managed to scream.

I felt rough fingers on my legs; then they found the fastening of my shorts and broke the zipper in their haste to get them off. I barely noticed, watching in horror as Mac writhed on the ground, trying to pull out the wooden mass that had pierced his thigh. He managed to get the slender spike out with steady hands, ignoring the abrupt wash of blood that stained his clothes, but another immediately wound itself around his neck, choking him.

"No! Leave him alone—you're killing him!"

The roots either didn't understand or didn't care. The creature on top of me yanked at the gaping material of my shorts, baring my upper thighs, then in one swift movement jerked them halfway down my legs. I kicked at him, but it was like hitting wood instead of living flesh and I don't think he even noticed. I looked around wildly for help, but Tomas' limp form was being shoved less than gently into a large sack. And although Marlowe had regained consciousness, he was being held down by three giants while another tried to get a sack over his head.

Mac had managed to get the root loose and was struggling one-handed to unwind it from around his neck. His other hand was held over the ragged wound in his leg, which had already drenched the ground beneath him as if it had nicked an artery. But at least the other roots had backed off. If he wasn't struggling, he didn't seem to interest them. I could only hope he'd stay down, and maybe play dead before he really was.

I realized in a rush of adrenaline that I was on my own, and that none of my usual defenses would work here. My bracelet was no more than a decoration, and my ward was useless. Sheba had disappeared after attacking the Consul, and the *geis* was silent. Either its power didn't work in Faerie, or these creatures were too alien for it to recognize them as threats. My amulet might have helped, but it was caught under my shirt and I couldn't reach it with my arms stretched over my head.

The skinny creature tore the shorts the rest of the way off and flung them aside while the fat one started pawing at my top. The tank was a stretchy knit that resisted tearing, and his clumsy fingers couldn't seem to get it off. He paused to lick my face as if tasting me, and a rope of saliva dripped from his mouth onto my cheek. It slowly trickled down my neck, cold and viscous, completely unlike bodily fluids are supposed to be. I tried to scream but got only a mouthful of grimy, foul-tasting hair instead of air.

I was temporarily blinded to what was happening, trapped under the suffocating mass on his head, but I felt the tug of fabric and the sudden shock of air against me when my panties were ripped away. I tried to shift, at that moment not caring about the consequences, but although I felt a deep, sluggish pull of my power, it wasn't enough. I couldn't grasp hold, and it remained a lifeline hovering just out of reach.

I turned my face as far toward the path as I could, desperate to find some air, and then I saw it. One weapon did remain nearby, if not exactly within my grasp. The rune must have fallen out of my shorts when they were thrown into the bushes, and it was so small that no one had noticed. It lay tantalizingly near my head, a pale sliver of bone half buried in damp leaves. But although it was only inches away, I had no way to grab it.

While I struggled to figure out how to cross those few inches, two slender but strong roots wrapped around my ankles and started twining upwards. When they reached my knees, they began pulling outward. The living bonds curled up to my thighs, biting into the skin as they brutally forced my legs so wide that, for a minute, I thought they meant to tear me in two. They finally stopped when my hips would give no further. I tried to fight, but nothing I did made the slightest difference, and my rising panic made it almost impossible to think. A stick bearing a few bright green leaves tumbled through the air from high above and landed on my face, a whisper of a caress, while the things above me started to wrestle over who would get to rape me first.

It was a short fight. The skinny one picked up his companion and threw him against a tree, the branches of which trapped him in a wooden embrace, like a cage. Then he turned and fell on me. Two coarse, knotted hands grabbed my shoulders painfully and I stared up into flat gray eyes that had nothing human in them. He wriggled down my body, his tough, uneven skin scraping against mine except where the tank protected me.

I ignored the pain his movements were causing and grabbed the stick, my only tool, in my mouth. My eyes zeroed in on the thong threaded through the top of the bone disk, despite the fact that it was brown and barely poked out of the scattered leaves. I knew I might get only one chance at this, and I had to concentrate. I managed to get the end of the stick through the small loop and began trying to work it closer. If I could get it to touch my skin or even just my aura, it might be enough. Then I heard a squelch, and something slick and clammy nudged my belly. I froze.

It felt like something old that had been left underground to rot for a very long time, spongy and moist and bloated. But it moved sluggishly, twitching against my lower stomach. I couldn't see anything except my attacker's shoulder and the small patch of path, but my brain conjured up images of an enormous white grub or a fist-sized slug. When its chill dampness slithered eagerly between my legs, I swear my heart stopped.

I was so paralyzed with horror that I just lay there as the inhuman thing swelled against me, like a rotten fruit about to burst. Its sodden cold raised goose bumps across my entire body as it leeched away my heat, numbing me as if an icicle was being rubbed over sensitive areas. Through the shudder-inducing revulsion, I understood that the horrible gelatinous shifting was it changing forms, trying to find one

compatible with my body. But the one it came up with bore
no resemblance to human virility. It suddenly grew firmer,
its slimy consistency congealing into a fat, rigid shape as un-
yielding as a wooden stake. If the thing pierced me, I knew
I wouldn't survive, that it would eat my heat and replace it
with its damp chill. The green man, some part of my brain
recalled: the old Celtic peoples had sacrificed one of their
own to the land, so it would grow rich and fertile off his
flesh. Only it looked like this forest preferred a green
woman.

When the parody of an organ began to thrust, the action
so very male, so very *human*, my paralysis broke. I screamed
and jerked my head in a violent negative motion. I hadn't
planned it, had almost forgotten what I'd been doing, but the
action caused something small and hard to land on my
cheek. My crossed eyes identified it as the rune disk and my
heart started up again. I wasn't sure how to cast it, wasn't
convinced that it would work at all. But I screamed the name
inside my head because my mouth didn't seem to work.

I don't know whether that was the right procedure, but it
did the trick. Sort of. With no warning, I found myself, not
twenty minutes back in time, but maybe two. The oak men
were coming for me, and Mac was leaping to intercept them,
so focused on saving me that he didn't see the roots straightening themselves into spears, coming for him. I didn't hesitate this time, but yelled a warning and fled down the path
towards his discarded backpack.

I was sobbing now that I could breathe freely again, and
my hands were shaking so hard that I wasn't sure I'd be able
to get the pack open. The shorter creature reached me when
I had only one buckle undone. He grabbed the front of my
shirt and pulled, and he must have had better leverage on his

feet because this time, the tank ripped. My amulet tumbled into view, jostling Billy's necklace for space between my breasts, and my attacker let out a screech and jumped back. He cradled the hand that had brushed against the charm as if it been burned, and a black mark appeared on his skin in the shape of the rowan cross. I plunged my hand into the half-open pack and finally clutched the gun.

I am not the world's greatest shot. In fact, I suck. But even I don't usually miss when my targets are three feet away. I didn't worry about aiming, just let off a barrage of bullets that splintered the barklike skin of the oak men as if I was firing at actual wood. The taller let out a squeal and took off down the trail, while his fat companion huddled on the ground, hands over his mossy head. The iron bullets obviously caused them pain, but although they were oozing a syrupy substance from every wound, they were both alive and moving when my clip ran out. I stared at them in disbelief; what did it take to stop one of these things?

The coat Pritkin had given me was lying nearby, where I had dropped it alongside the pack when we stopped to rest. But I had no time to search for the right bullets. The short Fey realized that I had stopped shooting and grabbed for me. I flattened the rowan charm against his forehead, pushing it into his skin as hard as I could. The flesh around it immediately turned black and start smoking, giving off a smell exactly like a burning campfire.

He tore away from me, clutching his head and screaming. I don't know whether he would have tried again, because the pixie suddenly appeared and, despite the fact that he was momentarily incapacitated, slapped him with the flat of her sword. The blow must have been more forceful than it looked, because he went sailing into the forest until he was stopped by an overhanging limb. He hit the ground hard, unconscious or worse. I didn't wait to find out, my only thought to get to Mac.

Huge hands descended on me at the same time that a scream reverberated through the forest. I looked down the path in time to see a root as large as a small tree erupt from the scarred ground right under Mac's feet. Time seemed to stop—I couldn't even feel my heart beating anymore—and then everything suddenly sped up. The root ripped out of the ground, piercing Mac through the center of his back. "No," I breathed, but no one heard, no one cared. Mac's body strained upward until his spine left the grass completely, his fingers digging into the hard-packed dirt, then the root burst out of his torso in a great gush of blood.

The pixie nodded once to the guards and they released me. I shot down the path, but Mac was already limp by the time I reached him, sightless eyes staring up without recognition. "Mac," I shook the unresponsive body gently. "Mac, please . . ."

Unresisting, his head lolled to the side just as a shower of gold hit the dark ground. My blood ran cold when I realized what had happened. Mac's wards had solidified and fallen away, leaving the skin between the unmoving leaves as pink and unmarked as a newborn's. I picked up one of the small shapes with a shaking hand. It was the tiny lizard, frozen in midleap. Next to my knee was a snake as long as my arm, uncurled from its usual place around his neck. And beside his ruined chest lay an eagle the size of my hand.

I stared at them numbly, knowing what it meant that his wards had deserted him, but not willing to let my brain shape the word. A deafening din rose up from the assembled spectators, but I didn't even look up at the screeching and howling. Until the roots came back.

If I had thought there were a lot before, I was instantly reminded how many are needed to feed even a small tree. They were suddenly everywhere, shooting out of the forest, erupting from the ground, diving from the underbrush. A few paused to leech Mac's blood from the spreading puddle that had almost covered the path, but most dove for him like hungry sharks. The flailing mass flogged my body like bark-covered whips, while the earth around Mac boiled with activity. Dozens of roots wrapped around him, binding him, as thick as a shroud. Then a huge knotted specimen slammed into my stomach, driving the air out of my lungs. I fell to my knees, and when I looked again, Mac had disappeared. The only sign that anything had happened was the golden wards that stuck up here and there out of the churned-up dirt.

The pixie said something to the lumbering giant standing behind her. He would have made a couple dozen of her, but he moved at her command without question. His bulk coming towards me down the path was the last thing I saw before the world went black and I realized that I'd been stuffed into a sack. I remember being slung over someone's back; then my brain shut down completely and I fell into darkness.

I awoke in a cold sweat, gasping for air, my heart hammering in my side. I stared into absolute blackness in dry-mouthed terror. I was sure something was about to grab me and that it would all start again. But minutes passed and nothing happened, and I couldn't hear any breaths except my own labored ones. My chest hurt as though I'd run for miles and I wanted nothing more than to curl around the

pain until it vanished, but I couldn't afford the luxury. I had
to find out where I was, had to know what had happened.

By feel I discovered that I was on a crudely made cot in
a stone cell, naked, with only a short, scratchy wool blanket
as a covering. I guess the tank top hadn't been worth saving.
I was thick-headed, bleary-eyed and trembling with the
memory of what had almost happened. I examined myself,
but other than being bruised, grubby and severely shaken, I
seemed to be okay, although the welts the roots had given
me throbbed in time with the eagle's claw mark on my hand,
making it feel like my rapid heartbeat was echoing throughout my body.

More than anything, I wanted a bath. I groped around
until I found a large bucket of water that had been left by the
door along with a sponge, a bar of homemade soap and a
towel. The floor was bare except for a little straw that had
leaked from a tear in the mattress, and there was a drain in
the center of the slightly sloping stones. I threw off the blanket and scrubbed my skin until it was raw in places and I
couldn't smell anything but the sharp tang of the soap.

I tipped the rest of the water over my head, but despite all
my efforts I didn't feel clean. I toweled off, trying not to
think about Mac, but it was impossible. The Fey must have
gathered up his charms and brought them along, because
they were in a pile on the end of the cot, recognizable by
their shapes, but cold and lifeless under my hands. I wondered if they were supposed to be some kind of message—
a reminder of how helpless our best magic was here. If so, I
didn't need it.

I still felt disoriented and could not quite believe what I'd
just seen. But the image was seared onto my eyes. I could
hear Mac's last scream, see his fingers clawing at the

ground, seeking a weapon he didn't have because he'd given his only Fey charm to me.

And I'd lost it.

I tried to summon my power again, but although I could feel it like a great wave beating against a seawall, it couldn't quite reach me. Maybe there was a way of compensating for the dampening effect but if so I couldn't figure it out. Now that my eyes had adjusted, I could see a faint light outlining the cell's door, so dim that when I blinked it disappeared. As far as escape went, it didn't help, and there wasn't a lot of inspiration in the bare cell. Other than the cot, there was no furniture, and except for the heavy, locked door and a high, barred window, there was no way out. I wrapped the blanket around me in lieu of clothes and dragged the cot over a few feet, wincing at the sound it made on the stones. When I clambered on top, I could just reach the windowsill, but when I felt around with my fingertips, I found only dust and what felt like a dead spider. No moon or stars were visible, but by feel I discovered that the bars were metal and as big around as my wrist.

I sat back down on the cot and wrapped my arms around me to keep from shivering in the chill night air. Bathing and checking out escape possibilities had given my brain something to do, but now it kept trying to go back to the horror in the forest. The more I tried not to think about Mac, the more the other images crowded my mind. I could smell the awful breath in my face, see the hunger in their expressions and feel that decayed mass squirming between my legs, seeking, thrusting, invading.

Despite my efforts, I was shivering anyway, so much that my teeth started to chatter. I used anger to push away the panic, to let me draw a deep breath, to let me think. I was alone and defenseless, and I hated it. Fear was an old companion, familiar in its way, but this wasn't fear. What I was feeling went beyond words, a bone-deep chill and a certainty that, even if I survived, I would never feel secure again.

I drew the blanket further around me, but it did little good. The cold that permeated me didn't come from the outside. I walked up and down the confines of the cell anyway, trying to force circulation into my icy center. It didn't warm me, but it did clear my head. I could examine my mistakes later. I could grieve later. Right now, I had to get out of here. And, somehow, I had to make sure that I was never, ever this helpless again.

I was about to try to access my power one more time when I heard a familiar, off-key voice from somewhere nearby. "I'll take you home again, Kathleen, across the ocean wild and wide," it warbled mournfully. It was faint and slurred, but unmistakable.

"Billy!" I almost cried in relief.

The singing stopped abruptly. "Cassie, me darlin'. I've got one for ya. I thought it up at the pub."

> *There once was a ghost name of Billy,*
> *Who got in a jam rather silly,*
> *He found a beautiful lass*
> *And quick made a pass*
> *Forgetting he only had mist for a willy.*

"Where are we?" I yelled. "What's going on?" The only answer I got was a rousing chorus of "The Belle of Belfast City." Trust Billy to make me want to strangle him when he wasn't even in the same room. "You're drunk!"

"That I am," he agreed, "but I'm conscious, which is more than I can say for my orange friend, here. Can't hold his liquor, poor sod."

"Billy!"

"All right, Cass. Hold your horses and good old Billy will tell the tale. We've been taken by the Dark Fey. They snatched me out of a lovely pub and threw me in this dank hole, with only himself for company, to wait on the king's pleasure."

I sagged in relief. At least we weren't going to be beheaded in the morning or something equally medieval. That bought the others some time to find us, assuming they were still free. "Where is everyone?" I hoped they were doing better than me, or we were in a lot of trouble.

"Pritkin and Marlowe are trying to convince the captain of the guard—a nasty pixie—to let us go, but I don't know how well they're doing." He paused, then asked in a different tone. "Hey, Cass. What do you think would happen to me if I got killed here? They don't have any ghosts, have you noticed?"

I thought of Mac, his face sagging in death, his eyes dull. If there had been a sign of a ghost, a flare or spark anywhere around him, I hadn't noticed. A new wash of chills spread over me. My God, what had we done?

"What if I didn't come back?" Billy was saying, "What if that was it—I died and there was no loophole this time? What if—"

"Billy!" I tried to keep the hysterical note out of my voice, but I wasn't entirely successful. I swallowed and tried again. "You aren't going to die, Billy. We'll get out of this." I said it as much to reassure myself as to quiet him, but I don't think it worked for either of us.

I heard a jangle of keys outside my cell, and the huge door swung open on ancient hinges. I was almost blinded by the lantern light that flooded the room, but blinking through my fingers, I made out who the guard was carrying. "Tomas!"

The guard, who was only about five feet tall, carried the six-foot-something vampire as if he was weightless. He dropped his burden on the bunk and turned to me, and for the first time I noticed the boar's tusks protruding from his wide mouth. *Ogre*, some part of my brain piped up as he thrust a stubby finger in my chest and grunted. His voice sounded like gravel being rolled over by a tank, and if it was supposed to contain words, I couldn't understand them.

"He want that you heal him," came a voice from the doorway. Behind the bulk of the jailer stood a slim brunette wearing an elaborate green dress covered in red embroidery. It took me a second to place her.

"Françoise?" It was bizarre. Every time I turned around, there she was. The first time we met had been in seventeenth century France, when Tomas and I had saved her from the Inquisition. Then she'd turned up again at Dante's with the pixie, where she was about to be sold to the Fey. I'd released her, but it looked like Destiny snapped at her heels as closely as it did at mine, because here she was anyway. "What are you doing here?" I asked, bewildered.

"You and *le monsieur* 'elped me once," she answered quickly. "I 'ave come, 'ow do you say? To return the favor."

"What about the others?" I asked quickly, "I came with a group—"

"*Oui, je sais.* The mage, 'ee make a deal with Radella. She is captain of the night guard, *une grande baroudeuse*, a warrior of skill."

"What kind of deal?"

"The mage 'ave a rune of power. Radella has long searched for such. Above all, she want a child, but is *inféconde*, barren. The mage say, 'ee cast it for her, if she aid us."

"Jera." Damn it if it hadn't come in handy after all.

"*C'est ça.*" She glanced at the ogre, who was looking between the two of us suspiciously. I got the impression that he didn't speak English, at least not well enough to follow the conversation. "They do not know why *le vampire* will not wake. I tell them you are a great healer—that you can save 'eem."

"He's in a healing trance. He'll save himself, hopefully."

"Eet does not matter," she said, smiling and nodding at the ogre. "I want only to 'ave the two of you together, near the portal. I return soon, after the guards change."

"The portal? But—"

"I weel do what I can," she said as the ogre lumbered past her, apparently deciding the conversation had lasted long enough. "But you must promise to take me with you. Please, I 'ave been here so long . . ."

"You've been here a week," I said, confused. I wanted to explain that I didn't need the portal. I needed to find Myra, not go right back where I'd started from, especially not with the *geis* in place and the Senate and Circle both hunting me. Worst of all, if we turned back now, Mac had died for nothing. But the ogre, who had paused to place the lantern on the floor, was now pulling the door shut. Françoise stared at me over his shoulder, looking panicked. "Okay, I promise!" I said. Even a week would feel like an eternity here, and I'd never leave anyone to face what had almost happened to me.

I stood in the middle of the room, hearing the ogre's footsteps echo down the corridor as he walked away. I wanted to check on Tomas but was afraid. What if he was no better? What if he'd never been in a healing trance at all, and we'd been lugging around a corpse?

After a minute, I screwed up my courage and walked across to the cot. Tomas was lying on his back, highlighted by the lantern light, but I couldn't see his chest and abdomen for all the bandages that had been wrapped around him. Someone had done a better job than my hasty efforts—he was practically a mummy from just below his nipples to the tops of his hard-muscled thighs. The bandages were all he was wearing, but I barely noticed because I caught a glimmer of dark eyes behind the slitted lids.

"Tomas!" I bent over him and felt the chill of his skin. That wasn't good. I don't know where the rumor started that vampires are cold. Unless they're starving, they run as hot as a human—after all, it's human blood that feeds them. I stripped off the blanket and tucked it around him, trying to cover as much bare skin as possible.

He smiled and tugged weakly at my hand, pulling me down beside him. There was barely room for the two of us on the narrow cot, but he insisted. "I finally have you naked and in bed, and I'm too tired to do anything about it," he joked. I could have cried with relief.

I stroked the side of his face with my wrist, but he pulled away. He knew what I was offering, and he desperately needed it. I put my wrist back against his cheek and looked at him seriously. "Feed. You won't heal without it."

"You need your strength."

"Then don't take much, but heal. I don't know how much time we have." The door to the cell was heavy, but if he'd been at his usual strength, Tomas could have ripped it from its hinges. Under the circumstances, I'd settle for him being able to run or at least walk once Françoise came back. Unlike the ogre, I couldn't carry him.

Tomas looked stubborn, but he must have reached the same conclusion I had, because the next minute I felt a brief pull at my power. It settled into a steady drain as his overtaxed system started to revive, and I sighed slightly in pleasure. The feeding process can be sensual, but this one wasn't. It was warm and comforting, like wrapping up in an old, cuddly blanket on a cold night. It felt familiar, too, and I suddenly remembered another reason I had to be angry with Tomas.

He'd been feeding from me surreptitiously while we roomed together, taking blood through the skin without leaving any telltale marks and with enough of a suggestion to cloud my mind. He'd said it was because he needed to keep track of me—part of his job had been to guarantee my safety and the feedings created a bond—but I still viewed it as a violation. Technically, I could have brought charges against him with the Senate, although that seemed kind of redundant at the moment. They'd happily kill him if they got their hands on him, no additional allegations needed.

He watched me, the lamplight gilding his dark lashes, and a warm languor spread through my veins. I found it increasingly difficult to be angry. After everything that had happened today, a little thing like a minor power drain seemed incredibly unimportant, and the sensation of peace and familiarity was welcome no matter what was causing it. And it wasn't like we had another choice: if Fey blood was anything like their other fluids, I was pretty sure it wouldn't work as vampire food. Tomas would already have fed if so, without anyone knowing.

"You're all right?" I asked as he released me, far too soon

for a full feeding. "I didn't know if you were in a healing trance or—"

"I am far from all right, but thanks to you I'll recover." He sounded stronger already, which shouldn't have surprised me. There were only a few hundred first-level masters in the world, and what they could do often seemed miraculous. "There is something about this place," he said wonderingly. "It is as if every moment that passes is an hour of our time. I have never before healed so quickly."

The answer to a riddle that had been bugging me for two days suddenly clicked into place. I couldn't believe I hadn't thought of it earlier. If Myra had been hiding in Faerie, land of the radically unpredictable timeline, then instead of having a week to heal from her injuries, she could have had months, even years. No wonder she'd looked good!

Tomas kissed the side of my head, the only thing he could reach, and looked at me somberly. "You should not have come back for me—it was a terrible risk. You must promise never to do it again."

"I won't have to," I said, brushing his hair out of his eyes. It was always so beautiful, long and black and as soft as a child's. I picked a few leaves out of it with a slightly trembling hand. I was so glad to see him alive that I felt giddy. "We'll find some way to hide you from the Senate."

Tomas was shaking his head before I even finished speaking. "Beautiful Cassie," he murmured. "It has been a very long time since anyone was willing to risk themselves for me. Very few ever have. I will remember what you tried to do."

"I told you, we'll find somewhere for you to hide. The Senate won't find you!"

He laughed slightly, then stopped abruptly as if it hurt.

"Do you not understand? They did not find me this time. I went back to them, to him. I thought I could fight it, but I was wrong."

I didn't have to ask who he meant. Louis-César, on loan to the Consul from the European Senate, was Tomas' master. He had defeated Tomas' original master, the hated Alejandro, in a duel a century ago and then laid claim. Tomas was a first-level master, but even they vary in strength, and Louis-César simply outmatched him. He'd never been able to break the bond between them.

Tomas shuddered lightly. I couldn't see it, but I could feel the slight tremor against me. "Every moment, I heard him, an endless voice, deep in my head driving me half mad! I could never relax, not for a moment. I knew as soon as I did, my will would break and I would go crawling back like a beaten dog. I told myself that soon the war would distract him and he would let me go. But tonight I awoke in the Senate's holding cells, and a guard informed me that I had walked into the compound and surrendered myself. Yet I remember nothing of it, Cassie! Nothing!" He shook more violently, a visible shudder passing over his limbs. "He pulled me to him like a puppet. He will do it again."

I was confused. "You mean he's calling you now?"

Tomas smiled, and it was blissful. "No. There is something about Faerie—I have not heard him since we arrived. Not having to fend him off has helped me heal, now that I can use all my strength for it. I had not completely repaired lesser injuries than these in a week with his call draining me, but in this brief time my wounds are closed."

"You can't hear him here?"

"For the first time in a century, I am free of him," he said, and his voice held awe, as if he couldn't quite believe it. "I have no master." He looked at me, and there was a fierce joy in his face. "For four and a half centuries, I was someone's slave! My master's voice controlled me completely, until I thought I would never break free!" He stared around the dank little cell in wonder. "But here, none of our rules seem to apply."

I felt my eyes start to burn. "Yeah, I noticed." If our magic worked here, Mac would have wiped the floor with the Fey.

"What is it?"

I shook my head. I didn't want to think about it, much less talk. But suddenly everything came pouring out of me anyway. It took me less than half an hour to bring him up to speed on what had been happening since we last met. That seemed wrong somehow, that so much pain could be summed up in so few words. Not that Tomas seemed to understand.

"MacAdam was a warrior. He understood the risks. You all did."

I looked at him bleakly. "Yes, which is why he wasn't supposed to come with us. That was never the plan."

Tomas shrugged. "Plans change in battle. Every warrior knows this."

"You didn't know him, or you wouldn't sound so . . . indifferent!" I snapped.

His eyes flashed. "I am not indifferent, Cassie. The mage helped to bring me here, to get me away from the Senate. I owe him much that I will never be able to repay. But at least I can honor the sacrifice he made without belittling him."

"I'm not belittling him!"

"Aren't you?" Tomas held my eyes without flinching. "He was an old warrior. He had experience and courage and he knew his own mind. And he died for something he believed in—you. You do him no honor by questioning his judgment now."

"His judgment got him killed! He should have stayed down." And I should have searched for Myra on my own. I'd said that no one else was going to die because of me, yet here I was, adding another mark to my body count. "He shouldn't have believed in me. No one should."

"And why not?" Tomas looked genuinely confused.

I let out a half-bitter, half-hysterical laugh. "Because getting close to me is a one-way ticket to trouble. You ought to know." Tomas had brought a lot of his problems on himself, but I had to wonder whether he would have made those same bad decisions if he had never met me.

Tomas shook his head. "You take too much on yourself, Cassie. Not everything is your fault, not every crisis is yours to solve."

"I know that!" But however much I might like to think otherwise, I was to blame for what had happened to Mac. He'd been here because of me, he'd been vulnerable because of me, and ultimately, he'd died because of me.

"Do you?" I felt Tomas' arm slip around me. "Then you've changed." Warm lips ghosted against my hair. "Perhaps I see things clearer, because I've been a warrior longer."

"I'm not a warrior at all."

"I thought the same once. But when the Spaniards came to our village, I fought with the rest, to save the corn that would feed us through the winter. I lost many friends then, Cassie. The man who had been like a father to me was taken, and because he would not betray where we had hidden the harvest, they fed him to their dogs, piece by piece. Then they carried off the women and burned the village to the ground."

He sounded so matter-of-fact about it that I stared. He smiled sadly. "I grieved for him by honoring what he fought for, by keeping our small group together and free."

He stopped and I knew why. It was one of the few things he'd told me about his life. Alejandro had eventually finished what the conquistadors had begun, by killing Tomas' village in some sort of game. I'd never heard the whole story, only a few small fragments, but I didn't want to make him relive it.

I decided to change the subject. "Louis-César said your mother was a noblewoman. How did you end up in a village?"

"After the conquest, no one was noble, no one commoner. You were either European or nothing. My mother had been a priestess of Inti, the sun god, and had taken a vow of chastity for life, but a conquistador took her as booty after the fall of Cuzco. She had expected to be treated with honor, according to the rules of war, but he knew nothing of our customs and would not have cared if he did. He was merely a farmer's son from Extremadura out to make a fortune, and didn't care much how he did it. She hated him."

"How did she get away?"

"No one thought she could scale a wall ten feet high when seven months pregnant, and they failed to watch her closely. She got away, but she had no money, and her defilement made her an outcast from her former calling. Not that it mattered. The temple had been plundered and the land was ravaged by disease and war. She fled the capital, where the Spaniards were fighting among themselves, but found things no better in the countryside." Tomas smiled bitterly. "They forgot, you cannot eat gold. Most of the farmers who had not died had run away. Famine was everywhere. Grain became more valuable than the riches the conquistadors had wanted so badly."

"Yet your mother found a village that would take her in?"

"She hid in her family's chullpa—a crypt where food and offerings were left for mummified ancestors—and one of the palace servants found her. He had long loved her, but the priestesses were considered the wives of Inti. Sleeping with one of them was a terrible crime. The punishment was to be stripped and chained to a wall, and left to starve to death."

"So he had worshipped from afar?"

Tomas smiled. "Very afar. But he began looking for her as soon as he heard she had escaped. He persuaded her to go away with him to his family's village. It was almost fifty miles from the capital, and so small that they hoped the Spanish would overlook it. They lived there together until I was eight, when she died of smallpox along with half the village."

"I'm sorry." It seemed there were no safe topics, after all. I fingered the eagle charm that I'd unconsciously picked up. I couldn't volunteer to go back and get Tomas' mother out of danger, before disease carried her away. I couldn't even help my own mother without drastically changing time. For all my supposed power, I didn't seem to be able to do much at all.

Tomas bent over to kiss me gently. His lips were soft and warm, and before I realized it, I was kissing him back. I'd wanted to do that for so long, it seemed as natural as breathing. Just touching him pushed away the memories of the attack, cleansing some part of me the bathwater hadn't been able to reach. Tomas deepened the kiss until I could feel it all the way to my toes, like tendrils of sunshine were curling through me. He tasted like wine, dark and sweet and burning, and I felt like I could never get enough.

But after a moment, I pulled back. It wasn't easy—the *geis* had recognized Tomas and the Pythia's power agreed that he would do fine to complete the ritual. Their need overrode my aversion to even thinking about intimacy at the moment. I wanted to fill my mind with thoughts and sensations that didn't involve horror and pain. I wanted him to touch me with those long, elegant hands, to have his mouth hot and demanding on mine. The look in his eyes was a caress itself, and an invitation. But the consequences for a few moments of passion would be severe.

Tomas let me go, an expression that I couldn't name flashing across his face. "I'm sorry, Cassie. I know I am not the one you want."

What could Tomas know about what I wanted? Most of the time, I didn't know myself. "What I want isn't the point," I said, trying to ignore the way his hand was playing along my side from breast to hip, over and over in a lazy, sensual stroke. It made my heart speed up and breathing difficult, like someone had sucked all the oxygen out of the room. Oh, yeah, the *geis* liked him fine.

"What do you mean?" Tomas' hand stilled on my hip. That was not a great help to my blood pressure. Despite the fact that I had moved back, we were less than a foot apart. I struggled not to look down and failed miserably. The blanket had slipped off the front half of Tomas' body. Long legs shifted in the shadows, and between them was ample evidence of just how recovered he was.

"I can't," I said, trying to remember exactly why that was. My fingers traced a line down his high forehead to the tender eyelids that fluttered closed under my touch, to the

proud nose and warm, full lips. It was a perfect profile, burnished bronze in the lamplight like the head on an ancient
coin, but his appearance wasn't what had attracted me to
him. I'd loved his kindness, his strength and—I'd thought at
the time—his honesty. Now I merely craved a warm body
and soft skin next to mine, and a face that was familiar and
caring.

"You saved my life, Cassie, even though I once put yours
at risk. Let me do something for you." Tomas' voice was at
its best, whiskey deep and smoky, as if golden liquor had
been magically turned into sound. It had always been one of
his most attractive features, partly because, unlike the carefully contrived outfits and blatant attempts at seduction, it
was unconscious. It was more the real Tomas, and so alluring that I wondered why he'd bothered with the rest. But of
course I knew why—because Louis-César had ordered him
to, after Mircea decided that he would do to fulfill the ritual.
I suppose they'd worried about the possibility of me recog-
nizing one of Mircea's people after so many years at Tony's,
where they came and went on a regular basis. But it hadn't
been fair to Tomas, and for the first time I wondered whether
he'd resented being used.

"I don't see what you can do," I said, "unless you can talk
the king into letting us go, or make my power work here."

Tomas smiled. "Or lift the *geis*?"

Chapter 12

My brain came to a screeching halt. "Run that by me again."

"I was told that a *geis* had been placed on you to protect your virtue as your ward protected your life. But as a precaution against anything going wrong, an escape clause was added. If you slept with Mircea or someone of his choosing, the spell was broken."

My mind reeled. That was it? That was the big secret? It seemed ridiculously simple, not to mention undermining the whole point. "But why would he do that? He wants to control me!"

Tomas smiled bitterly. "No doubt. But through so clumsy a device as a spell?" He shook his head. "It would hurt his pride, Cassie. Not to mention that controlling someone as powerful as the Pythia with such a clumsy stratagem would be extremely dangerous. Why do you think the mages take initiates so young, and brainwash them throughout childhood? I am sure they would prefer to use a spell to keep them in line, if such a thing were possible. But the Pythia's power might override it, and the controller become the controlled. I cannot imagine Mircea risking that!"

"But why place the *geis* on me, then, if he never intended to use it?"

"To protect your chance to become Pythia. A brief affair could have ruined everything, for you and for him. The *geis* seemed the simplest way to ensure that didn't happen. And to afford you added protection at Antonio's. You did not know about this?"

"I didn't even know about the *geis* until yesterday!" I sat up abruptly, my mind racing at the implications. I could break the *geis* by sleeping with Tomas. It was so simple that it was ludicrous—if he was telling the truth. But Tomas didn't need to resort to lies to get a woman in his bed, and his explanation made sense. I'd thought it strange all along that Mircea would think he needed magical help to manipulate someone as young and clueless as me, especially when I was already infatuated with him. There were far more subtle ways of exercising control, and he was master of them all.

Of course, even if Tomas was right, there was no way to know whether Mircea's get-out-of-jail-free card would work on a double spell. And even if it did, there was a catch. A big one. If I broke the *geis*, I'd fulfill the ritual's requirements and be stuck with the Pythia's position permanently. That would put paid to any hope of passing the power on to someone else, or of working something out with the Circle. Heirs could be unseated, as Myra had found out, but the Pythia held the position for life. If I completed the ritual, the mages would have no choice but to kill me if they wanted their candidate on the throne. And the same was true of Pritkin, if he really did favor Myra.

Unfortunately, things didn't look any better if I kept the *geis*. It was almost certain that the Senate would find me sooner or later. They had too many resources, including Marlowe's intelligence network, for me to have any illusions about that. And even if Tomas was right and Mircea couldn't use the spell to control me—a big "if," in my opinion—he also couldn't break it. The *dúthracht* had lived up to its reputation and gone haywire, and there was no telling what would happen if the bond completed itself. It was supposed to be under the control of one of the participants, but what happened if, as seemed to be the case, neither of us was in the driver's seat? I didn't know what a *geis* in control of itself might do, and I didn't want to find out.

One thing was certain: if we met again, Mircea and I would certainly complete the bond. It was embarrassing to have to admit, but the only reason we hadn't done it already—and in front of about a thousand spectators—was his self-control, not mine. And that would complete the ritual, which would bring me back to square one.

"Damn it!" Both options were unacceptable, but there wasn't a third. There was no way to get rid of the *geis* and avoid completing the ritual. Or, if there was, I had no way of finding it stuck in a cell in Faerie.

Everywhere I looked, I hit a brick wall. I hated not having options, of having someone or something deciding my life for me. It had been that way as far back as I could remember. Either Tony or the Senate or the goddamned Fey were making me a victim, taking away my right to choose. I'd never had the power to fight back, to forge my own life or just to keep myself and the people I cared about safe. I couldn't even deal with one rogue initiate! And, I realized, if things continued as they were, I never would.

"What is it?" Tomas' hand was delicately stroking the small of my back, trying to soothe, to comfort. It was comforting, I admit, but not soothing. Neither the ritual nor the *geis* cared if he was hurt, or if I was ambiguous about the idea of having sex in a dank, chilly dungeon with Billy probably listening in. The compulsion to turn around and take Tomas up on the offer he'd been making ever since I met him was so strong, I had to bunch my fists in the coarse blanket beneath me to keep them still.

I forced my mind back to the problem. I'd been telling myself that I could pass the power on to someone else, but who exactly would that be? There didn't appear to be any other candidates for the job who could be trusted not to fall under the control of the Circle or of Pritkin's faction, neither of which I trusted. There was a war on, and even the thought of the power passing into the hands of someone like Myra made me cold.

Tomas wrapped his arms around me, drawing me against the sultry cocoon of his body. My hand moved of its own accord to caress the warm, golden skin at the side of his knee, just where the slope of that long, strong thigh began. It would be so easy to give in, to feed the hunger I'd felt for so long. And did it really make that much difference? The Circle was already trying to kill me. Could I believe them if they offered a deal? Wouldn't it be better from their point of view to do away with any competition for their initiates, rather than leave someone like me around? If I was going to be hunted anyway, I vastly preferred to be in the strongest position possible. And that was doubly true when dealing with Myra.

"Are you sure you've thought this through?" I asked

Tomas seriously. "There could be repercussions for helping me complete the ritual. The mages—"

Tomas tasted the inside of my wrist with the tip of his tongue. "I'm sure."

"But what about—"

He smiled wryly. "Cassie, you know what hunts me. Do you truly believe I am concerned about the Circle?"

He had a point. And, as much as I didn't want to admit it, I still had feelings for him—or, to be more precise, for the person I'd thought he was. I really doubted that someone old enough to remember the fall of the Incan Empire bore much resemblance to the sweet street kid I'd known. I didn't know the real Tomas, who he was when the Senate wasn't pulling his strings. But they weren't here now. For once, both of us were free of them, even if it was only because we were prisoners elsewhere. And despite that, he still seemed to want me.

"The choice is yours, Cassie. You know how I feel."

I looked at him searchingly. "Do I? Louis-César commanded you to come to me. All those months, you were doing a job."

Tomas' hands stilled. "And am I still doing that job, Cassie? Is this all an elaborate hoax to persuade you to accept a position you do not want?"

"No." Vamps might not have the same reaction to pain as humans, but no one would allow himself to be carved up like that, not for any reason.

He pulled me against him, his eyes burning. "Do you think I am trying to win back the Consul's good graces by completing my original mission? Is that it?"

I didn't answer immediately. Tomas had betrayed me before, and although I'd convinced myself that he'd done the wrong thing for the right reasons, what if he hadn't? I knew for a fact that he was a good actor—most of the old vamps were. If they weren't born that way, they acquired the skill through centuries of practice. But it didn't make sense for him to be playing me. Even if the Senate was willing to wipe the slate clean and take him back, that wasn't what Tomas wanted. His main goal was to be free of his master's control in order to kill Alejandro. No matter how much they wanted me back, the Senate wasn't going to make war on another sovereign vampire body—especially not when they already had a war on their hands. They couldn't give Tomas what he truly wanted, and I didn't believe he'd sell me out for less.

"No," I finally admitted. "I don't think that."

"But you don't trust me."

It wasn't a question, so I didn't answer it. What could I say? He was right.

Tomas laughed mirthlessly. "How can I blame you? You put your trust in me once, and I lied to you. Anything I say now would only be words."

"I'd still like to hear them," I said tentatively. Tomas had given me an explanation for the betrayal, but he'd said nothing about us. I needed to hear that not everything about our time together had been a lie.

He kissed me lightly, just below the indentation of my throat. "All my life, I only knew people who wanted something from me. When I was young, it was protection and a chance for revenge. After Alejandro turned me, it was skill in battle and a knowledge of the land that he didn't possess. For Louis-César, I was a living trophy, a testament to his power." He caressed my hair, lightly, reverently. "Only you ever cared about me as a person, without wanting anything in return. *Te amo,* Cassie. *Te querré para siempre.*"

I don't speak Spanish, but I got the idea. Once I'd have given a lot to hear those words, in any language, but now my feelings were too confused to even begin sorting out. I didn't know what I felt, much less what to say. "Tomas, I—"

"Don't. I want to remember this, just as it is. I will have to go back soon and I do not want to take lies with me, no matter how sweet they sound. The Senate deals in lies. This"—he rested his cheek against my chest—"this is real."

"You don't have to go back, Tomas! I told you, we'll find a way to hide you."

He laughed, and it sounded more genuine this time. "Little Cassie, always looking out for everyone. I am the one supposed to be rescuing you, didn't you know? Is that not how the fairy tales go?" His expression darkened suddenly. "But why should you think that way? I have been little enough use so far!"

"You saved me from Tony's thugs, or doesn't that count?" Tony had sent a crew to the nightclub where I'd been working to take me out. They didn't succeed partly because the Senate had assigned Tomas to guard me. Despite everything, I hadn't forgotten that he'd saved my life. But apparently he had, because he brushed it away with a gesture.

"You would have managed. You always do." His expression grew fierce. "Cassie, if you doubt how I feel, let me show you! Let me do this for you!"

I let my hand comb through the silky mass of his hair. The Pythia's position might be a cage, but at least it was one over which I'd have some say. I'd be stuck with the job, but I'd retain control over the rest of my life—something the *geis* would deny me.

"You'll hurt yourself," I protested as Tomas' breath started to come faster. A first-level master could heal almost anything, but there was no way Tomas was over his injuries already.

A rumble of laughter sounded in my ear. "It hurt far more, seeing you every day, being surrounded by your scent for months, and not being allowed to touch you. I lived with you for half a year, yet I never saw your body. I will remember this," he said wonderingly, his hand gliding down my side.

"I won't risk hurting you," I insisted, trying to sound stronger than I felt.

Tomas laughed again, and laid me back against the cot. He bent over me, his hair forming a tent around our faces that was intimate instead of suffocating. Only his eyes were clearly visible, brimming with humor. "I think we can do this," he whispered, "if you promise to be gentle."

I couldn't help it—I laughed, and the next moment he was kissing me with an intensity that left me breathless. I slid my arms under the heavy mane of hair and clasped them around Tomas' neck. His grip was strong but careful, and although I could feel the weight of him against my leg, hot and hard and ready, he held back, waiting for me to make the first move. Suddenly, there was no more doubt. It wasn't just the *geis* tugging at me. It wasn't just that I wanted a way out of the current mess. I wanted him.

"Do it," I said, "quick, while we have time."

"Quick is not what I had in mind," Tomas said, frowning. "Particularly not the first time."

"We don't have time for anything else," I said impatiently. For once the *geis*, the power and I all agreed on something, and Tomas was being difficult.

I wrapped my hand around him and was rewarded with a

deep shiver and the wonderful feel of sweet, ardent flesh against my palm.

I desperately wanted to watch that thick shaft disappear into me. I knew it would stretch me to the limit, that the fit would be tight, the friction maddening, and that sounded perfect. I wanted to feel him work his way into me, wanted the pressure, craved the burn.

"It will hurt you," he protested, his voice ragged.

I ran my tongue up the column of his neck. "Let it."

Tomas was trembling but was stubbornly not giving in. I decided to forget about talking and persuade him another way. I kissed him, my mouth hungry against his, then slid down to fasten my teeth firmly on the joint of his neck and shoulder. It was exactly where a vampire would bite, but instead I sucked some of that taut skin into my mouth, marking him. I let my hands wander where they would, memorizing the contours of the muscle and sinew under that warm, satin skin. Then, without warning, I bit down.

Tomas' breath had been making low growls in his throat, but at the feel of my teeth sliding into his flesh, he groaned. Judging by the way the hardness pressing into my hip expanded in a sudden leap, it wasn't in protest. His narrowed eyes glittered when I finally released his neck. "You don't fight fair," he complained, his voice dark and heavy. He drew in a deep breath, released it and slid a finger inside me. I gasped at the unexpected invasion, and arched, tightening convulsively around him. "Not fair at all," he said hoarsely.

I tangled my hands in his hair as a talented tongue replaced the finger. He drew my flesh into his mouth, the suction pulling my hips with it, causing me to fall into a rhythm I couldn't even think about resisting. He pushed my legs wider for better access, until one was dangling inelegantly off the cot. I didn't care—the sight of him devouring my body made my breath catch almost as much as the sensation did.

My world narrowed to that luscious mouth; that slow, wet glide; those big, strong hands. Warm, rough palms smoothed again and again over the muscles of my abdomen as if they couldn't stop, then finally slid to my hip, slowly kneading the trembling muscle they found there. God, a girl could fall in love with those hands.

His mouth felt like liquid flame as he explored me, finding places that sent shock waves of ecstasy through my body. I gasped softly, amazed by the gentle, intimate examination, the deep, delicate touch. I collapsed back against the mattress and let those wet touches drag me under. Surges of pleasure rippled up my spine as he caressed me from the inside, and suddenly the angle and pressure were perfect. It seemed like his mouth was everywhere, tasting, sucking, touching, filling. He polished his performance quickly, picking up the clues from my body, noting what made me cry out and repeating it until sunbursts of pleasure started exploding behind my eyes. Every move of his lips seared along my nerves until it threatened to take the top of my head off.

"Tomas! Please!" Before I'd finished speaking, he had changed positions and was poised over me. He stopped, struggling for control, and I growled at him. Finally he moved forward, sinking slowly into me. And, God, it was good—no, better than good, if the sparks behind my eyelids were anything to go on. He had laid me open to a dance of sensation with his hands and tongue alone, but the feel of him moving into my body was even better, stretching, wonderfully filling, remaking my flesh until I fit him like a glove.

He was ample enough to be a tight fit, but his firm flesh was smooth and yielding, molding to mine with only a slight ache when he moved across skin abraded in the attack. But he bit his lip, keeping all that power on a thin leash, his breath coming in ragged gasps from the excruciating care he was taking. He slid forward a scant half-inch at a time, warming me by fractions when I wanted the whole searing length of him. But finally he was there, nestled fully within me, radiating heat to my very core. His eyes were closed, his long lashes sweeping his flushed cheeks as he held himself motionless for a long moment. He left me breathless.

His entrance hadn't hurt, but waiting for him to move, to shift position, to do something before I completely lost my mind, did. When he started withdrawing again, with that same agonizing slowness, my patience broke. I twined myself around him as he pulled out, then suddenly thrust up to meet him, sinking him completely inside me again in a single, groan-inducing stroke.

Tomas looked both surprised and vastly relieved, his breath coming out in a hiss of pleasure. He got the idea, and began to pick up speed. My hips shifted and began to rotate of their own accord as Tomas set up a slow circular motion, caressing, pleasuring, and stretching simultaneously.

I soon found that I couldn't control the sounds I was making. I was burning up, scored by sensation, sobbing with it. I was lightheaded and my breath was coming faster and my hips were bucking and my sight was going dark. A thundering sensation was building inside me and, before I even realized what was happening, orgasm was spilling over me, my body spasming helplessly under Tomas' steady rhythm. A lovely, yellow glow suddenly suffused the room, a color so pure, so lush, that it seemed as if happiness had been condensed and given form. For a moment, I thought it was all part of the sensations running through me, but it kept building, drowning out the lamplight as if a small star had burst to life around us. Wildly twining filaments of white and gold energy sizzled and writhed everywhere, building in intensity until, like grounded lightning, they blinded me.

Without warning, the world fell away. I was plunged into a maelstrom of sights and sounds and colors, all swirling together far too quickly to follow. I couldn't sense Tomas, couldn't see him or even feel him. A vortex was rushing towards me at terrific speed, and I was powerless to do anything but let it come.

Then, as suddenly as it had started, it was over. When the afterimages faded enough for me to see again, I found myself alone on a hill, looking up at a temple. Behind it, an ocean sparkled under a hot yellow sun. I felt the brush of lips on my neck and heard a rumble of rich masculine laughter in my ear.

"I approve of my avatar," a voice said. I knew it came from the man behind me, but it seemed to echo from all directions at once, as if the temple, sky and ocean were also speaking. "The son of another of my priestesses—really, a nice touch."

I blinked, dizzy and disbelieving, but the scene stayed the same. "Your what?" I finally croaked.

"The man chosen for the ceremony becomes my avatar for a time. His union with the heir consummates our marriage and confirms her in office."

I choked. "I am not your wife!"

That laughter bubbled again, rich and infectious. "Do not be afraid, Herophile. It's a spiritual union—you could not withstand me in my physical form."

"I'm not afraid," I said, and it was true. Compared to the visions I usually got, this one was a walk in the park. So far. "And my name is Cassandra."

"Not anymore."

I tried to turn around, but strong arms held me tight. They were the color of spring pollen, a bright true yellow that sparkled as if dusted with gold. The light danced over his skin the way it does on water, so dazzling that it hurt my eyes. It should have looked extremely strange on a human body, but somehow it didn't. Suddenly the surroundings made more sense.

"You don't miss a cliché, do you?"

"Your mind chooses how to perceive me," he chided. "If there are clichés, they are yours."

"Who are you?" I demanded.

"One who has waited long ages for someone like you. At last, things will begin to happen."

"What things?"

"You will see. I have great faith in you."

"Then you're crazy," I told him flatly. "I don't know how to use this power you've stuck me with, and Myra's going to kill me any minute now."

"I sincerely hope not. As for the other, the power goes where it will. Once I gave it into human hands, I lost control."

"But Myra—"

"Yes, for now, you must deal with your rival. We will speak again when that is done."

"But that's the point! I don't know how to—" I never got to finish the sentence. There was an outpouring of heat and a rush of wind, and all around me surged a terrible, ancient power that rumbled through the ground and sent currents sizzling along my entire body. Then I was back in the cell, blinking in the suddenly dim light, unsure what had just happened.

Tomas had let himself go, and the sensations he was

causing caught my breath in my throat and drove the questions from my mind. He pulled me closer to his chest, and I gasped as the length inside me shifted. His sweat-damp hair fell around me, and his teeth latched onto my throat. I felt my whole body constrict at the bite, and heard Tomas' pleased growl as my inner muscles tightened around him. Large hands gripped my hips, driving him into me as far as he could go. He released my throat without feeding, tongue swiping once along the abrasion; then his hips began pumping faster, his face slack with need, and I lost all ability to think for long minutes.

He finished inside me in a delicious rush that felt scorching next to the lingering bits of ice at my center. It ate that cold, consumed it, burnt the final vestiges of it away and filled me up with a heated languor that spread throughout my body. My own pleasure was less overpowering now, but deeper, more persistent and sweet. I felt boneless with Tomas draped over me like the best of heaters.

After a long moment, Tomas pulled back to gaze into my half-closed eyes. He searched my expression, but whatever he was looking for, he didn't seem to find. He kissed me anyway, and I arched into the sensual heat of his mouth, feeling somewhat bereft when he ended the contact too soon. "I'm sorry," he said softly, his thumb tracing my lower lip.

I smoothed one of his fine, dark eyebrows with a finger. "What's wrong?"

He took my face between his hands and gently kissed my forehead. "It's all right, Cassie. It will be all right."

"What will?" My afterglow was fast disappearing.

Tomas hesitated, then let his breath out in a sigh. "I can

still feel the *geis* around you, like a cloud." His jaw tight-ened. "It seems Mircea does not wish to release his claim."

I shook my head. "There was a complication with the spell. Mircea couldn't remove it, either." I'd known this was a possibility, but it was still a crushing disappointment.

Tomas started to say something else, but the door suddenly swung inward and there was Françoise, hands on hips, looking impatient. She tossed a bundle of clothes at me. "It's about time! It's supposed to be a ritual, not a marathon."

I scrambled to my feet, shivering in air that felt cold against my flushed skin. "What?"

"Well, come on! Get dressed! The king wants an audience, and he doesn't wait well. Piss him off, and none of us are getting out of here."

"Françoise?" I was getting a very bad feeling about this. The accent was suddenly gone, and the look on her face didn't remind me much of the French girl's usual nervousness.

She smiled grimly. "Françoise isn't home right now. Can I take a message?" Before I could come up with an answer to that, she grimaced and clutched the wall, her fingers clawed and white with strain, as if they were trying to dig into the stone. "Damn it! Not now, girl! Do you want to stay here forever?"

Tomas was looking back and forth between the two of us, but I could only shake my head at him. I had no idea what was wrong with her. "Um, Françoise," I finally said, as she began to vibrate as if her finger were stuck in a socket. "Is there something we can . . . do for you?"

She suddenly stopped, stock-still, and stared at me, impatience flooding her features. "Yes! You can get dressed! How many times do I have to say it?"

I was cold without Tomas' body heat, so I decided to

humor her. The dress was too large, and stiff with embroidery, but the dark red wool was warm. I decided that my best bet was to concentrate on one problem at a time, and Françoise's mental glitches weren't even close to top of the list.

"Françoise, do you have friends here? People who would help you?"

She narrowed her eyes. "Why?"

"It's Tomas. . . . If he leaves Faerie, he'll be killed. He can't go back, but he can't stay in this place, waiting to be executed, either. Do you know someone who can hide him?"

"Cassie." Tomas touched my elbow. "What are you doing?"

"I need to know that you're safe. What if the king orders us deported back to MAGIC? If you return, they'll kill you!" The Consul had offered me his life, but only in return for information I didn't have. I hadn't meant to place the *geis* on Mircea, and I certainly couldn't lift it.

"And if you go before the king without me, he may blame you for my escape. I won't endanger you further," Tomas said flatly. I would have argued, but the set of his jaw told me it would be a waste of time. Besides, Françoise was looking apoplectic.

"You're worried about a *vampire . . . now*, of all times?" She shook her head. "Cassie, he was a means to an end, that's all. He served his purpose; let him look after himself. They're pretty good at that, you know."

Okay, that clinched it. There was more going on here than Françoise having a fit. "You want to tell me who you are right now? Because I never told Françoise my name. Not to mention that she only used to speak French."

"We don't have time for this!"

I sat on the bunk and looked at her mulishly. "I'm not going anywhere until I know who you are and what is going on." I'd had about enough of flying by the seat of my pants. The past week had taught me the hard way that I sucked at it.

She threw up her hands in an oddly familiar gesture. Somewhere, I'd seen someone use that movement in the same way, but it eluded me. "I told you once you'd be either the best of us all or the very worst. Want to bet which way I'm leaning?"

It took a few seconds to sink in, and even when it did, I didn't believe it. "*Agnes?* What . . . what the hell are you doing in there?"

"Existing," she said bitterly. "Some afterlife."

"But . . . but . . . I didn't know you could even do possessions! The mages said—"

"Right. Like we tell them everything!" She put her hands back on her hips in another eerily familiar gesture. "The less the Circle knows about our abilities, the better! Did you really believe you could do it and I couldn't?"

"But you don't have Billy Joe," I protested. It was something that had been bothering me, both with her and with Myra. "How can you shift in time without a spirit to babysit your body while you're gone?"

Agnes just stared at me; then she shook her head. "Well, that's an original approach, I'll grant you," she muttered. "We go back to our bodies at almost the same moment we left them, Cassie. Our bodies don't die, because as far as they're concerned, we never left."

"But . . . your body . . ." I stared at her, wondering how to phrase things. There didn't seem to be a lot of options. "Agnes, I'm sorry, but . . . it *is* dead."

She looked at me as if I'd lost my mind. "Of course it is! What do you think I'm doing here?"

"I have no idea," I told her honestly.

"Well, it certainly wasn't my first choice!" She looked pissed. "This is supposed to be my bonus life, my time to enjoy myself for a change. I left you intending to return to my body, to gather strength to migrate into a nice German girl. She was supposed to die in a rockfall—a hiking accident—and I was all set to take her over—"

"Take her over?" I don't know what my face looked like, but Agnes let out a laugh.

"She was going to *die*, Cassie! On the whole, I think she'd have preferred sharing a life with me to that!"

I felt dizzy. "I don't get it."

Tomas spoke up suddenly, startling me. "One to serve, one to live," he murmured.

Agnes shot him a less-than-kind look. "I don't know where you heard that, but just forget it."

"Then it's true," he said, apparently stunned. "There have been rumors, but no one believes—"

"Which is how it's going to stay." Agnes said emphatically.

It was my turn to look back and forth between the two of them. "Will somebody please tell me what is going on?"

"There is an old rumor," Tomas said, ignoring Agnes' frown, "that the Pythia is rewarded at the end of her service with another life—a type of compensation for the one she gave up to her calling."

I closed my mouth, which kept trying to hang open in shock. For a moment, I just stared at Agnes. "Is that true?" I finally managed to ask.

"Do you want to get out of here or not?" she demanded. "Just tell me!"

She sighed and threw up her hands again. I didn't know if that was a regular habit, or if it just happened a lot around me. "Okay, long story short—yes, it's true. We find some-one slated to die young, and cut a deal with them. We pos-sess them and feed off their energy, and in return we help them to avoid whatever catastrophe was about to occur."

"That's horrible!"

"No, it's practical. A shared life is better than none at all."

"But if you can do it once," Tomas said slowly, "why can you not continue to do it life after life, century after cen-tury?"

"That's why I hate vamps," Agnes said to the room in general. "They're so damn suspicious!"

"But can you do it?" Tomas asked.

"Of course not!" she snapped. "Think it through! Once our time in service is over, the power migrates to someone else. Without it, we have no way of knowing who is going to die, and therefore no way of choosing another body. It's a onetime deal."

Tomas gave a short laugh. "You expect us to believe that no one has ever tried to cheat death? To live through many lifetimes by taking whomever they wanted, whether they were doomed or not?"

Agnes shrugged. "That's one of the many duties of the reigning Pythia—to make sure it doesn't happen that way."

I shook my head. This was happening too fast, all of it. My brain just couldn't keep up. "But why Françoise?"

"I told you—I didn't have a choice! I started to return to my body but discovered that I'd wasted too much energy helping you. I hadn't planned to have to freeze time—that's not an easy trick, especially after a jump of more than three hundred years! I found that I didn't have enough left to jump the centuries one last time."

"But I could have taken you back with me!" Agnes had

helped me fight off Myra. If it wasn't for her help, I'd probably be dead already. I would certainly not have refused to give her a lift.

"If you recall, Cassie, you were in the middle of a room full of hungry ghosts. They were bent on devouring every spirit in sight! I couldn't risk it. Once time started up again, I had to get out of there fast. So I went into the only person I knew of in that time who was near death and might be willing to cut a deal."

"And did she?" Françoise wasn't just any old norm: she was a witch, and from one very memorable trick I'd seen her perform, a powerful one. And it looked to me like she was fighting.

Almost as if she'd heard my thoughts, Agnes made another grimace and clutched her stomach. "In a manner of speaking."

"How did you end up here?" Tomas asked before I could demand something a little less nebulous.

"I'd planned to get back to Cassie before she left that century, once I was in possession of a body to keep the spirits away. But the damn dark mages showed up."

"They kidnapped you for sale to the Fey," he reasoned. "And you have been here ever since? But that was centuries ago!"

"Years, actually," Agnes corrected.

"Time runs differently here," I reminded him. Marlowe had said it, but I hadn't realized just how big the difference could be. "You're saying you've been here continually, ever since we left France?"

Agnes nodded, then held up a hand to stop me when I tried to say something else. "If you've seen us since, don't

tell me about it. Françoise can hear us, and she doesn't need
to be influenced by knowing what will happen in her future."

Her future, I thought dizzily, but my past. She'd killed a
dark mage at Dante's a week ago, helping me escape. Or,
rather, she was going to kill one. . . . My head was starting
to hurt.

"Do you want to get out of here or not?" Agnes demanded.

"Yes, but we're going to talk later," I told her. Maybe by
then I'd have sorted some of this out and be able to think
straight.

"If there is a later," she said ominously. "Don't forget the
wards—I went to enough trouble to get them for you." She
grabbed the lantern and, in a swirl of skirts, vanished down
the hallway. Tomas and I looked at each other, then hurried
to follow her, Tomas still pulling on the clothes she'd
brought and me stuffing wards into every pocket I could
find.

We turned at the end of the hall to ascend a long flight of
stairs that was only occasionally lit by low-burning torches.
At the end was another thick oak door, but it opened easily
at the barest push from Françoise. Pritkin, Billy and Marlowe stood around a large round opening in a wall of rock,
beyond which a mass of color shifted in a kaleidoscope of
light.

"Is this all of them?" the pixie demanded, barely bothering to glance at us. "The cycle is almost complete."

Billy looked nervous. "Cass, do you think I'll keep this
body once we go back?"

"We're going back?"

"As soon as that thing cycles to blue. But we'll only have
about thirty seconds to get through at the right destination.

We're getting off at Dante's, but the Senate is next on the rotation, so we have to jump quick before it turns red."

I found it hard to keep up. "Why are we leaving?"

"Because you're going to retrieve something for me." A deep baritone echoed off the walls. I slowly realized that what I had taken to be a pillar draped in material was actually the biggest leg I'd ever seen. I looked up, and kept on doing so for a ridiculous length of time. A face as large as a searchlight beamed down at me from the shadowy vastness of the hall. The ceiling had to be thirty feet high, yet he was bent over slightly as if it cramped him. I did a double take, then just stared.

The huge head lowered itself to get a better look at me. Frizzy brown hair obscured much of it, leaving a bulbous nose and blue eyes the size of softballs visible. "So this is the new Pythia."

"We had to deal with the king," Billy explained in a low voice. "Our runes are used up until next month. Pritkin tried to caste Hagalaz and it didn't work—it just got a little colder and we ended up with a puddle of slush. Null bombs are great, but only against magic, and we're seriously outnumbered here. The Fey don't need mumbo jumbo to hit us over the head. We need more weapons and some allies or the only thing we're going to do here is die. Marlowe's agreed to cough up the weapons from the Senate's stash when we go back."

"How generous of him. What's the catch?"

Marlowe, for once, didn't have a glib reply. Instead he simply stood there staring at me, looking flabbergasted. Then he slowly sank to one knee. "The Senate is always delighted to aid the Pythia," he finally said, after several tries.

"She isn't Pythia," Pritkin remarked, turning at last to

acknowledge my presence. Then he stopped dead, his mouth working but no sound coming out. One hand remained raised halfway through a movement, as if he had simply forgotten to lower it.

"My lady, what shall we call you?" Marlowe asked reverently.

"No!" Pritkin broke out of his trance and stared between me and the kneeling vamp. "This is a trick—it must be!"

I glanced at Tomas, baffled. "What's going on?"

He smiled slightly. "Your aura has changed."

I tried to see for myself, but I couldn't concentrate well enough and just ended up cross-eyed. "What does it look like?"

Marlowe answered for him. "Power," he whispered, appearing dazzled.

"You need to proclaim a reign title, Cassie," Tomas said. "Your rule doesn't officially begin until then. Lady Phemonoe was named after the first of the line. You can take the same title if you wish or choose another."

Pritkin had come back to life and was striding across the room, looking outraged. "Herophile," I said quickly, the name from my vision coming automatically. I looked nervously at Tomas. "Is that okay?" Pritkin's hand, which had been reaching for me, stopped and dropped to his side.

"Where's the golem?" I asked Billy, keeping an eye on the mage. He had the look of an atheist who'd just had a visit from God: stunned, disbelieving and faintly ill.

"You don't want to know," Billy answered, staring fixedly at the portal, his throat working nervously.

"What do you mean?"

The king answered for him. It was hard to believe that, for a moment, I'd actually forgotten someone that large. "He was given to my steward as a gift. He very generously loaned him to me."

"They turned him loose a couple of hours ago," Billy said. "They're going to give him another hour, then go after him. Something about training their hunting dogs."

"What?" I was horrified. "But he could be killed!"

"Technically, he isn't alive," Billy pointed out, "so he can't die."

"He may not have been alive before, but he is now!" I looked around for support but didn't find any. Marlowe had moved up beside Pritkin, looking worried. Billy was staring at the swirls of color inside the portal and biting his lip, and I doubted the golem's fate was uppermost in his mind. "We can't leave him!"

"Of course," the king murmured, a sound as loud as anyone else's bellow, "you could save him, if you like."

I had a very bad feeling about this. "How would I do that?"

The king smiled, showing teeth the size of golf balls. "By making a trade."

"Careful, Cass," Billy muttered. "He wants something from you, but he wouldn't tell us what."

"Quiet, remnant!" The king thundered. "Keep your tongue behind your teeth, or someone may cut it out!" Then, as quick as a flash, his mood changed and he smiled angelically. " 'Tis only a book, lady, a trifling matter."

"Their destination is next," the pixie warned.

Pritkin suddenly come back to life. "Where is Mac?"

I stared at him blankly, and then it hit. Oh, my God. No one had told him.

The pixie answered before I could begin to think of a reply. "The forest demanded a sacrifice before it would let us through. It went for the girl, but the mage offered himself instead."

I transferred my stare to her. She must have seen Mac deliberately do something to draw attention to himself. He had understood—the forest wouldn't let me go, wouldn't stop attacking us, until it had a sacrifice.

So he gave it one.

Tomas squeezed my shoulder in silent sympathy, but I hardly felt it. There had been no blood on the ground when we left. The earth had absorbed it, had absorbed him. The wards I'd stuffed in my pocket suddenly felt like bricks.

Pritkin had looked confused at the pixie's offhand comment, but whatever he saw on my face was explanation enough. Comprehension flooded his eyes. "You planned this," he said in a strangely dead voice. "You tricked us into rescuing that . . . thing, so you could complete the ritual. The *geis* made any other candidate impossible."

"I didn't plan anything," I said. I wanted to tell him how horribly sorry I was, to say something worthy of Mac, but my brain didn't seem to be working.

"About the book," the king rumbled.

I looked up at him, confused. "What book?"

His face contorted slightly and I realized that he was trying to look innocent. It didn't appear to be an expression he employed very often, judging by the result. "The *Codex Merlini*."

"What?" The name meant nothing to me, but Pritkin jerked violently.

Marlowe looked intrigued. "But you can pick one up at any magical bookstore."

The king made a sound like boulders rubbing together. I finally realized that he was laughing. "Not that one. The lost volume." He looked down at me and his eyes were hungry. "Bring me the second volume of the *Codex*, and you can have the creature. You have my word."

"No!" Pritkin suddenly lunged for me, his face thunderous, but a second later he was skidding across the floor from the brutal shove Tomas gave him. He hit the wall but did an acrobatic flip back to his feet and started for us again. His eyes were ice-cold and promised pain for someone.

"Interrupt me again, mage, and I'll have your liver for dinner," the king warned. His voice left no doubt that he meant it. Pritkin skidded to a halt.

I glanced from Pritkin's furious face to Marlowe's interested one. "What am I missing?"

"The *Codex* is the . . . the primer, if you like, the text on which all modern magic is based," Marlowe informed me. "Merlin composed it, partly from his own work, and partly from his research into the available magical texts of his day—many of which are now lost to us. He was afraid that knowledge would be lost if someone didn't catalog it for future generations. But legend says that we only have half his work, that there was originally a second volume." He glanced at the king. "Even if it still exists, what good would it do you? Human magic doesn't work here."

"Some does," the king replied evasively. He was trying to look as if the conversation barely interested him, but doing a lousy job. His enormous eyes were fairly dancing with excitement, and the cheeks over the curly beard were flushed. "Merlin divided his spells into two parts for security. The spells themselves were in volume one, the counterspells in volume two. Most of the counterspells have been discovered by trial and error through the years, except the odd lot, like that *geis* of yours. I want—"

My brain stuttered to a halt at the magic word. "Wait a minute. You're telling me the *Codex* contains a spell to remove the *geis*?"

"It is said to contain the counters to all Merlin's spells. He invented the *dúthracht*, so it should be in there." He regarded me shrewdly. "Does that add incentive, seer?"

I put on my poker face and hoped it was better than his. "Some. But I don't see how I can help you. If the book was lost—"

"Are you Pythia or not?" he bellowed, shaking the rafters. "Go back in time and find it, before it disappeared!"

I took in the eagerness written on his huge face and made a swift decision. "I could try," I agreed. "But the price you offer is too low. What else will you give?"

Pritkin let out an expletive and leapt for me. His face was beet red and he looked like he was about to burst a vein. Tomas took a step forward, but it was Marlowe, moving in a blur, who got a choke hold around his throat. I met the furious green gaze helplessly. I would talk to Pritkin later, try to explain everything, but now was not the time.

The king looked like he was thinking about adding Pritkin to the evening menu, but I interrupted. "We were bargaining, Your Majesty, and there isn't much time." I gestured at the portal, which was glowing a bright, true blue, with swirls of peacock, teal, navy and royal moving in lazy patterns over the surface.

"What do you want?" he asked swiftly.

After years of watching Tony wheel and deal, this was almost too easy. "I need to find a vampire," I told him. "His name is Antonio, although he may be using an alias. He's said to be somewhere in Faerie. In addition to the golem, I want Antonio's location and enough aid from you to retrieve him." And anyone with him, I silently added. "And sanctuary for Tomas, here at your court, for as long as he needs it."

"The golem's life and the sanctuary are simple enough," the king said, "but the other . . ." He trailed off thoughtfully. "I know of the vampire of whom you speak," he finally admitted. "But reaching him will be difficult—and dangerous."

"As will finding your book," I pointed out.

He hesitated, but the color at the edge of the spiral was starting to bleed to purple. He was out of time and I was the only one who could retrieve the book he wanted so badly. "Done. Bring me the book, and you will have your vampire."

I nodded and started forward, only to collide with Billy, who was backing away. "I-I need to rethink this," he babbled. "I'll take the next bus."

"What's wrong with you?" I demanded.

His face was white, and his hands were sketching agitated patterns in the air. "What if I lose my body when we return? I just got it back, Cass!"

"A little while ago, you were worried about what might happen if you stayed!"

"And now I'm worried about what'll happen if I go." He looked genuinely terrified. "You don't understand what could be through there!"

"Billy! We don't have time for this! You already came through a portal on the way here."

"Yeah, and look what it got me! Think it through, Cass!"

I had no idea what he was talking about, and wasn't given the chance to find out. "Get in the portal, remnant," the pixie said. "We don't need your kind here."

"Stay out of this, dolly," Billy warned, swiping at her with his hat.

Suddenly, a blur shot in front of us, heading for the

portal, and I barely had a chance to recognize Françoise before a bright light flashed and she was gone. The king let out an enraged bellow. "Bring her back!" he ordered.

The pixie unsheathed her tiny sword. I'd seen what that thing could do, but Billy hadn't and he didn't even bother to dodge. The side of the sword caught him in the stomach, lifting him off his feet and smacking him backwards. I had a chance to see his wide-eyed shock, and then he was gone. The pixie flew straight into the portal after him, their flashes coming so close together that they almost looked like one.

I turned to see that Pritkin had collapsed to his knees, Marlowe on his back. I was moving forward to intervene when he suddenly hit the vamp in the temple and simultaneously brought his other elbow back in a savage jab to the ribs. Marlowe let go and staggered backwards, straight into the vortex. Pritkin stayed down for a second, a hand to his injured throat, trying to get his breath back. From his gasping wheezes, it sounded like Marlowe's choke hold had been closer to a strangulation.

"Cassie, you must go," Tomas said urgently. He paused, his expression an odd mix of tenderness and pain. "Try not to get killed."

"Yeah. You, too." I would have preferred time to say good-bye, but there wasn't any. I kissed him quickly, took a running start and threw myself at the swirl of color. At the last second Pritkin dove in beside me. There was a flash of light, then another, then only blackness.

Chapter 13

I came around because a pounding was reverberating in my head. I realized three things simultaneously: I was back at Dante's, the pounding was coming from large speakers masquerading as giant tiki heads and Elvis was looking really rough—even for a dead guy. I blinked and Kit Marlowe shoved a drink into my hand. "Try to look normal," he murmured as Elvis started on the chorus to "Jailhouse Rock."

I looked around dazedly but found it hard to concentrate on anything but the huge man in white sequins who was swaying in what I guess was meant to be an alluring fashion. The bullet that had recently scalped him had been large caliber, and I didn't think the emergency toupee was holding up too well. The ladies throwing everything from room keys to underwear onstage didn't seem to notice, though. I guess love really is blind.

I wanted to ask what was going on, but my brain and mouth didn't seem to be connected. I sat, swaying a little in my chair. Half the audience was doing the same, but their movements were an unconscious imitation of the performance and not because of an unclear concept of which way was up. What was wrong with me? I'd barely had the thought when I remembered: the portal. Unlike the unnoticeable transition at MAGIC, this one had packed a wallop. Trust Tony to cheap out. Judging by the way my head felt, he'd gone for the bargain-basement version since he hadn't planned to ever have to use it himself. I hoped it had given him a really big migraine.

Marlowe picked a blue lace thong off his ear, one of the offerings to the god of rock 'n' roll that hadn't quite made the stage, and tossed it over his shoulder. "We're in trouble," he said unnecessarily.

I raised an eyebrow. What else was new? Marlowe used his swizzle stick to poke the fist-sized shrunken head that was posing as a centerpiece. The fact that the ugly thing sat on a pretty nest of dark green palm fronds and orange birds of paradise helped not at all. A shriveled, raisinlike eye reluctantly opened and rotated in his direction. "Can't it wait? This is my favorite song."

"I need a refill," Marlowe told it tersely. "One of the same." The head closed its eyes, but its mouth kept moving.

"What—" I paused to swallow because my tongue felt about twice the usual size, then tried again. "What is it doing?"

"Communicating with the bar," Marlowe answered, glancing around surreptitiously.

"I'm going to pass out now," I informed him.

Marlowe shot me a reproving glance. "You will do no such thing. The Circle has us surrounded. Two of their operatives saw us flash in and now everyone they left at the casino is here. They're too wary of the internal defenses and your abilities to try anything without backup, so we have a few moments, but that's all. You have to be ready to move."

"Move where? You said we're surrounded."

"Casanova is going to arrange a diversion, but for the moment all we can do is sit tight. And have a drink," he added, as I tried valiantly to keep my eyes from crossing. "Alcohol usually helps in these cases."

I nodded, but his words made less of an impression on my fried brain than the little head in the center of the table. It had finished talking to the bar and was now humming along with the music, which was quite a trick for a piece of plastic. I guess normal tourists thought there was some sort of microphone hidden inside the things that relayed their orders, but I knew better. I'd seen one of these before.

We were in Dante's zombie bar—the one known as Headliners because of the gruesome decorations and top-notch, if sadly deceased, entertainers. From past experience, I knew that the heads posing as centerpieces were fake, but not the way the tourists thought. They were enchanted copies designed to look like the only real one in the place, whose desiccated remains were suspended between two carved wooden masks behind the bar. It was rumored to have belonged to a gambler who had unwisely welshed on a bet. I heard him warn one guy that, at this casino, gambling money you didn't have wouldn't get you a little ahead. It would get you "a little head."

The woman who had thrown the thong, a buxom blonde who had about five pounds to go before another adjective would be required, snatched her property off the floor and gave Marlowe an evil look. She stood by the stage and flapped the tiny piece of lace like it was a handkerchief, but Elvis' eyes were far too glazed to notice. His face was the color of mildewed grout and his jet-black toupee had slid to the right, exposing a line of greenish white flesh over his left ear. Fortunately, he'd segued into "Love Me Tender," which didn't require so many gyrations. Maybe the toupee would last the night after all.

The head stopped humming when the song ended and rolled its eyes around to me. "Did you hear about the comedian who entertained at a werewolves' party?" it asked chattily. Marlowe and I ignored it. "He had them howling in the aisles!"

A zombie waiter dressed in a Hawaiian shirt that clashed with his gray skin and Bermuda shorts that showed off his shriveled legs was threading his way through the tables in our direction. I watched him come closer and realized that without knowing it I'd finished off the martini Marlowe had given me. The alcohol did seem to have helped my head, but not my mood, which was getting darker by the minute. I had a good reason: Tomas had been right; the *geis* was still there.

That constant miserable pressure was back. I could feel it, a shimmering cord stretching from me across the desert to MAGIC. I tried strengthening my shields, but the glimmering strands shot right through them. But at least there was no crushing pain this time. Maybe becoming Pythia had gained me something, after all, or maybe the *geis* just needed time to compensate for my new power level. In any case, I was grateful for the reprieve.

"Where are the others?" I asked. Billy could be a real help letting us know when the Circle's reinforcements were coming.

"I have not seen the pixie or the girl. But the mage came through the portal with you," Marlowe said, keeping an eye on the six figures that had fanned out on either side of the entrance. They were all weaving long leather topcoats that had to be stifling even in air-conditioning. Coats that looked like copies of Pritkin's. Several more, I noticed now, were in a similar position near the small side exit. "I rendered him unconscious and locked him in the back room."

"That won't hold him for long."

"Cassie, if we're here much longer, Pritkin will be the least of our worries." The waiter sat a pitcher of martinis and a dish of olives on the table. Marlowe appropriated the pitcher, leaving me only a coconut carved to resemble one of the shrunken heads. The pina colada inside had possibly had a bottle of rum waved over it at some point, but none had made it inside. I sighed and drank it anyway.

"Okay, how about a riddle," the head burbled. "What's the best way to a vampire's heart?" It paused for a couple of beats. "Through his rib cage!"

The big blonde, who'd been getting increasingly strident in her attempts to gain the King's attention, finally decided the heck with it and crawled up onstage. Despite wearing stiletto heels, she managed to get within a few feet of him before the bar's discreetly dressed security people grabbed her. Casanova, who was standing next to the stage, smoothed over the potential debacle by sending in a handsome Latino. The no-doubt incubus-possessed man led the woman off to the bar with a smile that promised to make her forget all about dead rock stars.

"If that was Casanova's idea of a diversion, he falls really short of his reputation."

"It wasn't." Marlowe sounded sure.

"How do you know?"

"Because, unless I miss my guess, the cavalry has arrived."

I followed his gaze to where a trio of terribly old Greeks had just toddled into view, bearing gifts. They didn't come through the main entrance, where the mages had visibly

stiffened at the sight of them, but from the side door near the
bar. The guards for that door had disappeared. One of the
bartenders, a gorgeous guy wearing only a pith helmet and a
tiny pair of khaki shorts, caught sight of the threesome and
poured half a bottle of Chivas on the bar before he noticed.

"A tough audience, huh?" the head asked. "Okay, but did
you hear the one about the guy who couldn't keep up pay-
ments to his exorcist? He was repossessed. Ha! Now, go
ahead, tell me that's not funny!"

"It's not funny," Marlowe said, unfolding his napkin.

"Hey, wait! I got a thousand of them! How about the—"
Thankfully, the heavy cotton folds of the napkin cut the
thing off before I kicked it across the room.

Deino approached our table with a toothless grin. "Birt'
Day!" she said, beaming at me. I started in surprise: they
were the first English words I'd heard her use, and it was obvious that she was proud of herself. I might have been more
admiring if she hadn't followed her greeting by plopping a
bucket of bloody entrails on the table right under my nose.

I looked at Marlowe fearfully. "Please tell me that isn't—"

"It's not human," he said, wrinkling up his nose. "Cow, I
think."

Pemphredo plopped a newspaper full of casino chips
onto the table beside her sister's gift. None were the red and
blue ones I use: most were black, with a few five-hundred-
dollar purple ones scattered about here and there. I counted
more than four thousand dollars at just a glance. I closed my
eyes in despair—all I needed were the human police after
me, too. Not to be outdone, Enyo placed a large three-tiered
cake beside the other two gifts. It was covered in something
slimy and green, which I guessed was supposed to be icing.
I decided not to ask why it smelled like pesto.

Deino dumped the remaining piña colada out of my coconut shell and filled it with a generous measure of blood
and guts. She shoved it under my nose and beamed at me.
"Birt' Day!"

I managed not to gag. "Why are they doing this?" I asked
Marlowe, who was looking almost as disgusted as I felt.
Vamps don't drink animal blood. It does nothing for them
and many find it actually repugnant.

"As a guess? They are making an offering. In the ancient
world, blood sacrifices were common. If I were you, I'd be
grateful they aren't slicing up a virgin on the table. Perhaps
they couldn't find one in Vegas."

"Ha, ha. What am I supposed to do with—" That was as
far as I got. If I hadn't been so grossed out, I'd have noticed
earlier that zombie Elvis had stopped singing halfway through
a lackluster rendition of "All Shook Up" and was now trying
to climb down from the stage.

Marlowe was on his feet. "We have to get rid of the
bucket!"

I looked around at the close-packed tables full of clueless
tourists. "How?"

Elvis scattered the handful of security types who had
rushed forward and lurched toward our table. His eyes were
no longer dull, but were filled with a burning hunger as they
zeroed in on the bloody bucket. Then one of the guards with
more muscle than sense grabbed him by the shoulder and
tried to whirl him around. All he succeeded in doing was
knocking the toupee the rest of the way off, revealing the top
of an exposed brain. I guessed the voodoo types Casanova
kept on staff had been a little overworked after the recent
raid and had skimped on the repair work. That probably
hadn't been a good business decision.

The sight of a gray-faced, slack-jawed zombie glowering from under a pulsing, bloody brain pretty much tore it for the people at nearby tables. Several of them let out screams, and they collectively knocked over chairs and one another in the stampede to get away. Other customers, who were too far back to get the full effect, began clapping, assuming that this was part of the night's entertainment. I wondered whether they'd still think so after Elvis downed the appetizer and started looking for a main course.

"Cassie!" Dimly, like an echo of an echo, I heard Billy's voice. I looked around but couldn't see him anywhere in the pandemonium.

Marlowe tugged me backwards, but my equilibrium hadn't returned and I lost my footing. I clutched at the table, trying to steady myself, while Elvis got a grip on the bucket's handle. Deino screeched and grabbed her offering, starting a furious tug of war. It slopped blood all over the tabletop, which was only a circle of glass perched on top of a grinning tiki head. Clots of coagulating blood spattered Françoise's beautiful dress and I instinctively grabbed a napkin to wipe them off but was stopped by an angry vampire.

"Forget that!" Marlowe gave me a little shake. "We have to get out of here!"

I gestured at the flood of mages who'd started pouring in the door. Ours wasn't the only cavalry to have come charging over the hill. "How?" I screamed.

"Can't you shift?"

The realization hit me that there was no longer any reason not to use my power. Whether I liked it or not, I was Pythia. I nodded, but before I could get an image of the street outside the casino, I heard Billy's voice again, and he sounded desperate. "Billy! Get in here!"

"What is it?" Marlowe demanded.

"Be quiet!" It was hard enough to hear as it was, without him bellowing in my ear. Billy had said something else, but I'd missed it. "Billy! I can't hear you!"

"Don't shift! I'm stuck."

"He says he's stuck," I told Marlowe, just as the blonde got loose from her keeper and jogged over to be nearer her idol. A guard intercepted her, and in her struggle to get away she knocked into me. I lost my footing and went down just as a fireball from one of the mages sizzled overhead, barely missing me and setting Marlowe's doublet ablaze on its way to destroy the tiki bar. He had the garment off faster than I could blink, then looked around frantically for somewhere to dispose of it safely. Magical fire burns like phosphorus, so the options were kind of limited. He solved the problem by whipping it back the way it had come, where it sizzled out against the mage's shields.

Marlowe didn't appear injured, but his fangs were out and his eyes were furious. "It's going to get very hot around here very soon, Cassie. I can't think of a better time to make our exit. The ghost can catch up with us later."

Billy must have overheard, because he began babbling like crazy. I couldn't make out most of what he was saying, but I got the gist. "Billy says not to shift."

Marlowe looked incredulous, but my expression must have warned him not to argue. "Stay here. I'll arrange something," he said abruptly before vanishing in a blur of color.

I was left huddled under the table to escape the stampeding crowd. Through the transparent tabletop I could see that the female fan had finally fought her way to her idol, a look of devotion on her features. I could only assume that she was drunk or legally blind, because the object of her affection was looking pretty damn scary. The glowing eyes, pulsing brain and salivating mouth didn't seem to register with her, however, and she lunged for him just as Deino gave a mighty heave and ripped the bucket away. The force of the movement caused the contents to splash all over the woman, drenching her from head to foot and leaving what looked like a piece of liver wedged in her cleavage.

She screamed, which was the worse possible reaction, because it got the zombie's attention. It ignored Deino, who was yelling in an unknown language and repeatedly clouting it over the head with the empty bucket. Instead, it dove for the gory girl.

Casanova was trying to evacuate the lounge and direct the fight away from the remaining norms. "Get the damn bocors in here!" I heard him bellow, just as three security men threw themselves on Elvis. He went down on the blood-slick floor barely a yard away from me, with the woman underneath him. Wherever the voodoo workers who usually controlled the acts were, it didn't look like they'd be quick enough to prevent her from becoming a midnight snack for the King.

"Help her!" I screamed at the Graeae. Enyo didn't need to be told twice. In a blink she switched from old-lady mode to her alter ego, covered in her own blanket of blood. It's supposed to contain remnants of every enemy she'd ever slaughtered, and either the variety or sheer amount got the zombie's attention. He dragged himself to his feet, despite having three security guards hanging off him. He didn't let go of the woman, but tucked her under his arm and stumbled after his new prey.

At a frantic look from me, Pemphredo snatched the girl and shoved her at Deino before jumping on the zombie's back. He gave a very nonmusical hiss when she started digging in his open cranium, tossing out handfuls of bloody brains. Enyo stayed just out of reach, leading the stumbling creature on a zigzag course through the tables, while her sister continued the impromptu lobotomy.

Marlowe appeared at my elbow, hair wild and pantaloons scorched, but otherwise unharmed. I grabbed his shirt with both hands. "Tell me you have a plan!"

"There's a trapdoor under the stage, we just have to make sure none of the mages see us go through it."

I didn't think that would be an issue. The zombies were a little short on fighting technique, but they made up for it in resilience. As Marlowe spoke, a mage thrust his arm completely through our waiter's abdomen, but despite the fact that his fist came out the other side, it didn't even slow the zombie down. Elvis, on the other hand, had either tired out or lost enough cognitive ability to forget what he'd been doing, because he had simply stopped three or four tables away. Enyo and Pemphredo abandoned him for the mages, leaving the newly arrived security people to deal with the King.

Casanova ran over at the head of the squad. "What are you two waiting for?" he screeched in a very unsexy voice. "Go!"

"I'll check out the exit and make sure there are no surprises," Marlowe said, slipping into the crowd. I started to follow when I was stopped in my tracks by a very unwelcome sight. A livid-looking Pritkin was standing by the smoldering remains of the bar, scanning the room. Marlowe's vermilion pantaloons must have caught his eye, because he zeroed in on him and, a second later, on me.

Uh-oh.

Casanova followed the direction of my gaze and said something a little stronger. He gave me a panicked look. "Mircea ordered me to help you, but there are limits! Locking the mage in an office while he recovered was one thing, but I cannot inflict actual harm. Not even if I'm staked for it!"

I stared at him. "What are you talking about?" I didn't get an answer because several mages had crashed through the undead lineup and were headed our way. He motioned for his security people, half of whom were vampires, to intercept them and started to follow, but I grabbed his arm. "When did you talk to Mircea?"

"He called a few hours ago, after you pulled your little stunt at MAGIC. He asked if I'd spoken to you and what we'd discussed. I told him." He saw my expression and his own grew even more irritable. "Did you really expect me to lie? I may serve two masters, Cassie, but I try to do it well."

With that cryptic remark, he was off, leaving me to handle Pritkin on my own. I judged the distance to the stage and knew I wouldn't make it. The tables that weren't on fire had overturned, and a few had begun to liquefy under the barrage of spells, sending rivers of melted glass everywhere. There was nothing else for it; Billy's warning notwithstanding, I was going to have to shift. I called for my power, but it was sluggish. I wasn't sure whether that had to do with the portal scrambling my brains or the sight of Pritkin's face as he fought his way through the chaos. Either way, I was screwed if I couldn't concentrate better than this.

I felt a tap on my shoulder and whirled around to find Deino looking pleased. Her sisters were busy fighting war mages with unabashed glee, but she had stuck to my side like a burr. She still had a grip on the sobbing, half-crazed fan girl, whom she thrust at me. "Birt' Day!" she said hap-

pily, apparently pleased to have found a substitute for her ruined gift. I shook my head violently. A human sacrifice
wasn't on my wish list.

"You know why mummies don't take vacations?" a muf-
fled voice asked from under Marlowe's napkin. "They're
afraid they'll relax and unwind."

The girl, who had collapsed in a shaking heap, had the
presence of mind to start crawling off. Deino watched her
gift scurry away with an exasperated expression, and that
momentary loss of concentration was all Pritkin needed to
jump her and send her crashing headlong into the clump of
speakers. For an instant he had a straight shot at me but was
too busy sending a fireball into the towering heads to take it.
They exploded in a hail of flaming wood and flying mechan-
ical parts that scattered across the stage, marring the polished surface with ugly scorch marks. The flames turned the
area around the speakers into a leaping bonfire that quickly
spread to the nearby piano.

Before I could scream, Deino's grizzled head popped up
over the burning mass. She didn't appear to be so much as
singed, but she looked plenty pissed. A second later, I got to
see what the loopiest Graeae's special talent was. Deino
didn't change shape or make Pritkin shoot himself as I'd half
expected. She just turned those sightless eyes on him and he
stopped dead, as if he'd run into an invisible wall. He
dropped the gun he'd pulled, presumably for me, and stood
gazing blankly around the room. He didn't appear to be
harmed; it was as if he simply didn't know where, or even
who, he was. The burning piano top collapsed in a musical
crash behind him, but he didn't so much as flinch.

Deino kicked the blazing statues out of her way and
crossed to me. A mage threw a fireball at her from the

closest segment of the fight, and she turned it back on him with a rude gesture. She tapped Pritkin on the shoulder and, when he turned around, she decked him. From this close, I could see that those hollow folds of skin were not as empty as I'd thought. They held a dark, roiling mist that in no way looked like eyes, but somehow gave the impression of sight.

"That must work really well in battle," I said, awed. It would be hard to throw a spell when you couldn't remember it, or even why you were fighting. Deino preened. "Will it wear off?"

She shrugged noncommittally, gave me a kiss on the cheek and mumbled "Birt' Day" in my ear before wandering off to join her sisters. The mages had shredded the zombies, whose twitching body parts littered the ground around the door, and were holding their own against the vamps. But I had a feeling that was about to change.

I intended to follow Marlowe's example, but Pritkin suddenly came back to life. I looked from his icy green eyes to the gun he'd retrieved. "There's one advantage to my blood," he hissed. "Mind games don't work."

I decided not to bother trying to open a dialogue. I lashed out with my foot and caught him square on the knee. It probably wouldn't have done anything but piss him off under normal circumstances, but the surprise of it combined with the river of blood and slick entrails on the floor to send him sprawling. He slid into the piled-up tables, tumbling them like a bowling ball crashing into a bunch of pins. Heavy glass tabletops tumbled down everywhere, some rolling off to the side but a few landing on him.

The flaming orange spells were flying thick and fast now, with the last one slamming into the top of the stage, setting the overhanging canopy of silk leaves ablaze. It was the last straw for the stage's bamboo frame, which collapsed like a giant game of pickup sticks. I avoided being squashed only because I dove for cover under one of the last remaining upright tables. I was afraid the glass top wouldn't hold, but none of the bigger columns hit it, and the others merely rattled off.

When I looked back up, Pritkin had disappeared. I thought I saw Françoise's bright green dress for an instant, near the main entrance, but then it was lost to the black smoke boiling through the ruined nightclub. I did catch sight of another familiar face, though. "Billy!"

The almost transparent shape of a cowboy had appeared by the main doors. He saw me at almost the same moment, and a look of profound relief flooded his features. He zoomed straight at me. I was about to ask him where he'd been, but he slipped inside my skin without so much as a hello. All I got instead was some hysterical gibbering. Then I got a glimpse of the main fight and forgot about him.

Casanova threw the mage he'd been throttling into two others, then caught sight of me and shouted. I couldn't hear him over the din, but I didn't really need to—it was obvious what the problem was. The Graeae had left the building.

I did a quick mental survey and realized that, until a few minutes ago, Deino was the only one who had not saved my life. Enyo had held off the mages at Casanova's, Pemphredo had helped me in the kitchen afterwards and Deino had just made it a hat trick. They had paid their debt and now I was on my own. Casanova was yelling something again, while trying to hold off three mages at once. I still couldn't hear him, but I read the word on his lips easily enough. "Go!"

I nodded. The Graeae were my responsibility, but they would have to wait their turn. I wasn't sure whether it was okay to shift yet or not, and I couldn't get a thing out of Billy. I started to crawl off but was stopped by an iron grip on my foot. Pritkin was pulling his way out of the tables with one hand and holding on to me with the other. Damn it!

"Cassie!" I whipped around at the familiar voice and saw Marlowe's curly mop sticking out from under the remains of the stage. I couldn't imagine what he was still doing here. There was fire everywhere, and vamps have approximately the same flash point as lighter fluid. He gestured for me to get out of the way and I flattened myself without asking why. I glanced back in time to see Pritkin lifted off the ground by an unseen hand and thrown across the mass of overturned tables, close to the main fight. Marlowe beckoned for me to join him, but there was no way. Bits of burning green silk were raining down all around the stage, creating a minefield of magical fire. It was as dangerous to me as regular fire was to a vamp; I couldn't risk it.

I looked around quickly, but there were no other options. The fight going on behind me put the main entrance out of the question, the back room was a dead end and the side exit was a sheet of flame from where a fireball had hit the hanging bamboo curtain, setting it and half the wall ablaze. With no other choice, I did the only thing I could and reached again for my power.

This time it came readily, surging beneath my fingertips like someone had opened a floodgate. Almost dizzy with relief, I tried to think of the best place to go. Then Pritkin launched himself over the pile of tables, hands outstretched, and I freaked and shifted with no destination in mind. All I was thinking about was finding Myra. Wherever that led had to be better than hanging around while Dante's lived up to its name.

*   *   *

There was no bone-jarring landing this time—only a gradual darkening of the fiery scene until it disappeared altogether, to be slowly replaced by a very dark street. After a minute, my eyes adjusted enough to make out a large building with a sign proclaiming it to be the Lyceum Theatre. I didn't know what time it was—the street was deserted, but it could have been anywhere from midnight to close to dawn.

"I thought you'd be along," Myra said from behind me. I whirled, my hand jerking up automatically at the sound of that smug, childish voice. Two daggers sailed straight at her, but she just stood there in the middle of the street, unconcerned. A split second later I realized why as my own weapons came sailing back at me. They didn't wound me, but they hit with enough force to knock me off my feet and send me skidding back along the filthy street. Myra held up her hand. A gleaming bracelet that looked a lot like my own dangled from her thin wrist. Except, where mine had daggers, it had tiny interlocking shields. "A gift from some new friends. To level the playing field."

I clambered to my feet. "When have you ever believed in a level playing field?"

She grinned. "Good point." Then her face changed as she got a good look at me. "So, you managed to complete the ritual. Congratulations. Unfortunately, your reign is destined to be the shortest in history."

I got a good look at her, too. For the first time, she was solid. It made sense, considering that she'd been attacked last time in spirit form. It didn't make her eyes look any less creepy, I decided.

"Answer me one thing," I said wearily. "Why always London? Why 1889? It's starting to get tedious."

"Convocation is being held in London this year," Myra answered, sweetly obliging. "That's the biannual meeting of the European Senate."

"I know that!"

"Oh, of course. I keep forgetting, you grew up at a vampire's court, didn't you? Well, then, maybe you already know this, too. The Senate usually meets in Paris, but they've traveled to London this year to settle an old score. They got the idea that the crimes being reported in the newspapers as the work of Jack the Ripper were really being done by Dracula. He escaped their version of an asylum shortly before they began, so it seemed reasonable."

"What does that have to do with me, or Mircea?"

Myra looked entirely too pleased with herself. "Everything. Mircea and that vampire the North American Senate sent to help him—"

"Augusta."

"Yes. They proved that the crimes were the work of a human by capturing the man calling himself Jack."

"And Jack was punished." I'd seen part of that myself, firsthand.

"Yes, but it seems that Jack went on his killing spree in an effort to impress Dracula, hoping to win a spot in his new stable. So the Senate blames Dracula for what happened."

"And they want him dead."

"Finally, you're starting to get it!" Myra clapped her hands approvingly. "Mircea managed to convince the European Consul to grant him a few days to find and trap his brother before drastic measures were taken, but not everyone agreed with that decision. It seems Dracula made a few enemies through the years."

I had a very bad feeling that I'd heard this story before. And it didn't end well for Dracula. Some senators with long memories had lynched him one foggy night in London. This night.

"They plan to kill him."

Myra laughed. "They *do* kill him—it's part of that time-line you're so concerned with protecting, Cassie. Only this time, with a little help from me, Mircea found him before they did. And something tells me they aren't going to hesitate to take your vampire out as well, if he gets between them and their revenge."

And he would. Mircea had spent years arranging for me to become Pythia in order to save one brother. I couldn't see him standing aside while another was murdered.

"It's simple enough, Cassie," Myra said brightly. "You want the position? Not a problem. Just be better than me."

She flashed out, and at the same moment, I was tackled from behind. I hit the road again, this time face-first. That wasn't the reason I yelled, though. The *geis* was definitely still there, and it hadn't changed its mind about John Pritkin. Based on the spike of pain that jumped from my body to his, I was betting the *geis* had confused anger for passion. The mage was too macho to scream like a little girl, but he let me go fast enough.

I turned to find him lying on the sidewalk, looking dazed. He made no attempt to immediately come after me, but I didn't take much heart from the fact. He was probably just waiting to recover. He must have been near enough when I shifted to piggyback along for the ride. Great.

"I won't let you do it," he gasped. "No matter what the price!"

I was suddenly grateful for the *geis*, because he looked truly homicidal. But just because he couldn't touch me, didn't mean I was safe. He could still shoot me and not feel a thing. I decided to get out of there before that occurred to him, too.

I smashed one of the theatre's windows and wiggled inside, gaining a new respect for burglars on the way. I cut my hand, tore my dress and almost threw my shoulder out of joint, but I managed it before Pritkin could come after me. Unfortunately, I didn't manage it quietly.

"What do we have here?" Augusta's voice sounded in my ear a second before I was jerked off my feet and slammed against the wall. A tiny, blue-veined hand held me there effortlessly. She settled her blue woolen skirts into perfect folds with a few flicks of her wrist. They had an elaborate design in black braid around the bottom, which matched the frog closures and jet brooch on the front of the gown.

"Nice dress," I croaked.

"Thanks. Yours, too." She looked me over. "It is Fey, but you"—she squeezed a little and my vision started to darken—"you are not."

I didn't spend a lot of time debating options. Augusta could snap my neck with less effort than I would use to break a twig. I couldn't fight her, but I could use her. Pritkin would be far less of a problem with Augusta's strength on my side.

I didn't like possessions; they weirded me out and left me feeling faintly dirty. That wasn't surprising since they were, no matter how I might justify them, a violation. I had planned to avoid them in the future if at all possible, but not at the cost of my life. The only question was, could I do it?

I'd possessed a dark mage once, although I'd been shoved out of his body within a couple of minutes. And that was with Billy Joe to help me. I'd never brought Billy along on a shift before, but had foolishly hoped he might be a useful ally. He wasn't sounding real useful at the moment, however. He was still a gibbering wreck, and I couldn't even get his attention, much less ask for help.

But if Myra could do it, damn it, so could I.

Luckily, Augusta's knowledge of warding was amateurish: if she could ward with more than one element, I never saw any sign of it. Her shields looked impressive—towering slabs of steel riveted together like the side of a battleship— but a closer examination showed spots so weak with rust that they were almost transparent. That's what you get for not maintaining your shields with a little daily meditation. If Augusta's protection had been as strong as it looked, she might have been able to expel me before I could take over. As it was, my fire burned a hole through her metal with surprising ease.

Everything was suddenly brighter, sharper, and closer than before, and I found myself staring into my own frightened eyes. I put a hand over my mouth before Billy Joe could make a racket, but that seemed the wrong thing to do because he went berserk. I finally bit the bullet and slapped myself across the face. I tried to do it gently, but I think I miscalculated because Billy's eyes rolled up and for a second I thought he was going to pass out. "It's me," I hissed.

He slowly nodded. After a moment, he got his borrowed lips to work. "I need a drink," he told me in a shaky undertone. "I need a whole freaking brewery."

"Are you okay?" He didn't look it. My face was pasty white and my mouth was trembling. "If you're going to be sick, tell me now."

Billy laughed, and there was a disturbing hysterical note in it. "Sick? Yeah, I guess you could say I was sick. Ghost, human, ghost, human; hey, it's all good."

I stared at him in concern. "I don't understand—"

"What's there to understand? I just *died*, that's all!"

"Billy," I said slowly, "you died a long time ago."

"I died a long time ago," Billy repeated, mockingly. "I died *today*, Cass, in case you missed it! An encore performance, courtesy of Faerie! Oh, God."

His face crumpled and he sank to the floor, shaking. I hugged him, finally realizing why Billy was freaking out. When he went through the portal, his new body had been ripped away. I'd known that would probably happen but hadn't thought about the ramifications. He possessed people all the time, including me, and it had never seemed to bother him when he had to leave. But I guess it was different with his own body. He hadn't been possessed; he'd been alive. And when he went through the portal, he had, in fact, died all over again. I hugged him harder, forgetting whose strength I had now, but let go when he gave a bleat of protest.

"I almost didn't come back this time, Cass," he said weakly. "It's not automatic, you know."

"What isn't?"

"Becoming a ghost. Nobody keeps stats, or if they do, they're not telling me, but it's pretty damn rare! And I almost . . . I got lost . . . I wasn't here, I wasn't there and I couldn't see anything. All I could feel was a pull, trying to wash me away, and the only thing holding me was the sound of your voice. And then you started talking about leaving, and then I found out—" He broke off with a strangled gasp.

"Billy . . . I'm sorry." It seemed really inadequate, but what do you say to someone who has just died for the second time? Even Eugenie's upbringing fell short.

He grabbed hold of me, and I hadn't known my arms were that strong. "Never. Leave. Again."

I nodded, but inwardly I was having a crisis only slightly less intense than Billy Joe's. I couldn't let go of Augusta unless I wanted a very pissed-off master vampire gunning for me, but I couldn't babysit a traumatized Billy all night while Myra ran loose. Something had to give.

I started to get up, hauling Billy with me, when someone grabbed me by the hair and put a knife to my throat. It really annoyed me. Augusta's ears could pick up the sound of rats scurrying in the theatre walls, the fact that its roof had a leak and the argument a cabbie was having several streets over with a drunken customer. So why hadn't I heard anyone sneaking up on me?

"Try anything, and I kill you," Pritkin said. I rolled my eyes. Of course.

"What do they teach you in mage school?" I demanded. "To kill a master vamp, you'd need to stake her—with wood, not metal—hack her head completely off, reduce the body to ashes and sprinkle them over a stream of moving water. Cutting her throat would only piss her off."

Pritkin ignored me. "You will have to find somewhere else to feed tonight. The girl goes with me."

"What girl?"

Billy was sitting with his back to the ticket booth, knees drawn up, red dress so big that it almost swallowed him. He looked up at me and his mouth gave a slight quirk. "He means me, Cass."

Then I understood. "I don't know if the *geis* works when I'm in this form or not," I told Pritkin. "But I'd rather you let go before we find out the hard way."

He released me so fast I stumbled. "I won't let you do it," he said, leveling a shotgun at me.

"That won't kill me, either," I informed him before snatching the gun away and breaking it in two. "But it would leave a nasty hole." Pritkin frowned at his ruined weapon, and I could almost see him reassessing matters. I decided to help him out. "Look, I'm Pythia now, whether either of us likes it or not. And FYI, whatever my faults, at least I'm sane. Which is a hell of a lot more than I can say for your precious Myra."

Pritkin seemed confused, and I had to hand it to him—it looked real. "What are you talking about?"

I couldn't believe he was trying that. "You want her as Pythia. I've known about your agenda all along, so you can drop the incredulous look."

"I would prefer to see neither of you in the position. Lady Phemonoe must have been senile to have anything to do with either of you!"

"So Marlowe was right! You *are* working with the Circle!" All that stuff at Dante's had been a blind after all. I shook my head at him, half in disbelief, half in admiration. "You know, it takes a real lunatic to risk bleeding to death just so I'd believe you."

Pritkin ran his hands through his hair with the air of a man trying not to wrap them around my neck. "I am not working with the Circle," he said slowly, as if talking to a four-year-old. "And I have only one agenda, as you call it."

I eyed him suspiciously. "And that would be?"

"That whoever holds the position be someone with intelligence, ability and experience!" he replied savagely. "Myra is obviously mad and, based upon what I saw in Faerie, I have my doubts about you!"

"And exactly what is it you think you saw?"

He frowned. "You made a deal with the Fey king to retrieve the *Codex*."

"So what? You said it yourself: most of the counterspells have already been discovered."

"But not all of them."

"What, there's some mystery spell you don't want found?" All I got was stony silence. I sighed. "Let me guess. You aren't going to tell me."

"You don't need to know. You will not give that book to the king. We will find another way to get to your vampire."

"Yeah, because we did so great last time." Our brief visit had made one thing very clear: I'd never survive the beautiful hell known as Faerie long enough to find Tony without Fey help. And there was only one way to get it. I decided to try to reason with the lunatic, as the only alternative was force—something that scared me with Augusta's strength. "Don't you think that trying to kill me to keep me away from a book was a bit extreme?"

Pritkin looked disgusted. "If I had wanted you dead, you would be dead," he said flatly. "I simply want to talk sense into you. That book is dangerous. It must not be found!"

"It *will* be found—I don't have another choice." Pritkin's eyes, usually a pale, icy green, went almost emerald in fury. "But if you help me," I hastened to add, "I'll let you have first crack at it. You can take out whatever you feel is so dangerous, give me the counterspell for the *geis* and then we turn the rest over to the king."

He looked at me as if I were speaking Martian. "Do you not realize what you did? You gave the Fey your word—they will hold you to it."

"I said I'd give them the book. I didn't make any promises about the contents."

"And you think that specious argument will hold up?"

"Yeah." I really wondered what world Pritkin had been living in, because it sure wasn't the supernatural one. "Anything not specifically spelled out in a contract is open to interpretation. If the king didn't want me gutting the book, he should have said so."

Pritkin looked at me for a long minute. "One of the functions of the war mages is to protect the Pythia at all costs," he finally said. "Mac believed in you, or he wouldn't have died for you. But you were brought up by a vampire, by a creature with no moral compass at all, and have received no training. Why should I fight for you? What kind of Pythia will you be?"

It was the big question, the same one I'd been asking myself. I'd taken the power hoping to break the *geis*, or at least give me an edge over Myra. So far, it had done neither. The truth was, I didn't know what kind of Pythia I'd be. But I did know one thing without any doubt at all. "A better one than Myra."

"So I am being given the choice of the lesser of two evils? You do not make much of a case for yourself."

"Maybe I'm not trying too hard," I said truthfully. I needed Pritkin. I knew next to nothing about magic on the grand scale, and had no idea where to even start looking for the book. But I didn't think I could stand another Mac on my conscience. "If you're smart, you'll lay low until this is over. Let me fight my own battles. You might get lucky and Myra and I will kill each other off."

"And why should I not kill both of you myself, and hope the next in line will be better?"

Billy's eyes got big, and I realized that while I was relatively safe in Augusta's body, he was still vulnerable in mine. I stepped in front of him. "There is no next in line," I told Pritkin flatly. "If there were another contender who could do a decent job, I'd have given her the damn power already! But the initiates are all under the control of your Circle, who I don't trust any more than the Black. I'm not going to hand world-shattering power to someone who can be manipulated, controlled or corrupted!"

Pritkin regarded me narrowly. "You expect me to believe you would give up the power, just like that, if there was a fit receptacle to receive it? You dragged us into Faerie to complete the ritual. Of course you want it."

"I didn't drag you anywhere! You *volunteered* to go."

"To find the rogue!"

I took a deep breath. Augusta didn't need it, but I did. "I went into Faerie to get Myra before she could get me. Picking up Tomas was a fluke, and completing the ritual was a bid to stay alive."

"You told Mac you went after your father."

"I did. Tony has him, or what's left of him, and I want him back. But the main goal was always Myra. I had reason to believe that she was with Tony." It had seemed like killing two birds with one stone, but I should have known better. When was my life ever that simple? "But now she's here, trying to kill Mircea. If she succeeds, he won't be around to protect me while I grow up, and I doubt I'll make it long enough to be a pain in your side, or anyone else's. If you want to get rid of me, here's your big chance."

"Why are you telling me this? I could help Myra destroy you, and your vampire."

"I know." And, frankly, it wouldn't surprise me. I was gambling a lot on Mac's faith in his buddy, a faith that could very well have been misplaced. But then, is it a gamble if you don't have a choice? I had Myra and half the European Senate against me. And the only one on my side was a very stressed-out ghost in an all-too-vulnerable body. What was one more enemy?

Pritkin was giving me another of his patented glares. "What do you think you can do alone, against Myra and the Senate?"

So he had overheard my little chat with Myra. I shrugged. "Possibly nothing. In which case, your problem is solved." I looked down at Billy. "Will you be all right on your own for a while?"

He shrugged. "Sure. Hell, if I die a few more times, I might even get used to it."

"I am going with you," Pritkin announced.

"So you're what? Opting for the lesser of two evils, after all?"

"For the moment."

It wasn't exactly a ringing endorsement, but it was good enough. "You're hired."

Chapter 14

The street was still dark, even to Augusta's eyes, but I discovered other ways to see. All along the road were people, hidden in the night—in tenements, scurrying along the street or congregating in pubs. Many of them were amorphous, dark-clothed shapes against the night, but all of them had heartbeats, and it was those thousands of living, beating organs that called out to me like a siren song. Beyond the human river were darker spots, just a few streets back, but my skin prickled with awareness of their power. Vampires.

I pulled away so I wouldn't see Augusta's features reflected in the dark glass. "There's a lot of vamps in the area," I told Pritkin, "maybe a couple dozen." I had managed the sentence without my voice cracking, but my palms had started to sweat. Even in Augusta's body, there was no way I could fight those odds, and for all his toys, Pritkin wasn't likely to do much better.

"How long until they get here?" He sounded far too matter-of-fact for my frazzled nerves.

"What difference does it make?" I fought to keep from

screaming it at him. "We need to find Mircea and hide—fast. It's the only sensible plan."

Pritkin walked out the stage door and down the steps. I followed him, all the way to the front of the building, where he stopped, looking up and down the frost-covered road. "Humor me," he said.

"In case you've forgotten, the Senate isn't the only problem," I told him, low enough that I hoped no passing vamps would take notice. "I can't let Myra run loose—"

"Then don't. Deal with the rogue. I will handle this."

"You'll handle this?" I'd rested my hand on a lamppost and didn't realize until I tried to pull away that I'd sunk my fingers almost completely through the cast iron. I pulled them out cautiously and leaned the listing post against a building so it didn't fall over. Getting angry in a vampire body was obviously not a good idea. "A corpse isn't much of an ally!" I told Pritkin frankly. "Some of these are Senate members. I doubt you could even slow them down. We need to hide."

"They could track us by scent alone. Hiding isn't an option."

"And suicide is?"

I would have said more, but someone grabbed me from behind. Again. For a half second I thought it was a vamp, but then I felt the heartbeat against my back and smelled the stink of unwashed man and stale beer. I pulled away, but the man came with me. I gave what felt like a gentle push, hardly expending any energy at all, and he went sailing across the street to crash into the heavy glass window of a pub. I could see the frozen shock on his face, the half dozen glass slivers that pierced his skin, even trace the arc of blood on the air.

His friend, whom I hadn't even noticed, gave a bellow of rage and ran at me, fist pulled back. I ducked and managed to subdue him by slipping an arm around his throat, cutting off his air supply. It was absurdly easy—the bones in his muscular workman's neck felt brittle, like a baby bird's, and instead of it being difficult to hold him, the challenge lay in not accidentally breaking anything.

I had never really thought about how delicate humans are, especially not human men, most of whom tower over me. It was suddenly all too apparent how careful vamps had to be not to leave a trail of bodies behind them. The man was making what he probably thought of as a violent attempt to break free, but to me, it was like holding a fragile butterfly by the wings and trying not to tear it. Just a little pressure to cut off the air, but carefully, gently, or the windpipe would collapse and this brawny creature would crumple like paper in my hands.

He finally went limp and I laid him down to check for a pulse. I found one and breathed a sigh of relief. "You seem to be doing well enough on your own," Pritkin commented.

"Against humans! It isn't humans hunting us."

"No, but the principle is the same. When they looked at you, the two men saw only a weak woman, where they should have seen a predator." He gave me a brief, mirthless grin. "I often have that same advantage."

"You can't take them all, predator or not!"

"The principle is the same," he repeated, wrenching the heavy lamppost I'd ruined out of the ground, then shoving it back into the hole, hard. The gas main underneath the street ruptured and caught fire with a whoosh, sending a bright plume skyward. I jumped back, Augusta's instinctive terror running through me. But a vamp I hadn't even noticed caught

fire and ran screaming into another. Pritkin grinned viciously. "Never be what they expect."

He ran down the street after the fleeing vampires, whoop-
ing and generally making as much noise as possible, and the
dark wells of power in my vision began to turn the same
way. The vamps didn't know what was going on, but they'd
been looking for a fight, and Pritkin seemed ready to give
them one. And he called me insane.

I ran back into the theatre and found Billy cowering behind the ticket booth. I nodded approval. There was no safe
place at the moment, but it beat having him with me or the
maniac outside.

I turned my attention to finding Myra. There were three
people in the building, and only one was human. I could
hear the strong, steady heartbeat, could feel it at the back of
my throat as something thick and sweet. The vamps weren't
bothering with trivialities like having a pulse, but I could
smell them. And even at this distance Augusta's keen nose
could pick out the crisp scent of pine.

I followed Augusta's hunger through the backstage areas,
trying to zero in on Myra's exact location, but the place was
a rabbit warren of tiny rooms and dead-end corridors, with
props stuck here and there haphazardly. I fumbled out of a
forest of painted trees to find myself in the wings of the
stage. The theatre was dark, enough so that to a human's
eyes little would have been visible. I could make out a few
props—a chest, a couple of flags and some blunted lances—
waiting for the next performance. There was no sign of activity, however, and the human's heartbeat was still a good
way off.

I finally located my target in a room behind the stage,
down a stairway filled with dust and old suits of armor. I

kept a wary eye on the battered knights as I slipped by, but none so much as twitched. The first room I reached was set up like a dining room, with a large shiny wood table that practically reeked of beeswax. It was oak to match the paneling on the walls and the beams on the ceiling. There were a bunch of portraits scattered around and a big stone fireplace. It had a gothic feel to it that would have served as a good backdrop for a couple of vamps, only there weren't any.

The still-glowing embers in the fireplace and the decanter and two used glasses on the table told me that they hadn't been gone long. I peered into the next room, drawn by an odd smell, and found the human. It wasn't Myra.

A tall, portly guy with dark hair and, oddly enough, a red beard, stood by a counter with his shirt open over a pale, hairy belly. He had a candle in his hand and I identified the odor: cooked human flesh. He appeared to be trying to melt the skin on his chest and stomach, patches of which were already a flaming, lobster red. A few that had received extra attention were starting to bubble. He was crying silently, tears coursing down his cheeks to soak his beard, but he didn't stop.

I ran forward and knocked the candle away. It rolled across the floor and went out, and he looked after it blankly. Then he reached to the shelf behind him, got another one and was in the process of lighting it when I jerked it away, too. I looked into his eyes, but there was no one home. Somebody had hit him with a suggestion, a strong one. I slapped him, but it didn't seem to help. I tried to catch his eyes with mine, but it was hard to get him to focus enough to get a hold. Vampires have a hard time influencing people who are really drunk, high or crazy, because their minds don't work right. Apparently that goes for those who've been hit with a prior suggestion as well.

In the end, I got his attention by throwing his candles and matches into a garbage pail and refusing to let him retrieve them. He woke up enough to notice I was there and along with the recognition went a wince of pain. That was going to get a whole lot worse as his brain unfogged, but for the moment he was just uncomfortable.

"Where's Myra?" I asked. He stared at me as if he was having a hard time remembering English. "Have you seen a girl, shorter than me, weird eyes—"

"The master and Lord Mircea are dueling," he said sadly. I tried repeating the question, but he just stared at me. There was only one thought in his head, and it wasn't about Myra.

"Where is this duel?" I didn't need to find Myra if I located Mircea—she'd find me.

"Onstage."

"I was just there—it's empty."

"They have gone to Lord Dracula's rooms for weapons." His face twisted in pain, but I think it was less from his wounds than from the thought of his master in jeopardy. I had never met Mircea's infamous younger brother and wasn't enthusiastic about the idea. But what really concerned me was the fight. Half the Senate was after them, and they were taking time out to duel?

"Why are they fighting?"

"If my lord wins, he goes free—his brother has sworn it. But if Lord Mircea wins, he must go back into captivity, possibly forever!" The big man started sobbing as if his heart would break. I sighed. I should have known. Of course Dracula wouldn't want to go back into jail or whatever asylum the Senate had fixed up for crazy vamps. But while he and Mircea battled it out, Myra and her new buddies would end the dispute by killing them both.

I turned the large man's face towards me. "Why were you burning yourself?"

"Lord Dracula commanded it, for my failure to keep Lord Mircea from learning his whereabouts. He came here an hour ago, and I meant to tell him nothing, but then everything I knew poured out of me."

"Mircea can be very persuasive."

"My lord was very generous not to end my life for such incompetence."

His eyes held the light of a true believer. I didn't even try to convince him that his god was really a monster. "What's your name?"

"Abraham Stoker, lady. I manage the theatre."

I did a double take. Okay, that explained a lot. "It has to be late. Go home and get some medical attention for your burns. If anyone asks, you were checking on a sauce here in the kitchen and pulled it off on you."

He nodded but looked torn, so I upped the amp on Augusta's suggestion. It used up a lot of energy, and I had to resist the impulse to snatch him to me for a quick bite. Being in a vampire body had its downsides.

Stoker started to leave, but jerked violently halfway to the door and came to a stop. His head swiveled around to face me, despite the fact that his body remained facing forward. Another inch and he'd break his neck. "Tell me, if you can, what sort of spirit are you, to so easily possess a master vampire?"

"I told you to go home!" I eyed him cautiously. His voice had sounded funny, lower and more in control.

"And I told him to stay. It seems we know who is the stronger here, do we not?"

I was getting a very bad feeling in the pit of my stomach. "Who are you?"

"I am one whom the vile blows and buffets of the world have so incensed that I am reckless what I do to spite the world."

I blinked. "What?" He laughed, and it was a full-throated, sexy sound, one that I was fairly sure the guy I'd met blubbering over his candles would never give. "Have you forgotten me so soon? When we met only last night?"

"Last night?" It took a second, but light dawned. "You're that spirit from the ball!"

"Incubus, please, my lady." I jerked in surprise. So that's what it was. I'd seen plenty of incubi, but never outside a host. "May I presume upon our acquaintance to ask why you are here?"

"You first."

He sighed. "I would prefer not to use this body any longer than necessary. It is in a large amount of discomfort. Trust the master to scupper my plans without even knowing what they are."

"What plans?" It was making my neck hurt just to look at him. I moved so Stoker's head wouldn't be at that crazy angle anymore.

"But that is what we need to discuss."

"Look, I really don't have time to chat!" I tried to move past him, but the large body was blocking the door. "Get out of my way." I could move him, of course—even without feeding recently, Augusta was stronger than a human—but I didn't want to hurt Stoker. He'd had enough of that for one night.

"No, I do not think so. As I recall, I did you something of a favor at our last meeting. I expect you to return it."

"Return it how?" I didn't like where this conversation was headed.

"I require a body for the evening, and this one has been rendered useless. It will collapse at any moment. I need a strong body, and yours will do nicely."

I backed up a step. "You can't invade vampires."

"No, but you can see me even without a body, as you proved at our first meeting. Very well. I will give directions, and you will follow them, and we will let this poor fellow go off to his soft bed and his shrewish wife."

"I don't have time to help you. I have my own job to do."

He smiled gently. "Yes. You wish to help Lord Mircea imprison his dastardly brother and make Europe safe from his fiendish ways once more, am I right?" He laughed at my expression, and again it was that goose-bump-inducing sound. "I saw you with Mircea at the ball. I see his mark on you now."

He paused because we both heard it at the same time—the ring of steel on steel from somewhere nearby. That would be all I needed, for Dracula to kill Mircea before Myra had the chance! I pushed at him, but he grasped my arm.

"Tell me, am I right? Is that why you are here—to save his life?"

I threw him off violently, not caring at the moment that poor Stoker's hand hit the wall with a bone-crunching thump. "Yes! Now get *out* of my *way*!"

I ran past him, fairly flying toward the stage, and reached the wings in record time. On the boards, two figures were engaged in a sword fight like nothing I'd ever seen. Power sizzled and crackled around them, brighter than the sparks that were struck off their swords. I concentrated on Mircea, but if he'd been hurt there was no sign of it. He wore a white shirt open at the throat, and there were no bloodstains on it that I could see. His hair had come out of its usual clip and it followed his motions, whip cracking around his lean form as he flowed through complex moves with deadly grace. I blinked and looked away, forcing myself to concentrate. When I looked back, I got my first glimpse of his legendary brother.

Usually, I get a tingle up my spine when I see a vamp, but there was nothing this time. I wasn't sure whether that was because I was in Augusta's body, or because my brain was too busy screaming to focus. There was a strong sense of wrongness emanating from the vamp like nothing I'd ever felt. It was like the danger in the room had coalesced into a red mist, as if there was blood in the air. It went well with his dead white face and burning green eyes, the color of emeralds on fire. It did not go well with Augusta's instincts, which were practically begging me to run.

The two vampires flowed through the motions of battle like it was silent, deadly poetry. Even with Augusta's senses I had trouble following them, their blades were striking so quickly. The sound of clashing metal echoed around the theatre like machine-gun fire, and every time I blinked they'd moved yards away from where they'd just been.

I clutched the curtains, watching with my stomach in my throat as Mircea flung himself to the ground, barely evading a savage slash from his brother's sword. He flicked his own saber at his assailant's ankles, but Dracula leaped, clearing the blade easily. By the time he landed, Mircea was back on his feet and they were off again.

"'Out, out brief candle! Life's but a walking shadow, a

poor player, that struts and frets his hour upon the stage, and then is heard no more.' " I had been so intent on the combat, I hadn't sensed the Stoker's arrival until he started quoting.

"What do you want?"

"I told you before, dear lady—your help."

"I'm busy," I snapped. Dracula flipped over his brother's head, his sword slashing downward, and if Mircea hadn't moved even faster than Augusta could see, it would have been over.

"Is it your plan to stand by and watch as they kill each other?" Dracula's blade had nicked Mircea's left arm, splattering his shoulder and chest with red, and I didn't think it would be the last time. Mircea was rumored to be a better-than-average duelist, but it looked to me like his younger brother was the faster of the two. It was a tiny difference, a fraction of a fraction of a second, maybe caused by the wound Dmitri had inflicted the night before. But sooner or later, it would be enough. And if Mircea lost, I somehow doubted Vlad had prison in mind for him.

"Who would have thought," the incubus murmured softly, a silken whisper in my ear, "the old man to have so much blood in him?"

Their shadows flickered in and out of the scenery, soaring against the back wall in a deadly dance. Something clicked as I watched them. I'd seen this before. It was the same scene as in my vision—the one that ended with Mircea's ghastly death. I swallowed thickly and turned to the incubus. "What's your plan?"

He pointed out a very familiar-looking box behind the curtains. I grabbed it with a sense of profound relief. I'd been wondering what to do about Myra since I'd left my box in a backpack somewhere in Faerie. She might be playing for the ultimate stakes, but I wasn't thrilled about having another death on my hands. Even hers.

"What's your interest in this?" I asked when I returned with the trap.

"The same as yours. We have much in common, I think. We both love dangerous creatures."

"You're Dracula's lover?" It looked like Stoker had gotten one thing right, after all. Only he'd put succubi in his novel. A nod to nineteenth-century morality, I guessed.

"I have waited many years for my master's release," the spirit said, "but it will profit neither of us if he is killed shortly thereafter. The Senate knows he is near—I spent most of the night laying false trails, but they will not work for long. They are coming. My master does not believe that imprisonment is better than death, but I feel otherwise."

Things suddenly made more sense. "That's why you helped me at the ball. You wanted Mircea alive so he can trap Dracula."

The spirit blinked Stoker's eyes at me. "Next year or next decade, I will find a way to free him again. As long as he is alive there is hope."

"So you want to trap him to save him? He won't thank you."

"Perhaps; perhaps not. What does it matter to you?"

He had a point. And with Dracula safely tucked away, Mircea would have no reason to hang around this death trap. I held out the box. "Okay, so tell me how to work this thing."

A couple of minutes later I was crawling behind the scenery, the box in my pocket and doubt in my mind. If the incubus was playing me I was in a lot of trouble; if not, I was still in a lot of trouble, but at least one problem would be solved. Of course, I should have known better—I never get one mess cleaned up before another makes an appearance.

This time was no exception. Myra flashed in so close to the fight that she might have been skewered had the two opponents not broken apart at just that moment, pulling back from an impasse. Dracula did something that caused Mircea to stumble—it was so fast I didn't see it—and he whirled to face the new threat. But before he could run her through, a dark shape plummeted from the rafters overhead and would have landed on him like an anvil if his reflexes hadn't been so sharp.

"Pritkin!"

He caught sight of me. "They're coming!"

"Oh, shit."

I looked around but saw no hordes of vamps. But Pritkin had his full arsenal out and his shields up, not something he did lightly. I finally got a chance to see Mac's handiwork in operation. The sword that slashed and danced around the mage's head had the same design as the one I'd seen Mac painstakingly carving into Pritkin's skin. But it was larger— easily half as long as me—and as solid and shiny as a real weapon. It also appeared to pack quite a punch. One swipe at Dracula threw him back almost ten feet, and if he hadn't deflected the blade, it would have bisected him.

Suddenly, Dracula and Mircea were fighting side by side, their own feud forgotten in the face of the new threat. Luckily, the two brothers were so busy concentrating on the mage and his bevy of flying weapons that they didn't notice me. Unluckily, they forgot about Myra, too, who had shrunk back from the fight, and her hands were clenched as if she held something. I reached her just as she threw the sphere in her left hand, and felt the effect slam into me like a tidal wave. Oh, joy. Little Myra had got herself a null bomb.

We went down in a tangle of Augusta's voluminous skirts, Myra screaming and me swearing. The thing in her other hand turned out to be another sphere, this one dull black and about the size of a softball. I didn't recognize it, but if it was magic it wouldn't work right now, so I ignored it. Myra raked her nails down my cheek, almost resulting in Augusta going through eternity with a less-than-fashionable eye patch. I turned my head at the last second, avoiding the worst, but the scratches still hurt like a bitch.

"Girlfriend," I told her, blinking to clear the blood out of my vision, "you so do not want to fuck with me today."

Her eyes got big, then her expression turned murderous. "You!" Myra didn't seem to like it that I'd been able to appropriate a stronger body, because she went for my throat, her reaching hands formed into claws. I managed to wrestle her hands off with minimal damage to either of us, but all I got in return was a snarl and a kick that caught me in the shin.

I slapped her hard enough that her head shot back and her eyes briefly lost focus, buying me a few seconds to check on the fight. The magical sword had disappeared and a few of Pritkin's knives were on the ground, their animation lost to the null's effects. The vamps had dealt with the others by simply allowing them to burrow so far into their flesh that they couldn't pull back out again. Both of them were a bloody mess, but they would survive. I was a lot less sure about Pritkin. He had his revolver out, but steel bullets wouldn't do much against master-level vampires, even assuming they connected.

Billy suddenly walked out onstage, in my body but with

his usual swagger. He was looking up and so was Myra, and she was laughing. One glance and I knew why—the rafters were suddenly swarming with vamps. They poured in from the roof, the windows, the doors—my God, there had to be a hundred of them. I stared in stupefied awe, Augusta's voice in my head telling me what I already knew. We were screwed.

A vamp dropped in front of me, plummeting the three floors from the rafters without even missing his footing on the landing. Before I got a good look at him, Billy reached into his pocket and tossed something at us. I caught a glint of gold as a tiny shape arced in the air, and then it changed.

Mac's eagle swooped down in a beautiful dive, gray feathers a blur against the dark theatre, but those glittering eyes just as bright as ever, and the vamp was suddenly not there anymore. A scream, a thud, and he landed in front of me again, this time missing a good chunk of his throat. He was a master—he'd live—but he wasn't going to be doing any fighting anytime soon.

The vamps attacked in a swarm, flooding the stage, and Billy threw the remaining wards into the air in a glittering arc. A wave of spitting, hissing and howling beasts tore into the vamps. A miniature tornado took out half a dozen, tearing along a rafter, tossing bodies everywhere before fading away. A snake the size of an anaconda dropped around another vamp's neck, winding its coils over his eyes, causing him to stagger blindly off the stage into the orchestra pit. A huge wolf jumped on one, snarling and tearing huge chunks out of his torso, while a spider the size of a Volkswagon had another wound up in silk, hanging him from the rafters with an air of pleased concentration.

Myra brought my attention back to earth by attempting to

stake me. Luckily, Augusta believed in whalebone—and lots of it—for stays. I ended up with a bruised rib and Myra with a blunt stake. I grabbed it out of her hand. "I'm already Pythia! There's no changing it!"

Myra only laughed. "I already killed one Pythia," she said viciously. "What's one more?"

"You killed Agnes?" I almost let her go in surprise. Not that it surprised me that she was capable of it, but what about the prohibition? "Then why are you after me? Even if I die, you'll never be Pythia!"

"If you're clever, there are ways around almost any problem." She glanced at the combatants. "We'll see what can't be changed!"

The other ball had become tangled in my skirts, but a kick from her started it rolling slowly across the floor toward the fight. I finally got a grip on her by grabbing a handful of hair, but although it must have hurt, she was smiling, her eyes following the black orb like it carried the secret to all her dreams. Considering that her dreams involved mayhem and death, and that she'd probably gotten that thing from her good buddy Rasputin, I decided that it would be very bad if it succeeded in crossing the stage.

It was just like my vision—Mircea covered in blood, fighting for his life, and someone tossing a weapon at him from the shadows. I knew what came next, but with Myra fighting me every inch of the way, I couldn't reach the ball in time to stop it. I dropped her in a heap and ran after her little contraption.

I hadn't gotten two steps before she tackled me, and it was like trying to get away from an enraged octopus— everywhere I moved, she seemed to be there first. Normally, Augusta would have been able to stow her under one arm and run with her or simply knock her unconscious. But the first idea would slow me down and the second was out because I didn't know Augusta's strength well enough to risk it.

Half walking, half crawling, I moved slowly toward the ball, but it was taking too much time. I caught sight of a flash of blue out of the corner of my eye and didn't hesitate. "She's going to destroy the theatre!" I screamed, pointing at Myra.

Myra looked at me like I was mad, but the theatre ghosts heard me just fine. The woman's face had already been screwed into a vicious snarl, watching the mess being made on her beloved stage, and now she had someone to blame. She threw the severed head, which was suddenly looking a lot less jolly, straight at Myra. When they merged, Myra gave a shriek and started convulsing. I shoved her away from me just as the woman joined her tiny partner. A whirl-wind started up that left me unable to see more than a thrash-ing tornado of white and blue.

This was no mere mugging—the ghosts had obviously given all the warnings they intended and had gotten down to business. A living person should have been stronger than they were, but it was two against one and they were on ground that had held generations of the bodies of their ances-tors. That's like an extra battery pack for a ghost, something Myra must have figured out. She screamed as they dove for her again, half in fear and half in rage, and vanished.

I lunged after the ball, but a vamp got in my way. I threw Myra's stake at him, more as a diversion than anything else, my aim being what it is. Apparently, Augusta's was better, because it connected.

A very pale and shaky-looking Stoker lurched out of the wings, staggering toward the ball as fast as his unsteady legs would carry him. It wasn't fast enough. The small sphere had reached the fight and rolled under the feet of the two combatants, who were now fighting against a circle of Senate members. It was getting pushed about as they shuffled and jockeyed for position, going first one way and then the other. The look of abject terror on Stoker's face was enough to make me run full-out after it.

I arrived just in time to get hit in the face by a sandbag on a rope that had fallen from the rafters. It was one of four that were swinging around, being dodged easily by most vamps, except the one who hadn't been paying attention. It had to have weighed fifty pounds, and had got up a lot of momentum on its arc. By the time I noticed it, there was no time to do anything but take it. It knocked me off my feet and I went skidding on my back for several yards.

"Dislocator!" Stoker had collapsed onto the stage, and unfortunately it was on his stomach. He screamed, but it was the same odd word, over and over.

I scrambled back up as the duelists paused, looking down at the small sphere at their feet. Everyone froze for half a second. Then the Senators melted away, flowing out of the theatre as quickly as they'd come into it, Mircea grabbed Billy and jumped straight up to the rafters, and Dracula ran towards us after snatching up Stoker. Pritkin threw an arm around my waist and took a flying leap off the stage. We landed in the orchestra pit, and because he'd rolled us at the last minute, he took the brunt of the impact.

It knocked him out and rattled my teeth, and the next second, a wave of power shot over our heads from stage level. The bomb must have found something to connect with, maybe some of the fallen vamps. If so, I didn't think they'd be getting up again. The impact had felt nothing like a null bomb. It was darker and almost greasy, and in no way would ever be mistaken for a defensive weapon.

I raised my head to find that I was almost nose to nose with Dracula. He looked strangely pleased to see me; then I was staring at the knife hilt sticking out of my chest, right between the third and fourth ribs. It hurt, but not like I would have expected. There was no bright, searing pain, and very little blood. That might have been because Augusta hadn't fed recently or because the bastard had missed her heart by a fraction of an inch.

Vlad was preparing to take off her head, why I couldn't imagine. Maybe because she was helping Mircea? Maybe because he was a nut? Who knew? But he was taking his time about unsheathing the long knife at his side. The one he'd used on me was one of Pritkin's—he must have pulled it out of his own flesh—but this one looked like an old family weapon, with a heavy, inlaid grip and a fine, polished blade. Too bad he wouldn't get a chance to use it.

"Billy, you're about to have company!" My yell echoed off the theatre walls. "Get down here."

"You have caused me a great deal of trouble," Dracula was telling me as my body tore towards us across the stage. "I will enjoy this."

"I doubt it," I said, and shifted.

A very confusing split second later, I ended up almost running off the stage. Billy screamed in my head and I stopped, balancing on the very edge. It gave me a perfect view of Dracula getting acquainted with Senate member Augusta. He should have decapitated her without the fanfare while he had the chance. As it was, she was more than happy to give a demonstration of exactly how she'd gotten onto the Senate in the first place. What she lacked in fighting skill she made up for in ruthlessness and utter practicality. She tore Pritkin's knife out of her chest, ignoring the splitting, fleshy sound it made, and stabbed it into Dracula's while he was still gloating over his kill.

Unlike him, she didn't miss.

I saw the shock on his face as the heart was pierced, and heard the sound of metal splitting wood when the knife hit the floor below. She sank it deeply enough to trap him like a bug on a pin, then snatched off the arm from one of the first-row seats nearby, using his heirloom to carve the end into a nice, jagged point. The metal weapon wouldn't kill him, although it didn't seem to be doing him any good, but the stake would. Augusta glanced up, as if waiting for me to intervene, but I just looked at her. I'd saved one of Mircea's brothers; I didn't owe him two.

Augusta's arm flashed down, almost too fast to see. But the makeshift stake hit only the floor of the theatre, connecting in an arm-numbing jolt that echoed loudly in the empty space. Dracula was simply not there anymore. I didn't understand it and neither did Augusta, but then I saw Stoker clutching a small black box. He gave me a slight smile, then slid sideways and passed out. The incubus rose from his chest, looking as smug as a largely featureless spirit can.

Augusta snatched up the box, but hesitated when she saw the way the spirit's face changed. She glanced from its demon visage to me, then again demonstrated utter practicality. She dropped it and ran.

I looked around, but no vamps were visible. Weirdly enough, other than for the chair arm and some blood smears on the stage, the theatre looked like nothing had ever happened. Still, something was missing. "Where are the wards?" I asked Billy.

He drifted out of me slowly, as if reluctant to leave the shelter of my body. He peered around, but there was no sign of the theatre ghosts. They were probably recovering from the energy drain of whatever they'd done to Myra. "Destroyed—the dislocator took them out."

"They're gone? All of them?"

"They wouldn't have lasted anyway, Cass. They weren't offensive wards. They were designed to operate defensively on a body, as protection, not like some kind of weapon. What you saw was them self-destructing."

I thought of the eagle making one final dive and my throat got tight.

"Cassie!" Billy's voice was like a slap. "Don't do this—not now! We have no wards and the vamps will be back any minute. We need to get gone."

I searched around for Myra, but without Augusta's senses, it was futile. I didn't believe for a second that the ghosts had killed her. For one thing, it would take a lot more than one ghost, or even one and a half, to drain a healthy human. For another, I'm just not that lucky. I briefly contemplated trying to go back in time, to be there to catch her before she made her grand exit, but the presence of that other bomb made me hesitate. I'd seen what a dislocator could do in my vision; I didn't want to experience it first-hand.

I slid off the stage with considerably less than Augusta's undead grace and picked up the black box. It weighed no more than it had before. I shook it doubtfully, but the spirit only smiled. It looked rather strange with bloody eyes and fangs. "He is in there, I assure you."

"Now what?" I asked, as its features slipped back into benevolent vagueness.

"I wait," it said, with a lot more serenity than I'd have felt in its position. Still, if you were immortal, I guess the prospect of a few decades' delay didn't faze you much.

Pritkin's eyelashes were fluttering. "Myra's gone," I told him before he could ask. He nodded but didn't say anything. I looked back up at my nebulous ally. "Have you seen Mircea?" I assumed he'd survived, since the sequence of events from the vision had been interrupted, but I had to be sure.

"I believe he will be along." It started to fade, and I held out a hand to stop it.

"Thank you for your help. I know you didn't do it for me, but—well, anyway." I suddenly realized something. "I don't even know your name. I'm Cassie Palmer."

It fluctuated to a light pink. "So few people bother to ask," it said in a pleased voice. "I have used many names through the centuries. It varies, depending on the sex and culture of the body I am inhabiting. I was Aisling once in Ireland, Sapna in India, Amets in France. Call me what you will, Cassie."

It flushed a darker shade, almost a rose, which I guess was good because it started quoting Shakespeare again. " 'When shall we three meet again, in thunder, lightning, or in rain? When the hurlyburly's done, when the battle's lost and won.' " It started fading out once more, and this time I let it.

Pritkin grasped the side of the orchestra pit and hauled himself up onstage. He peered back over the side, holding out a hand, but I ignored it. Something was tickling the back of my mind. It felt like I'd just been handed a puzzle piece; only I didn't know what it was or where it fit.

"Are you hurt?" Pritkin's voice floated down to me.

"No." I finally took his hand and crawled back onto the stage. Almost the moment I did so, hysterical shrieks erupted from the pit behind me. Stoker had woken up, and with no incubus to deflect it, the full force of his wounds hit him all at once. Burns are painful, and ones as bad as his had to be excruciating. Pritkin jumped back in the hole, but the man's pitiful cries didn't stop.

I was about to follow him when a black box dangling in front of my face suddenly filled my vision. A low, rich voice purred in my ear. "Good evening, Trouble."

Chapter 15

I didn't answer, momentarily stunned at the immense wave of relief that swept through me at hearing that voice alive and well. I controlled my features, waiting for the *geis* to kick in, but nothing happened. There was a warm rush of pleasure, a happy frisson humming along my skin from just being near him, but nothing extreme. I'd forgotten—in this era, the horrid thing was still brand spanking new. It hadn't had time to grow teeth yet.

But it would. Big ones.

I caught the box. It looked just like mine. "What is this?"

Dark eyes met mine, glittering wickedly. "I offer a trade."

Stoker, crazed from pain, suddenly scrambled out of the pit and took off up the center aisle. Pritkin went after him, why I couldn't imagine. Maybe so Mircea could wipe his memory, although that seemed unnecessary. When he'd written a confused version of everything years later, it had sold as fiction.

"Hurry up," I called, and Pritkin waved an arm before disappearing through the doors to the lobby.

Mircea smiled, and it was one of his better efforts, despite the fact that he was covered in blood, most of it his. "Are you not interested in pursuing your quarrel with the young hoyden who was here earlier?"

"What?" I stared at the box for a moment, uncomprehending. Then what he'd said sunk in. No. No way. I'd been trying so hard to find Myra, and now she was being dumped in my lap? Or, to be more precise, waved under my nose? It was bizarre.

"I intended the trap for my brother," Mircea said. "But when I saw that he had been captured already, I decided to employ it for other purposes. The young . . . woman . . . made the mistake of running to the balcony to watch the effects of her device. I found her there."

He put Myra's box on the boards, and put a hand on Dracula's. "The Senators will be back," I said, unable to tear my eyes away from the small black container that imprisoned my rival. For some reason, my ears were ringing. "They'll just kill him anyway."

"Kill who?" Mircea was mildly curious. "You cannot mean my brother. Tragically, he died in the blast."

"They'll smell him."

"Not in this." Mircea sounded like he knew. And it wasn't as if they'd search him for the box. They might risk war over Dracula himself, but over a suspicion? I didn't think so.

"Why do you cry?" he asked suddenly, his hand on my cheek. His thumb wiped away a tear I couldn't remember shedding. As mild as the contact was, it woke up the *geis*. I caught my breath, and Mircea's eyes widened.

I pulled away. "Please . . . don't." Unlike in my own time, there was no physical pain at withdrawal. But the emotional price was still there, and it was high.

Mircea waited, but I offered no explanation. To my

surprise, he let it drop. "Unless I am mistaken, you won," was his only comment. "Victory is usually a reason for smiles, not tears."

"Victory came at too high a price." Way too high.

"They often do." Something moved on my arm, and I jumped. I looked down to find a small green lizard on my forearm, quivering in fear. It stared at me out of big black eyes for a second, then scurried off to hide behind my elbow. Mircea laughed.

"Where did that come from?" It was one of Mac's; I recognized it.

"It must have hid out, Cass," Billy murmured. "I guess it latched on to me when I threw the others. It looks like we saved something, after all." Its tail was ticklish as it scurried up my inner arm, but I let it alone. I'd learned a long time ago; something, however small, was better than nothing.

Pritkin slammed open the theatre doors, dragging in Stoker's six-foot-two frame, and I snatched up Myra's box. Mircea took the one containing his brother, and I didn't protest. For all I knew, this was how it had happened all along. Maybe Mircea carried his brother home in secret, letting everyone believe that the lynching had gone off as planned. In any case, I wouldn't have won a struggle, and Pritkin was too close to risk it. He'd said he didn't want Myra as Pythia—and after what she'd just pulled, I assumed he meant it, even if he hadn't before. But I still didn't trust him. There were far too many unanswered questions about Mage Pritkin.

I shoved Myra into a pocket of Françoise's voluminous skirts, well out of sight. Mircea saw, but said nothing. He went to the edge of the stage and took Stoker's limp body from Pritkin, hefting it out of the pit as if it were weightless.

"One thing further," he said, after laying Stoker on the boards. He pulled something out of his coat and slipped it onto my foot.

"My shoe." It shone with all the glory a $14.99 special could hope to achieve.

"You dropped it at our first meeting, in your haste to leave. Something told me I might have a chance to return it." His eyes met mine, and the smile edged perilously close to a grin. "That is a lovely gown, but I must say, I preferred your other ensemble. Or lack of it."

I gave a wry smile and removed the shoe. With my life, I needed combat boots, not heels. Besides, this Cinderella had the Circle, the Senate and the Dark Fey to deal with. She wasn't going to be living happily ever after anytime soon. I handed it to him, careful to avoid actual contact. "Keep it."

He looked at me quizzically. "What would I do with such a thing?"

I shrugged. "You never know."

Mircea searched my face for a moment, then moved as if to take my hand. I snatched it back, and a frown line formed on his forehead. "May I assume that we will meet again?"

I hesitated. He would meet me, and make the mistake that would lead us to this. Whether I would see him in my future was another story. If I didn't break the *geis*, I'd never be able to risk it, and the thought twisted my insides into a tight knot. I was so tempted to warn him not to lay the *geis* that I had to bite my cheek to stay quiet. But as much as I hated it, the damned thing had played a big part in getting me where I was. It had protected me from unwanted advances as a teenager, helped Mircea find me before Tony did as an adult, and convinced him to let me go in the Senate chamber. If I changed that one thing, what would my life be like? I just didn't know.

I finally decided on a literal interpretation. "I think that's safe to say."

Mircea nodded, picked up Stoker and bowed. He somehow made it graceful despite having a two-hundred-fifty-pound man draped over one shoulder. "I look forward to it, little witch."

"I'm not a witch."

He smiled slightly. "I know." He walked offstage without another word. I gritted my teeth and let him go.

"You do make interesting allies," Pritkin commented, vaulting up onstage. "How did you persuade that creature to aid you? They are usually extremely self-interested." I thought he meant Mircea, and was about to explain the extreme folly of referring to any vamp, especially a master, by that term. He saw my expression and elaborated. "The incubus, the one called Dream."

My brain skidded to a halt. "What?"

"You didn't know what it was?" Pritkin asked, incredulous. "Are you in the habit of taking aid from strange spirits?"

Billy laughed. "No," I said, ignoring him. "The name—what did you call him?"

"It," Pritkin corrected.

"But the name—"

"Appropriate," he agreed, "an incubus called Dream." I goggled at him, and he frowned. "That is what the names it gave you mean. They are all variations of the same word. Why do you ask?"

I sat frozen in stunned comprehension, hearing a rich Spanish accent telling me that his name was Chavez, and exactly what that name meant. I rolled onto my back, staring sightlessly at the high ceiling. I'd handed three boxes from the Senate's prison into Chavez's manicured hands outside the ice rink. It would, of course, be too much to hope that none of them had been Dracula's.

I briefly wondered if the incubus had been playing me all the time, or if it had been luck that he ended up as my driver. Not that it mattered—either way, I was screwed. There was no way those boxes had made it to Casanova. Which meant that, in my time, Dracula was on the loose again. And it was my fault.

"Finally!" someone said behind me. For a moment, it barely registered. I was adding Dracula to my to-do list and trying not to think about how long that list was getting. But there was something very familiar about that voice. "I didn't think that vampire would ever leave! Now we finish this."

I turned slowly to find a ghostly outline of a young brunette hovering a few feet off the stage. I remembered those big blue eyes and the long white dress from the last time I'd seen this particular spirit. She'd informed me that she preferred appearing as she had been when traveling in spirit form, rather than duplicating her actual appearance. As a result, she still looked about fifteen.

"Agnes." For some reason, I wasn't even surprised. Or maybe my nerves were just too worn down to react much. "How did you get here?"

"She hitched a ride." Billy sounded aggrieved. "She wouldn't let me tell you, but she was already in the necklace when I fought my way back to your body. She must've been hiding around Headliners, and jumped from Françoise to you."

"Why?"

He shrugged. "We didn't talk much. I'd bet payback figures in there somewhere, though."

"Top of the list," Agnes agreed. She looked at me. "Set her free." It was a command, and spoken in the tones of one used to being immediately obeyed.

I didn't even try to pretend I wasn't following her. "You're after Myra, too."

Agnes crossed almost transparent arms and scowled at me. "Being murdered does tend to irritate me. Imagine that."

I shook my head. "I heard her confess, but I still don't understand how she did it."

"She gave me a solstice gift shortly before she went missing. To help keep me safe, she said." Agnes' lips twisted sardonically.

"The Sebastian medallion, I know. It contained arsenic—the mages found it and cut it open. But I still don't see how it could have been dangerous. The poison was welded inside!"

"She bored a tiny hole in the top before giving it to me. She knew my habits, knew I always dunked a charm or talisman of some sort in my beverages before I drank. It was a habit bequeathed me by my predecessor, who swore my life would end with poison if I wasn't cautious! Of course," Agnes said, drifting closer, "she also told me to buy stocks in '29. Herophile was a nutter."

"Herophile?"

"Yes, named after the second Pythia at Delphi. By all accounts, she was a little cracked, too."

I'd been named after a nut. Why didn't that surprise me? "But I still don't see why Myra wanted to kill you. If the power can't go to the assassin of a Pythia—"

"Technically, she didn't kill me."

"She gave you a poisoned medallion knowing what you'd do with it!" That sounded like murder to me.

"But she didn't force me to use it," Agnes pointed out. She held up a hand as I started to protest. "Yes, I know. Any modern court would convict her, but the power comes from a time before circumstantial evidence and reasonable doubt. She didn't take a sword to me or bash in my head with a club. She didn't even poison my wine—I did that. From its perspective, she's blameless."

"So what now?" I didn't know what Agnes had meant by finishing this, but it sounded kind of ominous.

"I said the power considers Myra to be blameless. Not that I did," she said viciously. "The little bitch murdered me. Why do you think I'm here?"

"And you're planning to do what?" Now that she was a disembodied spirit, her options seemed pretty limited.

"Let her loose and find out."

It suddenly occurred to me that Agnes did have one escape route. If she could possess Myra, she could use her power to go back and try to change things. I really hoped that wasn't the plan, because I had no idea how I was supposed to stop her if it was. I'd had enough trouble just dealing with her heir; there was no doubt Agnes could run circles around me if she felt like it.

"You can't intend to mess with the timeline yourself," I said slowly, "not after spending a lifetime protecting it!"

"Don't lecture me about the timeline!" she snapped.

"Who are you talking to?" Pritkin demanded.

I sighed. For a moment, I'd forgotten. Agnes was a spirit, so he couldn't see or hear her any better than he could Billy. "You wouldn't believe me if I told you."

"Try me." He wiped away the blood pouring from a cut

above his right eyebrow, I suppose to get it out of his eyes,
but all it did was smear it. He suddenly looked like he was
wearing war paint. I decided not to argue.

"Okay. Agnes is here in spirit form, and she's planning to
avenge her own murder. Do you understand anything better
now?"

"Yes." He immediately dropped to one knee. "Lady Phemonoe, it is an honor as always." I scowled at him. Way to
show me where I ranked.

Agnes barely glanced at him. She sent me a smile, but it
wasn't a very nice one. "Myra took away my life. The way
I see it, she owes me one."

Finally, something made sense. "Is that the deal you
struck with Françoise? To get you to this point so you could
take over Myra's body instead?" I narrowed my eyes. "Or
did you? Was she willing or not?"

"She would never have gotten away from the Light Fey
without my help," Agnes replied, avoiding the question.
"She probably wouldn't even have survived! My experience
kept us both alive. I think she owed me a few years for that!"

"That wasn't your call!"

"And speaking of debts, who do you think sent those
wards to your rescue earlier? Your ghost didn't know how
they worked. I'm the one who saved you. Again." She
looked at me pointedly. "So let her out!"

I clutched the box to my side. I could feel a tiny pulse
throbbing at the base of my throat. "What if you can't control her? You were supposed to pass into a norm, not someone like her. Françoise even made things hard on you
sometimes. What do you think a Seer of Myra's power
would do?"

"That's my problem."

"Not if she gets away from you!" I pulled out the box and shook it at her. "Do you have any idea what I went through to get this? Myra was trying to kill Mircea so he wouldn't be around to protect me. And she almost disrupted the entire timeline to do it! She almost killed me! And you're telling me it's not my problem?" I was yelling, but I didn't care.

"Let her go, Cassie," Agnes warned.

"Or what? You'll do to me what you did to Françoise?"

"Don't be ridiculous. I couldn't hold you."

"But you can control Myra?" I shook my head. "I don't think so. She's dangerous, Agnes. I got her in here because of luck, more than anything else. No way am I letting her go."

Agnes sighed. "You don't understand—" She broke off when Pritkin suddenly ripped the box out of my hand.

"Pritkin, no!" I made a grab for it, but before I got so much as a finger on it, there was a familiar flash and there stood Myra.

Agnes didn't waste any time. As soon as her old apprentice appeared, she flowed past me in a rush and slammed straight into Myra's shields. They spit and crackled as the two fought, Myra to keep her out, Agnes to find a way in.

"Do you know what you've done?" I asked Pritkin numbly. "She won't hold her. Not forever."

"She won't need to," he replied, watching the fight grimly.

Before I could ask what he meant, Myra screamed and Agnes disappeared, sinking through whatever chink she'd found in the girl's armor. The slight body shivered once, hard, and then looked up calmly. I suddenly realized that, except for their hair color and minor facial differences, the two women might have been twins. They had the same slight build and delicate bone structure, the same little-girl quality about them. But the eyes that had looked cold and opaque with Myra's mind behind them were now dancing with life.

"I did it!" Agnes announced, as if that was something to celebrate. She smiled at me. I didn't smile back. All that work, all that sacrifice had been for nothing. Agnes might be powerful, but it wasn't her body. Sooner or later, she would lose her grip, even if only for an instant. And that would be enough.

"You're crazy," I told her.

Pritkin started toward her, but Agnes held up a hand. "You don't have the right," she said simply.

His eyes cut to me and narrowed. "She won't."

"She must," Agnes said calmly. "You swore an oath."

Pritkin walked over and knelt by my side. I felt something cold touch my skin and looked down to find him pressing one of his knives into my hand. "Make it quick," he said grimly. "One slice, clean across the jugular."

I stared at him. "What?"

He closed my hand over the hilt. "Myra condemned herself from her own lips. You heard her. By every law—human, mage, or vampire—she deserves death."

The pieces finally all fell into place. I didn't much care for the picture they made. "This is why you really wanted me along, isn't it?"

He didn't try to deny it. "I swore an oath to protect the Pythia and her heir, with my life if necessary. The Circle believed I would disregard it on their order, that I would kill Myra with nothing to prove her guilt. But when I give my word, I keep it." His lips curled into a sour smile. "Which is why I don't give it often."

"You didn't bring me along to keep Myra from shifting," I accused. "You expect me to kill her!"

His expression didn't change. We might have been discussing anything—the weather, a football game. It was surreal. "If I could do it for you, I would," he told me calmly. "But Agnes is correct. Only the Pythia can discipline an initiate."

"We're not talking about discipline! Myra isn't being sent to bed without supper." I looked at Agnes, hoping to find support. "This is life and death!"

She shrugged Myra's slim shoulders, her face blank. She trained her for years and they must have been close once, but there was no sign of regret on her face. "You said it yourself. I can't hold her. Not for long."

"If this is what the job does to you," I told her bluntly, "I know I don't want it."

Blue eyes met mine, and suddenly they were a little sad. "But you have it."

I felt the knife blade bite into my hand, where my grip had slipped from the hilt, and the pain seemed to suddenly bring everything home. I shook my head violently. "No. We'll find another way."

Agnes regarded me gently. It was extremely weird to see that expression on Myra's face. "There isn't one. What were you planning to do? Keep her tucked up your sleeve? Carry her about with you? Sooner or later, she would get free. I taught her too much to doubt that." Her expression became more stern. "And dealing with rogues is part of your job. That's the rule."

"It isn't *my* rule," I said hoarsely.

"Someone has to do it," Agnes said implacably.

"Someone has to take responsibility. And whether you like it or not, that someone is you."

I swallowed hard. The tears I hadn't shed earlier were rolling down my face, but I didn't care. Another death, this time not only my fault but by my hand? That was not the plan. That was, in fact, the exact opposite of the plan. I'd wanted to win, but not like this. I was sick of death, especially death I helped to cause. A bitter taste flooded my mouth. "I can't."

Agnes bent down and a gentle hand cupped my face. "You haven't even started to learn what you can do yet. But you will." She stepped away from me, a small, sad smile on her face. "I would have liked to have trained you, Cassie." She looked at Pritkin. "She'll need help," she said simply.

Pritkin was back on his knees, his face white. "I know."

Agnes nodded and looked at me. A spasm passed over her face for a moment, but she regained control. "I will never teach you most of the lessons you will need," she continued, "but I find I have time for one."

I only realized that the knife was gone when I saw it in her small hand. "Agnes, no!" I scrambled to my feet, but it was too late. She didn't hesitate for a second. By the time I reached her, she'd already sunk to her knees, Myra's pristine white gown drenched in blood. She settled to the floor almost gracefully, her body a pale smear in the middle of all that vivid color.

I stared around frantically, but there was no sign of her spirit. Neither hers nor Myra's. I whirled on Pritkin, who was still on his knees, watching the blood spill across the boards in a widening stain. For a second, he looked lost, like a bewildered child. Then the expression was gone so quickly I wasn't sure it had been there at all.

"Where is she?" I demanded, my voice shrill with fear. "I can't see her!" He looked up at me, but it was almost as if his eyes didn't focus for a moment. I looked back at Myra's crumpled form, and my vision blurred to the point that it was hard to tell where the blood ended and the red fabric of the dress began. "Pritkin!"

"She's gone."

I rounded on him, stunned and disbelieving. "What do you mean, she's gone? Gone where? Into another host?"

"No." He got up and came over to her body, and with a whispered word, the area around her was engulfed in crimson flames. They cast a reddish glow on the old boards and sparked glints off the gilt frame of the stage, but it wasn't a normal fire. The slim figure at the heart of the blaze dusted to ashes in seconds, leaving only charred boards behind. Pritkin turned to me, and his eyes were pained. It was that look, more than his words, that got through. "Just gone."

I shook my head, blindly. "No! We could have found someplace safe for Myra. Agnes could have found another host. I'd have helped her. It didn't have to end this way!"

He gripped my arms painfully. "Do you still not understand?"

"Understand what? She died for nothing!" I was crying, but it was panic that clouded my vision, making the world run in streams of color. Agnes couldn't be gone. I'd believed I was on my own before, but I hadn't truly understood the odds against me. Now I did, and I knew I wouldn't be enough. "I'll go back, I'll save her—" I began, only to have him shake me so hard, my teeth rattled.

"Lady Phemonoe died doing her duty. She was one of the greatest of her line. You will *not* disgrace her!"

"Disgrace her? I'm talking about saving her!"

"There are some things even the Pythia cannot change," he said, his hard expression softening. "Myra had to die, and someone had to make sure that she couldn't use her power to jump into another body before her spirit was pulled away. And the only way to do that . . ."

Understanding finally dawned. "Was for someone to go with her," I whispered. I stared at the charred boards, disbelieving. It had all happened so fast. Maybe a fully trained Pythia wouldn't be plagued by doubts or worry, wouldn't second-guess her decisions or wonder what right she had to the power she held. But I hadn't been trained, and I didn't know what to do. Panic stopped my throat, froze my brain. I was on my own, and I was terrified.

"I assume you will go after the *Codex* no matter what I decide?" Pritkin asked.

It took a moment for my brain to catch up with my ears. And even then I didn't get it. Why was he asking about this *now*? A hundred problems were pulling at me, tugging me in different directions, to the point that I couldn't think clearly about any of them. All I knew was that Agnes was gone. And that it was all up to me now.

"What?" I asked stupidly.

"The *Codex*," he said patiently. "You are determined to seek it out?"

"I don't have a choice," I said, confused. "The *geis* won't budge. And I can't function if it gets much worse." At the moment I wasn't sure I could function anyway.

He nodded once, up and down. "Then I will help you."

I could feel the tears drying on my face, but I couldn't be bothered to wipe them away. "I always wondered if you have a death wish. I guess now I know."

"I promised Lady Phemonoe that I would help you."

I wrenched away from him, suddenly furious. "Agnes is gone! And I don't want another corpse on my hands. They're bloody enough!" I tried to move back, to get away from those burned boards, but my foot caught on the hem of the dress and I ended up on my hands and knees.

"I wasn't asking your permission," he informed me coolly.

I looked up at him through a curtain of tangled hair. "I'll never be the Pythia she was," I warned. "I may not be any good at all."

For the first time ever, I saw what looked like a genuine smile cross Pritkin's face. "Well, that's encouraging." He hauled me to my feet. "No one who wants power should ever be allowed to wield it."

"Then I'll be great," I said bitterly, "because no one could possibly want it any less than I do."

Pritkin didn't answer. Instead, to my disbelief, he sank to one knee in front of me. His clothes were torn and bloody, his face soot-stained, but there was still something impressive about him. "I don't recall the exact wording," he said. "And there should be witnesses—"

"What am I?" Billy asked, indignant, as he flowed back inside my necklace.

Pritkin ignored him. "But I believe it went something like this: I swear to defend you and your appointed successor against all malefactors present and to come, in peace and in war, for as long as I live and you continue to remain true to the ideals of your office."

I stared down at him, and suddenly a weight seemed to lift from my shoulders. However exasperating, annoying and just plain asinine Pritkin could be at times, he was a good man to have in a fight. And I had a feeling there was a lot of that ahead. "So I guess you'll be calling me Lady Herophile the Second from now on?"

"The Seventh." He was on his knees, but I received the same old arrogant look from those green eyes. "And don't count on it."

The main door slammed open and a stream of vamps poured in, murder in their eyes. I grabbed Pritkin's shoulder and gave him a weary smile. "I can live with that," I said, and shifted.